The Confidence-Man

The Confidence-Man was first published in 1857.

This edition published by Mint Editions 2021.

ISBN 9781513270036 | E-ISBN 9781513275031

Published by Mint Editions®

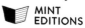
MINT
EDITIONS

minteditionbooks.com

Publishing Director: Jennifer Newens
Design & Production: Rachel Lopez Metzger
Typesetting: Westchester Publishing Services

The Confidence-Man

Herman Melville

MINT EDITIONS

Contents

I

A Mute Goes Aboard a Boat on the Mississippi

At sunrise on a first of April, there appeared, suddenly as Manco Capac at the lake Titicaca, a man in cream-colors, at the water-side in the city of St. Louis.

His cheek was fair, his chin downy, his hair flaxen, his hat a white fur one, with a long fleecy nap. He had neither trunk, valise, carpet-bag, nor parcel. No porter followed him. He was unaccompanied by friends. From the shrugged shoulders, titters, whispers, wonderings of the crowd, it was plain that he was, in the extremest sense of the word, a stranger.

In the same moment with his advent, he stepped aboard the favorite steamer Fidèle, on the point of starting for New Orleans. Stared at, but unsaluted, with the air of one neither courting nor shunning regard, but evenly pursuing the path of duty, lead it through solitudes or cities, he held on his way along the lower deck until he chanced to come to a placard nigh the captain's office, offering a reward for the capture of a mysterious impostor, supposed to have recently arrived from the East; quite an original genius in his vocation, as would appear, though wherein his originality consisted was not clearly given; but what purported to be a careful description of his person followed.

As if it had been a theatre-bill, crowds were gathered about the announcement, and among them certain chevaliers, whose eyes, it was plain, were on the capitals, or, at least, earnestly seeking sight of them from behind intervening coats; but as for their fingers, they were enveloped in some myth; though, during a chance interval, one of these chevaliers somewhat showed his hand in purchasing from another chevalier, ex-officio a peddler of money-belts, one of his popular safe-guards, while another peddler, who was still another versatile chevalier, hawked, in the thick of the throng, the lives of Measan, the bandit of Ohio, Murrel, the pirate of the Mississippi, and the brothers Harpe, the Thugs of the Green River country, in Kentucky—creatures, with others of the sort, one and all exterminated at the time, and for the most part, like the hunted generations of wolves in the same regions, leaving comparatively few successors; which would seem cause for unalloyed gratulation, and is such to all except those who think that in new countries, where the wolves are killed off, the foxes increase.

Pausing at this spot, the stranger so far succeeded in threading his way, as at last to plant himself just beside the placard, when, producing a small slate and tracing some words upon if, he held it up before him on a level with the placard, so that they who read the one might read the other. The words were these:—

"Charity thinketh no evil."

As, in gaining his place, some little perseverance, not to say persistence, of a mildly inoffensive sort, had been unavoidable, it was not with the best relish that the crowd regarded his apparent intrusion; and upon a more attentive survey, perceiving no badge of authority about him, but rather something quite the contrary—he being of an aspect so singularly innocent; an aspect too, which they took to be somehow inappropriate to the time and place, and inclining to the notion that his writing was of much the same sort: in short, taking him for some strange kind of simpleton, harmless enough, would he keep to himself, but not wholly unobnoxious as an intruder—they made no scruple to jostle him aside; while one, less kind than the rest, or more of a wag, by an unobserved stroke, dexterously flattened down his fleecy hat upon his head. Without readjusting it, the stranger quietly turned, and writing anew upon the slate, again held it up:—

"Charity suffereth long, and is kind."

Illy pleased with his pertinacity, as they thought it, the crowd a second time thrust him aside, and not without epithets and some buffets, all of which were unresented. But, as if at last despairing of so difficult an adventure, wherein one, apparently a non-resistant, sought to impose his presence upon fighting characters, the stranger now moved slowly away, yet not before altering his writing to this:—

"Charity endureth all things."

Shield-like bearing his slate before him, amid stares and jeers he moved slowly up and down, at his turning points again changing his inscription to—

> "Charity believeth all things."

and then—

> "Charity never faileth."

The word charity, as originally traced, remained throughout uneffaced, not unlike the left-hand numeral of a printed date, otherwise left for convenience in blank.

To some observers, the singularity, if not lunacy, of the stranger was heightened by his muteness, and, perhaps also, by the contrast to his proceedings afforded in the actions—quite in the wonted and sensible order of things—of the barber of the boat, whose quarters, under a smoking-saloon, and over against a bar-room, was next door but two to the captain's office. As if the long, wide, covered deck, hereabouts built up on both sides with shop-like windowed spaces, were some Constantinople arcade or bazaar, where more than one trade is plied, this river barber, aproned and slippered, but rather crusty-looking for the moment, it may be from being newly out of bed, was throwing open his premises for the day, and suitably arranging the exterior. With business-like dispatch, having rattled down his shutters, and at a palm-tree angle set out in the iron fixture his little ornamental pole, and this without overmuch tenderness for the elbows and toes of the crowd, he concluded his operations by bidding people stand still more aside, when, jumping on a stool, he hung over his door, on the customary nail, a gaudy sort of illuminated pasteboard sign, skillfully executed by himself, gilt with the likeness of a razor elbowed in readiness to shave, and also, for the public benefit, with two words not unfrequently seen ashore gracing other shops besides barbers':—

> "No Trust."

An inscription which, though in a sense not less intrusive than the contrasted ones of the stranger, did not, as it seemed, provoke any corresponding derision or surprise, much less indignation; and still less, to all appearances, did it gain for the inscriber the repute of being a simpleton.

Meanwhile, he with the slate continued moving slowly up and down, not without causing some stares to change into jeers, and some jeers into pushes, and some pushes into punches; when suddenly, in one of his turns, he was hailed from behind by two porters carrying a large trunk; but as the summons, though loud, was without effect, they accidentally or otherwise swung their burden against him, nearly overthrowing him; when, by a quick start, a peculiar inarticulate moan, and a pathetic telegraphing of his fingers, he involuntarily betrayed that he was not alone dumb, but also deaf.

Presently, as if not wholly unaffected by his reception thus far, he went forward, seating himself in a retired spot on the forecastle, nigh the foot of a ladder there leading to a deck above, up and down which ladder some of the boatmen, in discharge of their duties, were occasionally going.

From his betaking himself to this humble quarter, it was evident that, as a deck-passenger, the stranger, simple though he seemed, was not entirely ignorant of his place, though his taking a deck-passage might have been partly for convenience; as, from his having no luggage, it was probable that his destination was one of the small wayside landings within a few hours' sail. But, though he might not have a long way to go, yet he seemed already to have come from a very long distance.

Though neither soiled nor slovenly, his cream-colored suit had a tossed look, almost linty, as if, traveling night and day from some far country beyond the prairies, he had long been without the solace of a bed. His aspect was at once gentle and jaded, and, from the moment of seating himself, increasing in tired abstraction and dreaminess. Gradually overtaken by slumber, his flaxen head drooped, his whole lamb-like figure relaxed, and, half reclining against the ladder's foot, lay motionless, as some sugar-snow in March, which, softly stealing down over night, with its white placidity startles the brown farmer peering out from his threshold at daybreak.

II

SHOWING THAT MANY MEN HAVE MANY MINDS

O dd fish!"
"Poor fellow!"
"Who can he be?"
"Casper Hauser."
"Bless my soul!"
"Uncommon countenance."
"Green prophet from Utah."
"Humbug!"
"Singular innocence."
"Means something."
"Spirit-rapper."
"Moon-calf."
"Piteous."
"Trying to enlist interest."
"Beware of him."
"Fast asleep here, and, doubtless, pick-pockets on board."
"Kind of daylight Endymion."
"Escaped convict, worn out with dodging."
"Jacob dreaming at Luz."

Such the epitaphic comments, conflictingly spoken or thought, of a miscellaneous company, who, assembled on the overlooking, cross-wise balcony at the forward end of the upper deck near by, had not witnessed preceding occurrences.

Meantime, like some enchanted man in his grave, happily oblivious of all gossip, whether chiseled or chatted, the deaf and dumb stranger still tranquilly slept, while now the boat started on her voyage.

The great ship-canal of Ving-King-Ching, in the Flowery Kingdom, seems the Mississippi in parts, where, amply flowing between low, vine-tangled banks, flat as tow-paths, it bears the huge toppling steamers, bedizened and lacquered within like imperial junks.

Pierced along its great white bulk with two tiers of small embrasure-like windows, well above the waterline, the Fiddle, though, might at distance have been taken by strangers for some whitewashed fort on a floating isle.

Merchants on 'change seem the passengers that buzz on her decks, while, from quarters unseen, comes a murmur as of bees in the comb. Fine promenades, domed saloons, long galleries, sunny balconies, confidential passages, bridal chambers, state-rooms plenty as pigeon-holes, and out-of-the-way retreats like secret drawers in an escritoire, present like facilities for publicity or privacy. Auctioneer or coiner, with equal ease, might somewhere here drive his trade.

Though her voyage of twelve hundred miles extends from apple to orange, from clime to clime, yet, like any small ferry-boat, to right and left, at every landing, the huge Fidèle still receives additional passengers in exchange for those that disembark; so that, though always full of strangers, she continually, in some degree, adds to, or replaces them with strangers still more strange; like Rio Janeiro fountain, fed from the Cocovarde mountains, which is ever overflowing with strange waters, but never with the same strange particles in every part.

Though hitherto, as has been seen, the man in cream-colors had by no means passed unobserved, yet by stealing into retirement, and there going asleep and continuing so, he seemed to have courted oblivion, a boon not often withheld from so humble an applicant as he. Those staring crowds on the shore were now left far behind, seen dimly clustering like swallows on eaves; while the passengers' attention was soon drawn away to the rapidly shooting high bluffs and shot-towers on the Missouri shore, or the bluff-looking Missourians and towering Kentuckians among the throngs on the decks.

By-and-by—two or three random stoppages having been made, and the last transient memory of the slumberer vanished, and he himself, not unlikely, waked up and landed ere now—the crowd, as is usual, began in all parts to break up from a concourse into various clusters or squads, which in some cases disintegrated again into quartettes, trios, and couples, or even solitaires; involuntarily submitting to that natural law which ordains dissolution equally to the mass, as in time to the member.

As among Chaucer's Canterbury pilgrims, or those oriental ones crossing the Red Sea towards Mecca in the festival month, there was no lack of variety. Natives of all sorts, and foreigners; men of business and men of pleasure; parlor men and backwoodsmen; farm-hunters and fame-hunters; heiress-hunters, gold-hunters, buffalo-hunters,

HERMAN MELVILLE

bee-hunters, happiness-hunters, truth-hunters, and still keener hunters after all these hunters. Fine ladies in slippers, and moccasined squaws; Northern speculators and Eastern philosophers; English, Irish, German, Scotch, Danes; Santa Fé traders in striped blankets, and Broadway bucks in cravats of cloth of gold; fine-looking Kentucky boatmen, and Japanese-looking Mississippi cotton-planters; Quakers in full drab, and United States soldiers in full regimentals; slaves, black, mulatto, quadroon; modish young Spanish Creoles, and old-fashioned French Jews; Mormons and Papists Dives and Lazarus; jesters and mourners, teetotalers and convivialists, deacons and blacklegs; hard-shell Baptists and clay-eaters; grinning negroes, and Sioux chiefs solemn as high-priests. In short, a piebald parliament, an Anacharsis Cloots congress of all kinds of that multiform pilgrim species, man.

As pine, beech, birch, ash, hackmatack, hemlock, spruce, bass-wood, maple, interweave their foliage in the natural wood, so these mortals blended their varieties of visage and garb. A Tartar-like picturesqueness; a sort of pagan abandonment and assurance. Here reigned the dashing and all-fusing spirit of the West, whose type is the Mississippi itself, which, uniting the streams of the most distant and opposite zones, pours them along, helter-skelter, in one cosmopolitan and confident tide.

III

In Which a Variety of Characters Appear

In the forward part of the boat, not the least attractive object, for a time, was a grotesque negro cripple, in tow-cloth attire and an old coal-sifter of a tamborine in his hand, who, owing to something wrong about his legs, was, in effect, cut down to the stature of a Newfoundland dog; his knotted black fleece and good-natured, honest black face rubbing against the upper part of people's thighs as he made shift to shuffle about, making music, such as it was, and raising a smile even from the gravest. It was curious to see him, out of his very deformity, indigence, and houselessness, so cheerily endured, raising mirth in some of that crowd, whose own purses, hearths, hearts, all their possessions, sound limbs included, could not make gay.

"What is your name, old boy?" said a purple-faced drover, putting his large purple hand on the cripple's bushy wool, as if it were the curled forehead of a black steer.

"Der Black Guinea dey calls me, sar."

"And who is your master, Guinea?"

"Oh sar, I am der dog widout massa."

"A free dog, eh? Well, on your account, I'm sorry for that, Guinea. Dogs without masters fare hard."

"So dey do, sar; so dey do. But you see, sar, dese here legs? What ge'mman want to own dese here legs?"

"But where do you live?"

"All 'long shore, sar; dough now. I'se going to see brodder at der landing; but chiefly I libs in dey city."

"St. Louis, ah? Where do you sleep there of nights?"

"On der floor of der good baker's oven, sar."

"In an oven? whose, pray? What baker, I should like to know, bakes such black bread in his oven, alongside of his nice white rolls, too. Who is that too charitable baker, pray?"

"Dar he be," with a broad grin lifting his tambourine high over his head.

"The sun is the baker, eh?"

"Yes sar, in der city dat good baker warms der stones for dis ole darkie when he sleeps out on der pabements o' nights."

"But that must be in the summer only, old boy. How about winter, when the cold Cossacks come clattering and jingling? How about winter, old boy?"

"Den dis poor old darkie shakes werry bad, I tell you, sar. Oh sar, oh! don't speak ob der winter," he added, with a reminiscent shiver, shuffling off into the thickest of the crowd, like a half-frozen black sheep nudging itself a cozy berth in the heart of the white flock.

Thus far not very many pennies had been given him, and, used at last to his strange looks, the less polite passengers of those in that part of the boat began to get their fill of him as a curious object; when suddenly the negro more than revived their first interest by an expedient which, whether by chance or design, was a singular temptation at once to *diversion* and charity, though, even more than his crippled limbs, it put him on a canine footing. In short, as in appearance he seemed a dog, so now, in a merry way, like a dog he began to be treated. Still shuffling among the crowd, now and then he would pause, throwing back his head and, opening his mouth like an elephant for tossed apples at a menagerie; when, making a space before him, people would have a bout at a strange sort of pitch-penny game, the cripple's mouth being at once target and purse, and he hailing each expertly-caught copper with a cracked bravura from his tambourine. To be the subject of alms-giving is trying, and to feel in duty bound to appear cheerfully grateful under the trial, must be still more so; but whatever his secret emotions, he swallowed them, while still retaining each copper this side the esophagus. And nearly always he grinned, and only once or twice did he wince, which was when certain coins, tossed by more playful almoners, came inconveniently nigh to his teeth, an accident whose unwelcomeness was not unedged by the circumstance that the pennies thus thrown proved buttons.

While this game of charity was yet at its height, a limping, gimlet-eyed, sour-faced person—it may be some discharged custom-house officer, who, suddenly stripped of convenient means of support, had concluded to be avenged on government and humanity by making himself miserable for life, either by hating or suspecting everything and everybody—this shallow unfortunate, after sundry sorry observations of the negro, began to croak out something about his deformity being a sham, got up for financial purposes, which immediately threw a damp upon the frolic benignities of the pitch-penny players.

But that these suspicions came from one who himself on a wooden leg went halt, this did not appear to strike anybody present. That cripples, above all men should be companionable, or, at least, refrain from picking a fellow-limper to pieces, in short, should have a little sympathy in common misfortune, seemed not to occur to the company.

Meantime, the negro's countenance, before marked with even more than patient good-nature, drooped into a heavy-hearted expression, full of the most painful distress. So far abased beneath its proper physical level, that Newfoundland-dog face turned in passively hopeless appeal, as if instinct told it that the right or the wrong might not have overmuch to do with whatever wayward mood superior intelligences might yield to.

But instinct, though knowing, is yet a teacher set below reason, which itself says, in the grave words of Lysander in the comedy, after Puck has made a sage of him with his spell:—

"The will of man is by his reason swayed."

So that, suddenly change as people may, in their dispositions, it is not always waywardness, but improved judgment, which, as in Lysander's case, or the present, operates with them.

Yes, they began to scrutinize the negro curiously enough; when, emboldened by this evidence of the efficacy of his words, the wooden-legged man hobbled up to the negro, and, with the air of a beadle, would, to prove his alleged imposture on the spot, have stripped him and then driven him away, but was prevented by the crowd's clamor, now taking part with the poor fellow, against one who had just before turned nearly all minds the other way. So he with the wooden leg was forced to retire; when the rest, finding themselves left sole judges in the case, could not resist the opportunity of acting the part: not because it is a human weakness to take pleasure in sitting in judgment upon one in a box, as surely this unfortunate negro now was, but that it strangely sharpens human perceptions, when, instead of standing by and having their fellow-feelings touched by the sight of an alleged culprit severely handled by some one justiciary, a crowd suddenly come to be all justiciaries in the same case themselves; as in Arkansas once, a man proved guilty, by law, of murder, but whose condemnation was deemed unjust by the people, so that they rescued him to try him themselves; whereupon, they, as it turned out, found him even guiltier than the court had done, and forthwith proceeded to execution; so that the gallows presented the truly warning spectacle of a man hanged by his friends.

But not to such extremities, or anything like them, did the present crowd come; they, for the time, being content with putting the negro fairly and discreetly to the question; among other things, asking him, had he any documentary proof, any plain paper about him, attesting that his case was not a spurious one.

"No, no, dis poor ole darkie haint none o' dem waloable papers," he wailed.

"But is there not some one who can speak a good word for you?" here said a person newly arrived from another part of the boat, a young Episcopal clergyman, in a long, straight-bodied black coat; small in stature, but manly; with a clear face and blue eye; innocence, tenderness, and good sense triumvirate in his air.

"Oh yes, oh yes, ge'mmen," he eagerly answered, as if his memory, before suddenly frozen up by cold charity, as suddenly thawed back into fluidity at the first kindly word. "Oh yes, oh yes, dar is aboard here a werry nice, good ge'mman wid a weed, and a ge'mman in a gray coat and white tie, what knows all about me; and a ge'mman wid a big book, too; and a yarb-doctor; and a ge'mman in a yaller west; and a ge'mman wid a brass plate; and a ge'mman in a wiolet robe; and a ge'mman as is a sodjer; and ever so many good, kind, honest ge'mmen more aboard what knows me and will speak for me, God bress 'em; yes, and what knows me as well as dis poor old darkie knows hisself, God bress him! Oh, find 'em, find 'em," he earnestly added, "and let 'em come quick, and show you all, ge'mmen, dat dis poor ole darkie is werry well wordy of all you kind ge'mmen's kind confidence."

"But how are we to find all these people in this great crowd?" was the question of a bystander, umbrella in hand; a middle-aged person, a country merchant apparently, whose natural good-feeling had been made at least cautious by the unnatural ill-feeling of the discharged custom-house officer.

"Where are we to find them?" half-rebukefully echoed the young Episcopal clergymen. "I will go find one to begin with," he quickly added, and, with kind haste suiting the action to the word, away he went.

"Wild goose chase!" croaked he with the wooden leg, now again drawing nigh. "Don't believe there's a soul of them aboard. Did ever beggar have such heaps of fine friends? He can walk fast enough when he tries, a good deal faster than I; but he can lie yet faster. He's some white operator, betwisted and painted up for a decoy. He and his friends are all humbugs."

"Have you no charity, friend?" here in self-subdued tones, singularly contrasted with his unsubdued person, said a Methodist minister, advancing; a tall, muscular, martial-looking man, a Tennessean by birth, who in the Mexican war had been volunteer chaplain to a volunteer rifle-regiment.

"Charity is one thing, and truth is another," rejoined he with the wooden leg: "he's a rascal, I say."

"But why not, friend, put as charitable a construction as one can upon the poor fellow?" said the soldierlike Methodist, with increased difficulty maintaining a pacific demeanor towards one whose own asperity seemed so little to entitle him to it: "he looks honest, don't he?"

"Looks are one thing, and facts are another," snapped out the other perversely; "and as to your constructions, what construction can you put upon a rascal, but that a rascal he is?"

"Be not such a Canada thistle," urged the Methodist, with something less of patience than before. "Charity, man, charity."

"To where it belongs with your charity! to heaven with it!" again snapped out the other, diabolically; "here on earth, true charity dotes, and false charity plots. Who betrays a fool with a kiss, the charitable fool has the charity to believe is in love with him, and the charitable knave on the stand gives charitable testimony for his comrade in the box."

"Surely, friend," returned the noble Methodist, with much ado restraining his still waxing indignation—"surely, to say the least, you forget yourself. Apply it home," he continued, with exterior calmness tremulous with inkept emotion. "Suppose, now, I should exercise no charity in judging your own character by the words which have fallen from you; what sort of vile, pitiless man do you think I would take you for?"

"No doubt"—with a grin—"some such pitiless man as has lost his piety in much the same way that the jockey loses his honesty."

"And how is that, friend?" still conscientiously holding back the old Adam in him, as if it were a mastiff he had by the neck.

"Never you mind how it is"—with a sneer; "but all horses aint virtuous, no more than all men kind; and come close to, and much dealt with, some things are catching. When you find me a virtuous jockey, I will find you a benevolent wise man."

"Some insinuation there."

"More fool you that are puzzled by it."

"Reprobate!" cried the other, his indignation now at last almost boiling over; "godless reprobate! if charity did not restrain me, I could call you by names you deserve."

HERMAN MELVILLE

"Could you, indeed?" with an insolent sneer.

"Yea, and teach you charity on the spot," cried the goaded Methodist, suddenly catching this exasperating opponent by his shabby coat-collar, and shaking him till his timber-toe clattered on the deck like a nine-pin. "You took me for a non-combatant did you?—thought, seedy coward that you are, that you could abuse a Christian with impunity. You find your mistake"—with another hearty shake.

"Well said and better done, church militant!" cried a voice.

"The white cravat against the world!" cried another.

"Bravo, bravo!" chorused many voices, with like enthusiasm taking sides with the resolute champion.

"You fools!" cried he with the wooden leg, writhing himself loose and inflamedly turning upon the throng; "you flock of fools, under this captain of fools, in this ship of fools!"

With which exclamations, followed by idle threats against his admonisher, this condign victim to justice hobbled away, as disdaining to hold further argument with such a rabble. But his scorn was more than repaid by the hisses that chased him, in which the brave Methodist, satisfied with the rebuke already administered, was, to omit still better reasons, too magnanimous to join. All he said was, pointing towards the departing recusant, "There he shambles off on his one lone leg, emblematic of his one-sided view of humanity."

"But trust your painted decoy," retorted the other from a distance, pointing back to the black cripple, "and I have my revenge."

"But we aint agoing to trust him!" shouted back a voice.

"So much the better," he jeered back. "Look you," he added, coming to a dead halt where he was; "look you, I have been called a Canada thistle. Very good. And a seedy one: still better. And the seedy Canada thistle has been pretty well shaken among ye: best of all. Dare say some seed has been shaken out; and won't it spring though? And when it does spring, do you cut down the young thistles, and won't they spring the more? It's encouraging and coaxing 'em. Now, when with my thistles your farms shall be well stocked, why then—you may abandon 'em!"

"What does all that mean, now?" asked the country merchant, staring.

"Nothing; the foiled wolf's parting howl," said the Methodist. "Spleen, much spleen, which is the rickety child of his evil heart of unbelief: it has made him mad. I suspect him for one naturally reprobate. Oh, friends," raising his arms as in the pulpit, "oh beloved, how are we admonished by the melancholy spectacle of this raver. Let us profit by the lesson; and is it not this: that if, next to mistrusting Providence, there be aught that man should pray against, it is against mistrusting his fellow-man. I have been in mad-houses full of tragic mopers, and seen there the end of suspicion: the cynic, in the moody madness muttering in the corner; for years a barren fixture there; head lopped over, gnawing his own lip, vulture of himself; while, by fits and starts, from the corner opposite came the grimace of the idiot at him."

"What an example," whispered one.

"Might deter Timon," was the response.

"Oh, oh, good ge'mmen, have you no confidence in dis poor ole darkie?" now wailed the returning negro, who, during the late scene, had stumped apart in alarm.

"Confidence in you?" echoed he who had whispered, with abruptly changed air turning short round; "that remains to be seen."

"I tell you what it is, Ebony," in similarly changed tones said he who had responded to the whisperer, "yonder churl," pointing toward the wooden leg in the distance, "is, no doubt, a churlish fellow enough, and I would not wish to be like him; but that is no reason why you may not be some sort of black Jeremy Diddler."

"No confidence in dis poor ole darkie, den?"

"Before giving you our confidence," said a third, "we will wait the report of the kind gentleman who went in search of one of your friends who was to speak for you."

"Very likely, in that case," said a fourth, "we shall wait here till Christmas. Shouldn't wonder, did we not see that kind gentleman again. After seeking awhile in vain, he will conclude he has been made a fool of, and so not return to us for pure shame. Fact is, I begin to feel a little qualmish about the darkie myself. Something queer about this darkie, depend upon it."

Once more the negro wailed, and turning in despair from the last speaker, imploringly caught the Methodist by the skirt of his coat. But a change had come over that before impassioned intercessor. With an irresolute and troubled air, he mutely eyed the suppliant; against whom, somehow, by what seemed instinctive influences, the distrusts first set on foot were now generally reviving, and, if anything, with added severity.

"No confidence in dis poor ole darkie," yet again wailed the negro, letting go the coat-skirts and turning appealingly all round him.

"Yes, my poor fellow *I* have confidence in you," now exclaimed the country merchant before named, whom the negro's appeal, coming so piteously on the heel of pitilessness, seemed at last humanely to have decided in his favor. "And here, here is some proof of my trust," with which, tucking his umbrella under his arm, and diving down his hand into his pocket, he fished forth a purse, and, accidentally, along with it, his business card, which, unobserved, dropped to the deck. "Here, here, my poor fellow," he continued, extending a half dollar.

Not more grateful for the coin than the kindness, the cripple's face glowed like a polished copper saucepan, and shuffling a pace nigher, with one upstretched hand he received the alms, while, as unconsciously, his one advanced leather stump covered the card.

Done in despite of the general sentiment, the good deed of the merchant was not, perhaps, without its unwelcome return from the crowd, since that good deed seemed somehow to convey to them a sort of reproach. Still again, and more pertinaciously than ever, the cry arose against the negro, and still again he wailed forth his lament and appeal among other things, repeating that the friends, of whom already he had partially run off the list, would freely speak for him, would anybody go find them.

"Why don't you go find 'em yourself?" demanded a gruff boatman.

"How can I go find 'em myself? Dis poor ole game-legged darkie's friends must come to him. Oh, whar, whar is dat good friend of dis darkie's, dat good man wid de weed?"

At this point, a steward ringing a bell came along, summoning all persons who had not got their tickets to step to the captain's office; an announcement which speedily thinned the throng about the black cripple, who himself soon forlornly stumped out of sight, probably on much the same errand as the rest.

IV

Renewal of Old Acquaintance

"How do you do, Mr. Roberts?"

"Eh?"

"Don't you know me?"

"No, certainly."

The crowd about the captain's office, having in good time melted away, the above encounter took place in one of the side balconies astern, between a man in mourning clean and respectable, but none of the glossiest, a long weed on his hat, and the country-merchant before-mentioned, whom, with the familiarity of an old acquaintance, the former had accosted.

"Is it possible, my dear sir," resumed he with the weed, "that you do not recall my countenance? why yours I recall distinctly as if but half an hour, instead of half an age, had passed since I saw you. Don't you recall me, now? Look harder."

"In my conscience—truly—I protest," honestly bewildered, "bless my soul, sir, I don't know you—really, really. But stay, stay," he hurriedly added, not without gratification, glancing up at the crape on the stranger's hat, "stay—yes—seems to me, though I have not the pleasure of personally knowing you, yet I am pretty sure I have at least *heard* of you, and recently too, quite recently. A poor negro aboard here referred to you, among others, for a character, I think."

"Oh, the cripple. Poor fellow. I know him well. They found me. I have said all I could for him. I think I abated their distrust. Would I could have been of more substantial service. And apropos, sir," he added, "now that it strikes me, allow me to ask, whether the circumstance of one man, however humble, referring for a character to another man, however afflicted, does not argue more or less of moral worth in the latter?"

The good merchant looked puzzled.

"Still you don't recall my countenance?"

"Still does truth compel me to say that I cannot, despite my best efforts," was the reluctantly-candid reply.

"Can I be so changed? Look at me. Or is it I who am mistaken?—Are you not, sir, Henry Roberts, forwarding merchant, of Wheeling, Pennsylvania?

Pray, now, if you use the advertisement of business cards, and happen to have one with you, just look at it, and see whether you are not the man I take you for."

"Why," a bit chafed, perhaps, "I hope I know myself."

"And yet self-knowledge is thought by some not so easy. Who knows, my dear sir, but for a time you may have taken yourself for somebody else? Stranger things have happened."

The good merchant stared.

"To come to particulars, my dear sir, I met you, now some six years back, at Brade Brothers & Co's office, I think. I was traveling for a Philadelphia house. The senior Brade introduced us, you remember; some business-chat followed, then you forced me home with you to a family tea, and a family time we had. Have you forgotten about the urn, and what I said about Werter's Charlotte, and the bread and butter, and that capital story you told of the large loaf. A hundred times since, I have laughed over it. At least you must recall my name—Ringman, John Ringman."

"Large loaf? Invited you to tea? Ringman? Ringman? Ring? Ring?"

"Ah sir," sadly smiling, "don't ring the changes that way. I see you have a faithless memory, Mr. Roberts. But trust in the faithfulness of mine."

"Well, to tell the truth, in some things my memory aint of the very best," was the honest rejoinder. "But still," he perplexedly added, "still I—"

"Oh sir, suffice it that it is as I say. Doubt not that we are all well acquainted."

"But—but I don't like this going dead against my own memory; I—"

"But didn't you admit, my dear sir, that in some things this memory of yours is a little faithless? Now, those who have faithless memories, should they not have some little confidence in the less faithless memories of others?"

"But, of this friendly chat and tea, I have not the slightest—"

"I see, I see; quite erased from the tablet. Pray, sir," with a sudden illumination, "about six years back, did it happen to you to receive any injury on the head? Surprising effects have arisen from such a cause. Not alone unconsciousness as to events for a greater or less time immediately subsequent to the injury, but likewise—strange to add—oblivion, entire and incurable, as to events embracing a longer or shorter period immediately preceding it; that is, when the mind at the time was perfectly sensible of them, and fully competent also to register them in the memory, and did in fact so do; but all in vain, for all was afterwards bruised out by the injury."

After the first start, the merchant listened with what appeared more than ordinary interest. The other proceeded:

"In my boyhood I was kicked by a horse, and lay insensible for a long time. Upon recovering, what a blank! No faintest trace in regard to how I had come near the horse, or what horse it was, or where it was, or that it was a horse at all that had brought me to that pass. For the knowledge of those particulars I am indebted solely to my friends, in whose statements, I need not say, I place implicit reliance, since particulars of some sort there must have been, and why should they deceive me? You see sir, the mind is ductile, very much so: but images, ductilely received into it, need a certain time to harden and bake in their impressions, otherwise such a casualty as I speak of will in an instant obliterate them, as though they had never been. We are but clay, sir, potter's clay, as the good book says, clay, feeble, and too-yielding clay. But I will not philosophize. Tell me, was it your misfortune to receive any concussion upon the brain about the period I speak of? If so, I will with pleasure supply the void in your memory by more minutely rehearsing the circumstances of our acquaintance."

The growing interest betrayed by the merchant had not relaxed as the other proceeded. After some hesitation, indeed, something more than hesitation, he confessed that, though he had never received any injury of the sort named, yet, about the time in question, he had in fact been taken with a brain fever, losing his mind completely for a considerable interval. He was continuing, when the stranger with much animation exclaimed:

"There now, you see, I was not wholly mistaken. That brain fever accounts for it all."

"Nay; but—"

"Pardon me, Mr. Roberts," respectfully interrupting him, "but time is short, and I have something private and particular to say to you. Allow me."

Mr. Roberts, good man, could but acquiesce, and the two having silently walked to a less public spot, the manner of the man with the weed suddenly assumed a seriousness almost painful. What might be called a writhing expression stole over him. He seemed struggling with some disastrous necessity inkept. He made one or two attempts to speak, but words seemed to choke him. His companion stood in

　　　　　HERMAN MELVILLE

humane surprise, wondering what was to come. At length, with an effort mastering his feelings, in a tolerably composed tone he spoke:

"If I remember, you are a mason, Mr. Roberts?"

"Yes, yes."

Averting himself a moment, as to recover from a return of agitation, the stranger grasped the other's hand; "and would you not loan a brother a shilling if he needed it?"

The merchant started, apparently, almost as if to retreat.

"Ah, Mr. Roberts, I trust you are not one of those business men, who make a business of never having to do with unfortunates. For God's sake don't leave me. I have something on my heart—on my heart. Under deplorable circumstances thrown among strangers, utter strangers. I want a friend in whom I may confide. Yours, Mr. Roberts, is almost the first known face I've seen for many weeks."

It was so sudden an outburst; the interview offered such a contrast to the scene around, that the merchant, though not used to be very indiscreet, yet, being not entirely inhumane, remained not entirely unmoved.

The other, still tremulous, resumed:

"I need not say, sir, how it cuts me to the soul, to follow up a social salutation with such words as have just been mine. I know that I jeopardize your good opinion. But I can't help it: necessity knows no law, and heeds no risk. Sir, we are masons, one more step aside; I will tell you my story."

In a low, half-suppressed tone, he began it. Judging from his auditor's expression, it seemed to be a tale of singular interest, involving calamities against which no integrity, no forethought, no energy, no genius, no piety, could guard.

At every disclosure, the hearer's commiseration increased. No sentimental pity. As the story went on, he drew from his wallet a bank note, but after a while, at some still more unhappy revelation, changed it for another, probably of a somewhat larger amount; which, when the story was concluded, with an air studiously disclamatory of alms-giving, he put into the stranger's hands; who, on his side, with an air studiously disclamatory of alms-taking, put it into his pocket.

Assistance being received, the stranger's manner assumed a kind and degree of decorum which, under the circumstances, seemed almost coldness. After some words, not over ardent, and yet not exactly inappropriate, he took leave, making a bow which had one knows not what of a certain chastened independence about it; as if misery, however burdensome, could not break down self-respect, nor gratitude, however deep, humiliate a gentleman.

He was hardly yet out of sight, when he paused as if thinking; then with hastened steps returning to the merchant, "I am just reminded that the president, who is also transfer-agent, of the Black Rapids Coal Company, happens to be on board here, and, having been subpoenaed as witness in a stock case on the docket in Kentucky, has his transfer-book with him. A month since, in a panic contrived by artful alarmists, some credulous stock-holders sold out; but, to frustrate the aim of the alarmists, the Company, previously advised of their scheme, so managed it as to get into its own hands those sacrificed shares, resolved that, since a spurious panic must be, the panic-makers should be no gainers by it. The Company, I hear, is now ready, but not anxious, to redispose of those shares; and having obtained them at their depressed value, will now sell them at par, though, prior to the panic, they were held at a handsome figure above. That the readiness of the Company to do this is not generally known, is shown by the fact that the stock still stands on the transfer-book in the Company's name, offering to one in funds a rare chance for investment. For, the panic subsiding more and more every day, it will daily be seen how it originated; confidence will be more than restored; there will be a reaction; from the stock's descent its rise will be higher than from no fall, the holders trusting themselves to fear no second fate."

Having listened at first with curiosity, at last with interest, the merchant replied to the effect, that some time since, through friends concerned with it, he had heard of the company, and heard well of it, but was ignorant that there had latterly been fluctuations. He added that he was no speculator; that hitherto he had avoided having to do with stocks of any sort, but in the present case he really felt something like being tempted. "Pray," in conclusion, "do you think that upon a pinch anything could be transacted on board here with the transfer-agent? Are you acquainted with him?"

"Not personally. I but happened to hear that he was a passenger. For the rest, though it might be somewhat informal, the gentleman might not object to doing a little business on board. Along the Mississippi, you know, business is not so ceremonious as at the East."

"True," returned the merchant, and looked down a moment in thought, then, raising his head quickly, said, in a tone not so benign as his wonted one, "This would seem a rare chance, indeed; why, upon first hearing it, did you not snatch at it? I mean for yourself!"

"I?—would it had been possible!"

Not without some emotion was this said, and not without some embarrassment was the reply. "Ah, yes, I had forgotten."

Upon this, the stranger regarded him with mild gravity, not a little disconcerting; the more so, as there was in it what seemed the aspect not alone of the superior, but, as it were, the rebuker; which sort of bearing, in a beneficiary towards his benefactor, looked strangely enough; none the less, that, somehow, it sat not altogether unbecomingly upon the beneficiary, being free from anything like the appearance of assumption, and mixed with a kind of painful conscientiousness, as though nothing but a proper sense of what he owed to himself swayed him. At length he spoke:

"To reproach a penniless man with remissness in not availing himself of an opportunity for pecuniary investment—but, no, no; it was forgetfulness; and this, charity will impute to some lingering effect of that unfortunate brain-fever, which, as to occurrences dating yet further back, disturbed Mr. Roberts's memory still more seriously."

"As to that," said the merchant, rallying, "I am not—"

"Pardon me, but you must admit, that just now, an unpleasant distrust, however vague, was yours. Ah, shallow as it is, yet, how subtle a thing is suspicion, which at times can invade the humanest of hearts and wisest of heads. But, enough. My object, sir, in calling your attention to this stock, is by way of acknowledgment of your goodness. I but seek to be grateful; if my information leads to nothing, you must remember the motive."

He bowed, and finally retired, leaving Mr. Roberts not wholly without self-reproach, for having momentarily indulged injurious thoughts against one who, it was evident, was possessed of a self-respect which forbade his indulging them himself.

V

The Man With the Weed Makes it an Even Question Whether He Be a Great Sage or a Great Simpleton

"Well, there is sorrow in the world, but goodness too; and goodness that is not greenness, either, no more than sorrow is. Dear good man. Poor beating heart!"

It was the man with the weed, not very long after quitting the merchant, murmuring to himself with his hand to his side like one with the heart-disease.

Meditation over kindness received seemed to have softened him something, too, it may be, beyond what might, perhaps, have been looked for from one whose unwonted self-respect in the hour of need, and in the act of being aided, might have appeared to some not wholly unlike pride out of place; and pride, in any place, is seldom very feeling. But the truth, perhaps, is, that those who are least touched with that vice, besides being not unsusceptible to goodness, are sometimes the ones whom a ruling sense of propriety makes appear cold, if not thankless, under a favor. For, at such a time, to be full of warm, earnest words, and heart-felt protestations, is to create a scene; and well-bred people dislike few things more than that; which would seem to look as if the world did not relish earnestness; but, not so; because the world, being earnest itself, likes an earnest scene, and an earnest man, very well, but only in their place—the stage. See what sad work they make of it, who, ignorant of this, flame out in Irish enthusiasm and with Irish sincerity, to a benefactor, who, if a man of sense and respectability, as well as kindliness, can but be more or less annoyed by it; and, if of a nervously fastidious nature, as some are, may be led to think almost as much less favorably of the beneficiary paining him by his gratitude, as if he had been guilty of its contrary, instead only of an indiscretion. But, beneficiaries who know better, though they may feel as much, if not more, neither inflict such pain, nor are inclined to run any risk of so doing. And these, being wise, are the majority. By which one sees how inconsiderate those persons are, who, from the absence of its officious manifestations in the world, complain that there is not much gratitude extant; when the truth is, that there is as much of it as there is of modesty; but, both being for the most part votarists of the shade, for the most part keep out of sight.

What started this was, to account, if necessary, for the changed air of the man with the weed, who, throwing off in private the cold garb of decorum, and so giving warmly loose to his genuine heart, seemed almost transformed into another being. This subdued air of softness, too, was toned with melancholy, melancholy unreserved; a thing which, however at variance with propriety, still the more attested his earnestness; for one knows not how it is, but it sometimes happens that, where earnestness is, there, also, is melancholy.

At the time, he was leaning over the rail at the boat's side, in his pensiveness, unmindful of another pensive figure near—a young gentleman with a swan-neck, wearing a lady-like open shirt collar, thrown back, and tied with a black ribbon. From a square, tableted-broach, curiously engraved with Greek characters, he seemed a collegian—not improbably, a sophomore—on his travels; possibly, his first. A small book bound in Roman vellum was in his hand.

Overhearing his murmuring neighbor, the youth regarded him with some surprise, not to say interest. But, singularly for a collegian, being apparently of a retiring nature, he did not speak; when the other still more increased his diffidence by changing from soliloquy to colloquy, in a manner strangely mixed of familiarity and pathos.

"Ah, who is this? You did not hear me, my young friend, did you? Why, you, too, look sad. My melancholy is not catching!"

"Sir, sir," stammered the other.

"Pray, now," with a sort of sociable sorrowfulness, slowly sliding along the rail, "Pray, now, my young friend, what volume have you there? Give me leave," gently drawing it from him. "Tacitus!" Then opening it at random, read: "In general a black and shameful period lies before me." "Dear young sir," touching his arm alarmedly, "don't read this book. It is poison, moral poison. Even were there truth in Tacitus, such truth would have the operation of falsity, and so still be poison, moral poison. Too well I know this Tacitus. In my college-days he came near souring me into cynicism. Yes, I began to turn down my collar, and go about with a disdainfully joyless expression."

"Sir, sir, I—I—"

"Trust me. Now, young friend, perhaps you think that Tacitus, like me, is only melancholy; but he's more—he's ugly. A vast difference, young sir, between the melancholy view and the ugly. The one may show the world still beautiful, not so the other. The one may be compatible with benevolence, the other not. The one may deepen insight, the other shallows it. Drop Tacitus. Phrenologically, my young friend, you would seem to have a well-developed head, and large; but cribbed within the ugly view, the Tacitus view, your large brain, like your large ox in the contracted field, will but starve the more. And don't dream, as some of you students may, that, by taking this same ugly view, the deeper meanings of the deeper books will so alone become revealed to you. Drop Tacitus. His subtlety is falsity, To him, in his double-refined anatomy of human nature, is well applied the Scripture saying—'There is a subtle man, and the same is deceived.' Drop Tacitus. Come, now, let me throw the book overboard."

"Sir, I—I—"

"Not a word; I know just what is in your mind, and that is just what I am speaking to. Yes, learn from me that, though the sorrows of the world are great, its wickedness—that is, its ugliness—is small. Much cause to pity man, little to distrust him. I myself have known adversity, and know it still. But for that, do I turn cynic? No, no: it is small beer that sours. To my fellow-creatures I owe alleviations. So, whatever I may have undergone, it but deepens my confidence in my kind. Now, then" (winningly), "this book—will you let me drown it for you?"

"Really, sir—I—"

"I see, I see. But of course you read Tacitus in order to aid you in understanding human nature—as if truth was ever got at by libel. My young friend, if to know human nature is your object, drop Tacitus and go north to the cemeteries of Auburn and Greenwood."

"Upon my word, I—I—"

"Nay, I foresee all that. But you carry Tacitus, that shallow Tacitus. What do *I* carry? See"—producing a pocket-volume—"Akenside—his 'Pleasures of Imagination.' One of these days you will know it. Whatever our lot, we should read serene and cheery books, fitted to inspire love and trust. But Tacitus! I have long been of opinion that these classics are the bane of colleges; for—not to hint of the immorality of Ovid, Horace, Anacreon, and the rest, and the dangerous theology of Eschylus and others—where will one find views so injurious to human nature as in Thucydides, Juvenal, Lucian, but more particularly Tacitus? When I consider that, ever since the revival of learning, these classics have been the favorites of successive generations of students and studious men,

I tremble to think of that mass of unsuspected heresy on every vital topic which for centuries must have simmered unsurmised in the heart of Christendom. But Tacitus—he is the most extraordinary example of a heretic; not one iota of confidence in his kind. What a mockery that such an one should be reputed wise, and Thucydides be esteemed the statesman's manual! But Tacitus—I hate Tacitus; not, though, I trust, with the hate that sins, but a righteous hate. Without confidence himself, Tacitus destroys it in all his readers. Destroys confidence, paternal confidence, of which God knows that there is in this world none to spare. For, comparatively inexperienced as you are, my dear young friend, did you never observe how little, very little, confidence, there is? I mean between man and man—more particularly between stranger and stranger. In a sad world it is the saddest fact. Confidence! I have sometimes almost thought that confidence is fled; that confidence is the New Astrea—emigrated—vanished—gone." Then softly sliding nearer, with the softest air, quivering down and looking up, "could you now, my dear young sir, under such circumstances, by way of experiment, simply have confidence in *me*?"

From the outset, the sophomore, as has been seen, had struggled with an ever-increasing embarrassment, arising, perhaps, from such strange remarks coming from a stranger—such persistent and prolonged remarks, too. In vain had he more than once sought to break the spell by venturing a deprecatory or leave-taking word. In vain. Somehow, the stranger fascinated him. Little wonder, then, that, when the appeal came, he could hardly speak, but, as before intimated, being apparently of a retiring nature, abruptly retired from the spot, leaving the chagrined stranger to wander away in the opposite direction.

VI

At the Outset of Which Certain Passengers Prove Deaf to the Call of Charity

—"You—pish! Why will the captain suffer these begging fellows on board?";

These pettish words were breathed by a well-to-do gentleman in a ruby-colored velvet vest, and with a ruby-colored cheek, a ruby-headed cane in his hand, to a man in a gray coat and white tie, who, shortly after the interview last described, had accosted him for contributions to a Widow and Orphan Asylum recently founded among the Seminoles. Upon a cursory view, this last person might have seemed, like the man with the weed, one of the less unrefined children of misfortune; but, on a closer observation, his countenance revealed little of sorrow, though much of sanctity.

With added words of touchy disgust, the well-to-do gentleman hurried away. But, though repulsed, and rudely, the man in gray did not reproach, for a time patiently remaining in the chilly loneliness to which he had been left, his countenance, however, not without token of latent though chastened reliance.

At length an old gentleman, somewhat bulky, drew nigh, and from him also a contribution was sought.

"Look, you," coming to a dead halt, and scowling upon him. "Look, you," swelling his bulk out before him like a swaying balloon, "look, you, you on others' behalf ask for money; you, a fellow with a face as long as my arm. Hark ye, now: there is such a thing as gravity, and in condemned felons it may be genuine; but of long faces there are three sorts; that of grief's drudge, that of the lantern-jawed man, and that of the impostor. You know best which yours is."

"Heaven give you more charity, sir."

"And you less hypocrisy, sir."

With which words, the hard-hearted old gentleman marched off.

While the other still stood forlorn, the young clergyman, before introduced, passing that way, catching a chance sight of him, seemed suddenly struck by some recollection; and, after a moment's pause, hurried up with: "Your pardon, but shortly since I was all over looking for you."

"For me?" as marveling that one of so little account should be sought for.

"Yes, for you; do you know anything about the negro, apparently a cripple, aboard here? Is he, or is he not, what he seems to be?"

"Ah, poor Guinea! have you, too, been distrusted? you, upon whom nature has placarded the evidence of your claims?"

"Then you do really know him, and he is quite worthy? It relieves me to hear it—much relieves me. Come, let us go find him, and see what can be done."

"Another instance that confidence may come too late. I am sorry to say that at the last landing I myself—just happening to catch sight of him on the gangway-plank—assisted the cripple ashore. No time to talk, only to help. He may not have told you, but he has a brother in that vicinity.

"Really, I regret his going without my seeing him again; regret it, more, perhaps, than you can readily think. You see, shortly after leaving St. Louis, he was on the forecastle, and there, with many others, I saw him, and put trust in him; so much so, that, to convince those who did not, I, at his entreaty, went in search of you, you being one of several individuals he mentioned, and whose personal appearance he more or less described, individuals who he said would willingly speak for him. But, after diligent search, not finding you, and catching no glimpse of any of the others he had enumerated, doubts were at last suggested; but doubts indirectly originating, as I can but think, from prior distrust unfeelingly proclaimed by another. Still, certain it is, I began to suspect."

"Ha, ha, ha!"

A sort of laugh more like a groan than a laugh; and yet, somehow, it seemed intended for a laugh.

Both turned, and the young clergyman started at seeing the wooden-legged man close behind him, morosely grave as a criminal judge with a mustard-plaster on his back. In the present case the mustard-plaster might have been the memory of certain recent biting rebuffs and mortifications.

"Wouldn't think it was I who laughed would you?"

"But who was it you laughed at? or rather, tried to laugh at?" demanded the young clergyman, flushing, "me?"

"Neither you nor any one within a thousand miles of you. But perhaps you don't believe it."

"If he were of a suspicious temper, he might not," interposed the man in gray calmly, "it is one of the imbecilities of the suspicious person to fancy that every stranger, however absent-minded, he sees so much as smiling or gesturing to himself in any odd sort of way, is secretly making him his butt. In some moods, the movements of an entire street, as the suspicious man walks down it, will seem an express pantomimic jeer at him. In short, the suspicious man kicks himself with his own foot."

"Whoever can do that, ten to one he saves other folks' sole-leather," said the wooden-legged man with a crusty attempt at humor. But with augmented grin and squirm, turning directly upon the young clergyman, "you still think it was *you* I was laughing at, just now. To prove your mistake, I will tell you what I *was* laughing at; a story I happened to call to mind just then."

Whereupon, in his porcupine way, and with sarcastic details, unpleasant to repeat, he related a story, which might, perhaps, in a good-natured version, be rendered as follows:

A certain Frenchman of New Orleans, an old man, less slender in purse than limb, happening to attend the theatre one evening, was so charmed with the character of a faithful wife, as there represented to the life, that nothing would do but he must marry upon it. So, marry he did, a beautiful girl from Tennessee, who had first attracted his attention by her liberal mould, and was subsequently recommended to him through her kin, for her equally liberal education and disposition. Though large, the praise proved not too much. For, ere long, rumor more than corroborated it, by whispering that the lady was liberal to a fault. But though various circumstances, which by most Benedicts would have been deemed all but conclusive, were duly recited to the old Frenchman by his friends, yet such was his confidence that not a syllable would he credit, till, chancing one night to return unexpectedly from a journey, upon entering his apartment, a stranger burst from the alcove: "Begar!" cried he, "now I *begin* to suspec."

His story told, the wooden-legged man threw back his head, and gave vent to a long, gasping, rasping sort of taunting cry, intolerable as that of a high-pressure engine jeering off steam; and that done, with apparent satisfaction hobbled away.

"Who is that scoffer," said the man in gray, not without warmth. "Who is he, who even were truth on his tongue, his way of speaking it would make truth almost offensive as falsehood. Who is he?"

"He who I mentioned to you as having boasted his suspicion of the

HERMAN MELVILLE

negro," replied the young clergyman, recovering from disturbance, "in short, the person to whom I ascribe the origin of my own distrust; he maintained that Guinea was some white scoundrel, betwisted and painted up for a decoy. Yes, these were his very words, I think."

"Impossible! he could not be so wrong-headed. Pray, will you call him back, and let me ask him if he were really in earnest?"

The other complied; and, at length, after no few surly objections, prevailed upon the one-legged individual to return for a moment. Upon which, the man in gray thus addressed him: "This reverend gentleman tells me, sir, that a certain cripple, a poor negro, is by you considered an ingenious impostor. Now, I am not unaware that there are some persons in this world, who, unable to give better proof of being wise, take a strange delight in showing what they think they have sagaciously read in mankind by uncharitable suspicions of them. I hope you are not one of these. In short, would you tell me now, whether you were not merely joking in the notion you threw out about the negro. Would you be so kind?"

"No, I won't be so kind, I'll be so cruel."

"As you please about that."

"Well, he's just what I said he was."

"A white masquerading as a black?"

"Exactly."

The man in gray glanced at the young clergyman a moment, then quietly whispered to him, "I thought you represented your friend here as a very distrustful sort of person, but he appears endued with a singular credulity.—Tell me, sir, do you really think that a white could look the negro so? For one, I should call it pretty good acting."

"Not much better than any other man acts."

"How? Does all the world act? Am I, for instance, an actor? Is my reverend friend here, too, a performer?"

"Yes, don't you both perform acts? To do, is to act; so all doers are actors."

"You trifle.—I ask again, if a white, how could he look the negro so?"

"Never saw the negro-minstrels, I suppose?"

"Yes, but they are apt to overdo the ebony; exemplifying the old saying, not more just than charitable, that 'the devil is never so black as he is painted.' But his limbs, if not a cripple, how could he twist his limbs so?"

"How do other hypocritical beggars twist theirs? Easy enough to see how they are hoisted up."

"The sham is evident, then?"

"To the discerning eye," with a horrible screw of his gimlet one.

"Well, where is Guinea?" said the man in gray; "where is he? Let us at once find him, and refute beyond cavil this injurious hypothesis."

"Do so," cried the one-eyed man, "I'm just in the humor now for having him found, and leaving the streaks of these fingers on his paint, as the lion leaves the streaks of his nails on a Caffre. They wouldn't let me touch him before. Yes, find him, I'll make wool fly, and him after."

"You forget," here said the young clergyman to the man in gray, "that yourself helped poor Guinea ashore."

"So I did, so I did; how unfortunate. But look now," to the other, "I think that without personal proof I can convince you of your mistake. For I put it to you, is it reasonable to suppose that a man with brains, sufficient to act such a part as you say, would take all that trouble, and run all that hazard, for the mere sake of those few paltry coppers, which, I hear, was all he got for his pains, if pains they were?"

"That puts the case irrefutably," said the young clergyman, with a challenging glance towards the one-legged man.

"You two green-horns! Money, you think, is the sole motive to pains and hazard, deception and deviltry, in this world. How much money did the devil make by gulling Eve?"

Whereupon he hobbled off again with a repetition of his intolerable jeer.

The man in gray stood silently eying his retreat a while, and then, turning to his companion, said: "A bad man, a dangerous man; a man to be put down in any Christian community.—And this was he who was the means of begetting your distrust? Ah, we should shut our ears to distrust, and keep them open only for its opposite."

"You advance a principle, which, if I had acted upon it this morning, I should have spared myself what I now feel.—That but one man, and he with one leg, should have such ill power given him; his one sour word leavening into congenial sourness (as, to my knowledge, it did) the dispositions, before sweet enough, of a numerous company. But, as I hinted, with me at the time his ill words went for nothing; the same as now; only afterwards they had effect; and I confess, this puzzles me."

"It should not. With humane minds, the spirit of distrust works something as certain potions do; it is a spirit which may enter such minds, and yet, for a time, longer or shorter, lie in them quiescent; but only the more deplorable its ultimate activity."

HERMAN MELVILLE

"An uncomfortable solution; for, since that baneful man did but just now anew drop on me his bane, how shall I be sure that my present exemption from its effects will be lasting?"

"You cannot be sure, but you can strive against it."

"How?"

"By strangling the least symptom of distrust, of any sort, which hereafter, upon whatever provocation, may arise in you."

"I will do so." Then added as in soliloquy, "Indeed, indeed, I was to blame in standing passive under such influences as that one-legged man's. My conscience upbraids me.—The poor negro: You see him occasionally, perhaps?"

"No, not often; though in a few days, as it happens, my engagements will call me to the neighborhood of his present retreat; and, no doubt, honest Guinea, who is a grateful soul, will come to see me there."

"Then you have been his benefactor?"

"His benefactor? I did not say that. I have known him."

"Take this mite. Hand it to Guinea when you see him; say it comes from one who has full belief in his honesty, and is sincerely sorry for having indulged, however transiently, in a contrary thought."

"I accept the trust. And, by-the-way, since you are of this truly charitable nature, you will not turn away an appeal in behalf of the Seminole Widow and Orphan Asylum?"

"I have not heard of that charity."

"But recently founded."

After a pause, the clergyman was irresolutely putting his hand in his pocket, when, caught by something in his companion's expression, he eyed him inquisitively, almost uneasily.

"Ah, well," smiled the other wanly, "if that subtle bane, we were speaking of but just now, is so soon beginning to work, in vain my appeal to you. Good-by."

"Nay," not untouched, "you do me injustice; instead of indulging present suspicions, I had rather make amends for previous ones. Here is something for your asylum. Not much; but every drop helps. Of course you have papers?"

"Of course," producing a memorandum book and pencil. "Let me take down name and amount. We publish these names. And now let me give you a little history of our asylum, and the providential way in which it was started."

VII

A Gentleman With Gold Sleeve-Buttons

At an interesting point of the narration, and at the moment when, with much curiosity, indeed, urgency, the narrator was being particularly questioned upon that point, he was, as it happened, altogether diverted both from it and his story, by just then catching sight of a gentleman who had been standing in sight from the beginning, but, until now, as it seemed, without being observed by him.

"Pardon me," said he, rising, "but yonder is one who I know will contribute, and largely. Don't take it amiss if I quit you."

"Go: duty before all things," was the conscientious reply.

The stranger was a man of more than winsome aspect. There he stood apart and in repose, and yet, by his mere look, lured the man in gray from his story, much as, by its graciousness of bearing, some full-leaved elm, alone in a meadow, lures the noon sickleman to throw down his sheaves, and come and apply for the alms of its shade.

But, considering that goodness is no such rare thing among men—the world familiarly know the noun; a common one in every language—it was curious that what so signalized the stranger, and made him look like a kind of foreigner, among the crowd (as to some it make him appear more or less unreal in this portraiture), was but the expression of so prevalent a quality. Such goodness seemed his, allied with such fortune, that, so far as his own personal experience could have gone, scarcely could he have known ill, physical or moral; and as for knowing or suspecting the latter in any serious degree (supposing such degree of it to be), by observation or philosophy; for that, probably, his nature, by its opposition, imperfectly qualified, or from it wholly exempted. For the rest, he might have been five and fifty, perhaps sixty, but tall, rosy, between plump and portly, with a primy, palmy air, and for the time and place, not to hint of his years, dressed with a strangely festive finish and elegance. The inner-side of his coat-skirts was of white satin, which might have looked especially inappropriate, had it not seemed less a bit of mere tailoring than something of an emblem, as it were; an involuntary emblem, let us say, that what seemed so good about him was not all outside; no, the fine covering had a still finer lining. Upon one hand he wore a white kid glove, but the other hand, which was ungloved, looked hardly less white. Now, as the Fidèle, like most steamboats, was upon deck a little soot-streaked here and there, especially about the railings, it was marvel how, under such circumstances, these hands retained their spotlessness. But, if you watched them a while, you noticed that they avoided touching anything; you noticed, in short, that a certain negro body-servant, whose hands nature had dyed black, perhaps with the same purpose that millers wear white, this negro servant's hands did most of his master's handling for him; having to do with dirt on his account, but not to his prejudices. But if, with the same undefiledness of consequences to himself, a gentleman could also sin by deputy, how shocking would that be! But it is not permitted to be; and even if it were, no judicious moralist would make proclamation of it.

This gentleman, therefore, there is reason to affirm, was one who, like the Hebrew governor, knew how to keep his hands clean, and who never in his life happened to be run suddenly against by hurrying house-painter, or sweep; in a word, one whose very good luck it was to be a very good man.

Not that he looked as if he were a kind of Wilberforce at all; that superior merit, probably, was not his; nothing in his manner bespoke him righteous, but only good, and though to be good is much below being righteous, and though there is a difference between the two, yet not, it is to be hoped, so incompatible as that a righteous man can not be a good man; though, conversely, in the pulpit it has been with much cogency urged, that a merely good man, that is, one good merely by his nature, is so far from there by being righteous, that nothing short of a total change and conversion can make him so; which is something which no honest mind, well read in the history of righteousness, will care to deny; nevertheless, since St. Paul himself, agreeing in a sense with the pulpit distinction, though not altogether in the pulpit deduction, and also pretty plainly intimating which of the two qualities in question enjoys his apostolic preference; I say, since St. Paul has so meaningly said, that, "scarcely for a righteous man will one die, yet peradventure for a good man some would even dare to die;" therefore, when we repeat of this gentleman, that he was only a good man, whatever else by severe censors may be objected to him, it is still to be hoped that his goodness will not at least be considered criminal in him. At all events, no man, not even a righteous man, would think it quite right to commit this gentleman to prison for the crime, extraordinary as he might deem it;

more especially, as, until everything could be known, there would be some chance that the gentleman might after all be quite as innocent of it as he himself.

It was pleasant to mark the good man's reception of the salute of the righteous man, that is, the man in gray; his inferior, apparently, not more in the social scale than in stature. Like the benign elm again, the good man seemed to wave the canopy of his goodness over that suitor, not in conceited condescension, but with that even amenity of true majesty, which can be kind to any one without stooping to it.

To the plea in behalf of the Seminole widows and orphans, the gentleman, after a question or two duly answered, responded by producing an ample pocket-book in the good old capacious style, of fine green French morocco and workmanship, bound with silk of the same color, not to omit bills crisp with newness, fresh from the bank, no muckworms' grime upon them. Lucre those bills might be, but as yet having been kept unspotted from the world, not of the filthy sort. Placing now three of those virgin bills in the applicant's hands, he hoped that the smallness of the contribution would be pardoned; to tell the truth, and this at last accounted for his toilet, he was bound but a short run down the river, to attend, in a festive grove, the afternoon wedding of his niece: so did not carry much money with him.

The other was about expressing his thanks when the gentleman in his pleasant way checked him: the gratitude was on the other side. To him, he said, charity was in one sense not an effort, but a luxury; against too great indulgence in which his steward, a humorist, had sometimes admonished him.

In some general talk which followed, relative to organized modes of doing good, the gentleman expressed his regrets that so many benevolent societies as there were, here and there isolated in the land, should not act in concert by coming together, in the way that already in each society the individuals composing it had done, which would result, he thought, in like advantages upon a larger scale. Indeed, such a confederation might, perhaps, be attended with as happy results as politically attended that of the states.

Upon his hitherto moderate enough companion, this suggestion had an effect illustrative in a sort of that notion of Socrates, that the soul is a harmony; for as the sound of a flute, in any particular key, will, it is said, audibly affect the corresponding chord of any harp in good tune, within hearing, just so now did some string in him respond, and with animation.

Which animation, by the way, might seem more or less out of character in the man in gray, considering his unsprightly manner when first introduced, had he not already, in certain after colloquies, given proof, in some degree, of the fact, that, with certain natures, a soberly continent air at times, so far from arguing emptiness of stuff, is good proof it is there, and plenty of it, because unwasted, and may be used the more effectively, too, when opportunity offers. What now follows on the part of the man in gray will still further exemplify, perhaps somewhat strikingly, the truth, or what appears to be such, of this remark.

"Sir," said he eagerly, "I am before you. A project, not dissimilar to yours, was by me thrown out at the World's Fair in London."

"World's Fair? You there? Pray how was that?"

"First, let me—"

"Nay, but first tell me what took you to the Fair?"

"I went to exhibit an invalid's easy-chair I had invented."

"Then you have not always been in the charity business?"

"Is it not charity to ease human suffering? I am, and always have been, as I always will be, I trust, in the charity business, as you call it; but charity is not like a pin, one to make the head, and the other the point; charity is a work to which a good workman may be competent in all its branches. I invented my Protean easy-chair in odd intervals stolen from meals and sleep."

"You call it the Protean easy-chair; pray describe it."

"My Protean easy-chair is a chair so all over bejointed, behinged, and bepadded, everyway so elastic, springy, and docile to the airiest touch, that in some one of its endlessly-changeable accommodations of back, seat, footboard, and arms, the most restless body, the body most racked, nay, I had almost added the most tormented conscience must, somehow and somewhere, find rest. Believing that I owed it to suffering humanity to make known such a chair to the utmost, I scraped together my little means and off to the World's Fair with it."

"You did right. But your scheme; how did you come to hit upon that?"

"I was going to tell you. After seeing my invention duly catalogued and placed, I gave myself up to pondering the scene about me. As I dwelt upon that shining pageant of arts, and moving concourse of nations, and reflected that here was the pride of the world glorying in a glass house, a sense of the fragility of worldly grandeur profoundly impressed me. And I said to myself, I will see if this occasion of vanity cannot supply a hint toward a better profit than was designed. Let some world-wide good to the world-wide cause be now done. In short, inspired by the scene, on the fourth day I issued at the World's Fair my prospectus of the World's Charity."

"Quite a thought. But, pray explain it."

"The World's Charity is to be a society whose members shall comprise deputies from every charity and mission extant; the one object of the society to be the methodization of the world's benevolence; to which end, the present system of voluntary and promiscuous contribution to be done away, and the Society to be empowered by the various governments to levy, annually, one grand benevolence tax upon all mankind; as in Augustus Cæsar's time, the whole world to come up to be taxed; a tax which, for the scheme of it, should be something like the income-tax in England, a tax, also, as before hinted, to be a consolidation-tax of all possible benevolence taxes; as in America here, the state-tax, and the county-tax, and the town-tax, and the poll-tax, are by the assessors rolled into one. This tax, according to my tables, calculated with care, would result in the yearly raising of a fund little short of eight hundred millions; this fund to be annually applied to such objects, and in such modes, as the various charities and missions, in general congress represented, might decree; whereby, in fourteen years, as I estimate, there would have been devoted to good works the sum of eleven thousand two hundred millions; which would warrant the dissolution of the society, as that fund judiciously expended, not a pauper or heathen could remain the round world over."

"Eleven thousand two hundred millions! And all by passing round a *hat*, as it were."

"Yes, I am no Fourier, the projector of an impossible scheme, but a philanthropist and a financier setting forth a philanthropy and a finance which are practicable."

"Practicable?"

"Yes. Eleven thousand two hundred millions; it will frighten none but a retail philanthropist. What is it but eight hundred millions for each of fourteen years? Now eight hundred millions—what is that, to average it, but one little dollar a head for the population of the planet? And who will refuse, what Turk or Dyak even, his own little dollar for sweet charity's sake? Eight hundred millions! More than that sum is yearly expended by mankind, not only in vanities, but miseries. Consider that bloody spendthrift, War. And are mankind so stupid, so wicked, that, upon the demonstration of these things they will not, amending their ways, devote their superfluities to blessing the world instead of cursing it? Eight hundred millions! They have not to make it, it is theirs already; they have but to direct it from ill to good. And to this, scarce a self-denial is demanded. Actually, they would not in the mass be one farthing the poorer for it; as certainly would they be all the better and happier. Don't you see? But admit, as you must, that mankind is not mad, and my project is practicable. For, what creature but a madman would not rather do good than ill, when it is plain that, good or ill, it must return upon himself?"

"Your sort of reasoning," said the good gentleman, adjusting his gold sleeve-buttons, "seems all reasonable enough, but with mankind it wont do."

"Then mankind are not reasoning beings, if reason wont do with them."

"That is not to the purpose. By-the-way, from the manner in which you alluded to the world's census, it would appear that, according to your world-wide scheme, the pauper not less than the nabob is to contribute to the relief of pauperism, and the heathen not less than the Christian to the conversion of heathenism. How is that?"

"Why, that—pardon me—is quibbling. Now, no philanthropist likes to be opposed with quibbling."

"Well, I won't quibble any more. But, after all, if I understand your project, there is little specially new in it, further than the magnifying of means now in operation."

"Magnifying and energizing. For one thing, missions I would thoroughly reform. Missions I would quicken with the Wall street spirit."

"The Wall street spirit?"

"Yes; for if, confessedly, certain spiritual ends are to be gained but through the auxiliary agency of worldly means, then, to the surer gaining of such spiritual ends, the example of worldly policy in worldly projects should not by spiritual projectors be slighted. In brief, the conversion of the heathen, so far, at least, as depending on human effort, would, by the world's charity, be let out on contract. So much by bid for converting India, so much for Borneo, so much for Africa. Competition allowed, stimulus would be given. There would be no lethargy of monopoly. We should have no mission-house or tract-house of which slanderers could, with any plausibility, say that it had degenerated in its clerkships into a sort of custom-house. But the main point is the Archimedean money-power that would be brought to bear."

"You mean the eight hundred million power?"

"Yes. You see, this doing good to the world by driblets amounts to just nothing. I am for doing good to the world with a will. I am for doing good to the world once for all and having done with it. Do but think, my dear sir, of the eddies and maëlstroms of pagans in China. People here have no conception of it. Of a frosty morning in Hong Kong, pauper pagans are found dead in the streets like so many nipped peas in a bin of peas. To be an immortal being in China is no more distinction than to be a snow-flake in a snow-squall. What are a score or two of missionaries to such a people? A pinch of snuff to the kraken. I am for sending ten thousand missionaries in a body and converting the Chinese *en masse* within six months of the debarkation. The thing is then done, and turn to something else."

"I fear you are too enthusiastic."

"A philanthropist is necessarily an enthusiast; for without enthusiasm what was ever achieved but commonplace? But again: consider the poor in London. To that mob of misery, what is a joint here and a loaf there? I am for voting to them twenty thousand bullocks and one hundred thousand barrels of flour to begin with. They are then comforted, and no more hunger for one while among the poor of London. And so all round."

"Sharing the character of your general project, these things, I take it, are rather examples of wonders that were to be wished, than wonders that will happen."

"And is the age of wonders passed? Is the world too old? Is it barren? Think of Sarah."

"Then I am Abraham reviling the angel (with a smile). But still, as to your design at large, there seems a certain audacity."

"But if to the audacity of the design there be brought a commensurate circumspectness of execution, how then?"

"Why, do you really believe that your world's charity will ever go into operation?"

"I have confidence that it will."

"But may you not be over-confident?"

"For a Christian to talk so!"

"But think of the obstacles!"

"Obstacles? I have confidence to remove obstacles, though mountains. Yes, confidence in the world's charity to that degree, that, as no better person offers to supply the place, I have nominated myself provisional treasurer, and will be happy to receive subscriptions, for the present to be devoted to striking off a million more of my prospectuses."

The talk went on; the man in gray revealed a spirit of benevolence which, mindful of the millennial promise, had gone abroad over all the countries of the globe, much as the diligent spirit of the husbandman, stirred by forethought of the coming seed-time, leads him, in March reveries at his fireside, over every field of his farm. The master chord of the man in gray had been touched, and it seemed as if it would never cease vibrating. A not unsilvery tongue, too, was his, with gestures that were a Pentecost of added ones, and persuasiveness before which granite hearts might crumble into gravel.

Strange, therefore, how his auditor, so singularly good-hearted as he seemed, remained proof to such eloquence; though not, as it turned out, to such pleadings. For, after listening a while longer with pleasant incredulity, presently, as the boat touched his place of destination, the gentleman, with a look half humor, half pity, put another bank-note into his hands; charitable to the last, if only to the dreams of enthusiasm.

VIII

A CHARITABLE LADY

If a drunkard in a sober fit is the dullest of mortals, an enthusiast in a reason-fit is not the most lively. And this, without prejudice to his greatly improved understanding; for, if his elation was the height of his madness, his despondency is but the extreme of his sanity. Something thus now, to all appearance, with the man in gray. Society his stimulus, loneliness was his lethargy. Loneliness, like the sea breeze, blowing off from a thousand leagues of blankness, he did not find, as veteran solitaires do, if anything, too bracing. In short, left to himself, with none to charm forth his latent lymphatic, he insensibly resumes his original air, a quiescent one, blended of sad humility and demureness.

Ere long he goes laggingly into the ladies' saloon, as in spiritless quest of somebody; but, after some disappointed glances about him, seats himself upon a sofa with an air of melancholy exhaustion and depression.

At the sofa's further end sits a plump and pleasant person, whose aspect seems to hint that, if she have any weak point, it must be anything rather than her excellent heart. From her twilight dress, neither dawn nor dark, apparently she is a widow just breaking the chrysalis of her mourning. A small gilt testament is in her hand, which she has just been reading. Half-relinquished, she holds the book in reverie, her finger inserted at the xiii. of 1st Corinthians, to which chapter possibly her attention might have recently been turned, by witnessing the scene of the monitory mute and his slate.

The sacred page no longer meets her eye; but, as at evening, when for a time the western hills shine on though the sun be set, her thoughtful face retains its tenderness though the teacher is forgotten.

Meantime, the expression of the stranger is such as ere long to attract her glance. But no responsive one. Presently, in her somewhat inquisitive survey, her volume drops. It is restored. No encroaching politeness in the act, but kindness, unadorned. The eyes of the lady sparkle. Evidently, she is not now unprepossessed. Soon, bending over, in a low, sad tone, full of deference, the stranger breathes, "Madam, pardon my freedom, but there is something in that face which strangely draws me. May I ask, are you a sister of the Church?"

"Why—really—you—"

In concern for her embarrassment, he hastens to relieve it, but, without seeming so to do. "It is very solitary for a brother here," eying the showy ladies brocaded in the background, "I find none to mingle souls with. It may be wrong—I *know* it is—but I cannot force myself to be easy with the people of the world. I prefer the company, however silent, of a brother or sister in good standing. By the way, madam, may I ask if you have confidence?"

"Really, sir—why, sir—really—I—"

"Could you put confidence in *me* for instance?"

"Really, sir—as much—I mean, as one may wisely put in a—a—stranger, an entire stranger, I had almost said," rejoined the lady, hardly yet at ease in her affability, drawing aside a little in body, while at the same time her heart might have been drawn as far the other way. A natural struggle between charity and prudence.

"Entire stranger!" with a sigh. "Ah, who would be a stranger? In vain, I wander; no one will have confidence in me."

"You interest me," said the good lady, in mild surprise. "Can I any way befriend you?"

"No one can befriend me, who has not confidence."

"But I—I have—at least to that degree—I mean that—"

"Nay, nay, you have none—none at all. Pardon, I see it. No confidence. Fool, fond fool that I am to seek it!"

"You are unjust, sir," rejoins the good lady with heightened interest; "but it may be that something untoward in your experiences has unduly biased you. Not that I would cast reflections. Believe me, I—yes, yes—I may say—that—that—"

"That you have confidence? Prove it. Let me have twenty dollars."

"Twenty dollars!"

"There, I told you, madam, you had no confidence."

The lady was, in an extraordinary way, touched. She sat in a sort of restless torment, knowing not which way to turn. She began twenty different sentences, and left off at the first syllable of each. At last, in desperation, she hurried out, "Tell me, sir, for what you want the twenty dollars?"

"And did I not—" then glancing at her half-mourning, "for the widow and the fatherless. I am traveling agent of the Widow and Orphan Asylum, recently founded among the Seminoles."

"And why did you not tell me your object before?" As not a little relieved. "Poor souls—Indians, too—those cruelly-used Indians. Here, here; how could I hesitate. I am so sorry it is no more."

"Grieve not for that, madam," rising and folding up the bank-notes. "This is an inconsiderable sum, I admit, but," taking out his pencil and book, "though I here but register the amount, there is another register, where is set down the motive. Good-bye; you have confidence. Yea, you can say to me as the apostle said to the Corinthians, 'I rejoice that I have confidence in you in all things.'"

IX

Two Business Men Transact a Little Business

—"Pray, sir, have you seen a gentleman with a weed hereabouts, rather a saddish gentleman? Strange where he can have gone to. I was talking with him not twenty minutes since."

By a brisk, ruddy-cheeked man in a tasseled traveling-cap, carrying under his arm a ledger-like volume, the above words were addressed to the collegian before introduced, suddenly accosted by the rail to which not long after his retreat, as in a previous chapter recounted, he had returned, and there remained.

"Have you seen him, sir?"

Rallied from his apparent diffidence by the genial jauntiness of the stranger, the youth answered with unwonted promptitude: "Yes, a person with a weed was here not very long ago."

"Saddish?"

"Yes, and a little cracked, too, I should say."

"It was he. Misfortune, I fear, has disturbed his brain. Now quick, which way did he go?"

"Why just in the direction from which you came, the gangway yonder."

"Did he? Then the man in the gray coat, whom I just met, said right: he must have gone ashore. How unlucky!"

He stood vexedly twitching at his cap-tassel, which fell over by his whisker, and continued: "Well, I am very sorry. In fact, I had something for him here."—Then drawing nearer, "you see, he applied to me for relief, no, I do him injustice, not that, but he began to intimate, you understand. Well, being very busy just then, I declined; quite rudely, too, in a cold, morose, unfeeling way, I fear. At all events, not three minutes afterwards I felt self-reproach, with a kind of prompting, very peremptory, to deliver over into that unfortunate man's hands a ten-dollar bill. You smile. Yes, it may be superstition, but I can't help it; I have my weak side, thank God. Then again," he rapidly went on, "we have been so very prosperous lately in our affairs—by we, I mean the Black Rapids Coal Company—that, really, out of my abundance, associative and individual, it is but fair that a charitable investment or two should be made, don't you think so?"

"Sir," said the collegian without the least embarrassment, "do I understand that you are officially connected with the Black Rapids Coal Company?"

"Yes, I happen to be president and transfer-agent."

"You are?"

"Yes, but what is it to you? You don't want to invest?"

"Why, do you sell the stock?"

"Some might be bought, perhaps; but why do you ask? you don't want to invest?"

"But supposing I did," with cool self-collectedness, "could you do up the thing for me, and here?"

"Bless my soul," gazing at him in amaze, "really, you are quite a business man. Positively, I feel afraid of you."

"Oh, no need of that.—You could sell me some of that stock, then?"

"I don't know, I don't know. To be sure, there are a few shares under peculiar circumstances bought in by the Company; but it would hardly be the thing to convert this boat into the Company's office. I think you had better defer investing. So," with an indifferent air, "you have seen the unfortunate man I spoke of?"

"Let the unfortunate man go his ways.—What is that large book you have with you?"

"My transfer-book. I am subpoenaed with it to court."

"Black Rapids Coal Company," obliquely reading the gilt inscription on the back; "I have heard much of it. Pray do you happen to have with you any statement of the condition of your company."

"A statement has lately been printed."

"Pardon me, but I am naturally inquisitive. Have you a copy with you?"

"I tell you again, I do not think that it would be suitable to convert this boat into the Company's office.—That unfortunate man, did you relieve him at all?"

"Let the unfortunate man relieve himself.—Hand me the statement."

"Well, you are such a business-man, I can hardly deny you. Here," handing a small, printed pamphlet.

The youth turned it over sagely.

"I hate a suspicious man," said the other, observing him; "but I must say I like to see a cautious one."

"I can gratify you there," languidly returning the pamphlet; "for, as I said before, I am naturally inquisitive; I am also circumspect. No appearances can deceive me. Your statement," he added "tells a very fine story; but pray, was not your stock a little heavy awhile ago? downward tendency? Sort of low spirits among holders on the subject of that stock?"

"Yes, there was a depression. But how came it? who devised it? The 'bears,' sir. The depression of our stock was solely owing to the growling, the hypocritical growling, of the bears."

"How, hypocritical?"

"Why, the most monstrous of all hypocrites are these bears: hypocrites by inversion; hypocrites in the simulation of things dark instead of bright; souls that thrive, less upon depression, than the fiction of depression; professors of the wicked art of manufacturing depressions; spurious Jeremiahs; sham Heraclituses, who, the lugubrious day done, return, like sham Lazaruses among the beggars, to make merry over the gains got by their pretended sore heads—scoundrelly bears!"

"You are warm against these bears?"

"If I am, it is less from the remembrance of their stratagems as to our stock, than from the persuasion that these same destroyers of confidence, and gloomy philosophers of the stock-market, though false in themselves, are yet true types of most destroyers of confidence and gloomy philosophers, the world over. Fellows who, whether in stocks, politics, bread-stuffs, morals, metaphysics, religion—be it what it may—trump up their black panics in the naturally-quiet brightness, solely with a view to some sort of covert advantage. That corpse of calamity which the gloomy philosopher parades, is but his Good-Enough-Morgan."

"I rather like that," knowingly drawled the youth. "I fancy these gloomy souls as little as the next one. Sitting on my sofa after a champagne dinner, smoking my plantation cigar, if a gloomy fellow come to me—what a bore!"

"You tell him it's all stuff, don't you?"

"I tell him it ain't natural. I say to him, you are happy enough, and you know it; and everybody else is as happy as you, and you know that, too; and we shall all be happy after we are no more, and you know that, too; but no, still you must have your sulk."

"And do you know whence this sort of fellow gets his sulk? not from life; for he's often too much of a recluse, or else too young to have seen anything of it. No, he gets it from some of those old plays he sees on the stage, or some of those old books he finds up in garrets. Ten to one, he has lugged home from auction a musty old Seneca, and sets about stuffing himself with that stale old hay; and, thereupon, thinks it looks wise and antique to be a croaker, thinks it's taking a stand-way above his kind."

"Just so," assented the youth. "I've lived some, and seen a good many such ravens at second hand. By the way, strange how that man with the weed, you were inquiring for, seemed to take me for some soft sentimentalist, only because I kept quiet, and thought, because I had a copy of Tacitus with me, that I was reading him for his gloom, instead of his gossip. But I let him talk. And, indeed, by my manner humored him."

"You shouldn't have done that, now. Unfortunate man, you must have made quite a fool of him."

"His own fault if I did. But I like prosperous fellows, comfortable fellows; fellows that talk comfortably and prosperously, like you. Such fellows are generally honest. And, I say now, I happen to have a superfluity in my pocket, and I'll just—"

"—Act the part of a brother to that unfortunate man?"

"Let the unfortunate man be his own brother. What are you dragging him in for all the time? One would think you didn't care to register any transfers, or dispose of any stock—mind running on something else. I say I will invest."

"Stay, stay, here come some uproarious fellows—this way, this way."

And with off-handed politeness the man with the book escorted his companion into a private little haven removed from the brawling swells without.

Business transacted, the two came forth, and walked the deck.

"Now tell me, sir," said he with the book, "how comes it that a young gentleman like you, a sedate student at the first appearance, should dabble in stocks and that sort of thing?"

"There are certain sophomorean errors in the world," drawled the sophomore, deliberately adjusting his shirt-collar, "not the least of which is the popular notion touching the nature of the modern scholar, and the nature of the modern scholastic sedateness."

"So it seems, so it seems. Really, this is quite a new leaf in my experience."

"Experience, sir," originally observed the sophomore, "is the only teacher."

"Hence am I your pupil; for it's only when experience speaks, that I can endure to listen to speculation."

"My speculations, sir," dryly drawing himself up, "have been chiefly governed by the maxim of Lord Bacon; I speculate in those philosophies which come home to my business and bosom—pray, do you know of any other good stocks?"

"You wouldn't like to be concerned in the New Jerusalem, would you?"

"New Jerusalem?"

"Yes, the new and thriving city, so called, in northern Minnesota. It was originally founded by certain fugitive Mormons. Hence the name. It stands on the Mississippi. Here, here is the map," producing a roll. "There—there, you see are the public buildings—here the landing—there the park—yonder the botanic gardens—and this, this little dot here, is a perpetual fountain, you understand. You observe there are twenty asterisks. Those are for the lyceums. They have lignum-vitae rostrums."

"And are all these buildings now standing?"

"All standing—bona fide."

"These marginal squares here, are they the water-lots?"

"Water-lots in the city of New Jerusalem? All terra firma—you don't seem to care about investing, though?"

"Hardly think I should read my title clear, as the law students say," yawned the collegian.

"Prudent—you are prudent. Don't know that you are wholly out, either. At any rate, I would rather have one of your shares of coal stock than two of this other. Still, considering that the first settlement was by two fugitives, who had swum over naked from the opposite shore—it's a surprising place. It is, *bona fide*.—But dear me, I must go. Oh, if by possibility you should come across that unfortunate man—"

"—In that case," with drawling impatience, "I will send for the steward, and have him and his misfortunes consigned overboard."

"Ha ha!—now were some gloomy philosopher here, some theological bear, forever taking occasion to growl down the stock of human nature (with ulterior views, d'ye see, to a fat benefice in the gift of the worshipers of Ariamius), he would pronounce that the sign of a hardening heart and a softening brain. Yes, that would be his sinister construction. But it's nothing more than the oddity of a genial humor—genial but dry. Confess it. Good-bye."

X

In the Cabin

S tools, settees, sofas, divans, ottomans; occupying them are clusters of men, old and young, wise and simple; in their hands are cards spotted with diamonds, spades, clubs, hearts; the favorite games are whist, cribbage, and brag. Lounging in arm-chairs or sauntering among the marble-topped tables, amused with the scene, are the comparatively few, who, instead of having hands in the games, for the most part keep their hands in their pockets. These may be the philosophes. But here and there, with a curious expression, one is reading a small sort of handbill of anonymous poetry, rather wordily entitled:—

> "Ode
> on the Intimations
> of
> Distrust in Man,
> Unwillingly Inferred from Repeated Repulses,
> In Disinterested Endeavors
> To Procure His
> Confidence."

On the floor are many copies, looking as if fluttered down from a balloon. The way they came there was this: A somewhat elderly person, in the quaker dress, had quietly passed through the cabin, and, much in the manner of those railway book-peddlers who precede their proffers of sale by a distribution of puffs, direct or indirect, of the volumes to follow, had, without speaking, handed about the odes, which, for the most part, after a cursory glance, had been disrespectfully tossed aside, as no doubt, the moonstruck production of some wandering rhapsodist.

In due time, book under arm, in trips the ruddy man with the traveling-cap, who, lightly moving to and fro, looks animatedly about him, with a yearning sort of gratulatory affinity and longing, expressive of the very soul of sociality; as much as to say, "Oh, boys, would that I were personally acquainted with each mother's son of you, since what a sweet world, to make sweet acquaintance in, is ours, my brothers; yea, and what dear, happy dogs are we all!"

And just as if he had really warbled it forth, he makes fraternally up to one lounging stranger or another, exchanging with him some pleasant remark.

"Pray, what have you there?" he asked of one newly accosted, a little, dried-up man, who looked as if he never dined.

"A little ode, rather queer, too," was the reply, "of the same sort you see strewn on the floor here."

"I did not observe them. Let me see;" picking one up and looking it over. "Well now, this is pretty; plaintive, especially the opening:—

> *'Alas for man, he hath small sense*
> *Of genial trust and confidence.'*

—If it be so, alas for him, indeed. Runs off very smoothly, sir. Beautiful pathos. But do you think the sentiment just?"

"As to that," said the little dried-up man, "I think it a kind of queer thing altogether, and yet I am almost ashamed to add, it really has set me to thinking; yes and to feeling. Just now, somehow, I feel as it were trustful and genial. I don't know that ever I felt so much so before. I am naturally numb in my sensibilities; but this ode, in its way, works on my numbness not unlike a sermon, which, by lamenting over my lying dead in trespasses and sins, thereby stirs me up to be all alive in well-doing."

"Glad to hear it, and hope you will do well, as the doctors say. But who snowed the odes about here?"

"I cannot say; I have not been here long."

"Wasn't an angel, was it? Come, you say you feel genial, let us do as the rest, and have cards."

"Thank you, I never play cards."

"A bottle of wine?"

"Thank you, I never drink wine."

"Cigars?"

"Thank you, I never smoke cigars."

"Tell stories?"

"To speak truly, I hardly think I know one worth telling."

"Seems to me, then, this geniality you say you feel waked in you, is as water-power in a land without mills. Come, you had better take a genial hand at the cards. To begin, we will play for as small a sum as you please; just enough to make it interesting."

"Indeed, you must excuse me. Somehow I distrust cards."

"What, distrust cards? Genial cards? Then for once I join with our sad Philomel here:—

> *'Alas for man, he hath small sense*
> *Of genial trust and confidence.'*

Good-bye!"

Sauntering and chatting here and there, again, he with the book at length seems fatigued, looks round for a seat, and spying a partly-vacant settee drawn up against the side, drops down there; soon, like his chance neighbor, who happens to be the good merchant, becoming not a little interested in the scene more immediately before him; a party at whist; two cream-faced, giddy, unpolished youths, the one in a red cravat, the other in a green, opposed to two bland, grave, handsome, self-possessed men of middle age, decorously dressed in a sort of professional black, and apparently doctors of some eminence in the civil law.

By-and-by, after a preliminary scanning of the new comer next him the good merchant, sideways leaning over, whispers behind a crumpled copy of the Ode which he holds: "Sir, I don't like the looks of those two, do you?"

"Hardly," was the whispered reply; "those colored cravats are not in the best taste, at least not to mine; but my taste is no rule for all."

"You mistake; I mean the other two, and I don't refer to dress, but countenance. I confess I am not familiar with such gentry any further than reading about them in the papers—but those two are—are sharpers, aint they?"

"Far be from us the captious and fault-finding spirit, my dear sir."

"Indeed, sir, I would not find fault; I am little given that way: but certainly, to say the least, these two youths can hardly be adepts, while the opposed couple may be even more."

"You would not hint that the colored cravats would be so bungling as to lose, and the dark cravats so dextrous as to cheat?—Sour imaginations, my dear sir. Dismiss them. To little purpose have you read the Ode you have there. Years and experience, I trust, have not sophisticated you. A fresh and liberal construction would teach us to regard those four players—indeed, this whole cabin-full of players—as playing at games in which every player plays fair, and not a player but shall win."

"Now, you hardly mean that; because games in which all may win, such games remain as yet in this world uninvented, I think."

"Come, come," luxuriously laying himself back, and casting a free glance upon the players, "fares all paid; digestion sound; care, toil, penury, grief, unknown; lounging on this sofa, with waistband relaxed, why not be cheerfully resigned to one's fate, nor peevishly pick holes in the blessed fate of the world?"

Upon this, the good merchant, after staring long and hard, and then rubbing his forehead, fell into meditation, at first uneasy, but at last composed, and in the end, once more addressed his companion: "Well, I see it's good to out with one's private thoughts now and then. Somehow, I don't know why, a certain misty suspiciousness seems inseparable from most of one's private notions about some men and some things; but once out with these misty notions, and their mere contact with other men's soon dissipates, or, at least, modifies them."

"You think I have done you good, then? may be, I have. But don't thank me, don't thank me. If by words, casually delivered in the social hour, I do any good to right or left, it is but involuntary influence—locust-tree sweetening the herbage under it; no merit at all; mere wholesome accident, of a wholesome nature.—Don't you see?"

Another stare from the good merchant, and both were silent again.

Finding his book, hitherto resting on his lap, rather irksome there, the owner now places it edgewise on the settee, between himself and neighbor; in so doing, chancing to expose the lettering on the back—"*Black Rapids Coal Company*"—which the good merchant, scrupulously honorable, had much ado to avoid reading, so directly would it have fallen under his eye, had he not conscientiously averted it. On a sudden, as if just reminded of something, the stranger starts up, and moves away, in his haste leaving his book; which the merchant observing, without delay takes it up, and, hurrying after, civilly returns it; in which act he could not avoid catching sight by an involuntary glance of part of the lettering.

"Thank you, thank you, my good sir," said the other, receiving the volume, and was resuming his retreat, when the merchant spoke: "Excuse me, but are you not in some way connected with the—the Coal Company I have heard of?"

"There is more than one Coal Company that may be heard of, my good sir," smiled the other, pausing with an expression of painful impatience, disinterestedly mastered.

"But you are connected with one in particular.—The 'Black Rapids,' are you not?"

"How did you find that out?"

"Well, sir, I have heard rather tempting information of your Company."

"Who is your informant, pray," somewhat coldly.

"A—a person by the name of Ringman."

"Don't know him. But, doubtless, there are plenty who know our Company, whom our Company does not know; in the same way that one may know an individual, yet be unknown to him.—Known this Ringman long? Old friend, I suppose.—But pardon, I must leave you."

"Stay, sir, that—that stock."

"Stock?"

"Yes, it's a little irregular, perhaps, but—"

"Dear me, you don't think of doing any business with me, do you? In my official capacity I have not been authenticated to you. This transfer-book, now," holding it up so as to bring the lettering in sight, "how do you know that it may not be a bogus one? And I, being personally a stranger to you, how can you have confidence in me?"

"Because," knowingly smiled the good merchant, "if you were other than I have confidence that you are, hardly would you challenge distrust that way."

"But you have not examined my book."

"What need to, if already I believe that it is what it is lettered to be?"

"But you had better. It might suggest doubts."

"Doubts, may be, it might suggest, but not knowledge; for how, by examining the book, should I think I knew any more than I now think I do; since, if it be the true book, I think it so already; and since if it be otherwise, then I have never seen the true one, and don't know what that ought to look like."

"Your logic I will not criticize, but your confidence I admire, and earnestly, too, jocose as was the method I took to draw it out. Enough, we will go to yonder table, and if there be any business which, either in my private or official capacity, I can help you do, pray command me."

XI

Only a Page or So

The transaction concluded, the two still remained seated, falling into familiar conversation, by degrees verging into that confidential sort of sympathetic silence, the last refinement and luxury of unaffected good feeling. A kind of social superstition, to suppose that to be truly friendly one must be saying friendly words all the time, any more than be doing friendly deeds continually. True friendliness, like true religion, being in a sort independent of works.

At length, the good merchant, whose eyes were pensively resting upon the gay tables in the distance, broke the spell by saying that, from the spectacle before them, one would little divine what other quarters of the boat might reveal. He cited the case, accidentally encountered but an hour or two previous, of a shrunken old miser, clad in shrunken old moleskin, stretched out, an invalid, on a bare plank in the emigrants' quarters, eagerly clinging to life and lucre, though the one was gasping for outlet, and about the other he was in torment lest death, or some other unprincipled cut-purse, should be the means of his losing it; by like feeble tenure holding lungs and pouch, and yet knowing and desiring nothing beyond them; for his mind, never raised above mould, was now all but mouldered away. To such a degree, indeed, that he had no trust in anything, not even in his parchment bonds, which, the better to preserve from the tooth of time, he had packed down and sealed up, like brandy peaches, in a tin case of spirits.

The worthy man proceeded at some length with these dispiriting particulars. Nor would his cheery companion wholly deny that there might be a point of view from which such a case of extreme want of confidence might, to the humane mind, present features not altogether welcome as wine and olives after dinner. Still, he was not without compensatory considerations, and, upon the whole, took his companion to task for evincing what, in a good-natured, round-about way, he hinted to be a somewhat jaundiced sentimentality. Nature, he added, in Shakespeare's words, had meal and bran; and, rightly regarded, the bran in its way was not to be condemned.

The other was not disposed to question the justice of Shakespeare's thought, but would hardly admit the propriety of the application in this instance, much less of the comment. So, after some further temperate discussion of the pitiable miser, finding that they could not entirely harmonize, the merchant cited another case, that of the negro cripple. But his companion suggested whether the alleged hardships of that alleged unfortunate might not exist more in the pity of the observer than the experience of the observed. He knew nothing about the cripple, nor had seen him, but ventured to surmise that, could one but get at the real state of his heart, he would be found about as happy as most men, if not, in fact, full as happy as the speaker himself. He added that negroes were by nature a singularly cheerful race; no one ever heard of a native-born African Zimmermann or Torquemada; that even from religion they dismissed all gloom; in their hilarious rituals they danced, so to speak, and, as it were, cut pigeon-wings. It was improbable, therefore, that a negro, however reduced to his stumps by fortune, could be ever thrown off the legs of a laughing philosophy.

Foiled again, the good merchant would not desist, but ventured still a third case, that of the man with the weed, whose story, as narrated by himself, and confirmed and filled out by the testimony of a certain man in a gray coat, whom the merchant had afterwards met, he now proceeded to give; and that, without holding back those particulars disclosed by the second informant, but which delicacy had prevented the unfortunate man himself from touching upon.

But as the good merchant could, perhaps, do better justice to the man than the story, we shall venture to tell it in other words than his, though not to any other effect.

XII

Story of the Unfortunate Man, from Which May Be Gathered Whether or No He Has Been Justly So Entitled

It appeared that the unfortunate man had had for a wife one of those natures, anomalously vicious, which would almost tempt a metaphysical lover of our species to doubt whether the human form be, in all cases, conclusive evidence of humanity, whether, sometimes, it may not be a kind of unpledged and indifferent tabernacle, and whether, once for all to crush the saying of Thrasea, (an unaccountable one, considering that he himself was so good a man) that "he who hates vice, hates humanity," it should not, in self-defense, be held for a reasonable maxim, that none but the good are human.

Goneril was young, in person lithe and straight, too straight, indeed, for a woman, a complexion naturally rosy, and which would have been charmingly so, but for a certain hardness and bakedness, like that of the glazed colors on stone-ware. Her hair was of a deep, rich chestnut, but worn in close, short curls all round her head. Her Indian figure was not without its impairing effect on her bust, while her mouth would have been pretty but for a trace of moustache. Upon the whole, aided by the resources of the toilet, her appearance at distance was such, that some might have thought her, if anything, rather beautiful, though of a style of beauty rather peculiar and cactus-like.

It was happy for Goneril that her more striking peculiarities were less of the person than of temper and taste. One hardly knows how to reveal, that, while having a natural antipathy to such things as the breast of chicken, or custard, or peach, or grape, Goneril could yet in private make a satisfactory lunch on hard crackers and brawn of ham. She liked lemons, and the only kind of candy she loved were little dried sticks of blue clay, secretly carried in her pocket. Withal she had hard, steady health like a squaw's, with as firm a spirit and resolution. Some other points about her were likewise such as pertain to the women of savage life. Lithe though she was, she loved supineness, but upon occasion could endure like a stoic. She was taciturn, too. From early morning till about three o'clock in the afternoon she would seldom speak—it taking that time to thaw her, by all accounts, into but talking terms with humanity. During the interval she did little but look, and keep looking out of her large, metallic eyes, which her enemies called cold as a cuttle-fish's, but which by her were esteemed gazelle-like; for Goneril was not without vanity. Those who thought they best knew her, often wondered what happiness such a being could take in life, not considering the happiness which is to be had by some natures in the very easy way of simply causing pain to those around them. Those who suffered from Goneril's strange nature, might, with one of those hyberboles to which the resentful incline, have pronounced her some kind of toad; but her worst slanderers could never, with any show of justice, have accused her of being a toady. In a large sense she possessed the virtue of independence of mind. Goneril held it flattery to hint praise even of the absent, and even if merited; but honesty, to fling people's imputed faults into their faces. This was thought malice, but it certainly was not passion. Passion is human. Like an icicle-dagger, Goneril at once stabbed and froze; so at least they said; and when she saw frankness and innocence tyrannized into sad nervousness under her spell, according to the same authority, inly she chewed her blue clay, and you could mark that she chuckled. These peculiarities were strange and unpleasing; but another was alleged, one really incomprehensible. In company she had a strange way of touching, as by accident, the arm or hand of comely young men, and seemed to reap a secret delight from it, but whether from the humane satisfaction of having given the evil-touch, as it is called, or whether it was something else in her, not equally wonderful, but quite as deplorable, remained an enigma.

Needless to say what distress was the unfortunate man's, when, engaged in conversation with company, he would suddenly perceive his Goneril bestowing her mysterious touches, especially in such cases where the strangeness of the thing seemed to strike upon the touched person, notwithstanding good-breeding forbade his proposing the mystery, on the spot, as a subject of discussion for the company. In these cases, too, the unfortunate man could never endure so much as to look upon the touched young gentleman afterwards, fearful of the mortification of meeting in his countenance some kind of more or less quizzingly-knowing expression. He would shudderingly shun the young gentleman. So that here, to the husband, Goneril's touch had the dread operation of the heathen taboo. Now Goneril brooked no chiding. So, at favorable times, he, in a wary manner, and not indelicately, would venture in private interviews gently to make distant allusions to this questionable propensity. She divined him. But, in her cold loveless way, said it was witless to be telling one's dreams, especially foolish ones; but if the unfortunate man liked connubially to rejoice his soul with such chimeras, much connubial joy might they give him. All this was sad—a touching case—but all might, perhaps, have been borne by the unfortunate man—conscientiously mindful of his vow—for better or for worse—to love and cherish his dear Goneril so long as kind heaven might spare her to him—but when, after all that had happened, the devil of jealousy entered her, a calm, clayey, cakey devil, for none other could possess her, and the object of that deranged jealousy, her own child, a little girl of seven, her father's consolation and pet; when he saw Goneril artfully torment the little innocent, and then play the maternal hypocrite with it, the unfortunate man's patient long-suffering gave way. Knowing that she would neither confess nor amend, and might, possibly, become even worse than she was, he thought it but duty as a father, to withdraw the child from her; but, loving it as he did, he could not do so without accompanying it into domestic exile himself. Which, hard though it was, he did. Whereupon the whole female neighborhood, who till now had little enough admired dame Goneril, broke out in indignation against a husband, who, without assigning a cause, could deliberately abandon the wife of his bosom, and sharpen the sting to her, too, by depriving her of the solace of retaining her offspring. To all this, self-respect, with Christian charity towards Goneril, long kept the unfortunate man dumb. And well had it been had he continued so; for when, driven to desperation, he hinted something of the truth of the case, not a soul would credit it; while for Goneril, she pronounced all he said to be a malicious invention. Ere long, at the suggestion of some woman's-rights women, the injured wife began a suit, and, thanks to able counsel and accommodating testimony, succeeded in such a way, as not only to recover custody of the child, but to get such a settlement awarded upon a separation, as to make penniless the unfortunate man (so he averred), besides, through the legal sympathy she enlisted, effecting a judicial blasting of his private reputation. What made it yet more lamentable was, that the unfortunate man, thinking that, before the court, his wisest plan, as well as the most Christian besides, being, as he deemed, not at variance with the truth of the matter, would be to put forth the plea of the mental derangement of Goneril, which done, he could, with less of mortification to himself, and odium to her, reveal in self-defense those eccentricities which had led to his retirement from the joys of wedlock, had much ado in the end to prevent this charge of derangement from fatally recoiling upon himself—especially, when, among other things, he alleged her mysterious teachings. In vain did his counsel, striving to make out the derangement to be where, in fact, if anywhere, it was, urge that, to hold otherwise, to hold that such a being as Goneril was sane, this was constructively a libel upon womankind. Libel be it. And all ended by the unfortunate man's subsequently getting wind of Goneril's intention to procure him to be permanently committed for a lunatic. Upon which he fled, and was now an innocent outcast, wandering forlorn in the great valley of the Mississippi, with a weed on his hat for the loss of his Goneril; for he had lately seen by the papers that she was dead, and thought it but proper to comply with the prescribed form of mourning in such cases. For some days past he had been trying to get money enough to return to his child, and was but now started with inadequate funds.

Now all of this, from the beginning, the good merchant could not but consider rather hard for the unfortunate man.

XIII

The Man With the Traveling-Cap Evinces Much Humanity, and in a Way Which Would Seem to Show Him to Be One of The Most Logical of Optimists

Years ago, a grave American savant, being in London, observed at an evening party there, a certain coxcombical fellow, as he thought, an absurd ribbon in his lapel, and full of smart persiflage, whisking about to the admiration of as many as were disposed to admire. Great was the savan's disdain; but, chancing ere long to find himself in a corner with the jackanapes, got into conversation with him, when he was somewhat ill-prepared for the good sense of the jackanapes, but was altogether thrown aback, upon subsequently being whispered by a friend that the jackanapes was almost as great a savan as himself, being no less a personage than Sir Humphrey Davy.

The above anecdote is given just here by way of an anticipative reminder to such readers as, from the kind of jaunty levity, or what may have passed for such, hitherto for the most part appearing in the man with the traveling-cap, may have been tempted into a more or less hasty estimate of him; that such readers, when they find the same person, as they presently will, capable of philosophic and humanitarian discourse—no mere casual sentence or two as heretofore at times, but solidly sustained throughout an almost entire sitting; that they may not, like the American savan, be thereupon betrayed into any surprise incompatible with their own good opinion of their previous penetration.

The merchant's narration being ended, the other would not deny but that it did in some degree affect him. He hoped he was not without proper feeling for the unfortunate man. But he begged to know in what spirit he bore his alleged calamities. Did he despond or have confidence?

The merchant did not, perhaps, take the exact import of the last member of the question; but answered, that, if whether the unfortunate man was becomingly resigned under his affliction or no, was the point, he could say for him that resigned he was, and to an exemplary degree: for not only, so far as known, did he refrain from any one-sided reflections upon human goodness and human justice, but there was observable in him an air of chastened reliance, and at times tempered cheerfulness.

Upon which the other observed, that since the unfortunate man's alleged experience could not be deemed very conciliatory towards a view of human nature better than human nature was, it largely redounded to his fair-mindedness, as well as piety, that under the alleged dissuasives, apparently so, from philanthropy, he had not, in a moment of excitement, been warped over to the ranks of the misanthropes. He doubted not, also, that with such a man his experience would, in the end, act by a complete and beneficent inversion, and so far from shaking his confidence in his kind, confirm it, and rivet it. Which would the more surely be the case, did he (the unfortunate man) at last become satisfied (as sooner or later he probably would be) that in the distraction of his mind his Goneril had not in all respects had fair play. At all events, the description of the lady, charity could not but regard as more or less exaggerated, and so far unjust. The truth probably was that she was a wife with some blemishes mixed with some beauties. But when the blemishes were displayed, her husband, no adept in the female nature, had tried to use reason with her, instead of something far more persuasive. Hence his failure to convince and convert. The act of withdrawing from her, seemed, under the circumstances, abrupt. In brief, there were probably small faults on both sides, more than balanced by large virtues; and one should not be hasty in judging.

When the merchant, strange to say, opposed views so calm and impartial, and again, with some warmth, deplored the case of the unfortunate man, his companion, not without seriousness, checked him, saying, that this would never do; that, though but in the most exceptional case, to admit the existence of unmerited misery, more particularly if alleged to have been brought about by unhindered arts of the wicked, such an admission was, to say the least, not prudent; since, with some, it might unfavorably bias their most important persuasions. Not that those persuasions were legitimately servile to such influences. Because, since the common occurrences of life could never, in the nature of things, steadily look one way and tell one story, as flags in the trade-wind; hence, if the conviction of a Providence, for instance, were in any way made dependent upon such variabilities as everyday events, the degree of that conviction would, in thinking minds, be subject to fluctuations akin to those of the

HERMAN MELVILLE

stock-exchange during a long and uncertain war. Here he glanced aside at his transfer-book, and after a moment's pause continued. It was of the essence of a right conviction of the divine nature, as with a right conviction of the human, that, based less on experience than intuition, it rose above the zones of weather.

When now the merchant, with all his heart, coincided with this (as being a sensible, as well as religious person, he could not but do), his companion expressed satisfaction, that, in an age of some distrust on such subjects, he could yet meet with one who shared with him, almost to the full, so sound and sublime a confidence.

Still, he was far from the illiberality of denying that philosophy duly bounded was not permissible. Only he deemed it at least desirable that, when such a case as that alleged of the unfortunate man was made the subject of philosophic discussion, it should be so philosophized upon, as not to afford handles to those unblessed with the true light. For, but to grant that there was so much as a mystery about such a case, might by those persons be held for a tacit surrender of the question. And as for the apparent license temporarily permitted sometimes, to the bad over the good (as was by implication alleged with regard to Goneril and the unfortunate man), it might be injudicious there to lay too much polemic stress upon the doctrine of future retribution as the vindication of present impunity. For though, indeed, to the right-minded that doctrine was true, and of sufficient solace, yet with the perverse the polemic mention of it might but provoke the shallow, though mischievous conceit, that such a doctrine was but tantamount to the one which should affirm that Providence was not now, but was going to be. In short, with all sorts of cavilers, it was best, both for them and everybody, that whoever had the true light should stick behind the secure Malakoff of confidence, nor be tempted forth to hazardous skirmishes on the open ground of reason. Therefore, he deemed it unadvisable in the good man, even in the privacy of his own mind, or in communion with a congenial one, to indulge in too much latitude of philosophizing, or, indeed, of compassionating, since this might, beget an indiscreet habit of thinking and feeling which might unexpectedly betray him upon unsuitable occasions. Indeed, whether in private or public, there was nothing which a good man was more bound to guard himself against than, on some topics, the emotional unreserve of his natural heart; for, that the natural heart, in certain points, was not what it might be, men had been authoritatively admonished.

But he thought he might be getting dry.

The merchant, in his good-nature, thought otherwise, and said that he would be glad to refresh himself with such fruit all day. It was sitting under a ripe pulpit, and better such a seat than under a ripe peach-tree.

The other was pleased to find that he had not, as he feared, been prosing; but would rather not be considered in the formal light of a preacher; he preferred being still received in that of the equal and genial companion. To which end, throwing still more of sociability into his manner, he again reverted to the unfortunate man. Take the very worst view of that case; admit that his Goneril was, indeed, a Goneril; how fortunate to be at last rid of this Goneril, both by nature and by law? If he were acquainted with the unfortunate man, instead of condoling with him, he would congratulate him. Great good fortune had this unfortunate man. Lucky dog, he dared say, after all.

To which the merchant replied, that he earnestly hoped it might be so, and at any rate he tried his best to comfort himself with the persuasion that, if the unfortunate man was not happy in this world, he would, at least, be so in another.

His companion made no question of the unfortunate man's happiness in both worlds; and, presently calling for some champagne, invited the merchant to partake, upon the playful plea that, whatever notions other than felicitous ones he might associate with the unfortunate man, a little champagne would readily bubble away.

At intervals they slowly quaffed several glasses in silence and thoughtfulness. At last the merchant's expressive face flushed, his eye moistly beamed, his lips trembled with an imaginative and feminine sensibility. Without sending a single fume to his head, the wine seemed to shoot to his heart, and begin soothsaying there. "Ah," he cried, pushing his glass from him, "Ah, wine is good, and confidence is good; but can wine or confidence percolate down through all the stony strata of hard considerations, and drop warmly and ruddily into the cold cave of truth? Truth will *not* be comforted. Led by dear charity, lured by sweet hope, fond fancy essays this feat; but in vain; mere dreams and ideals, they explode in your hand, leaving naught but the scorching behind!"

"Why, why, why!" in amaze, at the burst: "bless me, if *In vino veritas* be a true saying, then, for all the fine confidence you professed with me, just now, distrust, deep distrust, underlies it; and ten thousand strong, like the Irish Rebellion, breaks out in you now. That wine, good wine, should do it! Upon my soul," half seriously, half humorously, securing the bottle, "you shall drink no more of it. Wine was meant to gladden the heart, not grieve it; to heighten confidence, not depress it."

Sobered, shamed, all but confounded, by this raillery, the most telling rebuke under such circumstances, the merchant stared about him, and then, with altered mien, stammeringly confessed, that he was almost as much surprised as his companion, at what had escaped him. He did not understand it; was quite at a loss to account for such a rhapsody popping out of him unbidden. It could hardly be the champagne; he felt his brain unaffected; in fact, if anything, the wine had acted upon it something like white of egg in coffee, clarifying and brightening.

"Brightening? brightening it may be, but less like the white of egg in coffee, than like stove-lustre on a stove—black, brightening seriously, I repent calling for the champagne. To a temperament like yours, champagne is not to be recommended. Pray, my dear sir, do you feel quite yourself again? Confidence restored?"

"I hope so; I think I may say it is so. But we have had a long talk, and I think I must retire now."

So saying, the merchant rose, and making his adieus, left the table with the air of one, mortified at having been tempted by his own honest goodness, accidentally stimulated into making mad disclosures—to himself as to another—of the queer, unaccountable caprices of his natural heart.

XIV

Worth the Consideration of Those to Whom it May Prove Worth Considering

As the last chapter was begun with a reminder looking forwards, so the present must consist of one glancing backwards.

To some, it may raise a degree of surprise that one so full of confidence, as the merchant has throughout shown himself, up to the moment of his late sudden impulsiveness, should, in that instance, have betrayed such a depth of discontent. He may be thought inconsistent, and even so he is. But for this, is the author to be blamed? True, it may be urged that there is nothing a writer of fiction should more carefully see to, as there is nothing a sensible reader will more carefully look for, than that, in the depiction of any character, its consistency should be preserved. But this, though at first blush, seeming reasonable enough, may, upon a closer view, prove not so much so. For how does it couple with another requirement—equally insisted upon, perhaps—that, while to all fiction is allowed some play of invention, yet, fiction based on fact should never be contradictory to it; and is it not a fact, that, in real life, a consistent character is a *rara avis*? Which being so, the distaste of readers to the contrary sort in books, can hardly arise from any sense of their untrueness. It may rather be from perplexity as to understanding them. But if the acutest sage be often at his wits' ends to understand living character, shall those who are not sages expect to run and read character in those mere phantoms which flit along a page, like shadows along a wall? That fiction, where every character can, by reason of its consistency, be comprehended at a glance, either exhibits but sections of character, making them appear for wholes, or else is very untrue to reality; while, on the other hand, that author who draws a character, even though to common view incongruous in its parts, as the flying-squirrel and, at different periods, as much at variance with itself as the butterfly is with the caterpillar into which it changes, may yet, in so doing, be not false but faithful to facts.

If reason be judge, no writer has produced such inconsistent characters as nature herself has. It must call for no small sagacity in a reader unerringly to discriminate in a novel between the inconsistencies of conception and those of life as elsewhere. Experience is the only guide here; but as no one man can be coextensive with *what is*, it may be unwise in every ease to rest upon it. When the duck-billed beaver of Australia was first brought stuffed to England, the naturalists, appealing to their classifications, maintained that there was, in reality, no such creature; the bill in the specimen must needs be, in some way, artificially stuck on.

But let nature, to the perplexity of the naturalists, produce her duck-billed beavers as she may, lesser authors some may hold, have no business to be perplexing readers with duck-billed characters. Always, they should represent human nature not in obscurity, but transparency, which, indeed, is the practice with most novelists, and is, perhaps, in certain cases, someway felt to be a kind of honor rendered by them to their kind. But, whether it involve honor or otherwise might be mooted, considering that, if these waters of human nature can be so readily seen through, it may be either that they are very pure or very shallow. Upon the whole, it might rather be thought, that he, who, in view of its inconsistencies, says of human nature the same that, in view of its contrasts, is said of the divine nature, that it is past finding out, thereby evinces a better appreciation of it than he who, by always representing it in a clear light, leaves it to be inferred that he clearly knows all about it.

But though there is a prejudice against inconsistent characters in books, yet the prejudice bears the other way, when what seemed at first their inconsistency, afterwards, by the skill of the writer, turns out to be their good keeping. The great masters excel in nothing so much as in this very particular. They challenge astonishment at the tangled web of some character, and then raise admiration still greater at their satisfactory unraveling of it; in this way throwing open, sometimes to the understanding even of school misses, the last complications of that spirit which is affirmed by its Creator to be fearfully and wonderfully made.

At least, something like this is claimed for certain psychological novelists; nor will the claim be here disputed. Yet, as touching this point, it may prove suggestive, that all those sallies of ingenuity, having for their end the revelation of human nature on fixed principles, have, by the best judges, been excluded with contempt from the ranks of the sciences—palmistry, physiognomy, phrenology, psychology. Likewise, the fact, that in all ages such conflicting views have, by the most eminent minds, been taken of mankind, would, as with other topics, seem some presumption of a pretty general and pretty thorough ignorance of it. Which may appear the less improbable if it be considered that, after poring over the best novels professing to portray human nature, the studious youth will still run risk of being too often at fault upon actually entering the world; whereas, had he been furnished with a true delineation, it ought to fare with him something as with a stranger entering, map in hand, Boston town; the streets may be very crooked, he may often pause; but, thanks to his true map, he does not hopelessly lose his way. Nor, to this comparison, can it be an adequate objection, that the twistings of the town are always the same, and those of human nature subject to variation. The grand points of human nature are the same today they were a thousand years ago. The only variability in them is in expression, not in feature.

But as, in spite of seeming discouragement, some mathematicians are yet in hopes of hitting upon an exact method of determining the longitude, the more earnest psychologists may, in the face of previous failures, still cherish expectations with regard to some mode of infallibly discovering the heart of man.

But enough has been said by way of apology for whatever may have seemed amiss or obscure in the character of the merchant; so nothing remains but to turn to our comedy, or, rather, to pass from the comedy of thought to that of action.

XV

An Old Miser, Upon Suitable Representations, is Prevailed Upon to Venture an Investment

The merchant having withdrawn, the other remained seated alone for a time, with the air of one who, after having conversed with some excellent man, carefully ponders what fell from him, however intellectually inferior it may be, that none of the profit may be lost; happy if from any honest word he has heard he can derive some hint, which, besides confirming him in the theory of virtue, may, likewise, serve for a finger-post to virtuous action.

Ere long his eye brightened, as if some such hint was now caught. He rises, book in hand, quits the cabin, and enters upon a sort of corridor, narrow and dim, a by-way to a retreat less ornate and cheery than the former; in short, the emigrants' quarters; but which, owing to the present trip being a down-river one, will doubtless be found comparatively tenantless. Owing to obstructions against the side windows, the whole place is dim and dusky; very much so, for the most part; yet, by starts, haggardly lit here and there by narrow, capricious sky-lights in the cornices. But there would seem no special need for light, the place being designed more to pass the night in, than the day; in brief, a pine barrens dormitory, of knotty pine bunks, without bedding. As with the nests in the geometrical towns of the associate penguin and pelican, these bunks were disposed with Philadelphian regularity, but, like the cradle of the oriole, they were pendulous, and, moreover, were, so to speak, three-story cradles; the description of one of which will suffice for all.

Four ropes, secured to the ceiling, passed downwards through auger-holes bored in the corners of three rough planks, which at equal distances rested on knots vertically tied in the ropes, the lowermost plank but an inch or two from the floor, the whole affair resembling, on a large scale, rope book-shelves; only, instead of hanging firmly against a wall, they swayed to and fro at the least suggestion of motion, but were more especially lively upon the provocation of a green emigrant sprawling into one, and trying to lay himself out there, when the cradling would be such as almost to toss him back whence he came. In consequence, one less inexperienced, essaying repose on the uppermost shelf, was liable to serious disturbance, should a raw beginner select a shelf beneath. Sometimes a throng of poor emigrants, coming at night in a sudden rain to occupy these oriole nests, would—through ignorance of their peculiarity—bring about such a rocking uproar of carpentry, joining to it such an uproar of exclamations, that it seemed as if some luckless ship, with all its crew, was being dashed to pieces among the rocks. They were beds devised by some sardonic foe of poor travelers, to deprive them of that tranquility which should precede, as well as accompany, slumber.—Procrustean beds, on whose hard grain humble worth and honesty writhed, still invoking repose, while but torment responded. Ah, did any one make such a bunk for himself, instead of having it made for him, it might be just, but how cruel, to say, You must lie on it!

But, purgatory as the place would appear, the stranger advances into it: and, like Orpheus in his gay descent to Tartarus, lightly hums to himself an opera snatch.

Suddenly there is a rustling, then a creaking, one of the cradles swings out from a murky nook, a sort of wasted penguin-flipper is supplicatingly put forth, while a wail like that of Dives is heard:—"Water, water!"

It was the miser of whom the merchant had spoken.

Swift as a sister-of-charity, the stranger hovers over him:—

"My poor, poor sir, what can I do for you?"

"Ugh, ugh—water!"

Darting out, he procures a glass, returns, and, holding it to the sufferer's lips, supports his head while he drinks: "And did they let you lie here, my poor sir, racked with this parching thirst?"

The miser, a lean old man, whose flesh seemed salted cod-fish, dry as combustibles; head, like one whittled by an idiot out of a knot; flat, bony mouth, nipped between buzzard nose and chin; expression, flitting between hunks and imbecile—now one, now the other—he made no response. His eyes were closed, his cheek lay upon an old white moleskin coat, rolled under his head like a wizened apple upon a grimy snow-bank.

Revived at last, he inclined towards his ministrant, and, in a voice disastrous with a cough, said:—"I am old and miserable, a poor beggar, not worth a shoestring—how can I repay you?"

"By giving me your confidence."

HERMAN MELVILLE

"Confidence!" he squeaked, with changed manner, while the pallet swung, "little left at my age, but take the stale remains, and welcome."

"Such as it is, though, you give it. Very good. Now give me a hundred dollars."

Upon this the miser was all panic. His hands groped towards his waist, then suddenly flew upward beneath his moleskin pillow, and there lay clutching something out of sight. Meantime, to himself he incoherently mumbled:—"Confidence? Cant, gammon! Confidence? hum, bubble!—Confidence? fetch, gouge!—Hundred dollars?—hundred devils!"

Half spent, he lay mute awhile, then feebly raising himself, in a voice for the moment made strong by the sarcasm, said, "A hundred dollars? rather high price to put upon confidence. But don't you see I am a poor, old rat here, dying in the wainscot? You have served me; but, wretch that I am, I can but cough you my thanks,—ugh, ugh, ugh!"

This time his cough was so violent that its convulsions were imparted to the plank, which swung him about like a stone in a sling preparatory to its being hurled.

"Ugh, ugh, ugh!"

"What a shocking cough. I wish, my friend, the herb-doctor was here now; a box of his Omni-Balsamic Reinvigorator would do you good."

"Ugh, ugh, ugh!"

"I've a good mind to go find him. He's aboard somewhere. I saw his long, snuff-colored surtout. Trust me, his medicines are the best in the world."

"Ugh, ugh, ugh!"

"Oh, how sorry I am."

"No doubt of it," squeaked the other again, "but go, get your charity out on deck. There parade the pursy peacocks; they don't cough down here in desertion and darkness, like poor old me. Look how scaly a pauper I am, clove with this churchyard cough. Ugh, ugh, ugh!"

"Again, how sorry I feel, not only for your cough, but your poverty. Such a rare chance made unavailable. Did you have but the sum named, how I could invest it for you. Treble profits. But confidence—I fear that, even had you the precious cash, you would not have the more precious confidence I speak of."

"Ugh, ugh, ugh!" flightily raising himself. "What's that? How, how? Then you don't want the money for yourself?"

"My dear, *dear* sir, how could you impute to me such preposterous self-seeking? To solicit out of hand, for my private behoof, an hundred dollars from a perfect stranger? I am not mad, my dear sir."

"How, how?" still more bewildered, "do you, then, go about the world, gratis, seeking to invest people's money for them?"

"My humble profession, sir. I live not for myself; but the world will not have confidence in me, and yet confidence in me were great gain."

"But, but," in a kind of vertigo, "what do—do you do—do with people's money? Ugh, ugh! How is the gain made?"

"To tell that would ruin me. That known, every one would be going into the business, and it would be overdone. A secret, a mystery—all I have to do with you is to receive your confidence, and all you have to do with me is, in due time, to receive it back, thrice paid in trebling profits."

"What, what?" imbecility in the ascendant once more; "but the vouchers, the vouchers," suddenly hunkish again.

"Honesty's best voucher is honesty's face."

"Can't see yours, though," peering through the obscurity.

From this last alternating flicker of rationality, the miser fell back, sputtering, into his previous gibberish, but it took now an arithmetical turn. Eyes closed, he lay muttering to himself—

"One hundred, one hundred—two hundred, two hundred—three hundred, three hundred."

He opened his eyes, feebly stared, and still more feebly said—

"It's a little dim here, ain't it? Ugh, ugh! But, as well as my poor old eyes can see, you look honest."

"I am glad to hear that."

"If—if, now, I should put"—trying to raise himself, but vainly, excitement having all but exhausted him—"if, if now, I should put, put—"

"No ifs. Downright confidence, or none. So help me heaven, I will have no half-confidences."

He said it with an indifferent and superior air, and seemed moving to go.

"Don't, don't leave me, friend; bear with me; age can't help some distrust; it can't, friend, it can't. Ugh, ugh, ugh! Oh, I am so old and miserable. I ought to have a guardian. Tell me, if—"

"If? No more!"

"Stay! how soon—ugh, ugh!—would my money be trebled? How soon, friend?"

"You won't confide. Good-bye!"

"Stay, stay," falling back now like an infant, "I confide, I confide; help, friend, my distrust!"

From an old buckskin pouch, tremulously dragged forth, ten hoarded eagles, tarnished into the appearance of ten old horn-buttons, were taken, and half-eagerly, half-reluctantly, offered.

"I know not whether I should accept this slack confidence," said the other coldly, receiving the gold, "but an eleventh-hour confidence, a sick-bed confidence, a distempered, death-bed confidence, after all. Give me the healthy confidence of healthy men, with their healthy wits about them. But let that pass. All right. Good-bye!"

"Nay, back, back—receipt, my receipt! Ugh, ugh, ugh! Who are you? What have I done? Where go you? My gold, my gold! Ugh, ugh, ugh!"

But, unluckily for this final flicker of reason, the stranger was now beyond ear-shot, nor was any one else within hearing of so feeble a call.

XVI

A Sick Man, After Some Impatience, is Induced to Become a Patient

The sky slides into blue, the bluffs into bloom; the rapid Mississippi expands; runs sparkling and gurgling, all over in eddies; one magnified wake of a seventy-four. The sun comes out, a golden huzzar, from his tent, flashing his helm on the world. All things, warmed in the landscape, leap. Speeds the dædal boat as a dream.

But, withdrawn in a corner, wrapped about in a shawl, sits an unparticipating man, visited, but not warmed, by the sun—a plant whose hour seems over, while buds are blowing and seeds are astir. On a stool at his left sits a stranger in a snuff-colored surtout, the collar thrown back; his hand waving in persuasive gesture, his eye beaming with hope. But not easily may hope be awakened in one long tranced into hopelessness by a chronic complaint.

To some remark the sick man, by word or look, seemed to have just made an impatiently querulous answer, when, with a deprecatory air, the other resumed:

"Nay, think not I seek to cry up my treatment by crying down that of others. And yet, when one is confident he has truth on his side, and that is not on the other, it is no very easy thing to be charitable; not that temper is the bar, but conscience; for charity would beget toleration, you know, which is a kind of implied permitting, and in effect a kind of countenancing; and that which is countenanced is so far furthered. But should untruth be furthered? Still, while for the world's good I refuse to further the cause of these mineral doctors, I would fain regard them, not as willful wrong-doers, but good Samaritans erring. And is this—I put it to you, sir—is this the view of an arrogant rival and pretender?"

His physical power all dribbled and gone, the sick man replied not by voice or by gesture; but, with feeble dumb-show of his face, seemed to be saying "Pray leave me; who was ever cured by talk?"

But the other, as if not unused to make allowances for such despondency, proceeded; and kindly, yet firmly:

"You tell me, that by advice of an eminent physiologist in Louisville, you took tincture of iron. For what? To restore your lost energy. And

HERMAN MELVILLE

how? Why, in healthy subjects iron is naturally found in the blood, and iron in the bar is strong; ergo, iron is the source of animal invigoration. But you being deficient in vigor, it follows that the cause is deficiency of iron. Iron, then, must be put into you; and so your tincture. Now as to the theory here, I am mute. But in modesty assuming its truth, and then, as a plain man viewing that theory in practice, I would respectfully question your eminent physiologist: 'Sir,' I would say, 'though by natural processes, lifeless natures taken as nutriment become vitalized, yet is a lifeless nature, under any circumstances, capable of a living transmission, with all its qualities as a lifeless nature unchanged? If, sir, nothing can be incorporated with the living body but by assimilation, and if that implies the conversion of one thing to a different thing (as, in a lamp, oil is assimilated into flame), is it, in this view, likely, that by banqueting on fat, Calvin Edson will fatten? That is, will what is fat on the board prove fat on the bones? If it will, then, sir, what is iron in the vial will prove iron in the vein.' Seems that conclusion too confident?"

But the sick man again turned his dumb-show look, as much as to say, "Pray leave me. Why, with painful words, hint the vanity of that which the pains of this body have too painfully proved?"

But the other, as if unobservant of that querulous look, went on:

"But this notion, that science can play farmer to the flesh, making there what living soil it pleases, seems not so strange as that other conceit—that science is now-a-days so expert that, in consumptive cases, as yours, it can, by prescription of the inhalation of certain vapors, achieve the sublimest act of omnipotence, breathing into all but lifeless dust the breath of life. For did you not tell me, my poor sir, that by order of the great chemist in Baltimore, for three weeks you were never driven out without a respirator, and for a given time of every day sat bolstered up in a sort of gasometer, inspiring vapors generated by the burning of drugs? as if this concocted atmosphere of man were an antidote to the poison of God's natural air. Oh, who can wonder at that old reproach against science, that it is atheistical? And here is my prime reason for opposing these chemical practitioners, who have sought out so many inventions. For what do their inventions indicate, unless it be that kind and degree of pride in human skill, which seems scarce compatible with reverential dependence upon the power above? Try to rid my mind of it as I may, yet still these chemical practitioners with their tinctures, and fumes, and braziers, and occult incantations, seem to me like Pharaoh's vain sorcerers, trying to beat down the will of heaven. Day and night, in all charity, I intercede for them, that heaven may not, in its own language, be provoked to anger with their inventions; may not take vengeance of their inventions. A thousand pities that you should ever have been in the hands of these Egyptians."

But again came nothing but the dumb-show look, as much as to say, "Pray leave me; quacks, and indignation against quacks, both are vain."

But, once more, the other went on: "How different we herb-doctors! who claim nothing, invent nothing; but staff in hand, in glades, and upon hillsides, go about in nature, humbly seeking her cures. True Indian doctors, though not learned in names, we are not unfamiliar with essences—successors of Solomon the Wise, who knew all vegetables, from the cedar of Lebanon, to the hyssop on the wall. Yes, Solomon was the first of herb-doctors. Nor were the virtues of herbs unhonored by yet older ages. Is it not writ, that on a moonlight night,

> *"Medea gathered the enchanted herbs
> That did renew old Æson?"*

Ah, would you but have confidence, you should be the new Æson, and I your Medea. A few vials of my Omni-Balsamic Reinvigorator would, I am certain, give you some strength."

Upon this, indignation and abhorrence seemed to work by their excess the effect promised of the balsam. Roused from that long apathy of impotence, the cadaverous man started, and, in a voice that was as the sound of obstructed air gurgling through a maze of broken honey-combs, cried: "Begone! You are all alike. The name of doctor, the dream of helper, condemns you. For years I have been but a gallipot for you experimentizers to rinse your experiments into, and now, in this livid skin, partake of the nature of my contents. Begone! I hate ye."

"I were inhuman, could I take affront at a want of confidence, born of too bitter an experience of betrayers. Yet, permit one who is not without feeling—"

"Begone! Just in that voice talked to me, not six months ago, the German doctor at the water cure, from which I now return, six months and sixty pangs nigher my grave."

"The water-cure? Oh, fatal delusion of the well-meaning Preisnitz!—Sir, trust me—"

"Begone!"

"Nay, an invalid should not always have his own way. Ah, sir, reflect

HERMAN MELVILLE

how untimely this distrust in one like you. How weak you are; and weakness, is it not the time for confidence? Yes, when through weakness everything bids despair, then is the time to get strength by confidence."

Relenting in his air, the sick man cast upon him a long glance of beseeching, as if saying, "With confidence must come hope; and how can hope be?"

The herb-doctor took a sealed paper box from his surtout pocket, and holding it towards him, said solemnly, "Turn not away. This may be the last time of health's asking. Work upon yourself; invoke confidence, though from ashes; rouse it; for your life, rouse it, and invoke it, I say."

The other trembled, was silent; and then, a little commanding himself, asked the ingredients of the medicine.

"Herbs."

"What herbs? And the nature of them? And the reason for giving them?"

"It cannot be made known."

"Then I will none of you."

Sedately observant of the juiceless, joyless form before him, the herb-doctor was mute a moment, then said:—"I give up."

"How?"

"You are sick, and a philosopher."

"No, no;—not the last."

"But, to demand the ingredient, with the reason for giving, is the mark of a philosopher; just as the consequence is the penalty of a fool. A sick philosopher is incurable?"

"Why?"

"Because he has no confidence."

"How does that make him incurable?"

"Because either he spurns his powder, or, if he take it, it proves a blank cartridge, though the same given to a rustic in like extremity, would act like a charm. I am no materialist; but the mind so acts upon the body, that if the one have no confidence, neither has the other."

Again, the sick man appeared not unmoved. He seemed to be thinking what in candid truth could be said to all this. At length, "You talk of confidence. How comes it that when brought low himself, the herb-doctor, who was most confident to prescribe in other cases, proves least confident to prescribe in his own; having small confidence in himself for himself?"

"But he has confidence in the brother he calls in. And that he does so, is no reproach to him, since he knows that when the body is prostrated, the mind is not erect. Yes, in this hour the herb-doctor does distrust himself, but not his art."

The sick man's knowledge did not warrant him to gainsay this. But he seemed not grieved at it; glad to be confuted in a way tending towards his wish.

"Then you give me hope?" his sunken eye turned up.

"Hope is proportioned to confidence. How much confidence you give me, so much hope do I give you. For this," lifting the box, "if all depended upon this, I should rest. It is nature's own."

"Nature!"

"Why do you start?"

"I know not," with a sort of shudder, "but I have heard of a book entitled 'Nature in Disease.'"

"A title I cannot approve; it is suspiciously scientific. 'Nature in Disease?' As if nature, divine nature, were aught but health; as if through nature disease is decreed! But did I not before hint of the tendency of science, that forbidden tree? Sir, if despondency is yours from recalling that title, dismiss it. Trust me, nature is health; for health is good, and nature cannot work ill. As little can she work error. Get nature, and you get well. Now, I repeat, this medicine is nature's own."

Again the sick man could not, according to his light, conscientiously disprove what was said. Neither, as before, did he seem over-anxious to do so; the less, as in his sensitiveness it seemed to him, that hardly could he offer so to do without something like the appearance of a kind of implied irreligion; nor in his heart was he ungrateful, that since a spirit opposite to that pervaded all the herb-doctor's hopeful words, therefore, for hopefulness, he (the sick man) had not alone medical warrant, but also doctrinal.

"Then you do really think," hectically, "that if I take this medicine," mechanically reaching out for it, "I shall regain my health?"

"I will not encourage false hopes," relinquishing to him the box, "I will be frank with you. Though frankness is not always the weakness of the mineral practitioner, yet the herb doctor must be frank, or nothing. Now then, sir, in your case, a radical cure—such a cure, understand, as should make you robust—such a cure, sir, I do not and cannot promise."

"Oh, you need not! only restore me the power of being something else to others than a burdensome care, and to myself a droning grief. Only cure me of this misery of weakness; only make me so that I can

　　　　　　　　　　　　　　　HERMAN MELVILLE

walk about in the sun and not draw the flies to me, as lured by the coming of decay. Only do that—but that."

"You ask not much; you are wise; not in vain have you suffered. That little you ask, I think, can be granted. But remember, not in a day, nor a week, nor perhaps a month, but sooner or later; I say not exactly when, for I am neither prophet nor charlatan. Still, if, according to the directions in your box there, you take my medicine steadily, without assigning an especial day, near or remote, to discontinue it, then may you calmly look for some eventual result of good. But again I say, you must have confidence."

Feverishly he replied that he now trusted he had, and hourly should pray for its increase. When suddenly relapsing into one of those strange caprices peculiar to some invalids, he added: "But to one like me, it is so hard, so hard. The most confident hopes so often have failed me, and as often have I vowed never, no, never, to trust them again. Oh," feebly wringing his hands, "you do not know, you do not know."

"I know this, that never did a right confidence, come to naught. But time is short; you hold your cure, to retain or reject."

"I retain," with a clinch, "and now how much?"

"As much as you can evoke from your heart and heaven."

"How?—the price of this medicine?"

"I thought it was confidence you meant; how much confidence you should have. The medicine,—that is half a dollar a vial. Your box holds six."

The money was paid.

"Now, sir," said the herb-doctor, "my business calls me away, and it may so be that I shall never see you again; if then—"

He paused, for the sick man's countenance fell blank.

"Forgive me," cried the other, "forgive that imprudent phrase 'never see you again.' Though I solely intended it with reference to myself, yet I had forgotten what your sensitiveness might be. I repeat, then, that it may be that we shall not soon have a second interview, so that hereafter, should another of my boxes be needed, you may not be able to replace it except by purchase at the shops; and, in so doing, you may run more or less risk of taking some not salutary mixture. For such is the popularity of the Omni-Balsamic Reinvigorator—thriving not by the credulity of the simple, but the trust of the wise—that certain contrivers have not been idle, though I would not, indeed, hastily affirm of them that they are aware of the sad consequences to the public. Homicides and murderers, some call those contrivers; but I do not; for murder (if such a crime be possible) comes from the heart, and these men's motives come from the purse. Were they not in poverty, I think they would hardly do what they do. Still, the public interests forbid that I should let their needy device for a living succeed. In short, I have adopted precautions. Take the wrapper from any of my vials and hold it to the light, you will see water-marked in capitals the word '*confidence*,' which is the countersign of the medicine, as I wish it was of the world. The wrapper bears that mark or else the medicine is counterfeit. But if still any lurking doubt should remain, pray enclose the wrapper to this address," handing a card, "and by return mail I will answer."

At first the sick man listened, with the air of vivid interest, but gradually, while the other was still talking, another strange caprice came over him, and he presented the aspect of the most calamitous dejection.

"How now?" said the herb-doctor.

"You told me to have confidence, said that confidence was indispensable, and here you preach to me distrust. Ah, truth will out!"

"I told you, you must have confidence, unquestioning confidence, I meant confidence in the genuine medicine, and the genuine *me*."

"But in your absence, buying vials purporting to be yours, it seems I cannot have unquestioning confidence."

"Prove all the vials; trust those which are true."

"But to doubt, to suspect, to prove—to have all this wearing work to be doing continually—how opposed to confidence. It is evil!"

"From evil comes good. Distrust is a stage to confidence. How has it proved in our interview? But your voice is husky; I have let you talk too much. You hold your cure; I will leave you. But stay—when I hear that health is yours, I will not, like some I know, vainly make boasts; but, giving glory where all glory is due, say, with the devout herb-doctor, Japus in Virgil, when, in the unseen but efficacious presence of Venus, he with simples healed the wound of Æneas:—

> '*This is no mortal work, no cure of mine,*
> *Nor art's effect, but done by power divine.*'"

HERMAN MELVILLE

XVII

Towards the End of Which the Herb-Doctor Proves Himself a Forgiver of Injuries

In a kind of ante-cabin, a number of respectable looking people, male and female, way-passengers, recently come on board, are listlessly sitting in a mutually shy sort of silence.

Holding up a small, square bottle, ovally labeled with the engraving of a countenance full of soft pity as that of the Romish-painted Madonna, the herb-doctor passes slowly among them, benignly urbane, turning this way and that, saying:—

"Ladies and gentlemen, I hold in my hand here the Samaritan Pain Dissuader, thrice-blessed discovery of that disinterested friend of humanity whose portrait you see. Pure vegetable extract. Warranted to remove the acutest pain within less than ten minutes. Five hundred dollars to be forfeited on failure. Especially efficacious in heart disease and tic-douloureux. Observe the expression of this pledged friend of humanity.—Price only fifty cents."

In vain. After the first idle stare, his auditors—in pretty good health, it seemed—instead of encouraging his politeness, appeared, if anything, impatient of it; and, perhaps, only diffidence, or some small regard for his feelings, prevented them from telling him so. But, insensible to their coldness, or charitably overlooking it, he more wooingly than ever resumed: "May I venture upon a small supposition? Have I your kind leave, ladies and gentlemen?"

To which modest appeal, no one had the kindness to answer a syllable.

"Well," said he, resignedly, "silence is at least not denial, and may be consent. My supposition is this: possibly some lady, here present, has a dear friend at home, a bed-ridden sufferer from spinal complaint. If so, what gift more appropriate to that sufferer than this tasteful little bottle of Pain Dissuader?"

Again he glanced about him, but met much the same reception as before. Those faces, alien alike to sympathy or surprise, seemed patiently to say, "We are travelers; and, as such, must expect to meet, and quietly put up with, many antic fools, and more antic quacks."

"Ladies and gentlemen," (deferentially fixing his eyes upon their now self-complacent faces) "ladies and gentlemen, might I, by your kind leave, venture upon one other small supposition? It is this: that there is scarce a sufferer, this noonday, writhing on his bed, but in his hour he sat satisfactorily healthy and happy; that the Samaritan Pain Dissuader is the one only balm for that to which each living creature— who knows?—may be a draughted victim, present or prospective. In short:—Oh, Happiness on my right hand, and oh, Security on my left, can ye wisely adore a Providence, and not think it wisdom to provide?— Provide!" (Uplifting the bottle.)

What immediate effect, if any, this appeal might have had, is uncertain. For just then the boat touched at a houseless landing, scooped, as by a land-slide, out of sombre forests; back through which led a road, the sole one, which, from its narrowness, and its being walled up with story on story of dusk, matted foliage, presented the vista of some cavernous old gorge in a city, like haunted Cock Lane in London. Issuing from that road, and crossing that landing, there stooped his shaggy form in the door-way, and entered the ante-cabin, with a step so burdensome that shot seemed in his pockets, a kind of invalid Titan in homespun; his beard blackly pendant, like the Carolina-moss, and dank with cypress dew; his countenance tawny and shadowy as an iron-ore country in a clouded day. In one hand he carried a heavy walking-stick of swamp-oak; with the other, led a puny girl, walking in moccasins, not improbably his child, but evidently of alien maternity, perhaps Creole, or even Camanche. Her eye would have been large for a woman, and was inky as the pools of falls among mountain-pines. An Indian blanket, orange-hued, and fringed with lead tassel-work, appeared that morning to have shielded the child from heavy showers. Her limbs were tremulous; she seemed a little Cassandra, in nervousness.

No sooner was the pair spied by the herb-doctor, than with a cheerful air, both arms extended like a host's, he advanced, and taking the child's reluctant hand, said, trippingly: "On your travels, ah, my little May Queen? Glad to see you. What pretty moccasins. Nice to dance in." Then with a half caper sang—

> "*Hey diddle, diddle, the cat and the fiddle;*
> *The cow jumped over the moon.*'

Come, chirrup, chirrup, my little robin!"

HERMAN MELVILLE

Which playful welcome drew no responsive playfulness from the child, nor appeared to gladden or conciliate the father; but rather, if anything, to dash the dead weight of his heavy-hearted expression with a smile hypochondriacally scornful.

Sobering down now, the herb-doctor addressed the stranger in a manly, business-like way—a transition which, though it might seem a little abrupt, did not appear constrained, and, indeed, served to show that his recent levity was less the habit of a frivolous nature, than the frolic condescension of a kindly heart.

"Excuse me," said he, "but, if I err not, I was speaking to you the other day;—on a Kentucky boat, wasn't it?"

"Never to me," was the reply; the voice deep and lonesome enough to have come from the bottom of an abandoned coal-shaft.

"Ah!—But am I again mistaken, (his eye falling on the swamp-oak stick,) or don't you go a little lame, sir?"

"Never was lame in my life."

"Indeed? I fancied I had perceived not a limp, but a hitch, a slight hitch;—some experience in these things—divined some hidden cause of the hitch—buried bullet, may be—some dragoons in the Mexican war discharged with such, you know.—Hard fate!" he sighed, "little pity for it, for who sees it?—have you dropped anything?"

Why, there is no telling, but the stranger was bowed over, and might have seemed bowing for the purpose of picking up something, were it not that, as arrested in the imperfect posture, he for the moment so remained; slanting his tall stature like a mainmast yielding to the gale, or Adam to the thunder.

The little child pulled him. With a kind of a surge he righted himself, for an instant looked toward the herb-doctor; but, either from emotion or aversion, or both together, withdrew his eyes, saying nothing. Presently, still stooping, he seated himself, drawing his child between his knees, his massy hands tremulous, and still averting his face, while up into the compassionate one of the herb-doctor the child turned a fixed, melancholy glance of repugnance.

The herb-doctor stood observant a moment, then said:

"Surely you have pain, strong pain, somewhere; in strong frames pain is strongest. Try, now, my specific," (holding it up). "Do but look at the expression of this friend of humanity. Trust me, certain cure for any pain in the world. Won't you look?"

"No," choked the other.

"Very good. Merry time to you, little May Queen."

And so, as if he would intrude his cure upon no one, moved pleasantly off, again crying his wares, nor now at last without result. A new-comer, not from the shore, but another part of the boat, a sickly young man, after some questions, purchased a bottle. Upon this, others of the company began a little to wake up as it were; the scales of indifference or prejudice fell from their eyes; now, at last, they seemed to have an inkling that here was something not undesirable which might be had for the buying.

But while, ten times more briskly bland than ever, the herb-doctor was driving his benevolent trade, accompanying each sale with added praises of the thing traded, all at once the dusk giant, seated at some distance, unexpectedly raised his voice with—

"What was that you last said?"

The question was put distinctly, yet resonantly, as when a great clock-bell—stunning admonisher—strikes one; and the stroke, though single, comes bedded in the belfry clamor.

All proceedings were suspended. Hands held forth for the specific were withdrawn, while every eye turned towards the direction whence the question came. But, no way abashed, the herb-doctor, elevating his voice with even more than wonted self-possession, replied—

"I was saying what, since you wish it, I cheerfully repeat, that the Samaritan Pain Dissuader, which I here hold in my hand, will either cure or ease any pain you please, within ten minutes after its application."

"Does it produce insensibility?"

"By no means. Not the least of its merits is, that it is not an opiate. It kills pain without killing feeling."

"You lie! Some pains cannot be eased but by producing insensibility, and cannot be cured but by producing death."

Beyond this the dusk giant said nothing; neither, for impairing the other's market, did there appear much need to. After eying the rude speaker a moment with an expression of mingled admiration and consternation, the company silently exchanged glances of mutual sympathy under unwelcome conviction. Those who had purchased looked sheepish or ashamed; and a cynical-looking little man, with a thin flaggy beard, and a countenance ever wearing the rudiments of a grin, seated alone in a corner commanding a good view of the scene, held a rusty hat before his face.

But, again, the herb-doctor, without noticing the retort, overbearing though it was, began his panegyrics anew, and in a tone more assured

HERMAN MELVILLE

than before, going so far now as to say that his specific was sometimes almost as effective in cases of mental suffering as in cases of physical; or rather, to be more precise, in cases when, through sympathy, the two sorts of pain coöperated into a climax of both—in such cases, he said, the specific had done very well. He cited an example: Only three bottles, faithfully taken, cured a Louisiana widow (for three weeks sleepless in a darkened chamber) of neuralgic sorrow for the loss of husband and child, swept off in one night by the last epidemic. For the truth of this, a printed voucher was produced, duly signed.

While he was reading it aloud, a sudden side-blow all but felled him.

It was the giant, who, with a countenance lividly epileptic with hypochondriac mania, exclaimed—

"Profane fiddler on heart-strings! Snake!"

More he would have added, but, convulsed, could not; so, without another word, taking up the child, who had followed him, went with a rocking pace out of the cabin.

"Regardless of decency, and lost to humanity!" exclaimed the herb-doctor, with much ado recovering himself. Then, after a pause, during which he examined his bruise, not omitting to apply externally a little of his specific, and with some success, as it would seem, plained to himself:

"No, no, I won't seek redress; innocence is my redress. But," turning upon them all, "if that man's wrathful blow provokes me to no wrath, should his evil distrust arouse you to distrust? I do devoutly hope," proudly raising voice and arm, "for the honor of humanity—hope that, despite this coward assault, the Samaritan Pain Dissuader stands unshaken in the confidence of all who hear me!"

But, injured as he was, and patient under it, too, somehow his case excited as little compassion as his oratory now did enthusiasm. Still, pathetic to the last, he continued his appeals, notwithstanding the frigid regard of the company, till, suddenly interrupting himself, as if in reply to a quick summons from without, he said hurriedly, "I come, I come," and so, with every token of precipitate dispatch, out of the cabin the herb-doctor went.

XVIII

Inquest Into the True Character
of the Herb-Doctor

S ha'n't see that fellow again in a hurry," remarked an auburn-haired gentleman, to his neighbor with a hook-nose. "Never knew an operator so completely unmasked."

"But do you think it the fair thing to unmask an operator that way?"

"Fair? It is right."

"Supposing that at high 'change on the Paris Bourse, Asmodeus should lounge in, distributing hand-bills, revealing the true thoughts and designs of all the operators present—would that be the fair thing in Asmodeus? Or, as Hamlet says, were it 'to consider the thing too curiously?'"

"We won't go into that. But since you admit the fellow to be a knave—"

"I don't admit it. Or, if I did, I take it back. Shouldn't wonder if, after all, he is no knave at all, or, but little of one. What can you prove against him?"

"I can prove that he makes dupes."

"Many held in honor do the same; and many, not wholly knaves, do it too."

"How about that last?"

"He is not wholly at heart a knave, I fancy, among whose dupes is himself. Did you not see our quack friend apply to himself his own quackery? A fanatic quack; essentially a fool, though effectively a knave."

Bending over, and looking down between his knees on the floor, the auburn-haired gentleman meditatively scribbled there awhile with his cane, then, glancing up, said:

"I can't conceive how you, in anyway, can hold him a fool. How he talked—so glib, so pat, so well."

"A smart fool always talks well; takes a smart fool to be tonguey."

In much the same strain the discussion continued—the hook-nosed gentleman talking at large and excellently, with a view of demonstrating that a smart fool always talks just so. Ere long he talked to such purpose as almost to convince.

Presently, back came the person of whom the auburn-haired gentleman had predicted that he would not return. Conspicuous in the door-way he stood, saying, in a clear voice, "Is the agent of the Seminole Widow and Orphan Asylum within here?"

No one replied.

"Is there within here any agent or any member of any charitable institution whatever?"

No one seemed competent to answer, or, no one thought it worth while to.

"If there be within here any such person, I have in my hand two dollars for him."

Some interest was manifested.

"I was called away so hurriedly, I forgot this part of my duty. With the proprietor of the Samaritan Pain Dissuader it is a rule, to devote, on the spot, to some benevolent purpose, the half of the proceeds of sales. Eight bottles were disposed of among this company. Hence, four half-dollars remain to charity. Who, as steward, takes the money?"

One or two pair of feet moved upon the floor, as with a sort of itching; but nobody rose.

"Does diffidence prevail over duty? If, I say, there be any gentleman, or any lady, either, here present, who is in any connection with any charitable institution whatever, let him or her come forward. He or she happening to have at hand no certificate of such connection, makes no difference. Not of a suspicious temper, thank God, I shall have confidence in whoever offers to take the money."

A demure-looking woman, in a dress rather tawdry and rumpled, here drew her veil well down and rose; but, marking every eye upon her, thought it advisable, upon the whole, to sit down again.

"Is it to be believed that, in this Christian company, there is no one charitable person? I mean, no one connected with any charity? Well, then, is there no object of charity here?"

Upon this, an unhappy-looking woman, in a sort of mourning, neat, but sadly worn, hid her face behind a meagre bundle, and was heard to sob. Meantime, as not seeing or hearing her, the herb-doctor again spoke, and this time not unpathetically:

"Are there none here who feel in need of help, and who, in accepting such help, would feel that they, in their time, have given or done more than may ever be given or done to them? Man or woman, is there none such here?"

The sobs of the woman were more audible, though she strove to repress them. While nearly every one's attention was bent upon her, a man of the appearance of a day-laborer, with a white bandage across his face, concealing the side of the nose, and who, for coolness' sake, had been sitting in his red-flannel shirt-sleeves, his coat thrown across one shoulder, the darned cuffs drooping behind—this man shufflingly rose, and, with a pace that seemed the lingering memento of the lock-step of convicts, went up for a duly-qualified claimant.

"Poor wounded huzzar!" sighed the herb-doctor, and dropping the money into the man's clam-shell of a hand turned and departed.

The recipient of the alms was about moving after, when the auburn-haired gentleman staid him: "Don't be frightened, you; but I want to see those coins. Yes, yes; good silver, good silver. There, take them again, and while you are about it, go bandage the rest of yourself behind something. D'ye hear? Consider yourself, wholly, the scar of a nose, and be off with yourself."

Being of a forgiving nature, or else from emotion not daring to trust his voice, the man silently, but not without some precipitancy, withdrew.

"Strange," said the auburn-haired gentleman, returning to his friend, "the money was good money."

"Aye, and where your fine knavery now? Knavery to devote the half of one's receipts to charity? He's a fool I say again."

"Others might call him an original genius."

"Yes, being original in his folly. Genius? His genius is a cracked pate, and, as this age goes, not much originality about that."

"May he not be knave, fool, and genius altogether?"

"I beg pardon," here said a third person with a gossiping expression who had been listening, "but you are somewhat puzzled by this man, and well you may be."

"Do you know anything about him?" asked the hooked-nosed gentleman.

"No, but I suspect him for something."

"Suspicion. We want knowledge."

"Well, suspect first and know next. True knowledge comes but by suspicion or revelation. That's my maxim."

"And yet," said the auburn-haired gentleman, "since a wise man will keep even some certainties to himself, much more some suspicions, at least he will at all events so do till they ripen into knowledge."

"Do you hear that about the wise man?" said the hook-nosed gentleman, turning upon the new comer. "Now what is it you suspect of this fellow?"

HERMAN MELVILLE

"I shrewdly suspect him," was the eager response, "for one of those Jesuit emissaries prowling all over our country. The better to accomplish their secret designs, they assume, at times, I am told, the most singular masques; sometimes, in appearance, the absurdest."

This, though indeed for some reason causing a droll smile upon the face of the hook-nosed gentleman, added a third angle to the discussion, which now became a sort of triangular duel, and ended, at last, with but a triangular result.

XIX

A Soldier of Fortune

"M exico? Molino del Rey? Resaca de la Palma?"

"Resaca de la *Tomba*!"

Leaving his reputation to take care of itself, since, as is not seldom the case, he knew nothing of its being in debate, the herb-doctor, wandering towards the forward part of the boat, had there espied a singular character in a grimy old regimental coat, a countenance at once grim and wizened, interwoven paralyzed legs, stiff as icicles, suspended between rude crutches, while the whole rigid body, like a ship's long barometer on gimbals, swung to and fro, mechanically faithful to the motion of the boat. Looking downward while he swung, the cripple seemed in a brown study.

As moved by the sight, and conjecturing that here was some battered hero from the Mexican battle-fields, the herb-doctor had sympathetically accosted him as above, and received the above rather dubious reply. As, with a half moody, half surly sort of air that reply was given, the cripple, by a voluntary jerk, nervously increased his swing (his custom when seized by emotion), so that one would have thought some squall had suddenly rolled the boat and with it the barometer.

"Tombs? my friend," exclaimed the herb-doctor in mild surprise. "You have not descended to the dead, have you? I had imagined you a scarred campaigner, one of the noble children of war, for your dear country a glorious sufferer. But you are Lazarus, it seems."

"Yes, he who had sores."

"Ah, the *other* Lazarus. But I never knew that either of them was in the army," glancing at the dilapidated regimentals.

"That will do now. Jokes enough."

"Friend," said the other reproachfully, "you think amiss. On principle, I greet unfortunates with some pleasant remark, the better to call off their thoughts from their troubles. The physician who is at once wise and humane seldom unreservedly sympathizes with his patient. But come, I am a herb-doctor, and also a natural bone-setter. I may be sanguine, but I think I can do something for you. You look up now.

Give me your story. Ere I undertake a cure, I require a full account of the case."

"You can't help me," returned the cripple gruffly. "Go away."

"You seem sadly destitute of—"

"No I ain't destitute; today, at least, I can pay my way."

"The Natural Bone-setter is happy, indeed, to hear that. But you were premature. I was deploring your destitution, not of cash, but of confidence. You think the Natural Bone-setter can't help you. Well, suppose he can't, have you any objection to telling him your story? You, my friend, have, in a signal way, experienced adversity. Tell me, then, for my private good, how, without aid from the noble cripple, Epictetus, you have arrived at his heroic sang-froid in misfortune."

At these words the cripple fixed upon the speaker the hard ironic eye of one toughened and defiant in misery, and, in the end, grinned upon him with his unshaven face like an ogre.

"Come, come, be sociable—be human, my friend. Don't make that face; it distresses me."

"I suppose," with a sneer, "you are the man I've long heard of—The Happy Man."

"Happy? my friend. Yes, at least I ought to be. My conscience is peaceful. I have confidence in everybody. I have confidence that, in my humble profession, I do some little good to the world. Yes, I think that, without presumption, I may venture to assent to the proposition that I am the Happy Man—the Happy Bone-setter."

"Then, you shall hear my story. Many a month I have longed to get hold of the Happy Man, drill him, drop the powder, and leave him to explode at his leisure.".

"What a demoniac unfortunate" exclaimed the herb-doctor retreating. "Regular infernal machine!"

"Look ye," cried the other, stumping after him, and with his horny hand catching him by a horn button, "my name is Thomas Fry. Until my—"

—"Any relation of Mrs. Fry?" interrupted the other. "I still correspond with that excellent lady on the subject of prisons. Tell me, are you anyway connected with *my* Mrs. Fry?"

"Blister Mrs. Fry! What do them sentimental souls know of prisons or any other black fact? I'll tell ye a story of prisons. Ha, ha!"

The herb-doctor shrank, and with reason, the laugh being strangely startling.

"Positively, my friend," said he, "you must stop that; I can't stand that; no more of that. I hope I have the milk of kindness, but your thunder will soon turn it."

"Hold, I haven't come to the milk-turning part yet. My name is Thomas Fry. Until my twenty-third year I went by the nickname of Happy Tom—happy—ha, ha! They called me Happy Tom, d'ye see? because I was so good-natured and laughing all the time, just as I am now—ha, ha!"

Upon this the herb-doctor would, perhaps, have run, but once more the hyæna clawed him. Presently, sobering down, he continued:

"Well, I was born in New York, and there I lived a steady, hard-working man, a cooper by trade. One evening I went to a political meeting in the Park—for you must know, I was in those days a great patriot. As bad luck would have it, there was trouble near, between a gentleman who had been drinking wine, and a pavior who was sober. The pavior chewed tobacco, and the gentleman said it was beastly in him, and pushed him, wanting to have his place. The pavior chewed on and pushed back. Well, the gentleman carried a sword-cane, and presently the pavior was down—skewered."

"How was that?"

"Why you see the pavior undertook something above his strength."

"The other must have been a Samson then. 'Strong as a pavior,' is a proverb."

"So it is, and the gentleman was in body a rather weakly man, but, for all that, I say again, the pavior undertook something above his strength."

"What are you talking about? He tried to maintain his rights, didn't he?"

"Yes; but, for all that, I say again, he undertook something above his strength."

"I don't understand you. But go on."

"Along with the gentleman, I, with other witnesses, was taken to the Tombs. There was an examination, and, to appear at the trial, the gentleman and witnesses all gave bail—I mean all but me."

"And why didn't you?"

"Couldn't get it."

"Steady, hard-working cooper like you; what was the reason you couldn't get bail?"

"Steady, hard-working cooper hadn't no friends. Well, souse I went into a wet cell, like a canal-boat splashing into the lock; locked up in pickle, d'ye see? against the time of the trial."

HERMAN MELVILLE

"But what had you done?"

"Why, I hadn't got any friends, I tell ye. A worse crime than murder, as ye'll see afore long."

"Murder? Did the wounded man die?"

"Died the third night."

"Then the gentleman's bail didn't help him. Imprisoned now, wasn't he?"

"Had too many friends. No, it was *I* that was imprisoned.—But I was going on: They let me walk about the corridor by day; but at night I must into lock. There the wet and the damp struck into my bones. They doctored me, but no use. When the trial came, I was boosted up and said my say."

"And what was that?"

"My say was that I saw the steel go in, and saw it sticking in."

"And that hung the gentleman."

"Hung him with a gold chain! His friends called a meeting in the Park, and presented him with a gold watch and chain upon his acquittal."

"Acquittal?"

"Didn't I say he had friends?"

There was a pause, broken at last by the herb-doctor's saying: "Well, there is a bright side to everything. If this speak prosaically for justice, it speaks romantically for friendship! But go on, my fine fellow."

"My say being said, they told me I might go. I said I could not without help. So the constables helped me, asking *where* would I go? I told them back to the 'Tombs.' I knew no other place. 'But where are your friends?' said they. 'I have none.' So they put me into a hand-barrow with an awning to it, and wheeled me down to the dock and on board a boat, and away to Blackwell's Island to the Corporation Hospital. There I got worse—got pretty much as you see me now. Couldn't cure me. After three years, I grew sick of lying in a grated iron bed alongside of groaning thieves and mouldering burglars. They gave me five silver dollars, and these crutches, and I hobbled off. I had an only brother who went to Indiana, years ago. I begged about, to make up a sum to go to him; got to Indiana at last, and they directed me to his grave. It was on a great plain, in a log-church yard with a stump fence, the old gray roots sticking all ways like moose-antlers. The bier, set over the grave, it being the last dug, was of green hickory; bark on, and green twigs sprouting from it. Some one had planted a bunch of violets on the mound, but it was a poor soil (always choose the poorest soils for grave-yards), and they were all dried to tinder. I was going to sit and rest myself on the bier and think about my brother in heaven, but the bier broke down, the legs being only tacked. So, after driving some hogs out of the yard that were rooting there, I came away, and, not to make too long a story of it, here I am, drifting down stream like any other bit of wreck."

The herb-doctor was silent for a time, buried in thought. At last, raising his head, he said: "I have considered your whole story, my friend, and strove to consider it in the light of a commentary on what I believe to be the system of things; but it so jars with all, is so incompatible with all, that you must pardon me, if I honestly tell you, I cannot believe it."

"That don't surprise me."

"How?"

"Hardly anybody believes my story, and so to most I tell a different one."

"How, again?"

"Wait here a bit and I'll show ye."

With that, taking off his rag of a cap, and arranging his tattered regimentals the best he could, off he went stumping among the passengers in an adjoining part of the deck, saying with a jovial kind of air: "Sir, a shilling for Happy Tom, who fought at Buena Vista. Lady, something for General Scott's soldier, crippled in both pins at glorious Contreras."

Now, it so chanced that, unbeknown to the cripple, a prim-looking stranger had overheard part of his story. Beholding him, then, on his present begging adventure, this person, turning to the herb-doctor, indignantly said: "Is it not too bad, sir, that yonder rascal should lie so?"

"Charity never faileth, my good sir," was the reply. "The vice of this unfortunate is pardonable. Consider, he lies not out of wantonness."

"Not out of wantonness. I never heard more wanton lies. In one breath to tell you what would appear to be his true story, and, in the next, away and falsify it."

"For all that, I repeat he lies not out of wantonness. A ripe philosopher, turned out of the great Sorbonne of hard times, he thinks that woes, when told to strangers for money, are best sugared. Though the inglorious lock-jaw of his knee-pans in a wet dungeon is a far more pitiable ill than to have been crippled at glorious Contreras, yet he is of opinion that this lighter and false ill shall attract, while the heavier and real one might repel."

HERMAN MELVILLE

"Nonsense; he belongs to the Devil's regiment; and I have a great mind to expose him."

"Shame upon you. Dare to expose that poor unfortunate, and by heaven—don't you do it, sir."

Noting something in his manner, the other thought it more prudent to retire than retort. By-and-by, the cripple came back, and with glee, having reaped a pretty good harvest.

"There," he laughed, "you know now what sort of soldier I am."

"Aye, one that fights not the stupid Mexican, but a foe worthy your tactics—Fortune!"

"Hi, hi!" clamored the cripple, like a fellow in the pit of a sixpenny theatre, then said, "don't know much what you meant, but it went off well."

This over, his countenance capriciously put on a morose ogreness. To kindly questions he gave no kindly answers. Unhandsome notions were thrown out about "free Ameriky," as he sarcastically called his country. These seemed to disturb and pain the herb-doctor, who, after an interval of thoughtfulness, gravely addressed him in these words:

"You, my Worthy friend, to my concern, have reflected upon the government under which you live and suffer. Where is your patriotism? Where your gratitude? True, the charitable may find something in your case, as you put it, partly to account for such reflections as coming from you. Still, be the facts how they may, your reflections are none the less unwarrantable. Grant, for the moment, that your experiences are as you give them; in which case I would admit that government might be thought to have more or less to do with what seems undesirable in them. But it is never to be forgotten that human government, being subordinate to the divine, must needs, therefore, in its degree, partake of the characteristics of the divine. That is, while in general efficacious to happiness, the world's law may yet, in some cases, have, to the eye of reason, an unequal operation, just as, in the same imperfect view, some inequalities may appear in the operations of heaven's law; nevertheless, to one who has a right confidence, final benignity is, in every instance, as sure with the one law as the other. I expound the point at some length, because these are the considerations, my poor fellow, which, weighed as they merit, will enable you to sustain with unimpaired trust the apparent calamities which are yours."

"What do you talk your hog-latin to me for?" cried the cripple, who, throughout the address, betrayed the most illiterate obduracy; and, with an incensed look, anew he swung himself.

Glancing another way till the spasm passed, the other continued:

"Charity marvels not that you should be somewhat hard of conviction, my friend, since you, doubtless, believe yourself hardly dealt by; but forget not that those who are loved are chastened."

"Mustn't chasten them too much, though, and too long, because their skin and heart get hard, and feel neither pain nor tickle."

"To mere reason, your case looks something piteous, I grant. But never despond; many things—the choicest—yet remain. You breathe this bounteous air, are warmed by this gracious sun, and, though poor and friendless, indeed, nor so agile as in your youth, yet, how sweet to roam, day by day, through the groves, plucking the bright mosses and flowers, till forlornness itself becomes a hilarity, and, in your innocent independence, you skip for joy."

"Fine skipping with these 'ere horse-posts—ha ha!"

"Pardon; I forgot the crutches. My mind, figuring you after receiving the benefit of my art, overlooked you as you stand before me."

"Your art? You call yourself a bone-setter—a natural bone-setter, do ye? Go, bone-set the crooked world, and then come bone-set crooked me."

"Truly, my honest friend, I thank you for again recalling me to my original object. Let me examine you," bending down; "ah, I see, I see; much such a case as the negro's. Did you see him? Oh no, you came aboard since. Well, his case was a little something like yours. I prescribed for him, and I shouldn't wonder at all if, in a very short time, he were able to walk almost as well as myself. Now, have you no confidence in my art?"

"Ha, ha!"

The herb-doctor averted himself; but, the wild laugh dying away, resumed:

"I will not force confidence on you. Still, I would fain do the friendly thing by you. Here, take this box; just rub that liniment on the joints night and morning. Take it. Nothing to pay. God bless you. Good-bye."

"Stay," pausing in his swing, not untouched by so unexpected an act; "stay—thank'ee—but will this really do me good? Honor bright, now; will it? Don't deceive a poor fellow," with changed mien and glistening eye.

"Try it. Good-bye."

"Stay, stay! *Sure* it will do me good?"

"Possibly, possibly; no harm in trying. Good-bye."

HERMAN MELVILLE

"Stay, stay; give me three more boxes, and here's the money."

"My friend," returning towards him with a sadly pleased sort of air, "I rejoice in the birth of your confidence and hopefulness. Believe me that, like your crutches, confidence and hopefulness will long support a man when his own legs will not. Stick to confidence and hopefulness, then, since how mad for the cripple to throw his crutches away. You ask for three more boxes of my liniment. Luckily, I have just that number remaining. Here they are. I sell them at half-a-dollar apiece. But I shall take nothing from you. There; God bless you again; good-bye."

"Stay," in a convulsed voice, and rocking himself, "stay, stay! You have made a better man of me. You have borne with me like a good Christian, and talked to me like one, and all that is enough without making me a present of these boxes. Here is the money. I won't take nay. There, there; and may Almighty goodness go with you."

As the herb-doctor withdrew, the cripple gradually subsided from his hard rocking into a gentle oscillation. It expressed, perhaps, the soothed mood of his reverie.

XX

REAPPEARANCE OF ONE WHO MAY BE REMEMBERED

The herb-doctor had not moved far away, when, in advance of him, this spectacle met his eye. A dried-up old man, with the stature of a boy of twelve, was tottering about like one out of his mind, in rumpled clothes of old moleskin, showing recent contact with bedding, his ferret eyes, blinking in the sunlight of the snowy boat, as imbecilely eager, and, at intervals, coughing, he peered hither and thither as if in alarmed search for his nurse. He presented the aspect of one who, bed-rid, has, through overruling excitement, like that of a fire, been stimulated to his feet.

"You seek some one," said the herb-doctor, accosting him. "Can I assist you?"

"Do, do; I am so old and miserable," coughed the old man. "Where is he? This long time I've been trying to get up and find him. But I haven't any friends, and couldn't get up till now. Where is he?"

"Who do you mean?" drawing closer, to stay the further wanderings of one so weakly.

"Why, why, why," now marking the other's dress, "why you, yes you—you, you—ugh, ugh, ugh!"

"I?"

"Ugh, ugh, ugh!—you are the man he spoke of. Who is he?"

"Faith, that is just what I want to know."

"Mercy, mercy!" coughed the old man, bewildered, "ever since seeing him, my head spins round so. I ought to have a guard*ee*an. Is this a snuff-colored surtout of yours, or ain't it? Somehow, can't trust my senses any more, since trusting him—ugh, ugh, ugh!"

"Oh, you have trusted somebody? Glad to hear it. Glad to hear of any instance, of that sort. Reflects well upon all men. But you inquire whether this is a snuff-colored surtout. I answer it is; and will add that a herb-doctor wears it."

Upon this the old man, in his broken way, replied that then he (the herb-doctor) was the person he sought—the person spoken of by the other person as yet unknown. He then, with flighty eagerness, wanted to know who this last person was, and where he was, and whether he could be trusted with money to treble it.

"Aye, now, I begin to understand; ten to one you mean my worthy friend, who, in pure goodness of heart, makes people's fortunes for them—their everlasting fortunes, as the phrase goes—only charging his one small commission of confidence. Aye, aye; before intrusting funds with my friend, you want to know about him. Very proper—and, I am glad to assure you, you need have no hesitation; none, none, just none in the world; bona fide, none. Turned me in a trice a hundred dollars the other day into as many eagles."

"Did he? did he? But where is he? Take me to him."

"Pray, take my arm! The boat is large! We may have something of a hunt! Come on! Ah, is that he?"

"Where? where?"

"O, no; I took yonder coat-skirts for his. But no, my honest friend would never turn tail that way. Ah!—"

"Where? where?"

"Another mistake. Surprising resemblance. I took yonder clergyman for him. Come on!"

Having searched that part of the boat without success, they went to another part, and, while exploring that, the boat sided up to a landing, when, as the two were passing by the open guard, the herb-doctor suddenly rushed towards the disembarking throng, crying out: "Mr. Truman, Mr. Truman! There he goes—that's he. Mr. Truman, Mr. Truman!—Confound that steam-pipe., Mr. Truman! for God's sake, Mr. Truman!—No, no.—There, the plank's in—too late—we're off."

With that, the huge boat, with a mighty, walrus wallow, rolled away from the shore, resuming her course.

"How vexatious!" exclaimed the herb-doctor, returning. "Had we been but one single moment sooner.—There he goes, now, towards yon hotel, his portmanteau following. You see him, don't you?"

"Where? where?"

"Can't see him any more. Wheel-house shot between. I am very sorry. I should have so liked you to have let him have a hundred or so of your money. You would have been pleased with the investment, believe me."

"Oh, I *have* let him have some of my money," groaned the old man.

"You have? My dear sir," seizing both the miser's hands in both his own and heartily shaking them. "My dear sir, how I congratulate you. You don't know."

"Ugh, ugh! I fear I don't," with another groan. "His name is Truman, is it?"

"John Truman."

"Where does he live?"

"In St. Louis."

"Where's his office?"

"Let me see. Jones street, number one hundred and—no, no—anyway, it's somewhere or other up-stairs in Jones street."

"Can't you remember the number? Try, now."

"One hundred—two hundred—three hundred—"

"Oh, my hundred dollars! I wonder whether it will be one hundred, two hundred, three hundred, with them! Ugh, ugh! Can't remember the number?"

"Positively, though I once knew, I have forgotten, quite forgotten it. Strange. But never mind. You will easily learn in St. Louis. He is well known there."

"But I have no receipt—ugh, ugh! Nothing to show—don't know where I stand—ought to have a guardeean—ugh, ugh! Don't know anything. Ugh, ugh!"

"Why, you know that you gave him your confidence, don't you?"

"Oh, yes."

"Well, then?"

"But what, what—how, how—ugh, ugh!"

"Why, didn't he tell you?"

"No."

"What! Didn't he tell you that it was a secret, a mystery?"

"Oh—yes."

"Well, then?"

"But I have no bond."

"Don't need any with Mr. Truman. Mr. Truman's word is his bond."

"But how am I to get my profits—ugh, ugh!—and my money back? Don't know anything. Ugh, ugh!"

"Oh, you must have confidence."

"Don't say that word again. Makes my head spin so. Oh, I'm so old and miserable, nobody caring for me, everybody fleecing me, and my head spins so—ugh, ugh!—and this cough racks me so. I say again, I ought to have a guardeean."

"So you ought; and Mr. Truman is your guardian to the extent you invested with him. Sorry we missed him just now. But you'll hear from

HERMAN MELVILLE

him. All right. It's imprudent, though, to expose yourself this way. Let me take you to your berth."

Forlornly enough the old miser moved slowly away with him. But, while descending a stairway, he was seized with such coughing that he was fain to pause.

"That is a very bad cough."

"Church-yard—ugh, ugh!—church-yard cough.—Ugh!"

"Have you tried anything for it?"

"Tired of trying. Nothing does me any good—ugh! ugh! Not even the Mammoth Cave. Ugh! ugh! Denned there six months, but coughed so bad the rest of the coughers—ugh! ugh!—black-balled me out. Ugh, ugh! Nothing does me good."

"But have you tried the Omni-Balsamic Reinvigorator, sir?"

"That's what that Truman—ugh, ugh!—said I ought to take. Yarb-medicine; you are that yarb-doctor, too?"

"The same. Suppose you try one of my boxes now. Trust me, from what I know of Mr. Truman, he is not the gentleman to recommend, even in behalf of a friend, anything of whose excellence he is not conscientiously satisfied."

"Ugh!—how much?"

"Only two dollars a box."

"Two dollars? Why don't you say two millions? ugh, ugh! Two dollars, that's two hundred cents; that's eight hundred farthings; that's two thousand mills; and all for one little box of yarb-medicine. My head, my head!—oh, I ought to have a guardeean for; my head. Ugh, ugh, ugh, ugh!"

"Well, if two dollars a box seems too much, take a dozen boxes at twenty dollars; and that will be getting four boxes for nothing, and you need use none but those four, the rest you can retail out at a premium, and so cure your cough, and make money by it. Come, you had better do it. Cash down. Can fill an order in a day or two. Here now," producing a box; "pure herbs."

At that moment, seized with another spasm, the miser snatched each interval to fix his half distrustful, half hopeful eye upon the medicine, held alluringly up. "Sure—ugh! Sure it's all nat'ral? Nothing but yarbs? If I only thought it was a purely nat'ral medicine now—all yarbs—ugh, ugh!—oh this cough, this cough—ugh, ugh!—shatters my whole body. Ugh, ugh, ugh!"

"For heaven's sake try my medicine, if but a single box. That it is pure nature you may be confident, Refer you to Mr. Truman."

"Don't know his number—ugh, ugh, ugh, ugh! Oh this cough. He did speak well of this medicine though; said solemnly it would cure me—ugh, ugh, ugh, ugh!—take off a dollar and I'll have a box."

"Can't sir, can't."

"Say a dollar-and-half. Ugh!"

"Can't. Am pledged to the one-price system, only honorable one."

"Take off a shilling—ugh, ugh!"

"Can't."

"Ugh, ugh, ugh—I'll take it.—There."

Grudgingly he handed eight silver coins, but while still in his hand, his cough took him and they were shaken upon the deck.

One by one, the herb-doctor picked them up, and, examining them, said: "These are not quarters, these are pistareens; and clipped, and sweated, at that."

"Oh don't be so miserly—ugh, ugh!—better a beast than a miser—ugh, ugh!"

"Well, let it go. Anything rather than the idea of your not being cured of such a cough. And I hope, for the credit of humanity, you have not made it appear worse than it is, merely with a view to working upon the weak point of my pity, and so getting my medicine the cheaper. Now, mind, don't take it till night. Just before retiring is the time. There, you can get along now, can't you? I would attend you further, but I land presently, and must go hunt up my luggage."

XXI

A Hard Case

Yarbs, yarbs; natur, natur; you foolish old file you! He diddled you with that hocus-pocus, did he? Yarbs and natur will cure your incurable cough, you think."

It was a rather eccentric-looking person who spoke; somewhat ursine in aspect; sporting a shaggy spencer of the cloth called bear's-skin; a high-peaked cap of raccoon-skin, the long bushy tail switching over behind; raw-hide leggings; grim stubble chin; and to end, a double-barreled gun in hand—a Missouri bachelor, a Hoosier gentleman, of Spartan leisure and fortune, and equally Spartan manners and sentiments; and, as the sequel may show, not less acquainted, in a Spartan way of his own, with philosophy and books, than with woodcraft and rifles.

He must have overheard some of the talk between the miser and the herb-doctor; for, just after the withdrawal of the one, he made up to the other—now at the foot of the stairs leaning against the baluster there—with the greeting above.

"Think it will cure me?" coughed the miser in echo; "why shouldn't it? The medicine is nat'ral yarbs, pure yarbs; yarbs must cure me."

"Because a thing is nat'ral, as you call it, you think it must be good. But who gave you that cough? Was it, or was it not, nature?"

"Sure, you don't think that natur, Dame Natur, will hurt a body, do you?"

"Natur is good Queen Bess; but who's responsible for the cholera?"

"But yarbs, yarbs; yarbs are good?"

"What's deadly-nightshade? Yarb, ain't it?"

"Oh, that a Christian man should speak agin natur and yarbs—ugh, ugh, ugh!—ain't sick men sent out into the country; sent out to natur and grass?"

"Aye, and poets send out the sick spirit to green pastures, like lame horses turned out unshod to the turf to renew their hoofs. A sort of yarb-doctors in their way, poets have it that for sore hearts, as for sore lungs, nature is the grand cure. But who froze to death my teamster on the prairie? And who made an idiot of Peter the Wild Boy?"

"Then you don't believe in these 'ere yarb-doctors?"

"Yarb-doctors? I remember the lank yarb-doctor I saw once on a hospital-cot in Mobile. One of the faculty passing round and seeing who lay there, said with professional triumph, 'Ah, Dr. Green, your yarbs don't help ye now, Dr. Green. Have to come to us and the mercury now, Dr. Green.—Natur! Y-a-r-b-s!'"

"Did I hear something about herbs and herb-doctors?" here said a flute-like voice, advancing.

It was the herb-doctor in person. Carpet-bag in hand, he happened to be strolling back that way.

"Pardon me," addressing the Missourian, "but if I caught your words aright, you would seem to have little confidence in nature; which, really, in my way of thinking, looks like carrying the spirit of distrust pretty far."

"And who of my sublime species may you be?" turning short round upon him, clicking his rifle-lock, with an air which would have seemed half cynic, half wild-cat, were it not for the grotesque excess of the expression, which made its sincerity appear more or less dubious.

"One who has confidence in nature, and confidence in man, with some little modest confidence in himself."

"That's your Confession of Faith, is it? Confidence in man, eh? Pray, which do you think are most, knaves or fools?"

"Having met with few or none of either, I hardly think I am competent to answer."

"I will answer for you. Fools are most."

"Why do you think so?"

"For the same reason that I think oats are numerically more than horses. Don't knaves munch up fools just as horses do oats?"

"A droll, sir; you are a droll. I can appreciate drollery—ha, ha, ha!"

"But I'm in earnest."

"That's the drollery, to deliver droll extravagance with an earnest air—knaves munching up fools as horses oats.—Faith, very droll, indeed, ha, ha, ha! Yes, I think I understand you now, sir. How silly I was to have taken you seriously, in your droll conceits, too, about having no confidence in nature. In reality you have just as much as I have."

"*I* have confidence in nature? *I?* I say again there is nothing I am more suspicious of. I once lost ten thousand dollars by nature. Nature embezzled that amount from me; absconded with ten thousand dollars' worth of my property; a plantation on this stream, swept clean away by one of those sudden shiftings of the banks in a freshet; ten thousand dollars' worth of alluvion thrown broad off upon the waters."

"But have you no confidence that by a reverse shifting that soil will come back after many days?—ah, here is my venerable friend," observing the old miser, "not in your berth yet? Pray, if you *will* keep afoot, don't lean against that baluster; take my arm."

It was taken; and the two stood together; the old miser leaning against the herb-doctor with something of that air of trustful fraternity with which, when standing, the less strong of the Siamese twins habitually leans against the other.

The Missourian eyed them in silence, which was broken by the herb-doctor.

"You look surprised, sir. Is it because I publicly take under my protection a figure like this? But I am never ashamed of honesty, whatever his coat."

"Look you," said the Missourian, after a scrutinizing pause, "you are a queer sort of chap. Don't know exactly what to make of you. Upon the whole though, you somewhat remind me of the last boy I had on my place."

"Good, trustworthy boy, I hope?"

"Oh, very! I am now started to get me made some kind of machine to do the sort of work which boys are supposed to be fitted for."

"Then you have passed a veto upon boys?"

"And men, too."

"But, my dear sir, does not that again imply more or less lack of confidence?—(Stand up a little, just a very little, my venerable friend; you lean rather hard.)—No confidence in boys, no confidence in men, no confidence in nature. Pray, sir, who or what may you have confidence in?"

"I have confidence in distrust; more particularly as applied to you and your herbs."

"Well," with a forbearing smile, "that is frank. But pray, don't forget that when you suspect my herbs you suspect nature."

"Didn't I say that before?"

"Very good. For the argument's sake I will suppose you are in earnest. Now, can you, who suspect nature, deny, that this same nature not only kindly brought you into being, but has faithfully nursed you to your present vigorous and independent condition? Is it not to nature that you are indebted for that robustness of mind which you so unhandsomely use to her scandal? Pray, is it not to nature that you owe the very eyes by which you criticise her?"

"No! for the privilege of vision I am indebted to an oculist, who in my tenth year operated upon me in Philadelphia. Nature made me blind and would have kept me so. My oculist counterplotted her."

"And yet, sir, by your complexion, I judge you live an out-of-door life; without knowing it, you are partial to nature; you fly to nature, the universal mother."

"Very motherly! Sir, in the passion-fits of nature, I've known birds fly from nature to me, rough as I look; yes, sir, in a tempest, refuge here," smiting the folds of his bearskin. "Fact, sir, fact. Come, come, Mr. Palaverer, for all your palavering, did you yourself never shut out nature of a cold, wet night? Bar her out? Bolt her out? Lint her out?"

"As to that," said the herb-doctor calmly, "much may be said."

"Say it, then," ruffling all his hairs. "You can't, sir, can't." Then, as in apostrophe: "Look you, nature! I don't deny but your clover is sweet, and your dandelions don't roar; but whose hailstones smashed my windows?"

"Sir," with unimpaired affability, producing one of his boxes, "I am pained to meet with one who holds nature a dangerous character. Though your manner is refined your voice is rough; in short, you seem to have a sore throat. In the calumniated name of nature, I present you with this box; my venerable friend here has a similar one; but to you, a free gift, sir. Through her regularly-authorized agents, of whom I happen to be one, Nature delights in benefiting those who most abuse her. Pray, take it."

"Away with it! Don't hold it so near. Ten to one there is a torpedo in it. Such things have been. Editors been killed that way. Take it further off, I say."

"Good heavens! my dear sir—"

"I tell you I want none of your boxes," snapping his rifle.

"Oh, take it—ugh, ugh! do take it," chimed in the old miser; "I wish he would give me one for nothing."

"You find it lonely, eh," turning short round; "gulled yourself, you would have a companion."

"How can he find it lonely," returned the herb-doctor, "or how desire a companion, when here I stand by him; I, even I, in whom he has trust. For the gulling, tell me, is it humane to talk so to this poor old man? Granting that his dependence on my medicine is vain, is it kind to deprive him of what, in mere imagination, if nothing more, may

HERMAN MELVILLE

help eke out, with hope, his disease? For you, if you have no confidence, and, thanks to your native health, can get along without it, so far, at least, as trusting in my medicine goes; yet, how cruel an argument to use, with this afflicted one here. Is it not for all the world as if some brawny pugilist, aglow in December, should rush in and put out a hospital-fire, because, forsooth, he feeling no need of artificial heat, the shivering patients shall have none? Put it to your conscience, sir, and you will admit, that, whatever be the nature of this afflicted one's trust, you, in opposing it, evince either an erring head or a heart amiss. Come, own, are you not pitiless?"

"Yes, poor soul," said the Missourian, gravely eying the old man—"yes, it *is* pitiless in one like me to speak too honestly to one like you. You are a late sitter-up in this life; past man's usual bed-time; and truth, though with some it makes a wholesome breakfast, proves to all a supper too hearty. Hearty food, taken late, gives bad dreams."

"What, in wonder's name—ugh, ugh!—is he talking about?" asked the old miser, looking up to the herb-doctor.

"Heaven be praised for that!" cried the Missourian.

"Out of his mind, ain't he?" again appealed the old miser.

"Pray, sir," said the herb-doctor to the Missourian, "for what were you giving thanks just now?"

"For this: that, with some minds, truth is, in effect, not so cruel a thing after all, seeing that, like a loaded pistol found by poor devils of savages, it raises more wonder than terror—its peculiar virtue being unguessed, unless, indeed, by indiscreet handling, it should happen to go off of itself."

"I pretend not to divine your meaning there," said the herb-doctor, after a pause, during which he eyed the Missourian with a kind of pinched expression, mixed of pain and curiosity, as if he grieved at his state of mind, and, at the same time, wondered what had brought him to it, "but this much I know," he added, "that the general cast of your thoughts is, to say the least, unfortunate. There is strength in them, but a strength, whose source, being physical, must wither. You will yet recant."

"Recant?"

"Yes, when, as with this old man, your evil days of decay come on, when a hoary captive in your chamber, then will you, something like the dungeoned Italian we read of, gladly seek the breast of that confidence begot in the tender time of your youth, blessed beyond telling if it return to you in age."

"Go back to nurse again, eh? Second childhood, indeed. You are soft."

"Mercy, mercy!" cried the old miser, "what is all this!—ugh, ugh! Do talk sense, my good friends. Ain't you," to the Missourian, "going to buy some of that medicine?"

"Pray, my venerable friend," said the herb-doctor, now trying to straighten himself, "don't lean *quite* so hard; my arm grows numb; abate a little, just a very little."

"Go," said the Missourian, "go lay down in your grave, old man, if you can't stand of yourself. It's a hard world for a leaner."

"As to his grave," said the herb-doctor, "that is far enough off, so he but faithfully take my medicine."

"Ugh, ugh, ugh!—He says true. No, I ain't—ugh! a going to die yet— ugh, ugh, ugh! Many years to live yet, ugh, ugh, ugh!"

"I approve your confidence," said the herb-doctor; "but your coughing distresses me, besides being injurious to you. Pray, let me conduct you to your berth. You are best there. Our friend here will wait till my return, I know."

With which he led the old miser away, and then, coming back, the talk with the Missourian was resumed.

"Sir," said the herb-doctor, with some dignity and more feeling, "now that our infirm friend is withdrawn, allow me, to the full, to express my concern at the words you allowed to escape you in his hearing. Some of those words, if I err not, besides being calculated to beget deplorable distrust in the patient, seemed fitted to convey unpleasant imputations against me, his physician."

"Suppose they did?" with a menacing air.

"Why, then—then, indeed," respectfully retreating, "I fall back upon my previous theory of your general facetiousness. I have the fortune to be in company with a humorist—a wag."

"Fall back you had better, and wag it is," cried the Missourian, following him up, and wagging his raccoon tail almost into the herb-doctor's face, "look you!"

"At what?"

"At this coon. Can you, the fox, catch him?"

"If you mean," returned the other, not unselfpossessed, "whether I flatter myself that I can in any way dupe you, or impose upon you, or pass myself off upon you for what I am not, I, as an honest man, answer that I have neither the inclination nor the power to do aught of the kind."

HERMAN MELVILLE

"Honest man? Seems to me you talk more like a craven."

"You in vain seek to pick a quarrel with me, or put any affront upon me. The innocence in me heals me."

"A healing like your own nostrums. But you are a queer man—a very queer and dubious man; upon the whole, about the most so I ever met."

The scrutiny accompanying this seemed unwelcome to the diffidence of the herb-doctor. As if at once to attest the absence of resentment, as well as to change the subject, he threw a kind of familiar cordiality into his air, and said: "So you are going to get some machine made to do your work? Philanthropic scruples, doubtless, forbid your going as far as New Orleans for slaves?"

"Slaves?" morose again in a twinkling, "won't have 'em! Bad enough to see whites ducking and grinning round for a favor, without having those poor devils of niggers congeeing round for their corn. Though, to me, the niggers are the freer of the two. You are an abolitionist, ain't you?" he added, squaring himself with both hands on his rifle, used for a staff, and gazing in the herb-doctor's face with no more reverence than if it were a target. "You are an abolitionist, ain't you?"

"As to that, I cannot so readily answer. If by abolitionist you mean a zealot, I am none; but if you mean a man, who, being a man, feels for all men, slaves included, and by any lawful act, opposed to nobody's interest, and therefore, rousing nobody's enmity, would willingly abolish suffering (supposing it, in its degree, to exist) from among mankind, irrespective of color, then am I what you say."

"Picked and prudent sentiments. You are the moderate man, the invaluable understrapper of the wicked man. You, the moderate man, may be used for wrong, but are useless for right."

"From all this," said the herb-doctor, still forgivingly, "I infer, that you, a Missourian, though living in a slave-state, are without slave sentiments."

"Aye, but are you? Is not that air of yours, so spiritlessly enduring and yielding, the very air of a slave? Who is your master, pray; or are you owned by a company?"

"*My* master?"

"Aye, for come from Maine or Georgia, you come from a slave-state, and a slave-pen, where the best breeds are to be bought up at any price from a livelihood to the Presidency. Abolitionism, ye gods, but expresses the fellow-feeling of slave for slave."

"The back-woods would seem to have given you rather eccentric notions," now with polite superiority smiled the herb-doctor, still with manly intrepidity forbearing each unmanly thrust, "but to return; since, for your purpose, you will have neither man nor boy, bond nor free, truly, then some sort of machine for you is all there is left. My desires for your success attend you, sir.—Ah!" glancing shoreward, "here is Cape Girádeau; I must leave you."

XXII

In the Polite Spirit of the Tusculan Disputations

—"'Philosophical Intelligence Office'—novel idea! But how did you come to dream that I wanted anything in your absurd line, eh?"

About twenty minutes after leaving Cape Girádeau, the above was growled out over his shoulder by the Missourian to a chance stranger who had just accosted him; a round-backed, baker-kneed man, in a mean five-dollar suit, wearing, collar-wise by a chain, a small brass plate, inscribed P. I. O., and who, with a sort of canine deprecation, slunk obliquely behind.

"How did you come to dream that I wanted anything in your line, eh?"

"Oh, respected sir," whined the other, crouching a pace nearer, and, in his obsequiousness, seeming to wag his very coat-tails behind him, shabby though they were, "oh, sir, from long experience, one glance tells me the gentleman who is in need of our humble services."

"But suppose I did want a boy—what they jocosely call a good boy— how could your absurd office help me?—Philosophical Intelligence Office?"

"Yes, respected sir, an office founded on strictly philosophical and physio—"

"Look you—come up here—how, by philosophy or physiology either, make good boys to order? Come up here. Don't give me a crick in the neck. Come up here, come, sir, come," calling as if to his pointer. "Tell me, how put the requisite assortment of good qualities into a boy, as the assorted mince into the pie?"

"Respected sir, our office—"

"You talk much of that office. Where is it? On board this boat?"

"Oh no, sir, I just came aboard. Our office—"

"Came aboard at that last landing, eh? Pray, do you know a herb-doctor there? Smooth scamp in a snuff-colored surtout?"

"Oh, sir, I was but a sojourner at Cape Girádeau. Though, now that you mention a snuff-colored surtout, I think I met such a man as you speak of stepping ashore as I stepped aboard, and 'pears to me I have seen him somewhere before. Looks like a very mild Christian sort of person, I should say. Do you know him, respected sir?"

"Not much, but better than you seem to. Proceed with your business."

With a low, shabby bow, as grateful for the permission, the other began: "Our office—"

"Look you," broke in the bachelor with ire, "have you the spinal complaint? What are you ducking and groveling about? Keep still. Where's your office?"

"The branch one which I represent, is at Alton, sir, in the free state we now pass," (pointing somewhat proudly ashore).

"Free, eh? You a freeman, you flatter yourself? With those coat-tails and that spinal complaint of servility? Free? Just cast up in your private mind who is your master, will you?"

"Oh, oh, oh! I don't understand—indeed—indeed. But, respected sir, as before said, our office, founded on principles wholly new—"

"To the devil with your principles! Bad sign when a man begins to talk of his principles. Hold, come back, sir; back here, back, sir, back! I tell you no more boys for me. Nay, I'm a Mede and Persian. In my old home in the woods I'm pestered enough with squirrels, weasels, chipmunks, skunks. I want no more wild vermin to spoil my temper and waste my substance. Don't talk of boys; enough of your boys; a plague of your boys; chilblains on your boys! As for Intelligence Offices, I've lived in the East, and know 'em. Swindling concerns kept by low-born cynics, under a fawning exterior wreaking their cynic malice upon mankind. You are a fair specimen of 'em."

"Oh dear, dear, dear!"

"Dear? Yes, a thrice dear purchase one of your boys would be to me. A rot on your boys!"

"But, respected sir, if you will not have boys, might we not, in our small way, accommodate you with a man?"

"Accommodate? Pray, no doubt you could accommodate me with a bosom-friend too, couldn't you? Accommodate! Obliging word accommodate: there's accommodation notes now, where one accommodates another with a loan, and if he don't pay it pretty quickly, accommodates him, with a chain to his foot. Accommodate! God forbid that I should ever be accommodated. No, no. Look you, as I told that cousin-german of yours, the herb-doctor, I'm now on the road to get me made some sort of machine to do my work. Machines for me. My cider-mill—does that ever steal my cider? My mowing-machine—does that ever lay a-bed mornings? My corn-husker—does that ever give me insolence? No: cider-mill, mowing-machine, corn-husker—all faithfully attend to their business. Disinterested, too; no board, no wages; yet doing good all their lives long; shining examples that virtue is its own reward—the only practical Christians I know."

"Oh dear, dear, dear, dear!"

"Yes, sir:—boys? Start my soul-bolts, what a difference, in a moral point of view, between a corn-husker and a boy! Sir, a corn-husker, for its patient continuance in well-doing, might not unfitly go to heaven. Do you suppose a boy will?"

"A corn-husker in heaven! (turning up the whites of his eyes). Respected sir, this way of talking as if heaven were a kind of Washington patent-office museum—oh, oh, oh!—as if mere machine-work and puppet-work went to heaven—oh, oh, oh! Things incapable of free agency, to receive the eternal reward of well-doing—oh, oh, oh!"

"You Praise-God-Barebones you, what are you groaning about? Did I say anything of that sort? Seems to me, though you talk so good, you are mighty quick at a hint the other way, or else you want to pick a polemic quarrel with me."

"It may be so or not, respected sir," was now the demure reply; "but if it be, it is only because as a soldier out of honor is quick in taking affront, so a Christian out of religion is quick, sometimes perhaps a little too much so, in spying heresy."

"Well," after an astonished pause, "for an unaccountable pair, you and the herb-doctor ought to yoke together."

So saying, the bachelor was eying him rather sharply, when he with the brass plate recalled him to the discussion by a hint, not unflattering, that he (the man with the brass plate) was all anxiety to hear him further on the subject of servants.

"About that matter," exclaimed the impulsive bachelor, going off at the hint like a rocket, "all thinking minds are, now-a-days, coming to the conclusion—one derived from an immense hereditary experience—see what Horace and others of the ancients say of servants—coming to the conclusion, I say, that boy or man, the human animal is, for most work-purposes, a losing animal. Can't be trusted; less trustworthy than oxen; for conscientiousness a turn-spit dog excels him. Hence these thousand new inventions—carding machines, horseshoe machines, tunnel-boring machines, reaping machines, apple-paring machines, boot-blacking machines, sewing machines, shaving machines, run-of-errand machines, dumb-waiter machines, and the Lord-only-knows-what machines; all of which announce the era when that refractory animal, the working or serving man, shall be a buried by-gone, a superseded fossil. Shortly prior to which glorious time, I doubt not that a price will be put upon their peltries as upon the knavish 'possums,' especially the boys. Yes, sir (ringing his rifle down on the deck), I rejoice to think that the day is at hand, when, prompted to it by law, I shall shoulder this gun and go out a boy-shooting."

"Oh, now! Lord, Lord, Lord!—But *our* office, respected sir, conducted as I ventured to observe—"

"No, sir," bristlingly settling his stubble chin in his coon-skins. "Don't try to oil me; the herb-doctor tried that. My experience, carried now through a course—worse than salivation—a course of five and thirty boys, proves to me that boyhood is a natural state of rascality."

"Save us, save us!"

"Yes, sir, yes. My name is Pitch; I stick to what I say. I speak from fifteen years' experience; five and thirty boys; American, Irish, English, German, African, Mulatto; not to speak of that China boy sent me by one who well knew my perplexities, from California; and that Lascar boy from Bombay. Thug! I found him sucking the embryo life from my spring eggs. All rascals, sir, every soul of them; Caucasian or Mongol. Amazing the endless variety of rascality in human nature of the juvenile sort. I remember that, having discharged, one after another, twenty-nine boys—each, too, for some wholly unforeseen species of viciousness peculiar to that one peculiar boy—I remember saying to myself: Now, then, surely, I have got to the end of the list, wholly exhausted it; I have only now to get me a boy, any boy different from those twenty-nine preceding boys, and he infallibly shall be that virtuous boy I have so long been seeking. But, bless me! this thirtieth boy—by the way, having at the time long forsworn your intelligence offices, I had him sent to me from the Commissioners of Emigration, all the way from New York, culled out carefully, in fine, at my particular request, from a standing army of eight hundred boys, the flowers of all nations, so they wrote me, temporarily in barracks on an East River island—I say, this thirtieth boy was in person not ungraceful; his deceased mother a lady's maid, or something of that sort; and in manner, why, in a plebeian way, a perfect Chesterfield; very intelligent, too—quick as a flash. But, such suavity! 'Please sir! please sir!' always bowing and saying, 'Please sir.' In the strangest way, too, combining a filial affection with a menial respect. Took such warm, singular interest in my affairs. Wanted to be considered one of the family—sort of adopted son of mine, I suppose. Of a morning, when I would go out to my stable, with what childlike good nature he would trot out my nag, 'Please sir, I think he's getting fatter and fatter.' 'But, he don't look very clean, does he?' unwilling to be downright harsh with so affectionate a lad; 'and he seems a little hollow inside the haunch there, don't he? or no, perhaps I don't see plain this morning.' 'Oh, please sir, it's just there I think he's gaining so, please.' Polite scamp! I soon found he never gave that wretched nag his oats of nights; didn't bed him either. Was above that sort of chambermaid work. No end to his willful neglects. But the more he abused my service, the more polite he grew."

"Oh, sir, some way you mistook him."

"Not a bit of it. Besides, sir, he was a boy who under a Chesterfieldian exterior hid strong destructive propensities. He cut up my horse-blanket for the bits of leather, for hinges to his chest. Denied it point-blank. After he was gone, found the shreds under his mattress. Would slyly break his hoe-handle, too, on purpose to get rid of hoeing. Then be so gracefully penitent for his fatal excess of industrious strength. Offer to mend all by taking a nice stroll to the nighest settlement—cherry-trees in full bearing all the way—to get the broken thing cobbled. Very politely stole my pears, odd pennies, shillings, dollars, and nuts; regular squirrel at it. But I could prove nothing. Expressed to him my suspicions. Said I, moderately enough, 'A little less politeness, and a little more honesty would suit me better.' He fired up; threatened to sue for libel. I won't say anything about his afterwards, in Ohio, being found in the act of gracefully putting a bar across a rail-road track, for the reason that a stoker called him the rogue that he was. But enough: polite boys or saucy boys, white boys or black boys, smart boys or lazy boys, Caucasian boys or Mongol boys—all are rascals."

"Shocking, shocking!" nervously tucking his frayed cravat-end out of sight. "Surely, respected sir, you labor under a deplorable hallucination. Why, pardon again, you seem to have not the slightest confidence in boys, I admit, indeed, that boys, some of them at least, are but too prone to one little foolish foible or other. But, what then, respected sir, when, by natural laws, they finally outgrow such things, and wholly?"

Having until now vented himself mostly in plaintive dissent of canine whines and groans, the man with the brass-plate seemed beginning to summon courage to a less timid encounter. But, upon his maiden essay, was not very encouragingly handled, since the dialogue immediately continued as follows:

"Boys outgrow what is amiss in them? From bad boys spring good men? Sir, 'the child is father of the man;' hence, as all boys are rascals, so are all men. But, God bless me, you must know these things better than I; keeping an intelligence office as you do; a business which must furnish peculiar facilities for studying mankind. Come, come up here, sir; confess you know these things pretty well, after all. Do you not know that all men are rascals, and all boys, too?"

"Sir," replied the other, spite of his shocked feelings seeming to pluck up some spirit, but not to an indiscreet degree, "Sir, heaven be praised, I am far, very far from knowing what you say. True," he thoughtfully continued, "with my associates, I keep an intelligence office, and for ten years, come October, have, one way or other, been concerned in that line; for no small period in the great city of Cincinnati, too; and though, as you hint, within that long interval, I must have had more or less favorable opportunity for studying mankind—in a business way, scanning not only the faces, but ransacking the lives of several thousands of human beings, male and female, of various nations, both employers and employed, genteel and ungenteel, educated and uneducated; yet—of course, I candidly admit, with some random exceptions, I have, so far as my small observation goes, found that mankind thus domestically viewed, confidentially viewed, I may say; they, upon the whole—making some reasonable allowances for human imperfection—present as pure a moral spectacle as the purest angel could wish. I say it, respected sir, with confidence."

"Gammon! You don't mean what you say. Else you are like a landsman at sea: don't know the ropes, the very things everlastingly pulled before your eyes. Serpent-like, they glide about, traveling blocks too subtle for you. In short, the entire ship is a riddle. Why, you green ones wouldn't know if she were unseaworthy; but still, with thumbs stuck back into your arm-holes, pace the rotten planks, singing, like a fool, words put into your green mouth by the cunning owner, the man who, heavily insuring it, sends his ship to be wrecked—

'A wet sheet and a flowing sea!'—

and, sir, now that it occurs to me, your talk, the whole of it, is but a wet sheet and a flowing sea, and an idle wind that follows fast, offering a striking contrast to my own discourse."

HERMAN MELVILLE

"Sir," exclaimed the man with the brass-plate, his patience now more or less tasked, "permit me with deference to hint that some of your remarks are injudiciously worded. And thus we say to our patrons, when they enter our office full of abuse of us because of some worthy boy we may have sent them—some boy wholly misjudged for the time. Yes, sir, permit me to remark that you do not sufficiently consider that, though a small man, I may have my small share of feelings."

"Well, well, I didn't mean to wound your feelings at all. And that they are small, very small, I take your word for it. Sorry, sorry. But truth is like a thrashing-machine; tender sensibilities must keep out of the way. Hope you understand me. Don't want to hurt you. All I say is, what I said in the first place, only now I swear it, that all boys are rascals."

"Sir," lowly replied the other, still forbearing like an old lawyer badgered in court, or else like a good-hearted simpleton, the butt of mischievous wags, "Sir, since you come back to the point, will you allow me, in my small, quiet way, to submit to you certain small, quiet views of the subject in hand?"

"Oh, yes!" with insulting indifference, rubbing his chin and looking the other way. "Oh, yes; go on."

"Well, then, respected sir," continued the other, now assuming as genteel an attitude as the irritating set of his pinched five-dollar suit would permit; "well, then, sir, the peculiar principles, the strictly philosophical principles, I may say," guardedly rising in dignity, as he guardedly rose on his toes, "upon which our office is founded, has led me and my associates, in our small, quiet way, to a careful analytical study of man, conducted, too, on a quiet theory, and with an unobtrusive aim wholly our own. That theory I will not now at large set forth. But some of the discoveries resulting from it, I will, by your permission, very briefly mention; such of them, I mean, as refer to the state of boyhood scientifically viewed."

"Then you have studied the thing? expressly studied boys, eh? Why didn't you out with that before?"

"Sir, in my small business way, I have not conversed with so many masters, gentlemen masters, for nothing. I have been taught that in this world there is a precedence of opinions as well as of persons. You have kindly given me your views, I am now, with modesty, about to give you mine."

"Stop flunkying—go on."

"In the first place, sir, our theory teaches us to proceed by analogy from the physical to the moral. Are we right there, sir? Now, sir, take a young boy, a young male infant rather, a man-child in short—what sir, I respectfully ask, do you in the first place remark?"

"A rascal, sir! present and prospective, a rascal!"

"Sir, if passion is to invade, surely science must evacuate. May I proceed? Well, then, what, in the first place, in a general view, do you remark, respected sir, in that male baby or man-child?"

The bachelor privily growled, but this time, upon the whole, better governed himself than before, though not, indeed, to the degree of thinking it prudent to risk an articulate response.

"What do you remark? I respectfully repeat." But, as no answer came, only the low, half-suppressed growl, as of Bruin in a hollow trunk, the questioner continued: "Well, sir, if you will permit me, in my small way, to speak for you, you remark, respected sir, an incipient creation; loose sort of sketchy thing; a little preliminary rag-paper study, or careless cartoon, so to speak, of a man. The idea, you see, respected sir, is there; but, as yet, wants filling out. In a word, respected sir, the man-child is at present but little, every way; I don't pretend to deny it; but, then, he *promises* well, does he not? Yes, promises very well indeed, I may say. (So, too, we say to our patrons in reference to some noble little youngster objected to for being a *dwarf*.) But, to advance one step further," extending his thread-bare leg, as he drew a pace nearer, "we must now drop the figure of the rag-paper cartoon, and borrow one— to use presently, when wanted—from the horticultural kingdom. Some bud, lily-bud, if you please. Now, such points as the new-born man-child has—as yet not all that could be desired, I am free to confess—still, such as they are, there they are, and palpable as those of an adult. But we stop not here," taking another step. "The man-child not only possesses these present points, small though they are, but, likewise—now our horticultural image comes into play—like the bud of the lily, he contains concealed rudiments of others; that is, points at present invisible, with beauties at present dormant."

"Come, come, this talk is getting too horticultural and beautiful altogether. Cut it short, cut it short!"

"Respected sir," with a rustily martial sort of gesture, like a decayed corporal's, "when deploying into the field of discourse the vanguard of an important argument, much more in evolving the grand central forces of a new philosophy of boys, as I may say, surely you will kindly allow scope adequate to the movement in hand, small and humble in its way as that movement may be. Is it worth my while to go on, respected sir?"

"Yes, stop flunkying and go on."

Thus encouraged, again the philosopher with the brass-plate proceeded:

"Supposing, sir, that worthy gentleman (in such terms, to an applicant for service, we allude to some patron we chance to have in our eye), supposing, respected sir, that worthy gentleman, Adam, to have been dropped overnight in Eden, as a calf in the pasture; supposing that, sir—then how could even the learned serpent himself have foreknown that such a downy-chinned little innocent would eventually rival the goat in a beard? Sir, wise as the serpent was, that eventuality would have been entirely hidden from his wisdom."

"I don't know about that. The devil is very sagacious. To judge by the event, he appears to have understood man better even than the Being who made him."

"For God's sake, don't say that, sir! To the point. Can it now with fairness be denied that, in his beard, the man-child prospectively possesses an appendix, not less imposing than patriarchal; and for this goodly beard, should we not by generous anticipation give the man-child, even in his cradle, credit? Should we not now, sir? respectfully I put it."

"Yes, if like pig-weed he mows it down soon as it shoots," porcinely rubbing his stubble-chin against his coon-skins.

"I have hinted at the analogy," continued the other, calmly disregardful of the digression; "now to apply it. Suppose a boy evince no noble quality. Then generously give him credit for his prospective one. Don't you see? So we say to our patrons when they would fain return a boy upon us as unworthy: 'Madam, or sir, (as the case may be) has this boy a beard?' 'No.' 'Has he, we respectfully ask, as yet, evinced any noble quality?' 'No, indeed.' 'Then, madam, or sir, take him back, we humbly beseech; and keep him till that same noble quality sprouts; for, have confidence, it, like the beard, is in him.'"

"Very fine theory," scornfully exclaimed the bachelor, yet in secret, perhaps, not entirely undisturbed by these strange new views of the matter; "but what trust is to be placed in it?"

"The trust of perfect confidence, sir. To proceed. Once more, if you please, regard the man-child."

"Hold!" paw-like thrusting put his bearskin arm, "don't intrude that man-child upon me too often. He who loves not bread, dotes not on dough. As little of your man-child as your logical arrangements will admit."

"Anew regard the man-child," with inspired intrepidity repeated he with the brass-plate, "in the perspective of his developments, I mean. At first the man-child has no teeth, but about the sixth month—am I right, sir?"

"Don't know anything about it."

"To proceed then: though at first deficient in teeth, about the sixth month the man-child begins to put forth in that particular. And sweet those tender little puttings-forth are."

"Very, but blown out of his mouth directly, worthless enough."

"Admitted. And, therefore, we say to our patrons returning with a boy alleged not only to be deficient in goodness, but redundant in ill: 'The lad, madam or sir, evinces very corrupt qualities, does he? No end to them.' 'But, have confidence, there will be; for pray, madam, in this lad's early childhood, were not those frail first teeth, then his, followed by his present sound, even, beautiful and permanent set. And the more objectionable those first teeth became, was not that, madam, we respectfully submit, so much the more reason to look for their speedy substitution by the present sound, even, beautiful and permanent ones.' 'True, true, can't deny that.' 'Then, madam, take him back, we respectfully beg, and wait till, in the now swift course of nature, dropping those transient moral blemishes you complain of, he replacingly buds forth in the sound, even, beautiful and permanent virtues.'"

"Very philosophical again," was the contemptuous reply—the outward contempt, perhaps, proportioned to the inward misgiving. "Vastly philosophical, indeed, but tell me—to continue your analogy— since the second teeth followed—in fact, came from—the first, is there no chance the blemish may be transmitted?"

"Not at all." Abating in humility as he gained in the argument. "The second teeth follow, but do not come from, the first; successors, not sons. The first teeth are not like the germ blossom of the apple, at once the father of, and incorporated into, the growth it foreruns; but they are thrust from their place by the independent undergrowth of the succeeding set—an illustration, by the way, which shows more for me than I meant, though not more than I wish."

"What does it show?" Surly-looking as a thundercloud with the inkept unrest of unacknowledged conviction.

"It shows this, respected sir, that in the case of any boy, especially an ill one, to apply unconditionally the saying, that the 'child is father of the man', is, besides implying an uncharitable aspersion of the race, affirming a thing very wide of—"

"—Your analogy," like a snapping turtle.

"Yes, respected sir."

"But is analogy argument? You are a punster."

"Punster, respected sir?" with a look of being aggrieved.

"Yes, you pun with ideas as another man may with words."

"Oh well, sir, whoever talks in that strain, whoever has no confidence in human reason, whoever despises human reason, in vain to reason with him. Still, respected sir," altering his air, "permit me to hint that, had not the force of analogy moved you somewhat, you would hardly have offered to contemn it."

"Talk away," disdainfully; "but pray tell me what has that last analogy of yours to do with your intelligence office business?"

"Everything to do with it, respected sir. From that analogy we derive the reply made to such a patron as, shortly after being supplied by us with an adult servant, proposes to return him upon our hands; not that, while with the patron, said adult has given any cause of dissatisfaction, but the patron has just chanced to hear something unfavorable concerning him from some gentleman who employed said adult, long before, while a boy. To which too fastidious patron, we, taking said adult by the hand, and graciously reintroducing him to the patron, say: 'Far be it from you, madam, or sir, to proceed in your censure against this adult, in anything of the spirit of an ex-post-facto law. Madam, or sir, would you visit upon the butterfly the caterpillar? In the natural advance of all creatures, do they not bury themselves over and over again in the endless resurrection of better and better? Madam, or sir, take back this adult; he may have been a caterpillar, but is now a butterfly."

"Pun away; but even accepting your analogical pun, what does it amount to? Was the caterpillar one creature, and is the butterfly another? The butterfly is the caterpillar in a gaudy cloak; stripped of which, there lies the impostor's long spindle of a body, pretty much worm-shaped as before."

"You reject the analogy. To the facts then. You deny that a youth of one character can be transformed into a man of an opposite character.

Now then—yes, I have it. There's the founder of La Trappe, and Ignatius Loyola; in boyhood, and someway into manhood, both devil-may-care bloods, and yet, in the end, the wonders of the world for anchoritish self-command. These two examples, by-the-way, we cite to such patrons as would hastily return rakish young waiters upon us. 'Madam, or sir—patience; patience,' we say; 'good madam, or sir, would you discharge forth your cask of good wine, because, while working, it riles more or less? Then discharge not forth this young waiter; the good in him is working.' 'But he is a sad rake.' 'Therein is his promise; the rake being crude material for the saint.'"

"Ah, you are a talking man—what I call a wordy man. You talk, talk."

"And with submission, sir, what is the greatest judge, bishop or prophet, but a talking man? He talks, talks. It is the peculiar vocation of a teacher to talk. What's wisdom itself but table-talk? The best wisdom in this world, and the last spoken by its teacher, did it not literally and truly come in the form of table-talk?"

"You, you, you!" rattling down his rifle.

"To shift the subject, since we cannot agree. Pray, what is your opinion, respected sir, of St. Augustine?"

"St. Augustine? What should I, or you either, know of him? Seems to me, for one in such a business, to say nothing of such a coat, that though you don't know a great deal, indeed, yet you know a good deal more than you ought to know, or than you have a right to know, or than it is safe or expedient for you to know, or than, in the fair course of life, you could have honestly come to know. I am of opinion you should be served like a Jew in the middle ages with his gold; this knowledge of yours, which you haven't enough knowledge to know how to make a right use of, it should be taken from you. And so I have been thinking all along."

"You are merry, sir. But you have a little looked into St. Augustine I suppose."

"St. Augustine on Original Sin is my text book. But you, I ask again, where do you find time or inclination for these out-of-the-way speculations? In fact, your whole talk, the more I think of it, is altogether unexampled and extraordinary."

"Respected sir, have I not already informed you that the quite new method, the strictly philosophical one, on which our office is founded, has led me and my associates to an enlarged study of mankind. It was my fault, if I did not, likewise, hint, that these studies directed always to

HERMAN MELVILLE

the scientific procuring of good servants of all sorts, boys included, for the kind gentlemen, our patrons—that these studies, I say, have been conducted equally among all books of all libraries, as among all men of all nations. Then, you rather like St. Augustine, sir?"

"Excellent genius!"

"In some points he was; yet, how comes it that under his own hand, St. Augustine confesses that, until his thirtieth year, he was a very sad dog?"

"A saint a sad dog?"

"Not the saint, but the saint's irresponsible little forerunner—the boy."

"All boys are rascals, and so are all men," again flying off at his tangent; "my name is Pitch; I stick to what I say."

"Ah, sir, permit me—when I behold you on this mild summer's eve, thus eccentrically clothed in the skins of wild beasts, I cannot but conclude that the equally grim and unsuitable habit of your mind is likewise but an eccentric assumption, having no basis in your genuine soul, no more than in nature herself."

"Well, really, now—really," fidgeted the bachelor, not unaffected in his conscience by these benign personalities, "really, really, now, I don't know but that I may have been a little bit too hard upon those five and thirty boys of mine."

"Glad to find you a little softening, sir. Who knows now, but that flexile gracefulness, however questionable at the time of that thirtieth boy of yours, might have been the silky husk of the most solid qualities of maturity. It might have been with him as with the ear of the Indian corn."

"Yes, yes, yes," excitedly cried the bachelor, as the light of this new illustration broke in, "yes, yes; and now that I think of it, how often I've sadly watched my Indian corn in May, wondering whether such sickly, half-eaten sprouts, could ever thrive up into the stiff, stately spear of August."

"A most admirable reflection, sir, and you have only, according to the analogical theory first started by our office, to apply it to that thirtieth boy in question, and see the result. Had you but kept that thirtieth boy—been patient with his sickly virtues, cultivated them, hoed round them, why what a glorious guerdon would have been yours, when at last you should have had a St. Augustine for an ostler."

"Really, really—well, I am glad I didn't send him to jail, as at first I intended."

"Oh that would have been too bad. Grant he was vicious. The petty vices of boys are like the innocent kicks of colts, as yet imperfectly broken. Some boys know not virtue only for the same reason they know not French; it was never taught them. Established upon the basis of parental charity, juvenile asylums exist by law for the benefit of lads convicted of acts which, in adults, would have received other requital. Why? Because, do what they will, society, like our office, at bottom has a Christian confidence in boys. And all this we say to our patrons."

"Your patrons, sir, seem your marines to whom you may say anything," said the other, relapsing. "Why do knowing employers shun youths from asylums, though offered them at the smallest wages? I'll none of your reformado boys."

"Such a boy, respected sir, I would not get for you, but a boy that never needed reform. Do not smile, for as whooping-cough and measles are juvenile diseases, and yet some juveniles never have them, so are there boys equally free from juvenile vices. True, for the best of boys' measles may be contagious, and evil communications corrupt good manners; but a boy with a sound mind in a sound body—such is the boy I would get you. If hitherto, sir, you have struck upon a peculiarly bad vein of boys, so much the more hope now of your hitting a good one."

"That sounds a kind of reasonable, as it were—a little so, really. In fact, though you have said a great many foolish things, very foolish and absurd things, yet, upon the whole, your conversation has been such as might almost lead one less distrustful than I to repose a certain conditional confidence in you, I had almost added in your office, also. Now, for the humor of it, supposing that even I, I myself, really had this sort of conditional confidence, though but a grain, what sort of a boy, in sober fact, could you send me? And what would be your fee?"

"Conducted," replied the other somewhat loftily, rising now in eloquence as his proselyte, for all his pretenses, sunk in conviction, "conducted upon principles involving care, learning, and labor, exceeding what is usual in kindred institutions, the Philosophical Intelligence Office is forced to charge somewhat higher than customary. Briefly, our fee is three dollars in advance. As for the boy, by a lucky chance, I have a very promising little fellow now in my eye—a very likely little fellow, indeed."

"Honest?"

"As the day is long. Might trust him with untold millions. Such, at least, were the marginal observations on the phrenological chart of his head, submitted to me by the mother."

"How old?"

"Just fifteen."

"Tall? Stout?"

"Uncommonly so, for his age, his mother remarked."

"Industrious?"

"The busy bee."

The bachelor fell into a troubled reverie. At last, with much hesitancy, he spoke:

"Do you think now, candidly, that—I say candidly—candidly—could I have some small, limited—some faint, conditional degree of confidence in that boy? Candidly, now?"

"Candidly, you could."

"A sound boy? A good boy?"

"Never knew one more so."

The bachelor fell into another irresolute reverie; then said: "Well, now, you have suggested some rather new views of boys, and men, too. Upon those views in the concrete I at present decline to determine. Nevertheless, for the sake purely of a scientific experiment, I will try that boy. I don't think him an angel, mind. No, no. But I'll try him. There are my three dollars, and here is my address. Send him along this day two weeks. Hold, you will be wanting the money for his passage. There," handing it somewhat reluctantly.

"Ah, thank you. I had forgotten his passage;" then, altering in manner, and gravely holding the bills, continued: "Respected sir, never willingly do I handle money not with perfect willingness, nay, with a certain alacrity, paid. Either tell me that you have a perfect and unquestioning confidence in me (never mind the boy now) or permit me respectfully to return these bills."

"Put 'em up, put 'em up!"

"Thank you. Confidence is the indispensable basis of all sorts of business transactions. Without it, commerce between man and man, as between country and country, would, like a watch, run down and stop. And now, supposing that against present expectation the lad should, after all, evince some little undesirable trait, do not, respected sir, rashly dismiss him. Have but patience, have but confidence. Those transient vices will, ere long, fall out, and be replaced by the sound, firm, even and permanent virtues. Ah," glancing shoreward, towards a grotesquely-shaped bluff, "there's the Devil's Joke, as they call it: the bell for landing will shortly ring. I must go look up the cook I brought for the innkeeper at Cairo."

XXIII

In Which the Powerful Effect of Natural Scenery is Evinced in the Case of the Missourian, Who, in View of the Region Round-About Cairo, Has a Return of His Chilly Fit

At Cairo, the old established firm of Fever & Ague is still settling up its unfinished business; that Creole grave-digger, Yellow Jack—his hand at the mattock and spade has not lost its cunning; while Don Saturninus Typhus taking his constitutional with Death, Calvin Edson and three undertakers, in the morass, snuffs up the mephitic breeze with zest.

In the dank twilight, fanned with mosquitoes, and sparkling with fire-flies, the boat now lies before Cairo. She has landed certain passengers, and tarries for the coming of expected ones. Leaning over the rail on the inshore side, the Missourian eyes through the dubious medium that swampy and squalid domain; and over it audibly mumbles his cynical mind to himself, as Apermantus' dog may have mumbled his bone. He bethinks him that the man with the brass-plate was to land on this villainous bank, and for that cause, if no other, begins to suspect him. Like one beginning to rouse himself from a dose of chloroform treacherously given, he half divines, too, that he, the philosopher, had unwittingly been betrayed into being an unphilosophical dupe. To what vicissitudes of light and shade is man subject! He ponders the mystery of human subjectivity in general. He thinks he perceives with Crossbones, his favorite author, that, as one may wake up well in the morning, very well, indeed, and brisk as a buck, I thank you, but ere bed-time get under the weather, there is no telling how—so one may wake up wise, and slow of assent, very wise and very slow, I assure you, and for all that, before night, by like trick in the atmosphere, be left in the lurch a ninny. Health and wisdom equally precious, and equally little as unfluctuating possessions to be relied on.

But where was slipped in the entering wedge? Philosophy, knowledge, experience—were those trusty knights of the castle recreant? No, but unbeknown to them, the enemy stole on the castle's south side, its genial one, where Suspicion, the warder, parleyed. In fine, his too indulgent, too artless and companionable nature betrayed him. Admonished by which, he thinks he must be a little splenetic in his intercourse henceforth.

He revolves the crafty process of sociable chat, by which, as he fancies, the man with the brass-plate wormed into him, and made such a fool of him as insensibly to persuade him to waive, in his exceptional case, that general law of distrust systematically applied to the race. He revolves, but cannot comprehend, the operation, still less the operator. Was the man a trickster, it must be more for the love than the lucre. Two or three dirty dollars the motive to so many nice wiles? And yet how full of mean needs his seeming. Before his mental vision the person of that threadbare Talleyrand, that impoverished Machiavelli, that seedy Rosicrucian—for something of all these he vaguely deems him— passes now in puzzled review. Fain, in his disfavor, would he make out a logical case. The doctrine of analogies recurs. Fallacious enough doctrine when wielded against one's prejudices, but in corroboration of cherished suspicions not without likelihood. Analogically, he couples the slanting cut of the equivocator's coat-tails with the sinister cast in his eye; he weighs slyboot's sleek speech in the light imparted by the oblique import of the smooth slope of his worn boot-heels; the insinuator's undulating flunkyisms dovetail into those of the flunky beast that windeth his way on his belly.

From these uncordial reveries he is roused by a cordial slap on the shoulder, accompanied by a spicy volume of tobacco-smoke, out of which came a voice, sweet as a seraph's:

"A penny for your thoughts, my fine fellow."

A Philanthropist Undertakes to Convert a Misanthrope, But Does Not Get Beyond Confuting Him

H ands off!" cried the bachelor, involuntarily covering dejection with moroseness.

"Hands off? that sort of label won't do in our Fair. Whoever in our Fair has fine feelings loves to feel the nap of fine cloth, especially when a fine fellow wears it."

"And who of my fine-fellow species may you be? From the Brazils, ain't you? Toucan fowl. Fine feathers on foul meat."

This ungentle mention of the toucan was not improbably suggested by the parti-hued, and rather plumagy aspect of the stranger, no bigot it would seem, but a liberalist, in dress, and whose wardrobe, almost anywhere than on the liberal Mississippi, used to all sorts of fantastic informalities, might, even to observers less critical than the bachelor, have looked, if anything, a little out of the common; but not more so perhaps, than, considering the bear and raccoon costume, the bachelor's own appearance. In short, the stranger sported a vesture barred with various hues, that of the cochineal predominating, in style participating of a Highland plaid, Emir's robe, and French blouse; from its plaited sort of front peeped glimpses of a flowered regatta-shirt, while, for the rest, white trowsers of ample duck flowed over maroon-colored slippers, and a jaunty smoking-cap of regal purple crowned him off at top; king of traveled good-fellows, evidently. Grotesque as all was, nothing looked stiff or unused; all showed signs of easy service, the least wonted thing setting like a wonted glove. That genial hand, which had just been laid on the ungenial shoulder, was now carelessly thrust down before him, sailor-fashion, into a sort of Indian belt, confining the redundant vesture; the other held, by its long bright cherry-stem, a Nuremburgh pipe in blast, its great porcelain bowl painted in miniature with linked crests and arms of interlinked nations—a florid show. As by subtle saturations of its mellowing essence the tobacco had ripened the bowl, so it looked as if something similar of the interior spirit came rosily out on the cheek. But rosy pipe-bowl, or rosy countenance, all was lost on that unrosy man, the bachelor, who, waiting a moment till the commotion, caused by the boat's renewed progress, had a little abated, thus continued:

"Hark ye," jeeringly eying the cap and belt, "did you ever see Signor Marzetti in the African pantomime?"

"No;—good performer?"

"Excellent; plays the intelligent ape till he seems it. With such naturalness can a being endowed with an immortal spirit enter into that of a monkey. But where's your tail? In the pantomime, Marzetti, no hypocrite in his monkery, prides himself on that."

The stranger, now at rest, sideways and genially, on one hip, his right leg cavalierly crossed before the other, the toe of his vertical slipper pointed easily down on the deck, whiffed out a long, leisurely sort of indifferent and charitable puff, betokening him more or less of the mature man of the world, a character which, like its opposite, the sincere Christian's, is not always swift to take offense; and then, drawing near, still smoking, again laid his hand, this time with mild impressiveness, on the ursine shoulder, and not unamiably said: "That in your address there is a sufficiency of the *fortiter in re* few unbiased observers will question; but that this is duly attempered with the *suaviter in modo* may admit, I think, of an honest doubt. My dear fellow," beaming his eyes full upon him, "what injury have I done you, that you should receive my greeting with a curtailed civility?"

"Off hands;" once more shaking the friendly member from him. "Who in the name of the great chimpanzee, in whose likeness, you, Marzetti, and the other chatterers are made, who in thunder are you?"

"A cosmopolitan, a catholic man; who, being such, ties himself to no narrow tailor or teacher, but federates, in heart as in costume, something of the various gallantries of men under various suns. Oh, one roams not over the gallant globe in vain. Bred by it, is a fraternal and fusing feeling. No man is a stranger. You accost anybody. Warm and confiding, you wait not for measured advances. And though, indeed, mine, in this instance, have met with no very hilarious encouragement, yet the principle of a true citizen of the world is still to return good for ill.—My dear fellow, tell me how I can serve you."

"By dispatching yourself, Mr. Popinjay-of-the-world, into the heart of the Lunar Mountains. You are another of them. Out of my sight!"

"Is the sight of humanity so very disagreeable to you then? Ah, I may be foolish, but for my part, in all its aspects, I love it. Served up à la

Pole, or à la Moor, à la Ladrone, or à la Yankee, that good dish, man, still delights me; or rather is man a wine I never weary of comparing and sipping; wherefore am I a pledged cosmopolitan, a sort of London-Dock-Vault connoisseur, going about from Teheran to Natchitoches, a taster of races; in all his vintages, smacking my lips over this racy creature, man, continually. But as there are teetotal palates which have a distaste even for Amontillado, so I suppose there may be teetotal souls which relish not even the very best brands of humanity. Excuse me, but it just occurs to me that you, my dear fellow, possibly lead a solitary life."

"Solitary?" starting as at a touch of divination.

"Yes: in a solitary life one insensibly contracts oddities,—talking to one's self now."

"Been eaves-dropping, eh?"

"Why, a soliloquist in a crowd can hardly but be overheard, and without much reproach to the hearer."

"You are an eaves-dropper."

"Well. Be it so."

"Confess yourself an eaves-dropper?"

"I confess that when you were muttering here I, passing by, caught a word or two, and, by like chance, something previous of your chat with the Intelligence-office man;—a rather sensible fellow, by the way; much of my style of thinking; would, for his own sake, he were of my style of dress. Grief to good minds, to see a man of superior sense forced to hide his light under the bushel of an inferior coat.—Well, from what little I heard, I said to myself, Here now is one with the unprofitable philosophy of disesteem for man. Which disease, in the main, I have observed—excuse me—to spring from a certain lowness, if not sourness, of spirits inseparable from sequestration. Trust me, one had better mix in, and do like others. Sad business, this holding out against having a good time. Life is a pic-nic *en costume*; one must take a part, assume a character, stand ready in a sensible way to play the fool. To come in plain clothes, with a long face, as a wiseacre, only makes one a discomfort to himself, and a blot upon the scene. Like your jug of cold water among the wine-flasks, it leaves you unelated among the elated ones. No, no. This austerity won't do. Let me tell you too—*en confiance*—that while revelry may not always merge into ebriety, soberness, in too deep potations, may become a sort of sottishness. Which sober sottishness, in my way of thinking, is only to be cured by beginning at the other end of the horn, to tipple a little."

HERMAN MELVILLE

"Pray, what society of vintners and old topers are you hired to lecture for?"

"I fear I did not give my meaning clearly. A little story may help. The story of the worthy old woman of Goshen, a very moral old woman, who wouldn't let her shoats eat fattening apples in fall, for fear the fruit might ferment upon their brains, and so make them swinish. Now, during a green Christmas, inauspicious to the old, this worthy old woman fell into a moping decline, took to her bed, no appetite, and refused to see her best friends. In much concern her good man sent for the doctor, who, after seeing the patient and putting a question or two, beckoned the husband out, and said: 'Deacon, do you want her cured?' 'Indeed I do.' 'Go directly, then, and buy a jug of Santa Cruz.' 'Santa Cruz? my wife drink Santa Cruz?' 'Either that or die.' 'But how much?' 'As much as she can get down.' 'But she'll get drunk!' 'That's the cure.' Wise men, like doctors, must be obeyed. Much against the grain, the sober deacon got the unsober medicine, and, equally against her conscience, the poor old woman took it; but, by so doing, ere long recovered health and spirits, famous appetite, and glad again to see her friends; and having by this experience broken the ice of arid abstinence, never afterwards kept herself a cup too low."

This story had the effect of surprising the bachelor into interest, though hardly into approval.

"If I take your parable right," said he, sinking no little of his former churlishness, "the meaning is, that one cannot enjoy life with gusto unless he renounce the too-sober view of life. But since the too-sober view is, doubtless, nearer true than the too-drunken; I, who rate truth, though cold water, above untruth, though Tokay, will stick to my earthen jug."

"I see," slowly spirting upward a spiral staircase of lazy smoke, "I see; you go in for the lofty."

"How?"

"Oh, nothing! but if I wasn't afraid of prosing, I might tell another story about an old boot in a pieman's loft, contracting there between sun and oven an unseemly, dry-seasoned curl and warp. You've seen such leathery old garretteers, haven't you? Very high, sober, solitary, philosophic, grand, old boots, indeed; but I, for my part, would rather be the pieman's trodden slipper on the ground. Talking of piemen, humble-pie before proud-cake for me. This notion of being lone and lofty is a sad mistake. Men I hold in this respect to be like roosters; the one that betakes himself to a lone and lofty perch is the hen-pecked one, or the one that has the pip."

"You are abusive!" cried the bachelor, evidently touched.

"Who is abused? You, or the race? You won't stand by and see the human race abused? Oh, then, you have some respect for the human race."

"I have some respect for *myself*" with a lip not so firm as before.

"And what race may *you* belong to? now don't you see, my dear fellow, in what inconsistencies one involves himself by affecting disesteem for men. To a charm, my little stratagem succeeded. Come, come, think better of it, and, as a first step to a new mind, give up solitude. I fear, by the way, you have at some time been reading Zimmermann, that old Mr. Megrims of a Zimmermann, whose book on Solitude is as vain as Hume's on Suicide, as Bacon's on Knowledge; and, like these, will betray him who seeks to steer soul and body by it, like a false religion. All they, be they what boasted ones you please, who, to the yearning of our kind after a founded rule of content, offer aught not in the spirit of fellowly gladness based on due confidence in what is above, away with them for poor dupes, or still poorer impostors."

His manner here was so earnest that scarcely any auditor, perhaps, but would have been more or less impressed by it, while, possibly, nervous opponents might have a little quailed under it. Thinking within himself a moment, the bachelor replied: "Had you experience, you would know that your tippling theory, take it in what sense you will, is poor as any other. And Rabelais's pro-wine Koran no more trustworthy than Mahomet's anti-wine one."

"Enough," for a finality knocking the ashes from his pipe, "we talk and keep talking, and still stand where we did. What do you say for a walk? My arm, and let's a turn. They are to have dancing on the hurricane-deck tonight. I shall fling them off a Scotch jig, while, to save the pieces, you hold my loose change; and following that, I propose that you, my dear fellow, stack your gun, and throw your bearskins in a sailor's hornpipe—I holding your watch. What do you say?"

At this proposition the other was himself again, all raccoon.

"Look you," thumping down his rifle, "are you Jeremy Diddler No. 3?"

"Jeremy Diddler? I have heard of Jeremy the prophet, and Jeremy Taylor the divine, but your other Jeremy is a gentleman I am unacquainted with."

"You are his confidential clerk, ain't you?"

"*Whose*, pray? Not that I think myself unworthy of being confided in, but I don't understand."

"You are another of them. Somehow I meet with the most extraordinary metaphysical scamps today. Sort of visitation of them. And yet that herb-doctor Diddler somehow takes off the raw edge of the Diddlers that come after him."

"Herb-doctor? who is he?"

"Like you—another of them."

"*Who?*" Then drawing near, as if for a good long explanatory chat, his left hand spread, and his pipe-stem coming crosswise down upon it like a ferule, "You think amiss of me. Now to undeceive you, I will just enter into a little argument and—"

"No you don't. No more little arguments for me. Had too many little arguments today."

"But put a case. Can you deny—I dare you to deny—that the man leading a solitary life is peculiarly exposed to the sorriest misconceptions touching strangers?"

"Yes, I *do* deny it," again, in his impulsiveness, snapping at the controversial bait, "and I will confute you there in a trice. Look, you—"

"Now, now, now, my dear fellow," thrusting out both vertical palms for double shields, "you crowd me too hard. You don't give one a chance. Say what you will, to shun a social proposition like mine, to shun society in any way, evinces a churlish nature—cold, loveless; as, to embrace it, shows one warm and friendly, in fact, sunshiny."

Here the other, all agog again, in his perverse way, launched forth into the unkindest references to deaf old worldlings keeping in the deafening world; and gouty gluttons limping to their gouty gormandizings; and corseted coquets clasping their corseted cavaliers in the waltz, all for disinterested society's sake; and thousands, bankrupt through lavishness, ruining themselves out of pure love of the sweet company of man—no envies, rivalries, or other unhandsome motive to it.

"Ah, now," deprecating with his pipe, "irony is so unjust: never could abide irony: something Satanic about irony. God defend me from Irony, and Satire, his bosom friend."

"A right knave's prayer, and a right fool's, too," snapping his rifle-lock.

"Now be frank. Own that was a little gratuitous. But, no, no, you didn't mean it; any way, I can make allowances. Ah, did you but know it, how much pleasanter to puff at this philanthropic pipe, than still to keep fumbling at that misanthropic rifle. As for your worldling, glutton, and coquette, though, doubtless, being such, they may have their little foibles—as who has not?—yet not one of the three can be reproached with that awful sin of shunning society; awful I call it, for not seldom it presupposes a still darker thing than itself—remorse."

"Remorse drives man away from man? How came your fellow-creature, Cain, after the first murder, to go and build the first city? And why is it that the modern Cain dreads nothing so much as solitary confinement?

"My dear fellow, you get excited. Say what you will, I for one must have my fellow-creatures round me. Thick, too—I must have them thick."

"The pick-pocket, too, loves to have his fellow-creatures round him. Tut, man! no one goes into the crowd but for his end; and the end of too many is the same as the pick-pocket's—a purse."

"Now, my dear fellow, how can you have the conscience to say that, when it is as much according to natural law that men are social as sheep gregarious. But grant that, in being social, each man has his end, do you, upon the strength of that, do you yourself, I say, mix with man, now, immediately, and be your end a more genial philosophy. Come, let's take a turn."

Again he offered his fraternal arm; but the bachelor once more flung it off, and, raising his rifle in energetic invocation, cried: "Now the high-constable catch and confound all knaves in towns and rats in grain-bins, and if in this boat, which is a human grain-bin for the time, any sly, smooth, philandering rat be dodging now, pin him, thou high rat-catcher, against this rail."

"A noble burst! shows you at heart a trump. And when a card's that, little matters it whether it be spade or diamond. You are good wine that, to be still better, only needs a shaking up. Come, let's agree that we'll to New Orleans, and there embark for London—I staying with my friends nigh Primrose-hill, and you putting up at the Piazza, Covent Garden—Piazza, Covent Garden; for tell me—since you will not be a disciple to the full—tell me, was not that humor, of Diogenes, which led him to live, a merry-andrew, in the flower-market, better than that of the less wise Athenian, which made him a skulking scare-crow in pine-barrens? An injudicious gentleman, Lord Timon."

"Your hand!" seizing it.

"Bless me, how cordial a squeeze. It is agreed we shall be brothers, then?"

"As much so as a brace of misanthropes can be," with another and terrific squeeze. "I had thought that the moderns had degenerated

HERMAN MELVILLE

beneath the capacity of misanthropy. Rejoiced, though but in one instance, and that disguised, to be undeceived."

The other stared in blank amaze.

"Won't do. You are Diogenes, Diogenes in disguise. I say—Diogenes masquerading as a cosmopolitan."

With ruefully altered mien, the stranger still stood mute awhile. At length, in a pained tone, spoke: "How hard the lot of that pleader who, in his zeal conceding too much, is taken to belong to a side which he but labors, however ineffectually, to convert!" Then with another change of air: "To you, an Ishmael, disguising in sportiveness my intent, I came ambassador from the human race, charged with the assurance that for your mislike they bore no answering grudge, but sought to conciliate accord between you and them. Yet you take me not for the honest envoy, but I know not what sort of unheard-of spy. Sir," he less lowly added, "this mistaking of your man should teach you how you may mistake all men. For God's sake," laying both hands upon him, "get you confidence. See how distrust has duped you. I, Diogenes? I he who, going a step beyond misanthropy, was less a man-hater than a man-hooter? Better were I stark and stiff!"

With which the philanthropist moved away less lightsome than he had come, leaving the discomfited misanthrope to the solitude he held so sapient.

XXV

The Cosmopolitan Makes an Acquaintance

In the act of retiring, the cosmopolitan was met by a passenger, who with the bluff *abord* of the West, thus addressed him, though a stranger.

"Queer 'coon, your friend. Had a little skrimmage with him myself. Rather entertaining old 'coon, if he wasn't so deuced analytical. Reminded me somehow of what I've heard about Colonel John Moredock, of Illinois, only your friend ain't quite so good a fellow at bottom, I should think."

It was in the semicircular porch of a cabin, opening a recess from the deck, lit by a zoned lamp swung overhead, and sending its light vertically down, like the sun at noon. Beneath the lamp stood the speaker, affording to any one disposed to it no unfavorable chance for scrutiny; but the glance now resting on him betrayed no such rudeness.

A man neither tall nor stout, neither short nor gaunt; but with a body fitted, as by measure, to the service of his mind. For the rest, one less favored perhaps in his features than his clothes; and of these the beauty may have been less in the fit than the cut; to say nothing of the fineness of the nap, seeming out of keeping with something the reverse of fine in the skin; and the unsuitableness of a violet vest, sending up sunset hues to a countenance betokening a kind of bilious habit.

But, upon the whole, it could not be fairly said that his appearance was unprepossessing; indeed, to the congenial, it would have been doubtless not uncongenial; while to others, it could not fail to be at least curiously interesting, from the warm air of florid cordiality, contrasting itself with one knows not what kind of aguish sallowness of saving discretion lurking behind it. Ungracious critics might have thought that the manner flushed the man, something in the same fictitious way that the vest flushed the cheek. And though his teeth were singularly good, those same ungracious ones might have hinted that they were too good to be true; or rather, were not so good as they might be; since the best false teeth are those made with at least two or three blemishes, the more to look like life. But fortunately for better constructions, no such critics had the stranger now in eye; only the cosmopolitan, who, after, in the first place, acknowledging his advances with a mute salute—in which acknowledgment, if there seemed less of spirit than in his way of accosting the Missourian, it was probably because of the saddening sequel of that late interview—thus now replied: "Colonel John Moredock," repeating the words abstractedly; "that surname recalls reminiscences. Pray," with enlivened air, "was he anyway connected with the Moredocks of Moredock Hall, Northamptonshire, England?"

"I know no more of the Moredocks of Moredock Hall than of the Burdocks of Burdock Hut," returned the other, with the air somehow of one whose fortunes had been of his own making; "all I know is, that the late Colonel John Moredock was a famous one in his time; eye like Lochiel's; finger like a trigger; nerve like a catamount's; and with but two little oddities—seldom stirred without his rifle, and hated Indians like snakes."

"Your Moredock, then, would seem a Moredock of Misanthrope Hall—the Woods. No very sleek creature, the colonel, I fancy."

"Sleek or not, he was no uncombed one, but silky bearded and curly headed, and to all but Indians juicy as a peach. But Indians—how the late Colonel John Moredock, Indian-hater of Illinois, did hate Indians, to be sure!"

"Never heard of such a thing. Hate Indians? Why should he or anybody else hate Indians? *I* admire Indians. Indians I have always heard to be one of the finest of the primitive races, possessed of many heroic virtues. Some noble women, too. When I think of Pocahontas, I am ready to love Indians. Then there's Massasoit, and Philip of Mount Hope, and Tecumseh, and Red-Jacket, and Logan—all heroes; and there's the Five Nations, and Araucanians—federations and communities of heroes. God bless me; hate Indians? Surely the late Colonel John Moredock must have wandered in his mind."

"Wandered in the woods considerably, but never wandered elsewhere, that I ever heard."

"Are you in earnest? Was there ever one who so made it his particular mission to hate Indians that, to designate him, a special word has been coined—Indian-hater?"

"Even so."

"Dear me, you take it very calmly.—But really, I would like to know something about this Indian-hating, I can hardly believe such a thing to be. Could you favor me with a little history of the extraordinary man you mentioned?"

"With all my heart," and immediately stepping from the porch, gestured the cosmopolitan to a settee near by, on deck. "There, sir, sit you there, and I will sit here beside you—you desire to hear of Colonel John Moredock. Well, a day in my boyhood is marked with a white stone—the day I saw the colonel's rifle, powder-horn attached, hanging in a cabin on the West bank of the Wabash river. I was going westward a long journey through the wilderness with my father. It was nigh noon, and we had stopped at the cabin to unsaddle and bait. The man at the cabin pointed out the rifle, and told whose it was, adding that the colonel was that moment sleeping on wolf-skins in the corn-loft above, so we must not talk very loud, for the colonel had been out all night hunting (Indians, mind), and it would be cruel to disturb his sleep. Curious to see one so famous, we waited two hours over, in hopes he would come forth; but he did not. So, it being necessary to get to the next cabin before nightfall, we had at last to ride off without the wished-for satisfaction. Though, to tell the truth, I, for one, did not go away entirely ungratified, for, while my father was watering the horses, I slipped back into the cabin, and stepping a round or two up the ladder, pushed my head through the trap, and peered about. Not much light in the loft; but off, in the further corner, I saw what I took to be the wolf-skins, and on them a bundle of something, like a drift of leaves; and at one end, what seemed a moss-ball; and over it, deer-antlers branched; and close by, a small squirrel sprang out from a maple-bowl of nuts, brushed the moss-ball with his tail, through a hole, and vanished, squeaking. That bit of woodland scene was all I saw. No Colonel Moredock there, unless that moss-ball was his curly head, seen in the back view. I would have gone clear up, but the man below had warned me, that though, from his camping habits, the colonel could sleep through thunder, he was for the same cause amazing quick to waken at the sound of footsteps, however soft, and especially if human."

"Excuse me," said the other, softly laying his hand on the narrator's wrist, "but I fear the colonel was of a distrustful nature—little or no confidence. He *was* a little suspicious-minded, wasn't he?"

"Not a bit. Knew too much. Suspected nobody, but was not ignorant of Indians. Well: though, as you may gather, I never fully saw the man, yet, have I, one way and another, heard about as much of him as any other; in particular, have I heard his history again and again from my father's friend, James Hall, the judge, you know. In every company being called upon to give this history, which none could better do, the judge

HERMAN MELVILLE

grow not too potent; and, lastly, being the most immediate in authority with the common people, they do best temper popular commotions.

For their merchants, they are "vena porta:" and if they flourish not, a kingdom may have good limbs, but will have empty veins, and nourish little. Taxes and imposts upon them do seldom good to the king's revenue, for that which he wins in the hundred he loseth in the shire; the particular rates being increased, but the total bulk of trading rather decreased.

For their commons, there is little danger from them, except it be where they have great and potent heads; or where you meddle with the point of religion, or their customs, or means of life.

For their men of war, it is a dangerous state where they live and remain in a body, and are used to donatives; whereof we see examples in the Janizaries and Prætorian bands of Rome; but trainings of men, and arming them in several places, and under several commanders, and without donatives, are things of defence and no danger.

Princes are like to heavenly bodies, which cause good or evil times; and which have much veneration, but no rest. All precepts concerning kings are in effect comprehended in those two remembrances, "Memento quod es homo;" and "Memento quod es Deus," or "vice Dei;" the one bridleth their power and the other their will.

Chapter 20

OF COUNSEL

The greatest trust between man and man is the trust of giving counsel; for in other confidences men commit the parts of life, their lands, their goods, their children, their credit, some particular affair; but to such as they make their counsellors they commit the whole; by how much the more they are obliged to all faith and integrity. The wisest princes need not think it any diminution to their greatness, or derogation to their sufficiency to rely upon counsel. God himself is not without, but hath made it one of the great names of his blessed Son, "The Counsellor." Solomon hath pronounced that, "in counsel is stability." Things will have their first or second agitation: if they be not tossed upon the arguments of counsel, they will be tossed upon the waves of fortune, and be full of inconstancy, doing and undoing, like the reeling of a drunken man. Solomon's son found the force of counsel, as his father saw the necessity of it; for the beloved kingdom of God was first rent and broken by ill counsel; upon which counsel there are set for our instruction the two marks whereby bad counsel is forever best discerned, that it was young counsel for the persons, and violent counsel for the matter.

The ancient times do set forth in figure both the incorporation and inseparable conjunction of counsel with kings, and the wise and politic use of counsel by kings; the one, in that they say Jupiter did marry Metis, which signifieth counsel; whereby they intend that sovereignty is married to counsel; the other in that which followeth, which was thus: they say, after Jupiter was married to Metis, she conceived by him and was with child; but Jupiter suffered her not to stay till she brought forth, but eat her up; whereby he became himself with child, and was delivered of Pallas armed, out of his head. Which monstrous fable containeth a secret of empire, how kings are to make use of their council of state; that first, they ought to refer matters unto them, which is the first begetting or impregnation; but when they are elaborate, moulded, and shaped in the womb of their counsel, and grow ripe and ready to be brought forth, that then they suffer not their council to go through with the resolution and direction, as if it depended on them; but take the matter back into their own hands, and make it appear to the world, that the decrees and final directions (which, because they come forth with prudence and power, are resembled to Pallas armed), proceeded from themselves; and not only from their authority, but (the more to add reputation to themselves) from their head and device.

Let us now speak of the inconveniences of counsel, and of the remedies. The inconveniences that have been noted in calling and using counsel are three: first, the revealing of affairs, whereby they become less secret; secondly, the weakening of the authority of princes, as if they were less of themselves; thirdly, the danger of being unfaithfully counselled, and more for the good of them that counsel than of him that is counselled; for which inconveniences, the doctrine of Italy, and practice of France, in some kings' times, hath introduced cabinet councils; a remedy worse than the disease.

As to secrecy, princes are not bound to communicate all matters with all counsellors, but may extract and select; neither is it necessary that he that consulteth what he should do, should declare what he will do; but let princes beware that the unsecreting of their affairs comes not from themselves; and, as for cabinet councils, it may be their motto, "Plenus rimarum sum:" one futile person, that maketh it his glory to tell, will do more hurt than many that know it their duty to conceal. It is true, there be some affairs which require extreme secrecy, which will hardly go beyond one or two persons besides the king. Neither are those counsels unprosperous; for, besides the secrecy, they commonly go on constantly in one spirit of direction without distraction; but then it must be a prudent king, such as is able to grind with a hand-mill; and those inward counsellors had need also to be wise men, and especially true and trusty to the king's ends; as it was with King Henry the Seventh of England, who, in his greatest business, imparted himself to none, except it were to Morton and Fox.

For weakening of authority, the fable showeth the remedy; nay, the majesty of kings is rather exalted than diminished when they are in the chair of council; neither was there ever prince bereaved of his dependencies by his council, except where there hath been either an over-greatness in one counsellor, or an over-strict combination in divers, which are things soon found and holpen.

For the last inconvenience, that men will counsel with an eye to themselves; certainly, "non inveniet fidem super terram," is meant of the nature of times, and not of all particular persons. There be that are in nature faithful and sincere, and plain and direct, not crafty and involved: let princes, above all, draw to themselves such natures. Besides, counsellors are not commonly so united, but that one counsellor keepeth sentinel over another; so that if any do counsel out of faction or private ends, it commonly comes to the king's ear; but the best remedy is, if princes know their counsellors, as well as their counsellors know them:—

"Principis est virtus maxima nosse suos."

And on the other side, counsellors should not be too speculative into their sovereign's person. The true composition of a counsellor is, rather to be skilful in their master's business than in his nature; for then he is like to advise him, and not to feed his humor. It is of singular use to princes, if they take the opinions of their council both separately and together; for private opinion is more free, but opinion before others is more reverend. In private, men are more bold in their own humors; and in consort, men are more obnoxious to others' humors; therefore it is good to take both; and of the inferior sort rather in private, to preserve freedom; of the greater, rather in consort, to preserve respect. It is in vain for princes to take counsel concerning matters, if they take no counsel likewise concerning persons; for all matters are as dead images; and the life of the execution of affairs resteth in the good choice of persons. Neither is it enough to consult concerning persons, "secundum genera," as in an idea or mathematical description, what the kind and character of the person should be; for the greatest errors are committed, and the most judgment is shown, in the choice of individuals. It was truly said, "Optimi consiliarii mortui:" "books will speak plain when counsellors blanch;" therefore it is good to be conversant in them, specially the books of such as themselves have been actors upon the stage.

The councils at this day in most places are but familiar meetings, where matters are rather talked on than debated; and they run too swift to the order or act of council. It were better that in causes of weight, the matter were propounded one day and not spoken to till the next day; "In nocte consilium;" so was it done in the commission of union between England and Scotland, which was a grave and orderly assembly. I commend set days for petitions; for both it gives the suitors more certainty for their attendance, and it frees the meetings for matters of estate, that they may "hoc agere." In choice of committees for ripening business for the council, it is better to choose indifferent persons, than to make an indifferency by putting in those that are strong on both sides. I commend, also, standing commissions; as for trade, for treasure, for war, for suits, for some provinces; for where there be divers particular councils, and but one council of estate (as it is in Spain), they are in effect no more than standing commissions, save that they have greater authority. Let such as are to inform councils out of their particular professions (as lawyers, seamen, mintmen, and the like) be first heard before committees; and then, as occasion serves, before the council; and let them not come in multitudes, or in a tribunitious manner; for that is to clamor councils, not to inform them. A long table and a square table, or seats about the walls, seem things of form, but are things of substance; for at a long table a few at the upper end, in effect, sway all the business; but in the other form there is more use of the counsellors' opinions that sit lower. A king, when he presides in council, let him beware how he opens his own inclination too much in that which he propoundeth; for else counsellors will but take the wind of him, and, instead of giving free counsel, will sing him a song of "placebo."

Chapter 21

OF DELAYS

Fortune is like the market, where, many times, if you can stay a little, the price will fall; and again, it is sometimes like Sibylla's offer, which at first offereth the commodity at full, then consumeth part and part, and still holdeth up the price; for occasion (as it is in the common verse) "turneth a bald noddle, after she hath presented her locks in front, and no hold taken;" or, at least, turneth the handle of the bottle first to be received, and after the belly, which is hard to clasp. There is surely no greater wisdom than well to time the beginnings and onsets of things. Dangers are no more light, if they once seem light; and more dangers have deceived men than forced them; nay, it were better to meet some dangers half-way, though they come nothing near, than to keep too long a watch upon their approaches; for if a man watch too long, it is odds he will fall asleep. On the other side, to be deceived with too long shadows (as some have been when the moon was low, and shone on their enemies' back), and so to shoot off before the time; or to teach dangers to come on by over early buckling towards them, is another extreme. The ripeness or unripeness of the occasion (as we said) must ever be well weighed; and generally it is good to commit the beginnings of all great actions to Argus with his hundred eyes, and the ends to Briareus with his hundred hands, first to watch and then to speed; for the helmet of Pluto, which maketh the politic man go invisible, is secrecy in the council, and celerity in the execution; for when things are once come to the execution, there is no secrecy comparable to celerity; like the motion of a bullet in the air, which flieth so swift as it outruns the eye.

Chapter 22

Of Cunning

We take cunning for a sinister, or crooked wisdom; and, certainly, there is great difference between a cunning man and a wise man, not only in point of honesty, but in point of ability. There be that can pack the cards, and yet cannot play well; so there are some that are good in canvasses and factions, that are otherwise weak men. Again, it is one thing to understand persons, and another thing to understand matters; for many are perfect in men's humors that are not greatly capable of the real part of business, which is the constitution of one that hath studied men more than books. Such men are fitter for practice than for counsel, and they are good but in their own alley. Turn them to new men, and they have lost their aim; so as the old rule, to know a fool from a wise man, "Mitte ambos nudos ad ignotos, et videbis," doth scarce hold for them; and, because these cunning men are like haberdashers of small wares, it is not amiss to set forth their shop.

It is a point of cunning to wait upon him with whom you speak with your eye, as the Jesuits give it in precept; for there be many wise men that have secret hearts and transparent countenances; yet this would be done with a demure abasing of your eye sometimes, as the Jesuits also do use.

Another is, that when you have any thing to obtain of present dispatch, you entertain and amuse the party with whom you deal with some other discourse, that he be not too much awake to make objections. I knew a counsellor and secretary that never came to Queen Elizabeth of England, with bills to sign, but he would always first put her into some discourse of estate, that she might the less mind the bills.

The like surprise may be made by moving things when the party is in haste, and cannot stay to consider advisedly of that is moved.

If a man would cross a business that he doubts some other would handsomely and effectually move, let him pretend to wish it well, and move it himself, in such sort as may foil it.

The breaking off in the midst of that one was about to say, as if he took himself up, breeds a greater appetite in him with whom you confer to know more.

And because it works better when any thing seemeth to be gotten from you by question than if you offer it of yourself, you may lay a bait for a question, by showing another visage and countenance than you are wont; to the end, to give occasion for the party to ask what the matter is of the change, as Nehemiah did: "And I had not, before that time, been sad before the king."

In things that are tender and unpleasing, it is good to break the ice by some whose words are of less weight, and to reserve the more weighty voice to come in as by chance, so that he may be asked the question upon the other's speech; as Narcissus did, in relating to Claudius the marriage of Messalina and Silius.

In things that a man would not be seen in himself, it is a point of cunning to borrow the name of the world; as to say, "The world says," or "There is a speech abroad."

I knew one, that when he wrote a letter, he would put that which was most material in a postscript, as if it had been a by-matter.

I knew another, that when he came to have speech, he would pass over that that he intended most; and go forth and come back again, and speak of it as a thing that he had almost forgot.

Some procure themselves to be surprised at such times as it is like the party that they work upon will suddenly come upon them, and to be found with a letter in their hand, or doing somewhat which they are not accustomed, to the end they may be apposed of those things which of themselves they are desirous to utter.

It is a point of cunning to let fall those words in a man's own name, which he would have another man learn and use, and thereupon take advantage. I knew two that were competitors for the secretary's place in Queen Elizabeth's time, and yet kept good quarter between themselves, and would confer one with another upon the business; and the one of them said, that to be a secretary in the declination of a monarchy was a ticklish thing, and that he did not affect it; the other straight caught up those words, and discoursed with divers of his friends, that he had no reason to desire to be secretary in the declination of a monarchy. The first man took hold of it, and found means it was told the queen, who, hearing of a declination of a monarchy, took it so ill, as she would never after hear of the other's suit.

There is a cunning, which we in England call "the turning of the cat in the pan;" which is, when that which a man says to another, he lays it as if another had said it to him; and, to say truth, it is not easy, when such a matter passed between two, to make it appear from which of them it first moved and began.

It is a way that some men have, to glance and dart at others by justifying themselves by negatives; as to say, "This I do not;" as Tigellinus did towards Burrhus: "Se non diversas spes, sed incolumitatem imperatoris simpliciter spectare."

Some have in readiness so many tales and stories, as there is nothing they would insinuate, but they can wrap it into a tale; which serveth both to keep themselves more in guard, and to make others carry it with more pleasure.

It is a good point of cunning for a man to shape the answer he would have in his own words and propositions; for it makes the other party stick the less.

It is strange how long some men will lie in wait to speak somewhat they desire to say; and how far about they will fetch, and how many other matters they will beat over to come near it. It is a thing of great patience, but yet of much use.

A sudden, bold, and unexpected question doth many times surprise a man, and lay him open. Like to him, that, having changed his name, and walking in Paul's, another suddenly came behind him and called him by his true name, whereat straightways he looked back.

But these small wares and petty points of cunning are infinite, and it were a good deed to make a list of them; for that nothing doth more hurt in a state than that cunning men pass for wise.

But certainly, some there are that know the resorts and falls of business that cannot sink into the main of it; like a house that hath convenient stairs and entries, but never a fair room. Therefore you shall see them find out pretty looses in the conclusion, but are noways able to examine or debate matters; and yet commonly they take advantage of their inability, and would be thought wits of direction. Some build rather upon the abusing of others, and (as we now say) putting tricks upon them, than upon soundness of their own proceedings; but Solomon saith: "Prudens advertit ad gressus suos; stultus divertit ad dolos."

Chapter 23

Of Wisdom for a Man's Self

An ant is a wise creature for itself, but it is a shrewd thing in an orchard or garden; and certainly, men that are great lovers of themselves waste the public. Divide with reason between self-love and society; and be so true to thyself as thou be not false to others, specially to thy king and country. It is a poor centre of a man's actions, himself. It is right earth; for that only stands fast upon his own centre; whereas all things that have affinity with the heavens, move upon the centre of another, which they benefit. The referring of all to a man's self is more tolerable in a sovereign prince, because themselves are not only themselves, but their good and evil is at the peril of the public fortune; but it is a desperate evil in a servant to a prince, or a citizen in a republic; for whatsoever affairs pass such a man's hands, he crooketh them to his own ends, which must needs be often eccentric to the ends of his master or state. Therefore, let princes or states choose such servants as have not this mark; except they mean their service should be made but the accessary. That which maketh the effect more pernicious is, that all proportion is lost. It were disproportion enough for the servant's good to be preferred before the master's; but yet it is a greater extreme, when a little good of the servant shall carry things against a great good of the master. And yet that is the case of bad officers, treasurers, ambassadors, generals, and other false and corrupt servants; which set a bias upon their bowl, of their own petty ends and envies, to the overthrow of their master's great and important affairs; and, for the most part, the good such servants receive is after the model of their own fortune; but the hurt they sell for that good is after the model of their master's fortune. And certainly, it is the nature of extreme self-lovers, as they will set a house on fire, an it were but to roast their eggs; and yet these men many times hold credit with their masters, because their study is but to please them, and profit themselves; and for either respect they will abandon the good of their affairs.

Wisdom for a man's self is, in many branches thereof, a depraved thing. It is the wisdom of rats, that will be sure to leave a house somewhat before it fall; it is the wisdom of the fox, that thrusts out the badger who digged and made room for him; it is the wisdom of crocodiles, that shed tears when they would devour. But that which is specially to be noted is, that those which (as Cicero says of Pompey) are "sui amantes, sine rivali," are many times unfortunate; and whereas they have all their times sacrificed to themselves, they become in the end themselves sacrifices to the inconstancy of fortune, whose wings they thought by their self-wisdom to have pinioned.

Chapter 24

OF INNOVATIONS

As the births of living creatures at first are ill-shapen, so are all innovations, which are the births of time; yet, notwithstanding, as those that first bring honor into their family are commonly more worthy than most that succeed, so the first precedent (if it be good) is seldom attained by imitation; for ill to man's nature as it stands perverted, hath a natural motion strongest in continuance, but good, as a forced motion, strongest at first. Surely, every medicine is an innovation, and he that will not apply new remedies must expect new evils, for time is the greatest innovator; and if time, of course, alter things to the worse, and wisdom and counsel shall not alter them to the better, what shall be the end? It is true, that what is settled by custom, though it be not good, yet, at least, it is fit; and those things which have long gone together, are, as it were, confederate within themselves; whereas new things piece not so well; but, though they help by their utility, yet they trouble by their inconformity; besides, they are like strangers, more admired and less favored. All this is true, if time stood still, which, contrariwise, moveth so round, that a froward retention of custom is as turbulent a thing as an innovation; and they that reverence too much old times are but a scorn to the new. It were good, therefore, that men in their innovations would follow the example of time itself, which indeed innovateth greatly, but quietly, and by degrees scarce to be perceived; for, otherwise, whatsoever is new is unlooked for, and ever it mends some and pairs other; and he that is holpen, takes it for a fortune, and thanks the time; and he that is hurt, for a wrong, and imputeth it to the author. It is good, also, not to try experiments in states, except the necessity be urgent, or the utility evident; and well to beware that it be the reformation that draweth on the change, and not the desire of change that pretendeth the reformation; and lastly, that the novelty, though it be not rejected, yet be held for a suspect, and, as the Scripture saith, "That we make a stand upon the ancient way, and then look about us, and discover what is the straight and right way, and so to walk in it."

Chapter 25

OF DISPATCH

Affected dispatch is one of the most dangerous things to business that can be; it is like that which the physicians call predigestion, or hasty digestion, which is sure to fill the body full of crudities, and secret seeds of diseases. Therefore, measure not dispatch by the times of sitting, but by the advancement of the business; and as in races, it is not the large stride, or high lift, that makes the speed, so in business, the keeping close to the matter, and not taking of it too much at once, procureth dispatch. It is the care of some, only to come off speedily for the time, or to contrive some false periods of business, because they may seem men of dispatch; but it is one thing to abbreviate by contracting, another by cutting off; and business so handled at several sittings, or meetings, goeth commonly backward and forward in an unsteady manner. I knew a wise man that had it for a byword, when he saw men hasten to a conclusion, "Stay a little, that we may make an end the sooner."

On the other side, true dispatch is a rich thing; for time is the measure of business, as money is of wares; and business is bought at a dear hand where there is small dispatch. The Spartans and Spaniards have been noted to be of small dispatch: "Mi venga la muerte de Spagna;" "Let my death come from Spain;" for then it will be sure to be long in coming.

Give good hearing to those that give the first information in business, and rather direct them in the beginning, than interrupt them in the continuance of their speeches; for he that is put out of his own order will go forward and backward, and be more tedious while he waits upon his memory, than he could have been if he had gone on in his own course; but sometimes it is seen that the moderator is more troublesome than the actor.

Iterations are commonly loss of time; but there is no such gain of time as to iterate often the state of the question; for it chaseth away many a frivolous speech as it is coming forth. Long and curious speeches are as fit for dispatch as a robe, or mantle, with a long train, is for a race. Prefaces, and passages, and excusations, and other speeches of reference to the person, are great wastes of time; and though they seem to proceed of modesty, they are bravery. Yet beware of being too material when there is any impediment, or obstruction in men's wills; for preoccupation of mind ever requireth preface of speech, like a fomentation to make the unguent enter.

Above all things, order and distribution, and singling out of parts, is the life of dispatch, so as the distribution be not too subtile; for he that doth not divide will never enter well into business; and he that divideth too much will never come out of it clearly. To choose time is to save time; and an unseasonable motion is but beating the air. There be three parts of business,—the preparation; the debate, or examination; and the perfection. Whereof, if you look for dispatch, let the middle only be the work of many, and the first and last the work of few. The proceeding, upon somewhat conceived in writing, doth for the most part facilitate dispatch; for though it should be wholly rejected, yet that negative is more pregnant of direction than an indefinite, as ashes are more generative than dust.

Chapter 26

OF SEEMING WISE

I t hath been an opinion, that the French are wiser than they seem, and
the Spaniards seem wiser than they are; but howsoever it be between
nations, certainly it is so between man and man; for, as the apostle
saith of godliness, "Having a show of godliness, but denying the power
thereof," so certainly there are, in points of wisdom and sufficiency,
that do nothing, or little very solemnly,—"magno conatu nugas." It is a
ridiculous thing, and fit for a satire to persons of judgment, to see what
shifts these formalists have, and what prospectives to make superficies
to seem body, that hath depth and bulk. Some are so close and reserved,
as they will not show their wares but by a dark light, and seem always
to keep back somewhat; and when they know within themselves they
speak of that they do not well know, would nevertheless seem to others
to know of that which they may not well speak. Some help themselves
with countenance and gesture, and are wise by signs; as Cicero saith of
Piso, that when he answered him, he fetched one of his brows up to his
forehead, and bent the other down to his chin: "Respondes, altero ad
frontem sublato, altero ad mentum depresso supercilio; crudelitatem
tibi non placere." Some think to bear it by speaking a great word, and
being peremptory; and go on, and take by admittance that which they
cannot make good. Some, whatsoever is beyond their reach, will seem to
despise or make light of it as impertinent or curious, and so would have
their ignorance seem judgment. Some are never without a difference,
and commonly by amusing men with a subtilty, blanch the matter; of
whom A. Gellius saith, "Hominem delirum, qui verborum minutiis
rerum frangit pondera." Of which kind also Plato, in his Protagoras,
bringeth in Prodicus in scorn, and maketh him make a speech that
consisteth of distinctions from the beginning to the end. Generally
such men, in all deliberations, find ease to be of the negative side, and
affect a credit to object and foretell difficulties; for when propositions
are denied, there is an end of them, but if they be allowed, it requireth
a new work; which false point of wisdom is the bane of business. To
conclude, there is no decaying merchant, or inward beggar, hath so
many tricks to uphold the credit of their wealth, as these empty persons

have to maintain the credit of their sufficiency. Seeming wise men may make shift to get opinion, but let no man choose them for employment; for certainly, you were better take for business a man somewhat absurd than over-formal.

Chapter 27

OF FRIENDSHIP

It had been hard for him that spake it, to have put more truth and untruth together in few words than in that speech: "Whosoever is delighted in solitude, is either a wild beast or a god:" for it is most true, that a natural and secret hatred and aversion towards society in any man hath somewhat of the savage beast; but it is most untrue, that it should have any character at all of the divine nature, except it proceed, not out of a pleasure in solitude, but out of a love and desire to sequester a man's self for a higher conversation; such as is found to have been falsely and feignedly in some of the heathen; as Epimenides, the Candian; Numa, the Roman; Empedocles, the Sicilian; and Apollonius, of Tyana; and truly and really in divers of the ancient hermits and holy fathers of the church. But little do men perceive what solitude is, and how far it extendeth; for a crowd is not company, and faces are but a gallery of pictures, and talk but a tinkling cymbal, where there is no love. The Latin adage meeteth with it a little: "Magna civitas, magna solitudo:" because in a great town friends are scattered, so that there is not that fellowship, for the most part, which is in less neighborhoods: but we may go further, and affirm most truly, that it is a mere and miserable solitude to want true friends, without which the world is but a wilderness; and even in this sense also of solitude, whosoever in the frame of his nature and affections is unfit for friendship, he taketh it of the beasts, and not from humanity.

A principal fruit of friendship is the ease and discharge of the fulness and swellings of the heart, which passions of all kinds do cause and induce. We know diseases of stoppings and suffocations are the most dangerous in the body, and it is not much otherwise in the mind. You may take sarza to open the liver, steel to open the spleen, flower of sulphur for the lungs, castoreum for the brain, but no receipt openeth the heart but a true friend, to whom you may impart griefs, joys, fears, hopes, suspicions, counsels, and whatsoever lieth upon the heart to oppress it, in a kind of civil shrift or confession.

It is a strange thing to observe how high a rate great kings and monarchs do set upon this fruit of friendship whereof we speak; so great, as they purchase it many times at the hazard of their own safety and greatness; for princes, in regard of the distance of their fortune from that of their subjects and servants, cannot gather this fruit, except (to make themselves capable thereof) they raise some persons to be as it were companions, and almost equals to themselves, which many times sorteth to inconvenience. The modern languages give unto such persons the name of favorites, or privadoes, as if it were matter of grace or conversation; but the Roman name attaineth the true use and cause thereof, naming them "participes curarum;" for it is that which tieth the knot. And we see plainly that this hath been done, not by weak and passionate princes only, but by the wisest and most politic that ever reigned, who have oftentimes joined to themselves some of their servants, whom both themselves have called friends, and allowed others likewise to call them in the same manner, using the word which is received between private men.

L. Sylla, when he commanded Rome, raised Pompey (after surnamed the Great) to that height, that Pompey vaunted himself for Sylla's overmatch; for when he had carried the consulship for a friend of his, against the pursuit of Sylla, and that Sylla did a little resent thereat, and began to speak great, Pompey turned upon him again, and, in effect, bade him be quiet; for that more men adored the sun rising than the sun setting. With Julius Cæsar, Decimus Brutus had obtained that interest, as he set him down in his testament for heir in remainder after his nephew; and this was the man that had power with him to draw him forth to his death; for when Cæsar would have discharged the senate, in regard of some ill presages, and specially a dream of Calphurnia, this man lifted him gently by the arm out of his chair, telling him he hoped he would not dismiss the senate till his wife had dreamt a better dream; and it seemeth his favor was so great, as Antonius, in a letter which is recited verbatim in one of Cicero's Philippics, calleth him *venefica*, "witch," as if he had enchanted Cæsar. Augustus raised Agrippa (though of mean birth) to that height, as, when he consulted with Mæcenas about the marriage of his daughter Julia, Mæcenas took the liberty to tell him, that he must either marry his daughter to Agrippa, or take away his life; there was no third way, he had made him so great. With Tiberius Cæsar, Sejanus had ascended to that height, as they two were termed and reckoned as a pair of friends. Tiberius, in a letter to him, saith, "Hæc pro amicitiâ nostrâ non occultavi;" and the whole senate dedicated an altar to Friendship, as to a goddess, in respect of the great dearness of friendship between them two. The like, or more, was between Septimius Severus and Plautianus; for he forced his eldest son to marry the daughter of Plautianus, and would often maintain Plautianus in doing affronts to his son; and did write, also, in a letter to the senate, by these words: "I love the man so well, as I wish he may over-live me." Now, if these princes had been as a Trajan, or a Marcus Aurelius, a man might have thought that this had proceeded of an abundant goodness of nature; but being men so wise, of such strength and severity of mind, and so extreme lovers of themselves, as all these were, it proveth most plainly that they found their own felicity (though as great as ever happened to mortal men) but as an half-piece, except they might have a friend to make it entire; and yet, which is more, they were princes that had wives, sons, nephews; and yet all these could not supply the comfort of friendship.

It is not to be forgotten what Comineus observeth of his first master, Duke Charles the Hardy, namely, that he would communicate his secrets with none, and, least of all, those secrets which troubled him most. Whereupon he goeth on, and saith, that towards his latter time, that closeness did impair and a little perish his understanding. Surely, Comineus might have made the same judgment, also, if it had pleased him, of his second master, Louis the Eleventh, whose closeness was indeed his tormentor. The parable of Pythagoras is dark, but true: "Cor ne edito," "eat not the heart." Certainly, if a man would give it a hard phrase, those that want friends to open themselves unto are cannibals of their own hearts; but one thing is most admirable (wherewith I will conclude this first fruit of friendship), which is, that this communicating of a man's self to his friend works two contrary effects, for it redoubleth joys, and cutteth griefs in halves; for there is no man that imparteth his joys to his friend, but he joyeth the more; and no man that imparteth his griefs to his friend, but he grieveth the less. So that it is, in truth, of operation upon a man's mind of like virtue as the alchemists used to attribute to their stone for man's body, that it worketh all contrary effects, but still to the good and benefit of nature. But yet, without praying in aid of alchemists, there is a manifest image of this in the ordinary course of nature; for, in bodies, union strengtheneth and cherisheth any natural action; and, on the other side, weakeneth and dulleth any violent impression; and even so it is of minds.

The second fruit of friendship is healthful and sovereign for the understanding, as the first is for the affections; for friendship maketh indeed a fair day in the affections from storm and tempests, but it maketh daylight in the understanding, out of darkness and confusion of thoughts. Neither is this to be understood only of faithful counsel, which a man receiveth from his friend; but before you come to that, certain it is, that whosoever hath his mind fraught with many thoughts, his wits and understanding do clarify and break up in the communicating and discoursing with another; he tosseth his thoughts more easily; he marshalleth them more orderly; he seeth how they look when they are turned into words; finally, he waxeth wiser than himself; and that more by an hour's discourse than by a day's meditation. It was well said by Themistocles to the king of Persia: "That speech was like cloth of Arras, opened and put abroad, whereby the imagery doth appear in figure; whereas in thoughts they lie but as in packs." Neither is this second fruit of friendship, in opening the understanding, restrained only to such friends as are able to give a man counsel (they indeed are best), but even without that a man learneth of himself, and bringeth his own thoughts to light, and whetteth his wits as against a stone, which itself cuts not. In a word, a man were better relate himself to a statue or picture, than to suffer his thoughts to pass in smother.

Add now, to make this second fruit of friendship complete, that other point which lieth more open, and falleth within vulgar observation; which is faithful counsel from a friend. Heraclitus saith well, in one of his enigmas, "Dry light is ever the best;" and certain it is, that the light that a man receiveth by counsel from another, is drier and purer than that which cometh from his own understanding and judgment, which is ever infused and drenched in his affections and customs. So, as there is as much difference between the counsel that a friend giveth, and that a man giveth himself, as there is between the counsel of a friend and of a flatterer; for there is no such flatterer as is a man's self, and there is no such remedy against flattery of a man's self, as the liberty of a friend. Counsel is of two sorts,—the one concerning manners, the other concerning business; for the first, the best preservative to keep the mind in health, is the faithful admonition of a friend. The calling of a man's self to a strict account is a medicine sometimes too piercing and corrosive; reading good books of morality is a little flat and dead; observing our faults in others is sometimes improper for our case; but the best receipt (best, I say, to work, and best to take), is the admonition of a friend. It is a strange thing to behold what gross errors and extreme absurdities many (especially of the greater sort) do commit for want of a friend to tell them of them, to the great damage both of their fame and fortune; for, as St. James saith, they are as men "that look sometimes into a glass, and presently forget their own shape and favor." As for business, a man may think, if he will, that two eyes see no more than one; or, that a gamester seeth always more than a looker-on; or, that a man in anger is as wise as he that has said over the four and twenty letters; or, that a musket may be shot off as well upon the arm as upon a rest; and such other fond and high imaginations, to think himself all in all; but when all is done, the help of good counsel is that which setteth business straight. And if any man think that he will take counsel, but it shall be by pieces, asking counsel in one business of one man, and in another business of another man; it is well (that is to say, better, perhaps, than if he asked none at all); but he runneth two dangers,—one, that he shall not be faithfully counselled; for it is a rare thing, except it be from a perfect and entire friend, to have counsel given, but such as shall be bowed and crooked to some ends which he hath that giveth it; the other, that he shall have counsel given, hurtful and unsafe (though with good meaning), and mixed partly of mischief, and partly of remedy; even as if you would call a physician, that is thought good for the cure of the disease you complain of, but is unacquainted with your body; and, therefore, may put you in a way for a present cure, but overthroweth your health in some other kind, and so cure the disease and kill the patient. But a friend, that is wholly acquainted with a man's estate, will beware, by furthering any present business, how he dasheth upon other inconvenience; and, therefore, rest not upon scattered counsels; they will rather distract and mislead, than settle and direct.

After these two noble fruits of friendship (peace in the affections, and support of the judgment), followeth the last fruit, which is like the pomegranate, full of many kernels; I mean aid, and bearing a part in all actions and occasions. Here the best way to represent to life the manifold use of friendship, is to cast and see how many things there are which a man cannot do himself; and then it will appear that it was a sparing speech of the ancients to say, "that a friend is another himself," for that a friend is far more than himself. Men have their time, and die many times in desire of some things which they principally take to heart; the bestowing of a child, the finishing of a work, or the like. If a man have a true friend, he may rest almost secure that the care of those things will continue after him; so that a man hath, as it were, two lives in his desires. A man hath a body, and that body is confined to a place;

but where friendship is, all offices of life are, as it were, granted to him and his deputy, for he may exercise them by his friend. How many things are there, which a man cannot, with any face or comeliness, say or do himself? A man can scarce allege his own merits with modesty, much less extol them; a man cannot sometimes brook to supplicate, or beg, and a number of the like; but all these things are graceful in a friend's mouth, which are blushing in a man's own. So, again, a man's person hath many proper relations which he cannot put off. A man cannot speak to his son but as a father; to his wife but as a husband; to his enemy but upon terms; whereas, a friend may speak as the case requires, and not as it sorteth with the person. But to enumerate these things were endless; I have given the rule, where a man cannot fitly play his own part. If he have not a friend, he may quit the stage.

Chapter 28

OF EXPENSE

Riches are for spending, and spending for honor and good actions; therefore, extraordinary expense must be limited by the worth of the occasion; for voluntary undoing may be as well for a man's country as for the kingdom of heaven; but ordinary expense ought to be limited by a man's estate, and governed with such regard, as it be within his compass, and not subject to deceit and abuse of servants, and ordered to the best show, that the bills may be less than the estimation abroad. Certainly, if a man will keep but of even hand, his ordinary expenses ought to be but to the half of his receipts; and, if he think to wax rich, but to the third part. It is no baseness for the greatest to descend and look into their own estate. Some forbear it, not upon negligence alone, but doubting to bring themselves into melancholy, in respect they shall find it broken; but wounds cannot be cured without searching. He that cannot look into his own estate at all, had need both choose well those whom he employeth, and change them often; for new are more timorous, and less subtle. He that can look into his estate but seldom, it behooveth him to turn all to certainties. A man had need, if he be plentiful in some kind of expense, to be as saving again in some other: as, if he be plentiful in diet, to be saving in apparel; if he be plentiful in the hall, to be saving in the stable; and the like. For he that is plentiful in expenses of all kinds, will hardly be preserved from decay. In clearing of a man's estate, he may as well hurt himself in being too sudden, as in letting it run on too long; for hasty selling is commonly as disadvantageable as interest. Besides, he that clears at once will relapse; for, finding himself out of straits, he will revert to his customs; but he that cleareth by degrees induceth a habit of frugality, and gaineth as well upon his mind as upon his estate. Certainly, who hath a state to repair, may not despise small things; and, commonly, it is less dishonorable to abridge petty charges, than to stoop to petty gettings. A man ought warily to begin charges, which once begun will continue; but in matters that return not, he may be more magnificent.

Chapter 29

Of the True Greatness of Kingdoms and Estates

The speech of Themistocles, the Athenian, which was haughty and arrogant, in taking so much to himself, had been a grave and wise observation and censure, applied at large to others. Desired at a feast to touch a lute, he said, "He could not fiddle, but yet he could make a small town a great city." These words (holpen a little with a metaphor) may express two different abilities in those that deal in business of estate; for if a true survey be taken of counsellors and statesmen, there may be found (though rarely) those which can make a small state great, and yet cannot fiddle: as, on the other side there will be found a great many that can fiddle very cunningly, but yet are so far from being able to make a small state great, as their gift lieth the other way,—to bring a great and flourishing estate to ruin and decay. And certainly, those degenerate arts and shifts, whereby many counsellors and governors gain both favor with their masters and estimation with the vulgar, deserve no better name than fiddling; being things rather pleasing for the time, and graceful to themselves only, than tending to the weal and advancement of the state which they serve. There are also (no doubt) counsellors and governors which may be held sufficient, "negotiis pares," able to manage affairs, and to keep them from precipices and manifest inconveniences; which, nevertheless, are far from the ability to raise and amplify an estate in power, means, and fortune. But be the workmen what they may be, let us speak of the work; that is, the true greatness of kingdoms and estates, and the means thereof. An argument fit for great and mighty princes to have in their hand; to the end, that neither by overmeasuring their forces, they lose themselves in vain enterprises: nor, on the other side, by undervaluing them, they descend to fearful and pusillanimous counsels.

The greatness of an estate, in bulk and territory, doth fall under measure; and the greatness of finances and revenue doth fall under computation. The population may appear by musters, and the number and greatness of cities and towns by cards and maps; but yet there is not anything amongst civil affairs more subject to error than the right valuation and true judgment concerning the power and forces of an estate. The kingdom of heaven is compared, not to any great kernel, or nut, but to a grain of mustard-seed; which is one of the least grains, but hath in it a property and spirit hastily to get up and spread. So are there states great in territory, and yet not apt to enlarge or command; and some that have but a small dimension of stem, and yet apt to be the foundations of great monarchies.

Walled towns, stored arsenals and armories, goodly races of horse, chariots of war, elephants, ordnance, artillery, and the like; all this is but a sheep in a lion's skin, except the breed and disposition of the people be stout and warlike. Nay, number itself in armies importeth not much, where the people is of weak courage; for, as Virgil saith, "It never troubles a wolf how many the sheep be." The army of the Persians in the plains of Arbela was such a vast sea of people, as it did somewhat astonish the commanders in Alexander's army, who came to him, therefore, and wished him to set upon them by night; but he answered, "He would not pilfer the victory;" and the defeat was easy.— When Tigranes, the Armenian, being encamped upon a hill with four hundred thousand men, discovered the army of the Romans, being not above fourteen thousand, marching towards him, he made himself merry with it, and said, "Yonder men are too many for an ambassage, and too few for a fight;" but before the sun set, he found them enow to give him the chase with infinite slaughter. Many are the examples of the great odds between number and courage; so that a man may truly make a judgment, that the principal point of greatness in any state is to have a race of military men. Neither is money the sinews of war (as it is trivially said), where the sinews of men's arms, in base and effeminate people, are failing: for Solon said well to Crœsus (when in ostentation he showed him his gold), "Sir, if any other come that hath better iron than you, he will be master of all this gold." Therefore, let any prince or state, think soberly of his forces, except his militia of natives be of good and valiant soldiers; and let princes, on the other side, that have subjects of martial disposition, know their own strength, unless they be otherwise wanting unto themselves. As for mercenary forces (which is the help in this case), all examples show that, whatsoever estate or prince doth rest upon them, he may spread his feathers for a time, but he will mew them soon after.

The blessing of Judah and Issachar will never meet; that the same people, or nation, should be both the lion's whelp and the ass between burdens; neither will it be, that a people overlaid with taxes should ever become valiant and martial. It is true that taxes, levied by consent of the estate, do abate men's courage less; as it hath been seen notably in the excises of the Low Countries, and, in some degree, in the subsidies of England; for, you must note, that we speak now of the heart, and not of the purse; so that, although the same tribute and tax, laid by consent or by imposing, be all one to the purse, yet it works diversely upon the courage. So that you may conclude, that no people overcharged with tribute is fit for empire.

Let states that aim at greatness take heed how their nobility and gentlemen do multiply too fast; for that maketh the common subject grow to be a peasant and base swain, driven out of heart, and, in effect, but the gentleman's laborer. Even as you may see in coppice woods; if you leave your staddles too thick, you shall never have clean underwood, but shrubs and bushes. So in countries, if the gentlemen be too many, the commons will be base; and you will bring it to that, that not the hundred poll will be fit for a helmet, especially as to the infantry, which is the nerve of an army; and so there will be great population and little strength. This which I speak of, hath been nowhere better seen than by comparing of England and France; whereof England, though far less in territory and population, hath been, nevertheless, an overmatch; in regard, the middle people of England make good soldiers, which the peasants of France do not. And herein the device of King Henry the Seventh (whereof I have spoken largely in the history of his life) was profound and admirable; in making farms and houses of husbandry of a standard, that is, maintained with such a proportion of land unto them as may breed a subject to live in convenient plenty, and no servile condition, and to keep the plough in the hands of the owners, and not mere hirelings; and thus, indeed, you shall attain to Virgil's character, which he gives to ancient Italy:—

"Terra potens armis atque ubere glebæ."

Neither is that state (which, for anything I know, is almost peculiar to England, and hardly to be found anywhere else, except it be, perhaps, in Poland), to be passed over; I mean the state of free servants and attendants upon noblemen and gentlemen, which are noways inferior unto the yeomanry for arms; and, therefore, out of all question, the splendor and magnificence, and great retinues, and hospitality of noblemen and gentlemen received into custom, do much conduce unto martial greatness; whereas, contrariwise, the close and reserved living of noblemen and gentlemen causeth a penury of military forces.

By all means, it is to be procured that the trunk of Nebuchadnezzar's tree of monarchy be great enough to bear the branches and the boughs; that is, that the natural subjects of the crown, or state, bear a sufficient proportion to the stranger subjects that they govern. Therefore, all states that are liberal of naturalization towards strangers are fit for empire; for to think that a handful of people can, with the greatest courage and policy in the world, embrace too large extent of dominion, it may hold for a time, but it will fail suddenly. The Spartans were a nice people in point of naturalization; whereby, while they kept their compass, they stood firm; but when they did spread, and their boughs were becoming too great for their stem, they became a windfall upon the sudden. Never any state was, in this point, so open to receive strangers into their body as were the Romans; therefore, it sorted with them accordingly, for they grew to the greatest monarchy. Their manner was to grant naturalization (which they called "jus civitatis"), and to grant it in the highest degree, that is, not only "jus commercii," "jus connubii," "jus hæreditatis;" but, also, "jus suffragii," and "jus honorum;" and this not to singular persons alone, but likewise to whole families; yea, to cities and sometimes to nations. Add to this their custom of plantation of colonies, whereby the Roman plant was removed into the soil of other nations, and, putting both constitutions together, you will say, that it was not the Romans that spread upon the world, but it was the world that spread upon the Romans; and that was the sure way of greatness. I have marvelled sometimes at Spain, how they clasp and contain so large dominions with so few natural Spaniards; but sure the whole compass of Spain is a very great body of a tree, far above Rome and Sparta at the first; and, besides, though they have not had that usage to naturalize liberally, yet they have that which is next to it; that is, to employ, almost indifferently, all nations in their militia of ordinary soldiers; yea, and sometimes in their highest commands; nay, it seemeth at this instant they are sensible of this want of natives, as by the pragmatical sanction, now published, appeareth.

It is certain that sedentary and within-door arts, and delicate manufactures (that require rather the finger than the arm), have in their nature a contrariety to a military disposition; and, generally, all warlike people are a little idle, and love danger better than travail; neither must they be too much broken of it, if they shall be preserved in vigor. Therefore, it was great advantage in the ancient states of Sparta, Athens, Rome, and others, that they had the use of slaves, which commonly did rid those manufactures; but that is abolished, in greatest part, by the Christian law. That which cometh nearest to it is, to leave those arts chiefly to strangers (which, for that purpose, are the more easily to be received), and to contain the principal bulk of the vulgar natives within those three kinds, tillers of the ground, free servants, and handicraftsmen of strong and manly arts; as smiths, masons, carpenters, &c., not reckoning professed soldiers.

But, above all, for empire and greatness, it importeth most, that a nation do profess arms as their principal honor, study, and occupation; for the things which we formerly have spoken of are but habilitations towards arms; and what is habilitation without intention and act? Romulus, after his death (as they report or feign), sent a present to the Romans, that, above all, they should intend arms, and then they should prove the greatest empire of the world. The fabric of the state of Sparta was wholly (though not wisely) framed and composed to that scope and end; the Persians and Macedonians had it for a flash; the Gauls, Germans, Goths, Saxons, Normans, and others, had it for a time; the Turks have it at this day, though in great declination. Of Christian Europe, they that have it are in effect only the Spaniards; but it is so plain, that every man profiteth in that he most intendeth, that it needeth not to be stood upon. It is enough to point at it, that no nation which doth not directly profess arms, may look to have greatness fall into their mouths; and, on the other side, it is a most certain oracle of time, that those states that continue long in that profession (as the Romans and Turks principally have done), do wonders; and those that have professed arms but for an age have, notwithstanding, commonly attained that greatness in that age which maintained them long after, when their profession and exercise of arms had grown to decay.

Incident to this point is, for a state to have those laws or customs which may reach forth unto them just occasions (as may be pretended) of war; for there is that justice imprinted in the nature of men, that they enter not upon wars (whereof so many calamities do ensue), but upon some, at the least specious grounds and quarrels. The Turk hath at hand, for cause of war, the propagation of his law or sect, a quarrel that he may always command. The Romans, though they esteemed the extending the limits of their empire to be great honor to their generals when it was done, yet they never rested upon that alone to begin a war. First, therefore, let nations that pretend to greatness have this, that they be sensible of wrongs, either upon borderers, merchants, or politic ministers; and that they sit not too long upon a provocation: secondly, let them be pressed, and ready to give aids and succors to their confederates, as it ever was with the Romans; insomuch, as if the confederate had leagues defensive with divers other states, and, upon invasion offered, did implore their aids severally, yet the Romans would ever be the foremost, and leave it to none other to have the honor. As for the wars, which were anciently made on the behalf of a kind of party, or tacit conformity of estate, I do not see how they may be well justified: as when the Romans made a war for the liberty of Græcia; or, when the Lacedæmonians and Athenians made wars to set up or pull down democracies and oligarchies; or when wars were made by foreigners, under the pretence of justice or protection, to deliver the subjects of others from tyranny and oppression, and the like. Let it suffice, that no estate expect to be great, that is not awake upon any just occasion of arming.

Nobody can be healthful without exercise, neither natural body nor politic; and, certainly, to a kingdom, or estate, a just and honorable war is the true exercise. A civil war, indeed, is like the heat of a fever; but a foreign war is like the heat of exercise, and serveth to keep the body in health; for, in a slothful peace, both courages will effeminate and manners corrupt. But, howsoever it be for happiness, without all question for greatness, it maketh to be still, for the most part, in arms; and the strength of a veteran army (though it be a chargeable business) always on foot, is that which commonly giveth the law, or, at least, the reputation amongst all neighbor states, as may well be seen in Spain, which hath had, in one part or other, a veteran army, almost continually, now by the space of sixscore years.

To be master of the sea is an abridgment of a monarchy. Cicero, writing to Atticus, of Pompey's preparation against Cæsar, saith, "Consilium Pompeii plane Themistocleum est; putat enim, qui mari potitur, eum rerum potiri; and, without doubt, Pompey had tired out Cæsar, if upon vain confidence he had not left that way. We see the great effects of battles by sea. The battle of Actium decided the empire of the world: the battle of Lepanto arrested the greatness of the Turk. There be many examples where sea-fights have been final to the war; but this is when princes, or states, have set up their rest upon the battles.

But thus much is certain, that he that commands the sea is at great liberty, and may take as much and as little of the war as he will; whereas, those that be strongest by land are many times, nevertheless, in great straits. Surely, at this day, with us of Europe, the vantage of strength at sea (which is one of the principal dowries of this kingdom of Great Britain) is great; both because most of the kingdoms of Europe are not merely inland, but girt with the sea most part of their compass; and because the wealth of both Indies seems, in great part, but an accessary to the command of the seas.

The wars of latter ages seem to be made in the dark, in respect of the glory and honor which reflected upon men from the wars in ancient time. There be now, for martial encouragement, some degrees and orders of chivalry, which, nevertheless, are conferred promiscuously upon soldiers and no soldiers; and some remembrance, perhaps, upon the escutcheon, and some hospitals for maimed soldiers, and such like things; but in ancient times, the trophies erected upon the place of the victory; the funeral laudatives, and monuments for those that died in the wars; the crowns and garlands personal; the style of emperor which the great kings of the world after borrowed; the triumphs of the generals upon their return; the great donatives and largesses upon the disbanding of the armies; were things able to inflame all men's courages. But, above all, that of the triumph amongst the Romans was not pageants or gaudery, but one of the wisest and noblest institutions that ever was; for it contained three things: honor to the general, riches to the treasury out of the spoils, and donatives to the army. But that honor, perhaps, were not fit for monarchies, except it be in the person of the monarch himself, or his sons; as it came to pass in the times of the Roman emperors, who did impropriate the actual triumphs to themselves and their sons, for such wars as they did achieve in person, and left only for wars achieved by subjects, some triumphal garments and ensigns to the general.

To conclude. No man can by care-taking (as the Scripture saith) "add a cubit to his stature," in this little model of a man's body; but in the great frame of kingdoms and commonwealths, it is in the power of princes, or estates, to add amplitude and greatness to their kingdom; for, by introducing such ordinances, constitutions, and customs, as we have now touched, they may sow greatness to their posterity and succession: but these things are commonly not observed, but left to take their chance.

Chapter 30

OF REGIMEN OF HEALTH

There is a wisdom in this beyond the rules of physic. A man's own observation, what he finds good of, and what he finds hurt of, is the best physic to preserve health; but it is a safer conclusion to say, "This agreeth not well with me, therefore I will not continue it;" than this, "I find no offence of this, therefore I may use it;" for strength of nature in youth passeth over many excesses which are owing a man till his age. Discern of the coming on of years, and think not to do the same things still; for age will not be defied. Beware of sudden change in any great point of diet, and, if necessity enforce it, fit the rest to it; for it is a secret both in nature and state, that it is safer to change many things than one. Examine thy customs of diet, sleep, exercise, apparel, and the like; and try, in any thing thou shalt judge hurtful, to discontinue it by little and little; but so, as if thou dost find any inconvenience by the change, thou come back to it again; for it is hard to distinguish that which is generally held good and wholesome, from that which is good particularly, and fit for thine own body. To be free-minded and cheerfully disposed at hours of meat, and of sleep, and of exercise, is one of the best precepts of long lasting. As for the passions and studies of the mind, avoid envy, anxious fears, anger fretting inwards, subtle and knotty inquisitions, joys, and exhilarations in excess, sadness not communicated. Entertain hopes, mirth rather than joy, variety of delights, rather than surfeit of them; wonder and admiration, and therefore novelties; studies that fill the mind with splendid and illustrious objects, as histories, fables, and contemplations of nature. If you fly physic in health altogether, it will be too strange for your body when you shall need it; if you make it too familiar, it will work no extraordinary effect when sickness cometh. I commend rather some diet, for certain seasons, than frequent use of physic, except it be grown into a custom; for those diets alter the body more, and trouble it less. Despise no new accident in your body, but ask opinion of it. In sickness, respect health principally; and in health, action; for those that put their bodies to endure in health, may, in most sicknesses which are not very sharp, be cured only with diet and tendering. Celsus could never have spoken it as a physician, had he not been a wise man withal, when he giveth it for one of the great precepts of health and lasting, that a man do vary and interchange contraries, but with an inclination to the more benign extreme. Use fasting and full eating, but rather full eating; watching and sleep, but rather sleep; sitting and exercise, but rather exercise, and the like; so shall nature be cherished, and yet taught masteries. Physicians are some of them so pleasing and conformable to the humor of the patient, as they press not the true cure of the disease; and some other are so regular in proceeding according to art for the disease, as they respect not sufficiently the condition of the patient. Take one of a middle temper; or, if it may not be found in one man, combine two of either sort; and forget not to call as well the best acquainted with your body, as the best reputed of for his faculty.

Chapter 31

OF SUSPICION

Suspicions amongst thoughts are like bats amongst birds, they ever fly by twilight. Certainly they are to be repressed, or at the least well guarded; for they cloud the mind, they lose friends, and they check with business, whereby business cannot go on currently and constantly. They dispose kings to tyranny, husbands to jealousy, wise men to irresolution and melancholy. They are defects, not in the heart but in the brain; for they take place in the stoutest natures, as in the example of Henry the Seventh of England. There was not a more suspicious man, nor a more stout, and in such a composition they do small hurt; for commonly they are not admitted, but with examination, whether they be likely or no; but in fearful natures they gain ground too fast. There is nothing makes a man suspect much, more than to know little; and, therefore, men should remedy suspicion by procuring to know more, and not to keep their suspicions in smother. What would men have? Do they think those they employ and deal with are saints? Do they not think they will have their own ends, and be truer to themselves than to them? Therefore, there is no better way to moderate suspicions, than to account upon such suspicions as true, and yet to bridle them as false: for so far a man ought to make use of suspicions as to provide, as if that should be true that he suspects, yet it may do him no hurt. Suspicions that the mind of itself gathers are but buzzes; but suspicions that are artificially nourished, and put into men's heads by the tales and whisperings of others, have stings. Certainly, the best mean, to clear the way in this same wood of suspicions, is frankly to communicate them with the party that he suspects: for thereby he shall be sure to know more of the truth of them than he did before; and, withal, shall make that party more circumspect, not to give further cause of suspicion. But this would not be done to men of base natures; for they, if they find themselves once suspected, will never be true. The Italian says, "Sospetto licentia fede;" as if suspicion did give a passport to faith; but it ought rather to kindle it to discharge itself.

Chapter 32

OF DISCOURSE

Some in their discourse desire rather commendation of wit, in being able to hold all arguments, than of judgment, in discerning what is true; as if it were a praise to know what might be said and not what should be thought. Some have certain commonplaces and themes, wherein they are good, and want variety; which kind of poverty is for the most part tedious, and, when it is once perceived, ridiculous. The honorablest part of talk is to give the occasion, and again to moderate and pass to somewhat else; for then a man leads the dance. It is good in discourse, and speech of conversation, to vary and intermingle speech of the present occasion with arguments, tales with reasons, asking of questions with telling of opinions, and jest with earnest; for it is a dull thing to tire, and, as we say now, to jade any thing too far. As for jest, there be certain things which ought to be privileged from it; namely, religion, matters of state, great persons, any man's present business of importance, and any case that deserveth pity; yet there be some that think their wits have been asleep, except they dart out somewhat that is piquant, and to the quick; that is a vein which would be bridled:—

"Parce, puer, stimulis, et fortius utere loris."

And, generally, men ought to find the difference between saltness and bitterness. Certainly, he that hath a satirical vein, as he maketh others afraid of his wit, so he had need be afraid of others' memory. He that questioneth much, shall learn much, and content much, but especially if he apply his questions to the skill of the persons whom he asketh: for he shall give them occasion to please themselves in speaking, and himself shall continually gather knowledge; but let his questions not be troublesome, for that is fit for a poser. And let him be sure to leave other men their turns to speak; nay, if there be any that would reign and take up all the time, let him find means to take them off, and to bring others on, as musicians used to do with those that dance too long galliards. If you dissemble sometimes your knowledge of that you are thought to know, you shall be thought, another time, to know that you know not. Speech of a man's self ought to be seldom, and well chosen. I knew one was wont to say in scorn, "He must needs be a wise man, he speaks so much of himself;" and there is but one case wherein a man may commend himself with good grace, and that is in commending virtue in another, especially if it be such a virtue whereunto himself pretendeth. Speech of touch towards others should be sparingly used; for discourse ought to be as a field, without coming home to any man. I knew two noblemen, of the west part of England, whereof the one was given to scoff, but kept ever royal cheer in his house; the other would ask of those that had been at the other's table, "Tell truly, was there never a flout or dry blow given?" To which the guest would answer, "Such and such a thing passed." The lord would say, "I thought he would mar a good dinner." Discretion of speech is more than eloquence; and to speak agreeably to him with whom we deal, is more than to speak in good words, or in good order. A good continued speech, without a good speech of interlocution, shows slowness; and a good reply, or second speech, without a good settled speech, showeth shallowness and weakness. As we see in beasts, that those that are weakest in the course, are yet nimblest in the turn; as it is betwixt the greyhound and the hare. To use too many circumstances, ere one come to the matter, is wearisome; to use none at all, is blunt.

Chapter 33

Of Plantations

Plantations are amongst ancient, primitive, and heroical works. When the world was young, it begat more children; but now it is old, it begets fewer; for I may justly account new plantations to be the children of former kingdoms. I like a plantation in a pure soil; that is, where people are not displanted, to the end to plant in others; for else it is rather an extirpation than a plantation. Planting of countries is like planting of woods; for you must make account to lose almost twenty years' profit, and expect your recompense in the end; for the principal thing that hath been the destruction of most plantations, hath been the base and hasty drawing of profit in the first years. It is true, speedy profit is not to be neglected, as far as may stand with the good of the plantation, but no further. It is a shameful and unblessed thing to take the scum of people and wicked condemned men, to be the people with whom you plant; and not only so, but it spoileth the plantation; for they will ever live like rogues, and not fall to work; but be lazy, and do mischief, and spend victuals, and be quickly weary, and then certify over to their country to the discredit of the plantation. The people wherewith you plant ought to be gardeners, ploughmen, laborers, smiths, carpenters, joiners, fishermen, fowlers, with some few apothecaries, surgeons, cooks, and bakers. In a country of plantations, first look about what kind of victual the country yields of itself to hand; as chestnuts, walnuts, pine-apples, olives, dates, plums, cherries, wild honey, and the like, and make use of them. Then consider what victual, or esculent things there are, which grow speedily, and within the year; as parsnips, carrots, turnips, onions, radish, artichokes of Jerusalem, maize, and the like. For wheat, barley, and oats, they ask too much labor; but with pease and beans you may begin, both because they ask less labor, and because they serve for meat as well as for bread; and of rice, likewise, cometh a great increase, and it is a kind of meat. Above all, there ought to be brought store of biscuit, oatmeal, flour, meal, and the like, in the beginning, till bread may be had. For beasts, or birds, take chiefly such as are least subject to diseases, and multiply fastest; as swine, goats, cocks, hens, turkeys, geese, house-doves, and the like. The victual in plantations ought to be expended almost as in a besieged town, that is, with certain allowance; and let the main part of the ground employed to gardens or corn, be to a common stock; and to be laid in, and stored up, and then delivered out in proportion; besides some spots of ground that any particular person will manure for his own private use. Consider, likewise, what commodities the soil where the plantation is doth naturally yield, that they may some way help to defray the charge of the plantation; so it be not, as was said, to the untimely prejudice of the main business, as it hath fared with tobacco in Virginia. Wood commonly aboundeth but too much; and therefore timber is fit to be one. If there be iron ore, and streams whereupon to set the mills, iron is a brave commodity where wood aboundeth. Making of bay-salt, if the climate be proper for it, would be put in experience; growing silk, likewise, if any be, is a likely commodity; pitch and tar, where store of firs and pines are, will not fail; so drugs and sweet woods, where they are, cannot but yield great profit; soap-ashes, likewise, and other things that may be thought of; but moil not too much under ground, for the hope of mines is very uncertain, and useth to make the planters lazy in other things. For government, let it be in the hands of one, assisted with some counsel; and let them have commission to exercise martial laws, with some limitation; and, above all, let men make that profit of being in the wilderness, as they have God always, and his service, before their eyes. Let not the government of the plantation depend upon too many counsellors and undertakers in the country that planteth, but upon a temperate number; and let those be rather noblemen and gentlemen, than merchants, for they look ever to the present gain. Let there be freedoms from custom, till the plantation be of strength; and not only freedom from custom, but freedom to carry their commodities where they may make their best of them, except there be some special cause of caution. Cram not in people, by sending too fast company after company; but rather hearken how they waste, and send supplies proportionably; but so as the number may live well in the plantation, and not by surcharge be in penury. It hath been a great endangering to the health of some plantations, that they have built along the sea and rivers, in marish and unwholesome grounds; therefore, though you begin there, to avoid carriage and other like discommodities, yet build still rather upwards from the streams than along. It concerneth, likewise, the health of the plantation, that they have good store of salt with them, that they may use it in their victuals when it shall be necessary. If you plant where savages are, do not only entertain them with trifles and gingles, but use them justly and graciously, with sufficient guard, nevertheless; and do not win their favor by helping them to invade their enemies, but for their defence it is not amiss; and send oft of them over to the country that plants, that they may see a better condition than their own, and commend it when they return. When the plantation grows to strength, then it is time to plant with women as well as with men; that the plantation may spread into generations, and not be ever pieced from without. It is the sinfullest thing in the world, to forsake or destitute a plantation once in forwardness; for, besides the dishonor, it is the guiltiness of blood of many commiserable persons.

Chapter 34

OF RICHES

I cannot call riches better than the baggage of virtue; the Roman word is better, "impedimenta;" for as the baggage is to an army, so is riches to virtue; it cannot be spared nor left behind, but it hindereth the march; yea, and the care of it sometimes loseth or disturbeth the victory. Of great riches there is no real use, except it be in the distribution; the rest is but conceit. So saith Solomon: "Where much is, there are many to consume it; and what hath the owner, but the sight of it with his eyes?" The personal fruition in any man cannot reach to feel great riches: there is a custody of them, or a power of dole and donative of them, or a fame of them, but no solid use to the owner. Do you not see what feigned prices are set upon little stones and rarities? and what works of ostentation are undertaken, because there might seem to be some use of great riches? But then you will say, they may be of use to buy men out of dangers or troubles; as Solomon saith: "Riches are as a strong-hold in the imagination of the rich man;" but this is excellently expressed, that it is in imagination, and not always in fact; for, certainly, great riches have sold more men than they have bought out. Seek not proud riches, but such as thou mayest get justly, use soberly, distribute cheerfully, and leave contentedly; yet have no abstract nor friarly contempt of them, but distinguish, as Cicero saith well of Rabirius Posthumus: "In studio rei amplificandæ apparebat, non avaritiæ prædam, sed instrumentum bonitati quæri." Hearken also to Solomon, and beware of hasty gathering of riches: "Qui festinat ad divitias, non erit insons." The poets feign, that when Plutus (which is riches) is sent from Jupiter, he limps, and goes slowly; but when he is sent from Pluto, he runs, and is swift of foot; meaning, that riches gotten by good means and just labor pace slowly; but when they come by the death of others (as by the course of inheritance, testaments, and the like), they come tumbling upon a man. But it might be applied likewise to Pluto, taking him for the devil; for when riches come from the devil (as by fraud and oppression, and unjust means), they come upon speed. The ways to enrich are many, and most of them foul: parsimony is one of the best, and yet is not innocent; for it withholdeth men from works of liberality and charity.

The improvement of the ground is the most natural obtaining of riches; for it is our great mother's blessing, the earth's, but it is slow; and yet, where men of great wealth do stoop to husbandry, it multiplieth riches exceedingly. I knew a nobleman, in England, that had the greatest audits of any man in my time, a great grazier, a great sheep-master, a great timber-man, a great collier, a great corn-master, a great lead-man, and so of iron, and a number of the like points of husbandry; so as the earth seemed a sea to him in respect of the perpetual importation. It was truly observed by one, "That himself came very hardly to a little riches, and very easily to great riches;" for when a man's stock is come to that, that he can expect the prime of markets, and overcome those bargains, which for their greatness are few men's money, and be partner in the industries of younger men, he cannot but increase mainly. The gains of ordinary trades and vocations are honest, and furthered by two things, chiefly: by diligence, and by a good name for good and fair dealing; but the gains of bargains are of a more doubtful nature, when men shall wait upon others' necessity: broke by servants and instruments to draw them on; put off others cunningly that would be better chapmen; and the like practices, which are crafty and naught. As for the chopping of bargains, when a man buys not to hold, but to sell over again, that commonly grindeth double, both upon the seller and upon the buyer. Sharings do greatly enrich, if the hands be well chosen that are trusted. Usury is the certainest means of gain, though one of the worst; as that whereby a man doth eat his bread, "in sudore vultûs alieni;" and, besides, doth plough upon Sundays; but yet certain though it be, it hath flaws, for that the scriveners and brokers do value unsound men to serve their own turn. The fortune, in being the first in an invention, or in a privilege, doth cause sometimes a wonderful overgrowth in riches, as it was with the first sugar-man in the Canaries; therefore, if a man can play the true logician, to have as well judgment as invention, he may do great matters, especially if the times be fit. He that resteth upon gains certain, shall hardly grow to great riches; and he that puts all upon adventures, doth oftentimes break and come to poverty; it is good, therefore, to guard adventures with certainties that may uphold losses. Monopolies, and coemption of wares for resale, where they are not restrained, are great means to enrich; especially if the party have intelligence what things are like to come into request, and so store himself beforehand. Riches gotten by service, though it be of the best rise, yet when they are gotten by flattery, feeding humors, and other servile conditions, they may be placed amongst the worst. As for fishing for testaments and executorships (as Tacitus saith of Seneca, "Testamenta et orbos tanquam indagine capi"), it is yet worse, by how much men submit themselves to meaner persons than in service. Believe not much them that seem to despise riches, for they despise them that despair of them; and none worse when they come to them. Be not penny-wise; riches have wings, and sometimes they fly away of themselves, sometimes they must be set flying to bring in more. Men leave their riches either to their kindred, or to the public; and moderate portions prosper best in both. A great state left to an heir, is as a lure to all the birds of prey round about to seize on him, if he be not the better stablished in years and judgment; likewise, glorious gifts and foundations are like sacrifices without salt, and but the painted sepulchres of alms, which soon will putrefy and corrupt inwardly. Therefore, measure not thine advancements by quantity, but frame them by measure, and defer not charities till death; for, certainly, if a man weigh it rightly, he that doth so is rather liberal of another man's than of his own.

Chapter 35

OF PROPHECIES

I mean not to speak of divine prophecies, nor of heathen oracles, nor of natural predictions; but only of prophecies that have been of certain memory, and from hidden causes. Saith the Pythonissa to Saul, "To-morrow thou and thy sons shall be with me." Virgil hath these verses from Homer:—

> *"Hic domus Æneæ cunctis dominabitur oris,*
> *Et nati natorum, et qui nascentur ab illis."*

A prophecy, as it seems, of the Roman empire. Seneca the tragedian hath these verses:—

> *"Venient annis*
> *Sæcula seris, quibus Oceanus*
> *Vincula rerum laxet, et ingens*
> *Pateat Tellus, Tiphysque novos*
> *Detegat orbes; nec sit terris*
> *Ultima Thule."*

A prophecy of the discovery of America. The daughter of Polycrates dreamed that Jupiter bathed her father, and Apollo anointed him; and it came to pass that he was crucified in an open place, where the sun made his body run with sweat, and the rain washed it. Philip of Macedon dreamed he sealed up his wife's belly, whereby he did expound it, that his wife should be barren; but Aristander the soothsayer told him his wife was with child, because men do not use to seal vessels that are empty. A phantasm that appeared to M. Brutus in his tent, said to him, "Philippis iterum me videbis." Tiberius said to Galba, "Tu quoque, Galba, degustabis imperium." In Vespasian's time, there went a prophecy in the East, that those that should come forth of Judea, should reign over the world; which, though it may be was meant of our Saviour, yet Tacitus expounds it of Vespasian. Domitian dreamed, the night before he was slain, that a golden head was growing out of the nape of his neck; and, indeed, the succession that followed him, for many years, made golden times. Henry the Sixth of England said of Henry the Seventh, when he was a lad, and gave him water, "This is the lad that shall enjoy the crown for which we strive." When I was in France, I heard from one Dr. Pena, that the queen mother, who was given to curious arts, caused the king her husband's nativity to be calculated under a false name; and the astrologer gave a judgment, that he should be killed in a duel; at which the queen laughed, thinking her husband to be above challenges and duels; but he was slain upon a course at tilt, the splinters of the staff of Montgomery going in at his beaver. The trivial prophecy which I heard when I was a child, and Queen Elizabeth was in the flower of her years, was,

> *"When hempe is spunne,*
> *England's done;"*

whereby it was generally conceived, that after the princes had reigned which had the principal letters of that word hempe (which were Henry, Edward, Mary, Philip, and Elizabeth), England should come to utter confusion; which, thanks be to God, is verified only in the change of the name; for that the king's style is now no more of England, but of Britain. There was also another prophecy before the year of eighty-eight, which I do not well understand.

> *"There shall be seen upon a day,*
> *Between the Baugh and the May,*
> *The black fleet of Norway.*
> *When that that is come and gone,*
> *England build houses of lime and stone,*
> *For after wars you shall have none."*

It was generally conceived to be meant of the Spanish fleet that came in eighty-eight; for that the king of Spain's surname, as they say, is Norway. The prediction of Regiomontanus,

> *"Octogesimus octavus mirabilis annus,"*

was thought likewise accomplished in the sending of that great fleet, being the greatest in strength, though not in number, of all that ever swam upon the sea. As for Cleon's dream, I think it was a jest; it was, that he was devoured of a long dragon; and it was expounded of a maker of sausages, that troubled him exceedingly. There are numbers of the like kind, especially if you include dreams, and predictions of astrology; but I have set down these few only of certain credit, for example. My judgment is, that they ought all to be despised, and ought to serve but for winter talk by the fireside; though, when I say despised, I mean it as for belief; for otherwise, the spreading or publishing of them is in no sort to be despised, for they have done much mischief; and I see many severe laws made to suppress them. That that hath given them grace, and some credit, consisteth in three things. First, that men mark when they hit, and never mark when they miss; as they do, generally, also of dreams. The second is, that probable conjectures, or obscure traditions, many times turn themselves into prophecies; while the nature of man, which coveteth divination, thinks it no peril to foretell that which indeed they do but collect, as that of Seneca's verse; for so much was then subject to demonstration, that the globe of the earth had great parts beyond the Atlantic, which might be probably conceived not to be all sea; and adding thereto the tradition in Plato's Timæus, and his Atlanticus, it might encourage one to turn it to a prediction. The third and last (which is the great one), is, that almost all of them, being infinite in number, have been impostures, and, by idle and crafty brains, merely contrived and feigned, after the event past.

Chapter 36

OF AMBITION

Ambition is like choler, which is a humor that maketh men active, earnest, full of alacrity, and stirring, if it be not stopped; but if it be stopped, and cannot have its way, it becometh adust, and thereby malign and venomous. So ambitious men, if they find the way open for their rising, and still get forward, they are rather busy than dangerous; but if they be checked in their desires, they become secretly discontent, and look upon men and matters with an evil eye, and are best pleased when things go backward; which is the worst property in a servant of a prince or state. Therefore, it is good for princes, if they use ambitious men, to handle it so, as they be still progressive, and not retrograde; which, because it cannot be without inconvenience, it is good not to use such natures at all; for if they rise not with their service, they will take order to make their service fall with them. But since we have said, it were good not to use men of ambitious natures, except it be upon necessity, it is fit we speak in what cases they are of necessity. Good commanders in the wars must be taken, be they never so ambitious; for the use of their service dispenseth with the rest; and to take a soldier without ambition, is to pull off his spurs. There is also great use of ambitious men in being screens to princes in matters of danger and envy; for no man will take that part, except he be like a seeled dove, that mounts and mounts, because he cannot see about him. There is use, also, of ambitious men, in pulling down the greatness of any subject that overtops; as Tiberius used Macro in the pulling down of Sejanus. Since, therefore, they must be used in such cases, there resteth to speak how they are to be bridled, that they may be less dangerous. There is less danger of them if they be of mean birth, than if they be noble; and if they be rather harsh of nature, than gracious and popular; and if they be rather new raised, than grown cunning and fortified in their greatness. It is counted by some a weakness in princes to have favorites; but it is, of all others, the best remedy against ambitious great ones; for when the way of pleasuring and displeasuring lieth by the favorite, it is impossible any other should be over-great. Another means to curb them, is, to balance them by others as proud as they; but then there must be some middle counsellors, to keep things steady, for without that ballast, the ship will roll too much. At the least, a prince may animate and inure some meaner persons to be, as it were, scourges to ambitious men. As for the having of them obnoxious to ruin, if they be of fearful natures, it may do well; but if they be stout and daring, it may precipitate their designs, and prove dangerous. As for the pulling of them down, if the affairs require it, and that it may not be done with safety suddenly, the only way is, the interchange continually of favors and disgraces, whereby they may not know what to expect, and be, as it were, in a wood. Of ambitions, it is less harmful the ambition to prevail in great things, than that other to appear in every thing; for that breeds confusion, and mars business; but yet, it is less danger to have an ambitious man stirring in business, than great in dependencies. He that seeketh to be eminent amongst able men, hath a great task, but that is ever good for the public; but he that plots to be the only figure amongst ciphers, is the decay of a whole age. Honor hath three things in it: the vantage-ground to do good; the approach to kings and principal persons; and the raising of a man's own fortunes. He that hath the best of these intentions, when he aspireth, is an honest man; and that prince that can discern of these intentions in another that aspireth, is a wise prince. Generally, let princes and states choose such ministers as are more sensible of duty than of rising, and such as love business rather upon conscience than upon bravery; and let them discern a busy nature from a willing mind.

Chapter 37

OF MASQUES AND TRIUMPHS

These things are but toys to come amongst such serious observations; but yet, since princes will have such things, it is better they should be graced with elegancy, than daubed with cost. Dancing to song is a thing of great state and pleasure. I understand it that the song be in choir, placed aloft, and accompanied with some broken music, and the ditty fitted to the device. Acting in song, especially in dialogues, hath an extreme good grace; I say acting, not dancing (for that is a mean and vulgar thing); and the voices of the dialogue would be strong and manly (a base and a tenor, no treble), and the ditty high and tragical, not nice or dainty. Several choirs, placed one over against another, and taking the voices by catches anthem-wise, give great pleasure. Turning dances into figure is a childish curiosity; and, generally, let it be noted, that those things which I here set down are such as do naturally take the sense, and not respect petty wonderments. It is true, the alterations of scenes, so it be quietly and without noise, are things of great beauty and pleasure: for they feed and relieve the eye before it be full of the same object. Let the scenes abound with light, specially colored and varied; and let the masquers, or any other that are to come down from the scene, have some motions upon the scene itself before their coming down; for it draws the eye strangely, and makes it with great pleasure to desire to see that it cannot perfectly discern. Let the songs be loud and cheerful, and not chirpings or pulings; let the music, likewise, be sharp and loud, and well placed. The colors that show best by candlelight, are white, carnation, and a kind of sea-water green; and ouches, or spangs, as they are of no great cost, so they are of most glory. As for rich embroidery, it is lost and not discerned. Let the suits of the masquers be graceful, and such as become the person when the vizors are off; not after examples of known attires, Turks, soldiers, mariners, and the like. Let anti-masques not be long; they have been commonly of fools, satyrs, baboons, wild men, antics, beasts, sprites, witches, Ethiopes, pigmies, turquets, nymphs, rustics, Cupids, statues moving, and the like. As for angels, it is not comical enough to put them in anti-masques; and any thing that is hideous, as devils, giants, is, on the other side, as unfit; but, chiefly, let the music of them be recreative, and with some strange changes. Some sweet odors suddenly coming forth, without any drops falling, are, in such a company as there is steam and heat, things of great pleasure and refreshment. Double masques, one of men, another of ladies, addeth state and variety; but all is nothing, except the room be kept clear and neat.

For justs, and tourneys, and barriers, the glories of them are chiefly in the chariots, wherein the challengers make their entry; especially if they be drawn with strange beasts, as lions, bears, camels, and the like; or in the devices of their entrance, or in the bravery of their liveries, or in the goodly furniture of their horses and armor. But enough of these toys.

Chapter 38

Of Nature in Men

Nature is often hidden, sometimes overcome, seldom extinguished. Force maketh nature more violent in the return; doctrine and discourse maketh nature less importune, but custom only doth alter and subdue nature. He that seeketh victory over his nature, let him not set himself too great nor too small tasks; for the first will make him dejected by often failings, and the second will make him a small proceeder, though by often prevailings. And at the first, let him practise with helps, as swimmers do with bladders, or rushes; but, after a time, let him practise with disadvantages, as dancers do with thick shoes; for it breeds great perfection, if the practice be harder than the use. Where nature is mighty, and therefore the victory hard, the degrees had need be, first, to stay and arrest nature in time; like to him that would say over the four and twenty letters when he was angry; then to go less in quantity: as if one should, in forbearing wine, come from drinking healths to a draught at a meal; and, lastly, to discontinue altogether; but if a man have the fortitude and resolution to enfranchise himself at once, that is the best:—

> *"Optimus ille animi vindex lædentia pectus*
> *Vincula qui rupit, dedoluitque semel."*

Neither is the ancient rule amiss, to bend nature as a wand to a contrary extreme, whereby to set it right; understanding it where the contrary extreme is no vice. Let not a man force a habit upon himself with a perpetual continuance, but with some intermission, for both the pause reinforceth the new onset; and if a man that is not perfect be ever in practice, he shall as well practise his errors as his abilities, and induce one habit of both; and there is no means to help this but by seasonable intermissions. But let not a man trust his victory over his nature too far; for nature will lie buried a great time, and yet revive upon the occasion or temptation; like as it was with Æsop's damsel, turned from a cat to a woman, who sat very demurely at the board's end till a mouse ran before her. Therefore, let a man either avoid the occasion altogether, or put himself often to it, that he may be little moved with it. A man's nature is best perceived in privateness, for there is no affectation; in passion, for that putteth a man out of his precepts; and in a new case or experiment, for there custom leaveth him. They are happy men whose natures sort with their vocations; otherwise they may say, "Multum incola fuit anima mea," when they converse in those things they do not affect. In studies, whatsoever a man commandeth upon himself, let him set hours for it: but whatsoever is agreeable to his nature, let him take no care for any set times; for his thoughts will fly to it of themselves, so as the spaces of other business or studies will suffice. A man's nature runs either to herbs or weeds; therefore, let him seasonably water the one, and destroy the other.

Chapter 39

OF CUSTOM AND EDUCATION

Men's thoughts are much according to their inclination; their discourse and speeches according to their learning and infused opinions; but their deeds are, after, as they have been accustomed; and, therefore, as Machiavel well noteth (though in an evil-favored instance), there is no trusting to the force of nature, nor to the bravery of words, except it be corroborate by custom. His instance is, that, for the achieving of a desperate conspiracy, a man should not rest upon the fierceness of any man's nature, or his resolute undertakings, but take such a one as hath had his hands formerly in blood; but Machiavel knew not of a Friar Clement, nor a Ravaillac, nor a Jaureguy, nor a Baltazar Gerard; yet his rule holdeth still, that nature, nor the engagement of words, are not so forcible as custom. Only superstition is now so well advanced, that men of the first blood are as firm as butchers by occupation; and votary resolution is made equipollent to custom, even in matter of blood. In other things, the predominancy of custom is everywhere visible, insomuch as a man would wonder to hear men profess, protest, engage, give great words, and then do just as they have done before, as if they were dead images and engines, moved only by the wheels of custom. We see, also, the reign or tyranny of custom, what it is.

The Indians (I mean the sect of their wise men) lay themselves quietly upon a stack of wood, and so sacrifice themselves by fire; nay, the wives strive to be burned with the corpses of their husbands. The lads of Sparta, of ancient time, were wont to be scourged upon the altar of Diana, without so much as quecking. I remember, in the beginning of Queen Elizabeth's time of England, an Irish rebel condemned, put up a petition to the deputy that he might be hanged in a withe, and not in a halter, because it had been so used with former rebels. There be monks in Russia for penance, that will sit a whole night in a vessel of water, till they be engaged with hard ice. Many examples may be put of the force of custom, both upon mind and body; therefore, since custom is the principal magistrate of man's life, let men, by all means, endeavor to obtain good customs. Certainly, custom is most perfect when it beginneth in young years: this we call education, which is, in effect, but an early custom. So we see, in languages, the tongue is more pliant to all expressions and sounds, the joints are more supple to all feats of activity and motions in youth, than afterwards; for it is true, that late learners cannot so well take the ply, except it be in some minds that have not suffered themselves to fix, but have kept themselves open and prepared to receive continual amendment, which is exceeding rare. But if the force of custom, simple and separate, be great, the force of custom, copulate and conjoined and collegiate, is far greater; for there example teacheth, company comforteth, emulation quickeneth, glory raiseth; so as in such places the force of custom is in his exaltation. Certainly, the great multiplication of virtues upon human nature resteth upon societies well ordained and disciplined; for commonwealths and good governments do nourish virtue grown, but do not much mend the seeds; but the misery is, that the most effectual means are now applied to the ends least to be desired.

Chapter 40

OF FORTUNE

It cannot be denied, but outward accidents conduce much to fortune; favor, opportunity, death of others, occasion fitting virtue; but, chiefly, the mould of a man's fortune is in his own hands: "Faber quisque fortunæ suæ," saith the poet; and the most frequent of external causes, is that the folly of one man is the fortune of another; for no man prospers so suddenly as by others' errors. "Serpens nisi serpentem comederit non fit draco." Overt and apparent virtues bring forth praise: but there be secret and hidden virtues that bring forth fortune; certain deliveries of a man's self, which have no name. The Spanish name, "disemboltura," partly expresseth them, when there be not stonds nor restiveness in a man's nature, but that the wheels of his mind keep way with the wheels of his fortune; for so Livy (after he had described Cato Major in these words, "In illo viro, tantum robur corporis et animi fuit, ut quocunque loco natus esset, fortunam sibi facturus videretur,") falleth upon that, that he had "versatile ingenium:" therefore, if a man look sharply and attentively, he shall see Fortune; for though she be blind, yet she is not invisible. The way of Fortune is like the milky way in the sky; which is a meeting, or knot, of a number of small stars, not seen asunder, but giving light together; so are there a number of little and scarce discerned virtues, or rather faculties and customs, that make men fortunate. The Italians note some of them, such as a man would little think. When they speak of one that cannot do amiss, they will throw in into his other conditions, that he hath "Poco di matto;" and, certainly, there be not two more fortunate properties, than to have a little of the fool, and not too much of the honest; therefore, extreme lovers of their country, or masters, were never fortunate; neither can they be, for when a man placeth his thoughts without himself, he goeth not his own way. A hasty fortune maketh an enterpriser and remover (the French hath it better, "entreprenant," or "remuant"); but the exercised fortune maketh the able man. Fortune is to be honored and respected, and it be but for her daughters, Confidence and Reputation; for those two Felicity breedeth; the first within a man's self, the latter in others towards him. All wise men, to decline the envy of their own virtues, use to ascribe them to

Providence and Fortune; for so they may the better assume them; and, besides, it is greatness in a man to be the care of the higher powers. So Cæsar said to the pilot in the tempest, "Cæsarem portas, et fortunam ejus." So Sylla chose the name of "Felix," and not of "Magnus;" and it hath been noted, that those who ascribe openly too much to their own wisdom and policy, end unfortunate. It is written, that Timotheus the Athenian, after he had, in the account he gave to the state of his government, often interlaced his speech, "and in this Fortune had no part," never prospered in any thing he undertook afterwards. Certainly there be, whose fortunes are like Homer's verses, that have a slide and easiness more than the verses of other poets; as Plutarch saith of Timoleon's fortune in respect of that of Agesilaus or Epaminondas; and that this should be, no doubt it is much in a man's self.

Chapter 41

Of Usury

M any have made witty invectives against usury. They say that it is pity the devil should have God's part, which is the tithe; that the usurer is the greatest Sabbath-breaker, because his plough goeth every Sunday; that the usurer is the drone that Virgil speaketh of:—

"Ignavum fucos pecus a præsepibus arcent;"

that the usurer breaketh the first law that was made for mankind after the fall, which was, "in sudore vultûs tui comedes panem tuum;" not, "in sudore vultûs alieni;" that usurers should have orange-tawny bonnets, because they do Judaize; that it is against nature for money to beget money, and the like. I say this only, that usury is a "concessum propter duritiem cordis;" for, since there must be borrowing and lending, and men are so hard of heart as they will not lend freely, usury must be permitted. Some others have made suspicious and cunning propositions of banks, discovery of men's estates, and other inventions; but few have spoken of usury usefully. It is good to set before us the incommodities and commodities of usury, that the good may be either weighed out, or culled out; and warily to provide, that, while we make forth to that which is better, we meet not with that which is worse.

The discommodities of usury are, first, that it makes fewer merchants; for were it not for this lazy trade of usury, money would not lie still, but would, in great part, be employed upon merchandising, which is the "vena porta" of wealth in a state. The second, that it makes poor merchants; for as a farmer cannot husband his ground so well if he sit at a great rent, so the merchant cannot drive his trade so well if he sit at great usury. The third is incident to the other two; and that is, the decay of customs of kings, or states, which ebb or flow with merchandising. The fourth, that it bringeth the treasure of a realm or state into a few hands; for the usurer being at certainties, and others at uncertainties, at the end of the game most of the money will be in the box; and ever a state flourisheth when wealth is more equally spread. The fifth, that it beats down the price of land; for the employment of money is chiefly either merchandising or purchasing, and usury waylays both. The sixth, that it doth dull and damp all industries, improvements, and new inventions, wherein money would be stirring, if it were not for this slug. The last, that it is the canker and ruin of many men's estates, which, in process of time, breeds a public poverty.

On the other side, the commodities of usury are, first, that, howsoever usury in some respect hindereth merchandising, yet in some other it advanceth it; for it is certain that the greatest part of trade is driven by young merchants upon borrowing at interest; so as if the usurer either call in, or keep back his money, there will ensue presently a great stand of trade. The second is, that, were it not for this easy borrowing upon interest, men's necessities would draw upon them a most sudden undoing, in that they would be forced to sell their means (be it lands or goods), far under foot; and so, whereas usury doth but gnaw upon them, bad markets would swallow them quite up. As for mortgaging or pawning, it will little mend the matter; for either men will not take pawns without use, or, if they do, they will look precisely for the forfeiture. I remember a cruel moneyed man in the country, that would say, "The devil take this usury, it keeps us from forfeitures of mortgages and bonds." The third and last is, that it is a vanity to conceive that there would be ordinary borrowing without profit; and it is impossible to conceive the number of inconveniences that will ensue, if borrowing be cramped. Therefore, to speak of the abolishing of usury is idle; all states have ever had it in one kind or rate, or other; so as that opinion must be sent to Utopia.

To speak now of the reformation and reglement of usury, how the discommodities of it may be best avoided, and the commodities retained. It appears, by the balance of commodities and discommodities of usury, two things are to be reconciled; the one, that the tooth of usury be grinded, that it bite not too much; the other, that there be left open a means to invite moneyed men to lend to the merchants, for the continuing and quickening of trade. This cannot be done, except you introduce two several sorts of usury, a less and a greater; for if you reduce usury to one low rate, it will ease the common borrower, but the merchant will be to seek for money; and it is to be noted that the trade of merchandise being the most lucrative, may bear usury at a good rate; other contracts not so.

To serve both intentions, the way would be briefly thus: that there be two rates of usury; the one free and general for all; the other under license only to certain persons, and in certain places of merchandising. First, therefore, let usury in general be reduced to five in the hundred, and let that rate be proclaimed to be free and current; and let the state shut itself out to take any penalty for the same. This will preserve borrowing from any general stop or dryness; this will ease infinite borrowers in the country; this will, in good part, raise the price of land, because land purchased at sixteen years' purchase will yield six in the hundred, and somewhat more, whereas this rate of interest yields but five. This, by like reason, will encourage and edge industrious and profitable improvements, because many will rather venture in that kind, than take five in the hundred, especially having been used to greater profit. Secondly, let there be certain persons licensed to lend to known merchants upon usury, at a higher rate, and let it be with the cautions following: Let the rate be, even with the merchant himself, somewhat more easy than that he used formerly to pay; for, by that means, all borrowers shall have some ease by this reformation, be he merchant, or whosoever; let it be no bank or common stock, but every man be master of his own money; not that I altogether mislike banks, but they will hardly be brooked, in regard of certain suspicions. Let the state be answered some small matter for the license, and the rest left to the lender; for if the abatement be but small, it will no whit discourage the lender; for he, for example, that took before ten or nine in the hundred, will sooner descend to eight in the hundred, than give over his trade of usury, and go from certain gains to gains of hazard. Let these licensed lenders be in number indefinite, but restrained to certain principal cities and towns of merchandising; for then they will be hardly able to color other men's moneys in the country, so as the license of nine will not suck away the current rate of five; for no man will send his moneys far off, nor put them into unknown hands.

If it be objected, that this doth in a sort authorize usury, which before was in some places but permissive; the answer is, that it is better to mitigate usury by declaration, than to suffer it to rage by connivance.

Chapter 42

OF YOUTH AND AGE

A man that is young in years may be old in hours, if he have lost no time; but that happeneth rarely. Generally, youth is like the first cogitations, not so wise as the second; for there is a youth in thoughts as well as in ages; and yet the invention of young men is more lively than that of old, and imaginations stream into their minds better, and, as it were, more divinely. Natures that have much heat, and great and violent desires and perturbations, are not ripe for action till they have passed the meridian of their years: as it was with Julius Cæsar and Septimius Severus; of the latter of whom it is said, "Juventutem egit erroribus, imo furoribus plenam;" and yet he was the ablest emperor, almost, of all the list; but reposed natures may do well in youth, as it is seen in Augustus Cæsar, Cosmus Duke of Florence, Gaston de Foix, and others. On the other side, heat and vivacity in age is an excellent composition for business. Young men are fitter to invent than to judge, fitter for execution than for counsel, and fitter for new projects than for settled business; for the experience of age, in things that fall within the compass of it, directeth them; but in new things abuseth them. The errors of young men are the ruin of business; but the errors of aged men amount but to this, that more might have been done, or sooner.

Young men, in the conduct and manage of actions, embrace more than they can hold, stir more than they can quiet; fly to the end, without consideration of the means and degrees; pursue some few principles which they have chanced upon absurdly; care not to innovate, which draws unknown inconveniences; use extreme remedies at first; and that, which doubleth all errors, will not acknowledge or retract them, like an unready horse, that will neither stop nor turn. Men of age object too much, consult too long, adventure too little, repent too soon, and seldom drive business home to the full period, but content themselves with a mediocrity of success. Certainly, it is good to compound employments of both; for that will be good for the present, because the virtues of either age may correct the defects of both; and good for succession, that young men may be learners, while men in age are actors; and, lastly, good for externe accidents, because authority followeth old men, and favor and popularity youth; but, for the moral part, perhaps, youth will have the preëminence, as age hath for the politic. A certain rabbin, upon the text, "Your young men shall see visions, and your old men shall dream dreams," inferreth that young men are admitted nearer to God than old, because vision is a clearer revelation than a dream; and, certainly, the more a man drinketh of the world, the more it intoxicateth; and age doth profit rather in the powers of understanding, than in the virtues of the will and affections. There be some have an over-early ripeness in their years, which fadeth betimes; these are, first, such as have brittle wits, the edge whereof is soon turned; such as was Hermogenes the rhetorician, whose books are exceedingly subtle; who afterwards waxed stupid. A second sort is of those that have some natural dispositions, which have better grace in youth than in age; such as is a fluent and luxuriant speech, which becomes youth well, but not age; so Tully saith of Hortensius: "Idem manebat, neque idem decebat." The third is of such as take too high a strain at the first, and are magnanimous more than tract of years can uphold; as was Scipio Africanus, of whom Livy saith, in effect, "Ultima primis cedebant."

Chapter 43

OF BEAUTY

Virtue is like a rich stone, best plain set; and surely virtue is best in a body that is comely, though not of delicate features, and that hath rather dignity of presence than beauty of aspect; neither is it always most seen, that very beautiful persons are otherwise of great virtue; as if nature were rather busy not to err, than in labor to produce excellency; and therefore they prove accomplished, but not of great spirit, and study rather behavior than virtue. But this holds not always; for Augustus Cæsar, Titus Vespasianus, Philip le Bel of France, Edward the Fourth of England, Alcibiades of Athens, Ismael the Sophy of Persia, were all high and great spirits, and yet the most beautiful men of their times. In beauty, that of favor is more than that of color; and that of decent and gracious motion, more than that of favor. That is the best part of beauty, which a picture cannot express; no, nor the first sight of the life. There is no excellent beauty that hath not some strangeness in the proportion. A man cannot tell whether Apelles, or Albert Durer, were the more trifler; whereof the one would make a personage by geometrical proportions; the other, by taking the best parts out of divers faces to make one excellent. Such personages, I think, would please nobody but the painter that made them: not but I think a painter may make a better face than ever was; but he must do it by a kind of felicity (as a musician that maketh an excellent air in music), and not by rule. A man shall see faces, that, if you examine them part by part, you shall find never a good, and yet altogether do well. If it be true that the principal part of beauty is in decent motion, certainly it is no marvel, though persons in years seem many times more amiable; "Pulchrorum autumnus pulcher;" for no youth can be comely but by pardon, and considering the youth as to make up the comeliness. Beauty is as summer fruits, which are easy to corrupt, and cannot last; and, for the most part, it makes a dissolute youth, and an age a little out of countenance; but yet certainly again, if it light well, it maketh virtues shine, and vices blush.

Chapter 44

OF DEFORMITY

Deformed persons are commonly even with nature; for, as nature hath done ill by them, so do they by nature, being for the most part (as the Scripture saith) "void of natural affection;" and so they have their revenge of nature. Certainly, there is a consent between the body and the mind, and where nature erreth in the one, she ventureth in the other: "Ubi peccat in uno, periclitatur in altero." But because there is in man an election, touching the frame of his mind, and a necessity in the frame of his body, the stars of natural inclination are sometimes obscured by the sun of discipline and virtue; therefore, it is good to consider of deformity, not as a sign which is more deceivable, but as a cause which seldom faileth of the effect. Whosoever hath any thing fixed in his person that doth induce contempt, hath also a perpetual spur in himself to rescue and deliver himself from scorn; therefore, all deformed persons are extreme bold; first, as in their own defence, as being exposed to scorn, but, in process of time, by a general habit. Also, it stirreth in them industry, and especially of this kind, to watch and observe the weakness of others, that they may have somewhat to repay. Again, in their superiors, it quencheth jealousy towards them, as persons that they think they may at pleasure despise; and it layeth their competitors and emulators asleep, as never believing they should be in possibility of advancement till they see them in possession; so that upon the matter, in a great wit, deformity is an advantage to rising. Kings in ancient times (and at this present in some countries) were wont to put great trust in eunuchs, because they that are envious towards all are more obnoxious and officious towards one; but yet their trust towards them hath rather been as to good spials, and good whisperers, than good magistrates and officers; and much like is the reason of deformed persons. Still the ground is, they will, if they be of spirit, seek to free themselves from scorn, which must be either by virtue or malice; and, therefore, let it not be marvelled, if sometimes they prove excellent persons; as was Agesilaüs, Zanger, the son of Solyman, Æsop, Gasca president of Peru; and Socrates may go likewise amongst them, with others.

Chapter 45

OF BUILDING

Houses are built to live in, and not to look on, therefore, let use be preferred before uniformity, except where both may be had. Leave the goodly fabrics of houses, for beauty only, to the enchanted palaces of the poets, who build them with small cost. He that builds a fair house upon an ill seat, committeth himself to prison; neither do I reckon it an ill seat only where the air is unwholesome, but likewise where the air is unequal. As you shall see many fine seats set upon a knap of ground environed with higher hills round about it, whereby the heat of the sun is pent in, and the wind gathereth as in troughs; so as you shall have, and that suddenly, as great diversity of heat and cold as if you dwelt in several places. Neither is it ill air only that maketh an ill seat; but ill ways, ill markets, and, if you will consult with Momus, ill neighbors. I speak not of many more: want of water, want of wood, shade, and shelter, want of fruitfulness, and mixture of grounds of several natures; want of prospect, want of level grounds, want of places at some near distance for sports of hunting, hawking, and races; too near the sea, too remote; having the commodity of navigable rivers, or the discommodity of their overflowing; too far off from great cities, which may hinder business; or too near them, which lurcheth all provisions, and maketh every thing dear; where a man hath a great living laid together, and where he is scanted; all which, as it is impossible perhaps to find together, so it is good to know them, and think of them, that a man may take as many as he can; and if he have several dwellings, that he sort them so, that what he wanteth in the one he may find in the other. Lucullus answered Pompey well, who, when he saw his stately galleries and rooms so large and lightsome, in one of his houses, said, "Surely, an excellent place for summer, but how do you do in winter?" Lucullus answered, "Why, do you not think me as wise as some fowls are, that ever change their abode towards the winter?"

To pass from the seat to the house itself, we will do as Cicero doth in the orator's art, who writes books De Oratore, and a book he entitles Orator; whereof the former delivers the precepts of the art, and the latter the perfection. We will therefore describe a princely palace, making a brief model thereof; for it is strange to see, now in Europe, such huge buildings as the Vatican and Escurial, and some others be, and yet scarce a very fair room in them.

First, therefore, I say, you cannot have a perfect palace, except you have two several sides; a side for the banquet, as is spoken of in the book of Esther, and a side for the household; the one for feasts and triumphs, and the other for dwelling. I understand both these sides to be not only returns, but parts of the front, and to be uniform without, though severally partitioned within; and to be on both sides of a great and stately tower in the midst of the front, that, as it were, joineth them together on either hand. I would have, on the side of the banquet in front, one only goodly room above stairs, of some forty foot high; and under it a room for a dressing or preparing place, at times of triumphs. On the other side, which is the household side, I wish it divided at the first into a hall and a chapel, (with a partition between), both of good state and bigness; and those not to go all the length, but to have at the further end a winter and a summer parlor, both fair; and under these rooms a fair and large cellar sunk under ground; and likewise some privy kitchens, with butteries, and pantries, and the like. As for the tower, I would have it two stories, of eighteen foot high apiece above the two wings; and a goodly leads upon the top, railed, with statues interposed; and the same tower to be divided into rooms, as shall be thought fit. The stairs likewise to the upper rooms, let them be upon a fair open newel, and finely railed in with images of wood cast into a brass color, and a very fair landing-place at the top. But this to be, if you do not point any of the lower rooms for a dining-place of servants; for, otherwise, you shall have the servants' dinner after your own; for the steam of it will come up as in a tunnel. And so much for the front; only I understand the height of the first stairs to be sixteen foot, which is the height of the lower room.

Beyond this front is there to be a fair court, but three sides of it of a far lower building than the front; and in all the four corners of that court fair staircases, cast into turrets on the outside, and not within the row of buildings themselves; but those towers are not to be of the height of the front, but rather proportionable to the lower building. Let the court not be paved, for that striketh up a great heat in summer, and much cold in winter; but only some side alleys with a cross, and the quarters to graze, being kept shorn, but not too near shorn. The row of return on the banquet side, let it be all stately galleries; in which galleries let there be three or five fine cupolas in the length of it, placed at equal distance, and fine colored windows of several works; on the household side, chambers of presence and ordinary entertainments, with some bedchambers; and let all three sides be a double house, without thorough lights on the sides, that you may have rooms from the sun, both for forenoon and afternoon. Cast it, also, that you may have rooms both for summer and winter; shady for summer, and warm for winter. You shall have sometimes fair houses so full of glass, that one cannot tell where to become to be out of the sun or cold. For imbowed windows, I hold them of good use; (in cities, indeed, upright do better, in respect of the uniformity towards the street;) for they be pretty retiring places for conference; and, besides, they keep both the wind and sun off; for that which would strike almost through the room doth scarce pass the window: but let them be but few, four in the court, on the sides only.

Beyond this court, let there be an inward court, of the same square and height, which is to be environed with the garden on all sides; and in the inside, cloistered on all sides upon decent and beautiful arches, as high as the first story; on the under story towards the garden, let it be turned to grotto, or place of shade, or estivation; and only have opening and windows towards the garden, and be level upon the floor, no whit sunk under ground to avoid all dampishness; and let there be a fountain, or some fair work of statues in the midst of this court, and to be paved as the other court was. These buildings to be for privy lodgings on both sides, and the end for privy galleries; whereof you must foresee that one of them be for an infirmary, if the prince or any special person should be sick, with chambers, bedchamber, "anticamera," and "recamera," joining to it; this upon the second story. Upon the ground story, a fair gallery, open, upon pillars; and upon the third story, likewise, an open gallery upon pillars, to take the prospect and freshness of the garden. At both corners of the further side, by way of return, let there be two delicate or rich cabinets, daintily paved, richly hanged, glazed with crystalline glass, and a rich cupola in the midst, and all other elegancy that can be thought upon. In the upper gallery, too, I wish that there may be, if the place will yield it, some fountains running in divers places from the wall, with some fine avoidances. And thus much for the model of the palace, save that you must have, before you come to the front, three courts: a green court plain, with a wall about it; a second court of the same, but more garnished with little turrets, or rather embellishments, upon the wall; and a third court, to make a square with the front, but not to be built, nor yet inclosed with a naked wall, but inclosed with terraces leaded aloft, and fairly garnished on the three sides, and cloistered on the inside with pillars, and not with arches below. As for offices, let them stand at distance, with some low galleries to pass from them to the palace itself.

Chapter 46

OF GARDENS

God Almighty first planted a garden; and, indeed, it is the purest of human pleasures; it is the greatest refreshment to the spirits of man; without which buildings and palaces are but gross handyworks; and a man shall ever see, that, when ages grow to civility and elegancy, men come to build stately, sooner than to garden finely; as if gardening were the greater perfection. I do hold it, in the royal ordering of gardens, there ought to be gardens for all the months in the year, in which, severally, things of beauty may be then in season. For December, and January, and the latter part of November, you must take such things as are green all winter: holly, ivy, bays, juniper, cypress-trees, yew, pineapple-trees; fir-trees, rosemary, lavender; periwinkle, the white, the purple, and the blue; germander, flags, orange-trees, lemon-trees, and myrtles, if they be stoved; and sweet marjoram, warm set. There followeth, for the latter part of January and February, the mezereon-tree, which then blossoms; crocus vernus, both the yellow and the gray; primroses, anemones, the early tulip, the hyacinthus orientalis, chamaïris fritellaria. For March, there come violets, especially the single blue, which are the earliest; the yellow daffodil, the daisy, the almond-tree in blossom, the peach-tree in blossom, the cornelian-tree in blossom, sweet-brier. In April, follow the double white violet, the wall-flower, the stock-gillyflower, the cowslip, flower-de-luces, and lilies of all natures; rosemary flowers, the tulip, the double peony, the pale daffodil, the French honeysuckle, the cherry-tree in blossom, the damascene and plum-trees in blossom, the white thorn in leaf, the lilac-tree. In May and June come pinks of all sorts, especially the blush-pink; roses of all kinds, except the musk, which comes later; honeysuckles, strawberries, bugloss, columbine, the French marigold, flos Africanus, cherry-tree in fruit, ribes, figs in fruit, rasps, vine-flowers, lavender in flowers, the sweet satyrian, with the white flower; herba muscaria, lilium convallium, the apple-tree in blossom. In July come gillyflowers of all varieties, musk-roses, the lime-tree in blossom, early pears, and plums in fruit, genitings, codlins. In August come plums of all sorts in fruit, pears, apricots, barberries, filberts, musk-melons, monks-hoods, of all colors. In September come grapes, apples, poppies of all colors, peaches, melocotones, nectarines, cornelians, wardens, quinces. In October, and the beginning of November, come services, medlars, bullaces, roses cut or removed to come late, hollyoaks, and such like. These particulars are for the climate of London; but my meaning is perceived, that you may have "ver perpetuum," as the place affords.

And because the breath of flowers is far sweeter in the air (where it comes and goes, like the warbling of music), than in the hand, therefore nothing is more fit for that delight, than to know what be the flowers and plants that do best perfume the air. Roses, damask and red, are fast flowers of their smell, so that you may walk by a whole row of them, and find nothing of their sweetness; yea, though it be in a morning's dew. Bays, likewise, yield no smell as they grow, rosemary little, nor sweet marjoram; that which, above all others, yields the sweetest smell in the air, is the violet, especially the white double violet, which comes twice a year, about the middle of April, and about Bartholomew-tide. Next to that is the musk-rose; then the strawberry leaves dying, with a most excellent cordial smell; then the flower of the vines, it is a little dust like the dust of a bent, which grows upon the cluster in the first coming forth; then sweet-brier, then wall-flowers, which are very delightful to be set under a parlor or lower chamber window; then pinks and gillyflowers, specially the matted pink and clove gillyflower; then the flowers of the lime-tree; then the honeysuckles, so they be somewhat afar off. Of bean-flowers I speak not, because they are field-flowers; but those which perfume the air most delightfully, not passed by as the rest, but being trodden upon and crushed, are three; that is, burnet, wild thyme, and water-mints; therefore you are to set whole alleys of them, to have the pleasure when you walk or tread.

For gardens (speaking of those which are indeed prince-like, as we have done of buildings), the contents ought not well to be under thirty acres of ground, and to be divided into three parts; a green in the entrance, a heath, or desert, in the going forth, and the main garden in the midst, besides alleys on both sides; and I like well that four acres of ground be assigned to the green, six to the heath, four and four to either side, and twelve to the main garden. The green hath two pleasures: the one, because nothing is more pleasant to the eye than green grass kept finely shorn; the other, because it will give you a fair alley in the midst, by which you may go in front upon a stately hedge, which is to inclose the garden. But because the alley will be long, and in great heat of the year, or day, you ought not to buy the shade in the garden by going in the sun through the green; therefore you are, of either side the green, to plant a covert alley, upon carpenter's work, about twelve foot in height, by which you may go in shade into the garden. As for the making of knots or figures, with divers colored earths, that they may lie under the windows of the house on that side which the garden stands, they be but toys; you may see as good sights many times in tarts. The garden is best to be square, encompassed on all the four sides with a stately arched hedge: the arches to be upon pillars of carpenter's work, of some ten foot high, and six foot broad, and the spaces between of the same dimension with the breadth of the arch. Over the arches let there be an entire hedge of some four foot high, framed also upon carpenter's work; and upon the upper hedge, over every arch a little turret, with a belly enough to receive a cage of birds; and over every space between the arches some other little figure, with broad plates of round colored glass gilt, for the sun to play upon; but this hedge I intend to be raised upon a bank, not steep, but gently slope, of some six foot, set all with flowers. Also, I understand that this square of the garden should not be the whole breadth of the ground, but to leave on either side ground enough for diversity of side alleys, unto which the two covert alleys of the green may deliver you; but there must be no alleys with hedges at either end of this great inclosure; not at the hither end, for letting your prospect upon this fair hedge from the green; nor at the further end for letting your prospect from the hedge through the arches upon the heath.

For the ordering of the ground within the great hedge, I leave it to variety of device; advising, nevertheless, that whatsoever form you cast it into first, it be not too bushy, or full of work; wherein I, for my part, do not like images cut out in juniper or other garden stuff; they be for children. Little low hedges, round like welts, with some pretty pyramids, I like well; and in some places fair columns, upon frames of carpenter's work. I would also have the alleys spacious and fair. You may have closer alleys upon the side grounds, but none in the main garden. I wish, also, in the very middle, a fair mount, with three ascents and alleys, enough for four to walk abreast; which I would have to be perfect circles, without any bulwarks or embossments; and the whole mount to be thirty foot high, and some fine banqueting-house, with some chimneys neatly cast, and without too much glass.

For fountains, they are a great beauty and refreshment; but pools mar all, and make the garden unwholesome, and full of flies and frogs. Fountains I intend to be of two natures; the one that sprinkleth or spouteth water;

the other, a fair receipt of water, of some thirty or forty foot square, but without fish, or slime, or mud. For the first, the ornaments of images, gilt or of marble, which are in use, do well; but the main matter is so to convey the water, as it never stay, either in the bowls or in the cistern; that the water be never by rest discolored, green, or red, or the like, or gather any mossiness or putrefaction; besides that, it is to be cleansed every day by the hand; also, some steps up to it, and some fine pavement about it, doth well. As for the other kind of fountain, which we may call a bathing-pool, it may admit much curiosity and beauty, wherewith we will not trouble ourselves: as, that the bottom be finely paved, and with images; the sides likewise; and, withal, embellished with colored glass, and such things of lustre; encompassed, also, with fine rails of low statues. But the main point is the same that we mentioned in the former kind of fountain; which is, that the water be in perpetual motion, fed by a water higher than the pool, and delivered into it by fair spouts, and then discharged away under ground, by some equality of bores, that it stay little; and for fine devices, of arching water without spilling, and making it rise in several forms (of feathers, drinking-glasses, canopies, and the like), they be pretty things to look on, but nothing to health and sweetness.

For the heath, which was the third part of our plot, I wish it to be framed as much as may be to a natural wildness. Trees I would have none in it, but some thickets made only of sweet-brier and honeysuckle, and some wild vine amongst; and the ground set with violets, strawberries, and primroses; for these are sweet, and prosper in the shade, and these to be in the heath here and there, not in any order. I like also little heaps, in the nature of molehills (such as are in wild heaths), to be set, some with wild thyme, some with pinks, some with germander, that gives a good flower to the eye; some with periwinkle, some with violets, some with strawberries, some with cowslips, some with daisies, some with red roses, some with lilium convallium, some with sweet-williams red, some with bear's-foot, and the like low flowers, being withal sweet and sightly; part of which heaps to be with standards of little bushes pricked upon their top, and part without; the standards to be roses, juniper, holly, barberries (but here and there, because of the smell of their blossom), red currants, gooseberries, rosemary, bays, sweetbrier, and such like; but these standards to be kept with cutting, that they grow not out of course.

For the side grounds, you are to fill them with variety of alleys, private, to give a full shade; some of them wheresoever the sun be. You are to frame some of them likewise for shelter, that when the wind blows sharp, you may walk as in a gallery: and those alleys must be likewise hedged at both ends, to keep out the wind; and these closer alleys must be ever finely gravelled, and no grass, because of going wet. In many of these alleys, likewise, you are to set fruit-trees of all sorts, as well upon the walls as in ranges; and this should be generally observed, that the borders wherein you plant your fruit-trees be fair, and large, and low, and not steep; and set with fine flowers, but thin and sparingly, lest they deceive the trees. At the end of both the side grounds I would have a mount of some pretty height, leaving the wall of the inclosure breast high, to look abroad into the fields.

For the main garden, I do not deny but there should be some fair alleys ranged on both sides with fruit-trees, and some pretty tufts of fruit-trees and arbors with seats, set in some decent order; but these to be by no means set too thick, but to leave the main garden so as it be not close, but the air open and free. For as for shade, I would have you rest upon the alleys of the side grounds, there to walk, if you be disposed, in the heat of the year or day; but to make account that the main garden is for the more temperate parts of the year, and in the heat of summer for the morning and the evening or overcast days.

For aviaries, I like them not, except they be of that largeness as they may be turfed, and have living plants and bushes set in them; that the birds may have more scope and natural nestling, and that no foulness appear in the floor of the aviary. So I have made a platform of a princely garden, partly by precept, partly by drawing; not a model, but some general lines of it; and in this I have spared for no cost. But it is nothing for great princes, that, for the most part, taking advice with workmen, with no less cost set their things together, and sometimes add statues and such things for state and magnificence, but nothing to the true pleasure of a garden.

Chapter 47

OF NEGOTIATING

It is generally better to deal by speech than by letter; and by the mediation of a third, than by a man's self. Letters are good, when a man would draw an answer by letter back again; or when it may serve for a man's justification afterwards to produce his own letter, or where it may be danger to be interrupted or heard by pieces. To deal in person is good, when a man's face breedeth regard, as commonly with inferiors; or in tender cases, where a man's eye upon the countenance of him with whom he speaketh, may give him a direction how far to go; and, generally, where a man will reserve to himself liberty, either to disavow or to expound. In choice of instruments, it is better to choose men of a plainer sort, that are like to do that that is committed to them, and to report back again faithfully the success, than those that are cunning to contrive out of other men's business somewhat to grace themselves, and will help the matter in report, for satisfaction sake. Use also such persons as affect the business wherein they are employed, for that quickeneth much; and such as are fit for the matter, as bold men for expostulation, fairspoken men for persuasion, crafty men for inquiry and observation, froward and absurd men for business that doth not well bear out itself. Use also such as have been lucky and prevailed before in things wherein you have employed them; for that breeds confidence, and they will strive to maintain their prescription. It is better to sound a person with whom one deals afar off, than to fall upon the point at first, except you mean to surprise him by some short question. It is better dealing with men in appetite, than with those that are where they would be. If a man deal with another upon conditions, the start of first performance is all; which a man cannot reasonably demand, except either the nature of the thing be such, which must go before; or else a man can persuade the other party, that he shall still need him in some other thing; or else that he be counted the honester man. All practice is to discover, or to work. Men discover themselves in trust, in passion, at unawares; and, of necessity, when they would have somewhat done, and cannot find an apt pretext. If you would work any man, you must either know his nature and fashions, and so lead him;

or his ends, and so persuade him; or his weakness and disadvantages, and so awe him; or those that have interest in him, and so govern him. In dealing with cunning persons, we must ever consider their ends, to interpret their speeches; and it is good to say little to them, and that which they least look for. In all negotiations of difficulty, a man may not look to sow and reap at once; but must prepare business, and so ripen it by degrees.

Chapter 48

Of Followers and Friends

Costly followers are not to be liked, lest, while a man maketh his train longer, he make his wings shorter. I reckon to be costly, not them alone which charge the purse, but which are wearisome and importune in suits. Ordinary followers ought to challenge no higher conditions than countenance, recommendation, and protection from wrongs. Factious followers are worse to be liked, which follow not upon affection to him with whom they range themselves, but upon discontentment conceived against some other; whereupon commonly ensueth that ill intelligence, that we many times see between great personages. Likewise glorious followers, who make themselves as trumpets of the commendations of those they follow, are full of inconvenience, for they taint business through want of secrecy; and they export honor from a man, and make him a return in envy. There is a kind of followers, likewise, which are dangerous, being indeed espials; which inquire the secrets of the house, and bear tales of them to others; yet such men, many times, are in great favor, for they are officious, and commonly exchange tales. The following, by certain estates of men, answerable to that which a great person himself professeth (as of soldiers to him that hath been employed in the wars, and the like), hath ever been a thing civil and well taken even in monarchies, so it be without too much pomp or popularity. But the most honorable kind of following, is to be followed as one that apprehendeth to advance virtue and desert in all sorts of persons; and yet, where there is no eminent odds in sufficiency, it is better to take with the more passable, than with the more able; and, besides, to speak truth in base times, active men are of more use than virtuous. It is true, that, in government, it is good to use men of one rank equally; for to countenance some extraordinarily, is to make them insolent, and the rest discontent, because they may claim a due: but, contrariwise, in favor, to use men with much difference and election is good: for it maketh the persons preferred more thankful, and the rest more officious, because all is of favor. It is good discretion not to make too much of any man at the first, because one cannot hold out that proportion. To be governed, as we call it, by one, is not safe, for it shows softness, and gives a freedom to scandal and disreputation; for those that would not censure, or speak ill of a man immediately, will talk more boldly of those that are so great with them, and thereby wound their honor; yet to be distracted with many is worse, for it makes men to be of the last impression, and full of change. To take advice of some few friends is ever honorable; for lookers-on many times see more than gamesters, and the vale best discovereth the hill. There is little friendship in the world, and least of all between equals, which was wont to be magnified. That that is, is between superior and inferior, whose fortunes may comprehend the one the other.

Chapter 49

OF SUITORS

Many ill matters and projects are undertaken; and private suits do putrefy the public good. Many good matters are undertaken with bad minds; I mean not only corrupt minds, but crafty minds, that intend not performance. Some embrace suits, which never mean to deal effectually in them; but if they see there may be life in the matter, by some other mean they will be content to win a thank, or take a second reward, or, at least, to make use, in the mean time, of the suitor's hopes. Some take hold of suits only for an occasion to cross some other, or to make an information, whereof they could not otherwise have apt pretext, without care what become of the suit when that turn is served; or, generally, to make other men's business a kind of entertainment to bring in their own: nay, some undertake suits with a full purpose to let them fall, to the end to gratify the adverse party, or competitor. Surely, there is in some sort a right in every suit; either a right of equity, if it be a suit of controversy, or a right of desert, if it be a suit of petition. If affection lead a man to favor the wrong side in justice, let him rather use his countenance to compound the matter than to carry it. If affection lead a man to favor the less worthy in desert, let him do it without depraving or disabling the better deserver. In suits which a man doth not well understand, it is good to refer them to some friend of trust and judgment, that may report whether he may deal in them with honor; but let him choose well his referendaries, for else he may be led by the nose. Suitors are so distasted with delays and abuses, that plain dealing in denying to deal in suits at first, and reporting the success barely, and in challenging no more thanks than one hath deserved, is grown not only honorable, but also gracious. In suits of favor, the first coming ought to take little place; so far forth consideration may be had of his trust, that if intelligence of the matter could not otherwise have been had but by him, advantage be not taken of the note, but the party left to his other means, and in some sort recompensed for his discovery. To be ignorant of the value of a suit is simplicity; as well as to be ignorant of the right thereof, is want of conscience. Secrecy in suits is a great mean of obtaining; for voicing them to be in forwardness may discourage some kind of suitors, but doth quicken and awake others. But timing of the suit is the principal; timing, I say, not only in respect of the person that should grant it, but in respect of those which are like to cross it. Let a man, in the choice of his mean, rather choose the fittest mean, than the greatest mean; and rather them that deal in certain things, than those that are general. The reparation of a denial is sometimes equal to the first grant, if a man show himself neither dejected nor discontented. "Iniquum petas, ut æquum feras," is a good rule, where a man hath strength of favor; but otherwise a man were better rise in his suit; for he that would have ventured at first to have lost the suitor, will not, in the conclusion, lose both the suitor and his own former favor. Nothing is thought so easy a request to a great person as his letter: and yet if it be not in a good cause, it is so much out of his reputation. There are no worse instruments than these general contrivers of suits; for they are but a kind of poison and infection to public proceedings.

Chapter 50

OF STUDIES

S tudies serve for delight, for ornament, and for ability. Their chief use for delight, is in privateness and retiring; for ornament, is in discourse; and for ability, is in the judgment and disposition of business; for expert men can execute, and perhaps judge of particulars one by one; but the general counsels, and the plots and marshalling of affairs, come best from those that are learned. To spend too much time in studies, is sloth; to use them too much for ornament, is affectation; to make judgment wholly by their rules, is the humor of a scholar. They perfect nature, and are perfected by experience; for natural abilities are like natural plants, that need pruning by study; and studies themselves do give forth directions too much at large, except they be bounded in by experience. Crafty men contemn studies, simple men admire them, and wise men use them; for they teach not their own use; but that is a wisdom without them and above them, won by observation. Read not to contradict and confute, nor to believe and take for granted, nor to find talk and discourse, but to weigh and consider. Some books are to be tasted, others to be swallowed, and some few to be chewed and digested; that is, some books are to be read only in parts; others to be read, but not curiously; and some few to be read wholly, and with diligence and attention. Some books also may be read by deputy, and extracts made of them by others; but that would be only in the less important arguments and the meaner sort of books; else distilled books are, like common distilled waters, flashy things. Reading maketh a full man; conference a ready man; and writing an exact man; and, therefore, if a man write little, he had need have a great memory; if he confer little, he had need have a present wit; and if he read little, he had need have much cunning, to seem to know that he doth not. Histories make men wise; poets, witty; the mathematics, subtile; natural philosophy, deep; moral, grave; logic and rhetoric, able to contend: "Abeunt studia in mores;" nay, there is no stand or impediment in the wit, but may be wrought out by fit studies. Like as diseases of the body may have appropriate exercises, bowling is good for the stone and reins, shooting for the lungs and breast, gentle walking for the stomach, riding for the head and the like; so, if a man's wit be wandering, let him study the mathematics; for in demonstrations, if his wit be called away never so little, he must begin again; if his wit be not apt to distinguish or find difference, let him study the schoolmen, for they are "Cymini sectores." If he be not apt to beat over matters, and to call up one thing to prove and illustrate another, let him study the lawyers' cases; so every defect of the mind may have a special receipt.

Chapter 51

OF FACTION

Many have an opinion not wise, that for a prince to govern his estate, or for a great person to govern his proceedings, according to the respect of factions, is a principal part of policy; whereas, contrariwise, the chiefest wisdom is, either in ordering those things which are general, and wherein men of several factions do nevertheless agree, or in dealing with correspondence to particular persons, one by one; but I say not, that the consideration of factions is to be neglected. Mean men in their rising must adhere; but great men, that have strength in themselves, were better to maintain themselves indifferent and neutral; yet, even in beginners, to adhere so moderately, as he be a man of the one faction, which is most passable with the other, commonly giveth best way. The lower and weaker faction is the firmer in conjunction; and it is often seen, that a few that are stiff, do tire out a great number that are more moderate. When one of the factions is extinguished, the remaining subdivideth; as the faction between Lucullus and the rest of the nobles of the senate (which they called "optimates"), held out a while against the faction of Pompey and Cæsar; but when the senate's authority was pulled down, Cæsar and Pompey soon after brake. The faction or party of Antonius and Octavianus Cæsar, against Brutus and Cassius, held out likewise for a time; but when Brutus and Cassius were overthrown, then soon after Antonius and Octavianus brake and subdivided. These examples are of wars, but the same holdeth in private factions; and, therefore, those that are seconds in factions do many times, when the faction subdivideth, prove principals; but many times also they prove ciphers, and cashiered, for many a man's strength is in opposition; and when that faileth, he groweth out of use. It is commonly seen, that men once placed, take in with the contrary faction to that by which they enter; thinking, belike, that they have the first sure, and now are ready for a new purchase. The traitor in faction lightly goeth away with it; for when matters have stuck long in balancing, the winning of some one man casteth them, and he getteth all the thanks. The even carriage between two factions proceedeth not always of moderation, but of a trueness to a man's self, with end to make use of both. Certainly, in

Italy, they hold it a little suspect in popes, when they have often in their mouth, "Padre commune;" and take it to be a sign of one that meaneth to refer all to the greatness of his own house. Kings had need beware how they side themselves, and make themselves as of a faction or party; for leagues within the state are ever pernicious to monarchies; for they raise an obligation paramount to obligation of sovereignty, and make the king "tanquam unus ex nobis," as was to be seen in the League of France. When factions are carried too high and too violently, it is a sign of weakness in princes, and much to the prejudice both of their authority and business. The motions of factions under kings, ought to be like the motions (as the astronomers speak) of the inferior orbs, which may have their proper motions, but yet still are quietly carried by the higher motion of "primum mobile."

Chapter 52

OF CEREMONIES AND RESPECTS

H e that is only real, had need have exceeding great parts of virtue; as the stone had need to be rich that is set without foil; but if a man mark it well, it is in praise and commendation of men, as it is in gettings and gains; for the proverb is true, that "Light gains make heavy purses;" for light gains come thick, whereas great come but now and then. So it is true, that small matters win great commendation, because they are continually in use and in note; whereas the occasion of any great virtue cometh but on festivals; therefore it doth much add to a man's reputation, and is (as Queen Isabella said) like perpetual letters commendatory, to have good forms. To attain them, it almost sufficeth not to despise them; for so shall a man observe them in others; and let him trust himself with the rest; for if he labor too much to express them, he shall lose their grace, which is to be natural and unaffected. Some men's behavior is like a verse, wherein every syllable is measured; how can a man comprehend great matters, that breaketh his mind too much to small observations? Not to use ceremonies at all, is to teach others not to use them again, and so diminisheth respect to himself; especially they be not to be omitted to strangers and formal natures; but the dwelling upon them, and exalting them above the moon, is not only tedious, but doth diminish the faith and credit of him that speaks; and, certainly, there is a kind of conveying of effectual and imprinting passages amongst compliments, which is of singular use, if a man can hit upon it. Amongst a man's peers, a man shall be sure of familiarity, and, therefore, it is good a little to keep state; amongst a man's inferiors, one shall be sure of reverence, and therefore it is good a little to be familiar. He that is too much in any thing, so that he giveth another occasion of satiety, maketh himself cheap. To apply one's self to others, is good, so it be with demonstration that a man doth it upon regard, and not upon facility. It is a good precept, generally in seconding another, yet to add somewhat of one's own; as, if you will grant his opinion, let it be with some distinction; if you will follow his motion, let it be with condition; if you allow his counsel, let it be with alleging further reason. Men had need beware how they be too perfect in compliments; for be they never so sufficient otherwise, their enviers will be sure to give them that attribute to the disadvantage of their greater virtues. It is loss, also, in business, to be too full of respects, or to be too curious in observing times and opportunities. Solomon saith, "He that considereth the wind shall not sow, and he that looketh to the clouds shall not reap." A wise man will make more opportunities than he finds. Men's behavior should be like their apparel, not too strait or point device, but free for exercise or motion.

Chapter 53

OF PRAISE

P raise is the reflection of virtue; but it is glass, or body, which giveth the reflection. If it be from the common people, it is commonly false and naught, and rather followeth vain persons than virtuous; for the common people understand not many excellent virtues. The lowest virtues draw praise from them, the middle virtues work in them astonishment or admiration, but of the highest virtues they have no sense or perceiving at all; but shows and "species virtutibus similes," serve best with them. Certainly, fame is like a river, that beareth up things light and swollen, and drowns things weighty and solid; but if persons of quality and judgment concur, then it is (as the Scripture saith), "Nomen bonum instar unguenti fragrantis:" it filleth all round about, and will not easily away; for the odors of ointments are more durable than those of flowers. There be so many false points of praise, that a man may justly hold it a suspect. Some praises proceed merely of flattery; and if he be an ordinary flatterer, he will have certain common attributes, which may serve every man; if he be a cunning flatterer, he will follow the arch-flatterer, which is a man's self, and wherein a man thinketh best of himself, therein the flatterer will uphold him most. But if he be an impudent flatterer, look wherein a man is conscious to himself that he is most defective, and is most out of countenance in himself, that will the flatterer entitle him to, perforce, "spretâ conscientiâ." Some praises come of good wishes and respects, which is a form due in civility to kings and great persons, "laudando præcipere;" when, by telling men what they are, they represent to them what they should be; some men are praised maliciously to their hurt, thereby to stir envy and jealousy towards them: "Pessimum genus inimicorum laudantium;" insomuch as it was a proverb amongst the Grecians, that "he that was praised to his hurt, should have a push rise upon his nose;" as we say that a blister will rise upon one's tongue that tells a lie; certainly, moderate praise, used with opportunity, and not vulgar, is that which doth the good. Solomon saith: "He that praiseth his friend aloud, rising early, it shall be to him no better than a curse." Too much magnifying of man or matter doth irritate contradiction, and procure envy and scorn. To praise a man's self cannot be decent, except it be in rare cases; but to praise a man's office or profession, he may do it with good grace, and with a kind of magnanimity. The cardinals of Rome, which are theologues, and friars, and schoolmen, have a phrase of notable contempt and scorn towards civil business; for they call all temporal business of wars, embassages, judicature, and other employments, sbirrerie, which is under-sheriffries, as if they were but matters for under-sheriffs and catchpoles; though many times those under-sheriffries do more good than their high speculations. St. Paul, when he boasts of himself, he doth oft interlace, "I speak like a fool:" but speaking of his calling, he saith, "Magnificabo apostolatum meum."

Chapter 54

OF VAINGLORY

It was prettily devised of Æsop, the fly sat upon the axle-tree of the chariot-wheel, and said, "What a dust do I raise!" So are there some vain persons, that, whatsoever goeth alone, or moveth upon greater means, if they have never so little hand in it, they think it is they that carry it. They that are glorious, must needs be factious; for all bravery stands upon comparisons. They must needs be violent, to make good their own vaunts; neither can they be secret, and therefore not effectual; but, according to the French proverb, "Beaucoup de bruit, peu de fruit;"— "much bruit, little fruit." Yet, certainly, there is use of this quality in civil affairs: where there is an opinion and fame to be created, either of virtue or greatness, these men are good trumpeters. Again, as Titus Livius noteth, in the case of Antiochus and the Ætolians, there are sometimes great effects of cross lies; as if a man that negotiates between two princes, to draw them to join in a war against the third, doth extol the forces of either of them above measure, the one to the other; and sometimes he that deals between man and man, raiseth his own credit with both, by pretending greater interest than he hath in either; and in these, and the like kinds, it often falls out, that somewhat is produced of nothing; for lies are sufficient to breed opinion, and opinion brings on substance. In military commanders and soldiers, vainglory is an essential point; for as iron sharpens iron, so by glory one courage sharpeneth another. In cases of great enterprise upon charge and adventure, a composition of glorious natures doth put life into business; and those that are of solid and sober natures, have more of the ballast than of the sail. In fame of learning, the flight will be slow without some feathers of ostentation: "Qui de contemnendâ gloriâ libros scribunt, nomen suum inscribunt." Socrates, Aristotle, Galen, were men full of ostentation: certainly, vainglory helpeth to perpetuate a man's memory; and virtue was never so beholden to human nature, as it received its due at the second hand. Neither had the fame of Cicero, Seneca, Plinius Secundus, borne her age so well if it had not been joined with some vanity in themselves; like unto varnish, that makes ceilings not only shine, but last. But all this while, when I speak of vainglory, I mean not of that property that

Tacitus doth attribute to Mucianus, "Omnium, quæ dixerat feceratque, arte quâdam ostentator;" for that proceeds not of vanity, but of natural magnanimity and discretion; and, in some persons, is not only comely, but gracious; for excusations, cessions, modesty itself, well governed, are but arts of ostentation; and amongst those arts there is none better than that which Plinius Secundus speaketh of, which is to be liberal of praise and commendation to others, in that wherein a man's self hath any perfection. For, saith Pliny, very wittily, "In commending another, you do yourself right; for he that you commend is either superior to you in that you commend, or inferior: if he be inferior, if he be to be commended, you much more; if he be superior, if he be not to be commended, you much less." Glorious men are the scorn of wise men, the admiration of fools, the idols of parasites, and the slaves of their own vaunts.

Chapter 55

OF HONOR AND REPUTATION

The winning of honor is but the revealing of a man's virtue and worth without disadvantage; for some in their actions do woo and affect honor and reputation; which sort of men are commonly much talked of, but inwardly little admired; and some, contrariwise, darken their virtue in the show of it, so as they be undervalued in opinion. If a man perform that which hath not been attempted before, or attempted and given over, or hath been achieved, but not with so good circumstance, he shall purchase more honor than by affecting a matter of greater difficulty or virtue, wherein he is but a follower. If a man so temper his actions, as in some one of them he doth content every faction or combination of people, the music will be the fuller. A man is an ill husband of his honor that entereth into any action, the failing wherein may disgrace him more than the carrying of it through can honor him. Honor that is gained and broken upon another hath the quickest reflection, like diamonds cut with facets; and therefore let a man contend to excel any competitors of his in honor, in outshooting them, if he can, in their own bow. Discreet followers and servants help much to reputation: "Omnis fama a domesticis emanat." Envy, which is the canker of honor, is best extinguished by declaring a man's self in his ends, rather to seek merit than fame; and by attributing a man's successes rather to Divine providence and felicity, than to his own virtue or policy. The true marshalling of the degrees of sovereign honor are these. In the first place are "conditores imperiorum," founders of states and commonwealths; such as were Romulus, Cyrus, Cæsar, Ottoman, Ismael: in the second place are "legislatores," lawgivers, which are also called second founders, or "perpetui principes," because they govern by their ordinances after they are gone; such were Lycurgus, Solon, Justinian, Edgar, Alphonsus of Castile, the Wise, that made the "Siete Partidas:" in the third place are "liberatores," or "salvatores," such as compound the long miseries of civil wars, or deliver their countries from servitude of strangers or tyrants, as Augustus Cæsar, Vespasianus, Aurelianus, Theodoricus, King Henry the Seventh of England, King Henry the Fourth of France: in the fourth place are "propagatores," or "propugnatores imperii," such as in honorable wars enlarge their territories, or make noble defence against invaders: and, in the last place are "patres patriæ," which reign justly, and make the times good wherein they live; both which last kinds need no examples, they are in such number. Degrees of honor in subjects are, first, "participes curarum," those upon whom princes do discharge the greatest weight of their affairs, their right hands, as we call them; the next are "duces belli," great leaders, such as are princes' lieutenants, and do them notable services in the wars; the third are "gratiosi," favorites, such as exceed not this scantling, to be solace to the sovereign, and harmless to the people; and the fourth, "negotiis pares," such as have great places under princes, and execute their places with sufficiency. There is an honor, likewise, which may be ranked amongst the greatest, which happeneth rarely; that is, of such as sacrifice themselves to death or danger for the good of their country; as was M. Regulus, and the two Decii.

Chapter 56

OF JUDICATURE

Judges ought to remember that their office is "jus dicere," and not "jus dare;" to interpret law, and not to make law, or give law; else will it be like the authority claimed by the Church of Rome, which, under pretext of exposition of Scripture, doth not stick to add and alter, and to pronounce that which they do not find, and, by show of antiquity, to introduce novelty. Judges ought to be more learned than witty, more reverend than plausible, and more advised than confident. Above all things, integrity is their portion and proper virtue. "Cursed (saith the law) is he that removeth the landmark." The mislayer of a mere stone is to blame; but it is the unjust judge that is the capital remover of landmarks, when he defineth amiss of lands and property. One foul sentence doth more hurt than many foul examples; for these do but corrupt the stream, the other corrupteth the fountain: so saith Solomon, "Fons turbatus et vena corrupta est justus cadens in causâ suâ coram adversario." The office of judges may have reference unto the parties that sue, unto the advocates that plead, unto the clerks and ministers of justice underneath them, and to the sovereign or state above them.

First, for the causes or parties that sue. "There be (saith the Scripture) that turn judgment into wormwood;" and surely there be, also, that turn it into vinegar; for injustice maketh it bitter, and delays make it sour. The principal duty of a judge is to suppress force and fraud; whereof force is the more pernicious when it is open, and fraud when it is close and disguised. Add thereto contentious suits, which ought to be spewed out, as the surfeit of courts. A judge ought to prepare his way to a just sentence, as God useth to prepare his way, by raising valleys and taking down hills; so when there appeareth on either side a high hand, violent prosecution, cunning advantages taken, combination, power, great counsel, then is the virtue of a judge seen to make inequality equal, that he may plant his judgment as upon an even ground. "Qui fortiter emungit, elicit sanguinem;" and where the wine-press is hard wrought, it yields a harsh wine, that tastes of the grape-stone. Judges must beware of hard constructions and strained inferences; for there is no worse torture than the torture of laws. Especially in case of laws penal, they ought to have care that that which was meant for terror be not turned into rigor; and that they bring not upon the people that shower whereof the Scripture speaketh, "Pluet super eos laqueos;" for penal laws pressed, are a shower of snares upon the people. Therefore let penal laws, if they have been sleepers of long, or if they be grown unfit for the present time, be by wise judges confined in the execution: "Judicis officium est, ut res, ita tempora rerum," &c. In causes of life and death, judges ought (as far as the law permitteth) in justice to remember mercy, and to cast a severe eye upon the example, but a merciful eye upon the person.

Secondly, for the advocates and counsel that plead. Patience and gravity of hearing is an essential part of justice, and an overspeaking judge is no well-tuned cymbal. It is no grace to a judge first to find that which he might have heard in due time from the bar; or to show quickness of conceit in cutting off evidence or counsel too short, or to prevent information by questions, though pertinent. The parts of a judge in hearing are four: to direct the evidence; to moderate length, repetition, of impertinency of speech; to recapitulate, select, and collate the material points of that which hath been said; and to give the rule or sentence. Whatsoever is above these is too much, and proceedeth either of glory, and willingness to speak, or of impatience to hear, or of shortness of memory, or of want of a staid and equal attention. It is a strange thing to see that the boldness of advocates should prevail with judges; whereas, they should imitate God in whose seat they sit, who represseth the presumptuous, and giveth grace to the modest; but it is more strange, that judges should have noted favorites, which cannot but cause multiplication of fees, and suspicion of by-ways. There is due from the judge to the advocate some commendation and gracing, where causes are well handled and fair pleaded, especially towards the side which obtaineth not; for that upholds in the client the reputation of his counsel, and beats down in him the conceit of his cause. There is likewise due to the public a civil reprehension of advocates, where there appeareth cunning counsel, gross neglect, slight information, indiscreet pressing, or an over-bold defence; and let not the counsel at the bar chop with the judge, nor wind himself into the handling of the cause anew after the judge hath declared his sentence; but, on the other side, let not the judge meet the cause half-way, nor give occasion to the party to say, his counsel or proofs were not heard.

Thirdly, for that that concerns clerks and ministers. The place of justice is a hallowed place; and, therefore, not only the bench, but the foot-pace and precincts, and purprise thereof, ought to be preserved without scandal and corruption; for, certainly, "Grapes (as the Scripture saith) will not be gathered of thorns or thistles;" neither can justice yield her fruit with sweetness amongst the briers and brambles of catching and polling clerks and ministers. The attendance of courts is subject to four bad instruments: first, certain persons that are sowers of suits, which make the court swell, and the country pine: the second sort is of those that engage courts in quarrels of jurisdiction, and are not truly "amici curiæ," but "parasiti curiæ," in puffing a court up beyond her bounds for their own scraps and advantage: the third sort is of those that may be accounted the left hands of courts; persons that are full of nimble and sinister tricks and shifts, whereby they pervert the plain and direct courses of courts, and bring justice into oblique lines and labyrinths: and the fourth is the poller and exacter of fees; which justifies the common resemblance of the courts of justice to the bush, whereunto while the sheep flies for defence in weather, he is sure to lose part of his fleece. On the other side, an ancient clerk, skilful in precedents, wary in proceeding, and understanding in the business of the court, is an excellent finger of a court, and doth many times point the way to the judge himself.

Fourthly, for that which may concern the sovereign and estate. Judges ought, above all, to remember the conclusion of the Roman Twelve Tables, "Salus populi suprema lex;" and to know that laws, except they be in order to that end, are but things captious, and oracles not well inspired; therefore it is a happy thing in a state, when kings and states do often consult with judges; and again, when judges do often consult with the king and state: the one, when there is matter of law intervenient in business of state; the other, when there is some consideration of state intervenient in matter of law; for many times the things deduced to judgment may be "meum" and "tuum," when the reason and consequence thereof may trench to point of estate. I call matter of estate, not only the parts of sovereignty, but whatsoever introduceth any great alteration, or dangerous precedent, or concerneth manifestly any great portion of people; and let no man weakly conceive, that just laws and true policy have any antipathy, for they are like the spirits and sinews, that one moves with the other. Let judges also remember, that Solomon's throne was supported by lions on both sides;

let them be lions, but yet lions under the throne, being circumspect that they do not check or oppose any points of sovereignty. Let not judges also be so ignorant of their own right, as to think there is not left to them, as a principal part of their office, a wise use and application of laws; for they may remember what the apostle saith of a greater law than theirs: "Nos scimus quia lex bona est, modo quis eâ utatur legitime."

Chapter 57

OF ANGER

To seek to extinguish anger utterly is but a bravery of the Stoics. We have better oracles: "Be angry, but sin not; let not the sun go down upon your anger." Anger must be limited and confined, both in race and in time. We will first speak how the natural inclination and habit, "to be angry," may be attempered and calmed; secondly, how the particular motions of anger may be repressed, or, at least, refrained from doing mischief; thirdly, how to raise anger, or appease anger in another.

For the first, there is no other way but to meditate and ruminate well upon the effects of anger, how it troubles man's life; and the best time to do this is, to look back upon anger when the fit is thoroughly over. Seneca saith well, "that anger is like ruin, which breaks itself upon that it falls." The Scripture exhorteth us "to possess our souls in patience;" whosoever is out of patience, is out of possession of his soul. Men must not turn bees:—

"animasque in vulnere ponunt."

Anger is certainly a kind of baseness; as it appears well in the weakness of those subjects in whom it reigns, children, women, old folks, sick folks. Only men must beware that they carry their anger rather with scorn than with fear; so that they may seem rather to be above the injury than below it; which is a thing easily done, if a man will give law to himself in it.

For the second point, the causes and motives of anger are chiefly three. First, to be too sensible of hurt, for no man is angry that feels not himself hurt; and therefore tender and delicate persons must needs be oft angry, they have so many things to trouble them, which more robust natures have little sense of: the next is, the apprehension and construction of the injury offered, to be, in the circumstances thereof, full of contempt; for contempt is that which putteth an edge upon anger, as much, or more, than the hurt itself; and therefore, when men are ingenious in picking out circumstances of contempt, they do kindle their anger much: lastly, opinion of the touch of a man's reputation doth multiply and sharpen anger; wherein the remedy is, that a man should have, as Gonsalvo was wont to say, "Telam honoris crassiorem." But in all refrainings of anger, it is the best remedy to win time, and to make a man's self believe that the opportunity of his revenge is not yet come; but that he foresees a time for it, and so to still himself in the mean time, and reserve it.

To contain anger from mischief, though it take hold of a man, there be two things whereof you must have special caution: the one, of extreme bitterness of words, especially if they be aculeate and proper, for "communia maledicta" are nothing so much; and, again, that in anger a man reveal no secrets, for that makes him not fit for society: the other, that you do not peremptorily break off in any business in a fit of anger; but, howsoever you show bitterness, do not act any thing that is not revocable.

For raising and appeasing anger in another, it is done chiefly by choosing of times when men are frowardest and worst disposed to incense them; again, by gathering (as was touched before) all that you can find out to aggravate the contempt: and the two remedies are by the contraries; the former to take good times, when first to relate to a man an angry business, for the first impression is much; and the other is, to sever, as much as may be, the construction of the injury from the point of contempt; imputing it to misunderstanding, fear, passion, or what you will.

Chapter 58

OF VICISSITUDE OF THINGS

S olomon saith, "There is no new thing upon the earth;" so that as Plato had an imagination that all knowledge was but remembrance, so Solomon giveth his sentence, "That all novelty is but oblivion;" whereby you may see, that the river of Lethe runneth as well above ground as below. There is an abstruse astrologer that saith, if it were not for two things that are constant (the one is, that the fixed stars ever stand at like distance one from another, and never come nearer together, nor go further asunder; the other, that the diurnal motion perpetually keepeth time), no individual would last one moment; certain it is, that the matter is in a perpetual flux, and never at a stay. The great winding-sheets that bury all things in oblivion, are two,—deluges and earthquakes. As for conflagrations and great droughts, they do not merely dispeople, but destroy. Phaeton's car went but a day; and the three years' drought in the time of Elias, was but particular, and left people alive. As for the great burnings by lightnings, which are often in the West Indies, they are but narrow; but in the other two destructions, by deluge and earthquake, it is further to be noted, that the remnant of people which happen to be reserved, are commonly ignorant and mountainous people, that can give no account of the time past; so that the oblivion is all one, as if none had been left. If you consider well of the people of the West Indies, it is very probable that they are a newer, or a younger people than the people of the old world; and it is much more likely that the destruction that hath heretofore been there, was not by earthquakes, (as the Egyptian priest told Solon, concerning the Island of Atlantis, that it was swallowed by an earthquake), but rather that it was desolated by a particular deluge, for earthquakes are seldom in those parts; but, on the other side, they have such pouring rivers, as the rivers of Asia, and Africa, and Europe, are but brooks to them. Their Andes, likewise, or mountains, are far higher than those with us; whereby it seems, that the remnants of generations of men were in such a particular deluge saved. As for the observation that Machiavel hath, that the jealousy of sects doth much extinguish the memory of things, traducing Gregory the Great, that he did what in him lay to extinguish all heathen antiquities, I do not find that those zeals do any great effects, nor last long; as it appeared in the succession of Sabinian, who did revive the former antiquities.

The vicissitude, or mutations, in the superior globe, are no fit matter for this present argument. It may be, Plato's great year, if the world should last so long, would have some effect, not in renewing the state of like individuals (for that is the fume of those that conceive the celestial bodies have more accurate influences upon these things below, than indeed they have), but in gross. Comets, out of question, have likewise power and effect over the gross and mass of things; but they are rather gazed, and waited upon in their journey, than wisely observed in their effects, especially in their respective effects; that is, what kind of comet for magnitude, color, version of the beams, placing in the region of heaven, or lasting, produceth what kind of effects.

There is a toy, which I have heard, and I would not have it given over, but waited upon a little. They say it is observed in the Low Countries (I know not in what part), that every five and thirty years the same kind and suit of years and weather comes about again; as great frosts, great wet, great droughts, warm winters, summers with little heat, and the like; and they call it the prime. It is a thing I do the rather mention, because, computing backwards, I have found some concurrence.

But to leave these points of nature, and to come to men. The greatest vicissitude of things amongst men, is the vicissitude of sects and religions; for those orbs rule in men's minds most. The true religion is built upon the rock; the rest are tossed upon the waves of time. To speak, therefore, of the causes of new sects, and to give some counsel concerning them, as far as the weakness of human judgment can give stay to so great revolutions.

When the religion formerly received is rent by discords, and when the holiness of the professors of religion is decayed and full of scandal, and, withal, the times be stupid, ignorant, and barbarous, you may doubt the springing up of a new sect; if then, also, there should arise any extravagant and strange spirit to make himself author thereof; all which points held when Mahomet published his law. If a new sect have not two properties, fear it not, for it will not spread. The one is the supplanting or the opposing of authority established, for nothing is more popular than that; the other is, the giving license to pleasures and a voluptuous life; for as for speculative heresies (such as were in ancient times the Arians, and now the Arminians), though they work mightily upon men's wits, yet they do not produce any great alterations in states, except it be by the help of civil occasions. There be three manner of plantations of new sects: by the power of signs and miracles; by the eloquence and wisdom of speech and persuasion; and by the sword. For martyrdoms, I reckon them amongst miracles, because they seem to exceed the strength of human nature; and I may do the like of superlative and admirable holiness of life. Surely, there is no better way to stop the rising of new sects and schisms, than to reform abuses; to compound the smaller differences; to proceed mildly, and not with sanguinary persecutions; and rather to take off the principal authors, by winning and advancing them, than to enrage them by violence and bitterness.

The changes and vicissitude in wars are many, but chiefly in three things: in the seats or stages of the war, in the weapons, and in the manner of the conduct. Wars, in ancient time, seemed more to move from east to west; for the Persians, Assyrians, Arabians, Tartars (which were the invaders), were all eastern people. It is true the Gauls were western; but we read but of two incursions of theirs, the one to Gallo-Græcia, the other to Rome: but east and west have no certain points of heaven; and no more have the wars, either from the east or west, any certainty of observation; but north and south are fixed; and it hath seldom or never been seen that the far southern people have invaded the northern, but contrariwise: whereby it is manifest that the northern tract of the world is in nature the more martial region, be it in respect of the stars of that hemisphere, or of the great continents that are upon the north; whereas, the south part, for aught that is known, is almost all sea; or (which is most apparent) of the cold of the northern parts, which is that which, without aid of discipline, doth make the bodies hardest, and the courage warmest.

Upon the breaking and shivering of a great state and empire, you may be sure to have wars; for great empires, while they stand, do enervate and destroy the forces of the natives which they have subdued, resting upon their own protecting forces; and then, when they fail also, all goes to ruin, and they become a prey. So was it in the decay of the Roman empire, and likewise in the empire of Almaigne, after Charles the Great, every bird taking a feather, and were not unlike to befall to Spain, if it should break. The great accessions and unions of kingdoms do likewise stir up wars; for when a state grows to an over-power, it is like a great flood, that will be sure to overflow, as it hath been seen in the states of Rome, Turkey,

Spain, and others. Look when the world hath fewest barbarous people, but such as commonly will not marry or generate, except they know means to live (as it is almost everywhere at this day, except Tartary), there is no danger of inundations of people; but when there be great shoals of people, which go on to populate, without foreseeing means of life and sustenation, it is of necessity that once in an age or two they discharge a portion of their people upon other nations, which the ancient northern people were wont to do by lot; casting lots what part should stay at home, and what should seek their fortunes. When a warlike state grows soft and effeminate, they may be sure of a war, for commonly such states are grown rich in the time of their degenerating; and so the prey inviteth, and their decay in valor encourageth a war.

As for the weapons, it hardly falleth under rule and observation, yet we see even they have returns and vicissitudes; for certain it is that ordnance was known in the city of the Oxidraces, in India, and was that which the Macedonians called thunder and lightning, and magic; and it is well known that the use of ordnance hath been in China above two thousand years. The conditions of weapons, and their improvements are, first, the fetching afar off, for that outruns the danger, as it is seen in ordnance and muskets; secondly, the strength of the percussion, wherein, likewise, ordnance do exceed all arietations, and ancient inventions; the third is, the commodious use of them, as that they may serve in all weathers, that the carriage may be light and manageable, and the like.

For the conduct of the war: at the first, men rested extremely upon number; they did put the wars likewise upon main force and valor, pointing days for pitched fields, and so trying it out upon an even match; and they were more ignorant in ranging and arraying their battles. After they grew to rest upon number, rather competent than vast, they grew to advantages of place, cunning diversions, and the like, and they grew more skilful in the ordering of their battles.

In the youth of a state, arms do flourish; in the middle age of a state, learning; and then both of them together for a time; in the declining age of a state, mechanical arts and merchandise. Learning hath its infancy when it is but beginning, and almost childish; then its youth, when it is luxuriant and juvenile; then its strength of years, when it is solid and reduced; and, lastly, its old age, when it waxeth dry and exhaust. But it is not good to look too long upon these turning wheels of vicissitude, lest we become giddy; as for the philology of them, that is but a circle of tales, and therefore not fit for this writing.

A Note About the Author

Francis Bacon (1561–1626) was an English philosopher, scientist, and statesman. Recognized for his intelligence from a young age, Bacon would develop the empirical basis for modern scientific inquiry—known today as the scientific method—by promoting skepticism and observational experimentation as essential for the discovery of truth and the growth of human knowledge. A central figure of the scientific revolution and the Renaissance, Bacon was recognized as Lord Verulam and Viscount St. Alban during his lifetime and was honored by both Queen Elizabeth I and King James VI for his contributions to society. Bacon was also an accomplished statesman, responsible for drafting early legal documents and charters for the British colonization of the Americas. His career was not without controversy, however, as accusations of bribery tarnished his reputation and barred him from government service toward the end of his life and career. Today, he is remembered as one of the founders of modern science whose theories and methods continue to form the basis of all scientific experimentation and inquiry.

A Note from the Publisher

Spanning many genres, from non-fiction essays to literature classics to children's books and lyric poetry, Mint Edition books showcase the master works of our time in a modern new package. The text is freshly typeset, is clean and easy to read, and features a new note about the author in each volume. Many books also include exclusive new introductory material. Every book boasts a striking new cover, which makes it as appropriate for collecting as it is for gift giving. Mint Edition books are only printed when a reader orders them, so natural resources are not wasted. We're proud that our books are never manufactured in excess and exist only in the exact quantity they need to be read and enjoyed.

bookfinity™

Discover more of your favorite classics with Bookfinity™.

- Track your reading with custom book lists.
- Get great book recommendations for your personalized Reader Type.
- Add reviews for your favorite books.
- AND MUCH MORE!

Visit **bookfinity.com** and take the fun Reader Type quiz to get started.

Enjoy our classic and modern companion pairings!

Classic & Modern

Printed in the USA
CPSIA information can be obtained
at www.ICGtesting.com
JSHW082347140824
68134JS00020B/1936

at last fell into a style so methodic, you would have thought he spoke less to mere auditors than to an invisible amanuensis; seemed talking for the press; very impressive way with him indeed. And I, having an equally impressible memory, think that, upon a pinch, I can render you the judge upon the colonel almost word for word."

"Do so, by all means," said the cosmopolitan, well pleased.

"Shall I give you the judge's philosophy, and all?"

"As to that," rejoined the other gravely, pausing over the pipe-bowl he was filling, "the desirableness, to a man of a certain mind, of having another man's philosophy given, depends considerably upon what school of philosophy that other man belongs to. Of what school or system was the judge, pray?"

"Why, though he knew how to read and write, the judge never had much schooling. But, I should say he belonged, if anything, to the free-school system. Yes, a true patriot, the judge went in strong for free-schools."

"In philosophy? The man of a certain mind, then, while respecting the judge's patriotism, and not blind to the judge's capacity for narrative, such as he may prove to have, might, perhaps, with prudence, waive an opinion of the judge's probable philosophy. But I am no rigorist; proceed, I beg; his philosophy or not, as you please."

"Well, I would mostly skip that part, only, to begin, some reconnoitering of the ground in a philosophical way the judge always deemed indispensable with strangers. For you must know that Indian-hating was no monopoly of Colonel Moredock's; but a passion, in one form or other, and to a degree, greater or less, largely shared among the class to which he belonged. And Indian-hating still exists; and, no doubt, will continue to exist, so long as Indians do. Indian-hating, then, shall be my first theme, and Colonel Moredock, the Indian-hater, my next and last."

With which the stranger, settling himself in his seat, commenced— the hearer paying marked regard, slowly smoking, his glance, meanwhile, steadfastly abstracted towards the deck, but his right ear so disposed towards the speaker that each word came through as little atmospheric intervention as possible. To intensify the sense of hearing, he seemed to sink the sense of sight. No complaisance of mere speech could have been so flattering, or expressed such striking politeness as this mute eloquence of thoroughly digesting attention.

XXVI

Containing the Metaphysics of Indian-Hating, According to the Views of One Evidently Not So Prepossessed as Rousseau in Favor of Savages

The judge always began in these words: 'The backwoodsman's hatred of the Indian has been a topic for some remark. In the earlier times of the frontier the passion was thought to be readily accounted for. But Indian rapine having mostly ceased through regions where it once prevailed, the philanthropist is surprised that Indian-hating has not in like degree ceased with it. He wonders why the backwoodsman still regards the red man in much the same spirit that a jury does a murderer, or a trapper a wild cat—a creature, in whose behalf mercy were not wisdom; truce is vain; he must be executed.

"'A curious point,' the judge would continue, 'which perhaps not everybody, even upon explanation, may fully understand; while, in order for any one to approach to an understanding, it is necessary for him to learn, or if he already know, to bear in mind, what manner of man the backwoodsman is; as for what manner of man the Indian is, many know, either from history or experience.

"'The backwoodsman is a lonely man. He is a thoughtful man. He is a man strong and unsophisticated. Impulsive, he is what some might call unprincipled. At any rate, he is self-willed; being one who less hearkens to what others may say about things, than looks for himself, to see what are things themselves. If in straits, there are few to help; he must depend upon himself; he must continually look to himself. Hence self-reliance, to the degree of standing by his own judgment, though it stand alone. Not that he deems himself infallible; too many mistakes in following trails prove the contrary; but he thinks that nature destines such sagacity as she has given him, as she destines it to the 'possum. To these fellow-beings of the wilds their untutored sagacity is their best dependence. If with either it prove faulty, if the 'possum's betray it to the trap, or the backwoodsman's mislead him into ambuscade, there

HERMAN MELVILLE

are consequences to be undergone, but no self-blame. As with the 'possum, instincts prevail with the backwoodsman over precepts. Like the 'possum, the backwoodsman presents the spectacle of a creature dwelling exclusively among the works of God, yet these, truth must confess, breed little in him of a godly mind. Small bowing and scraping is his, further than when with bent knee he points his rifle, or picks its flint. With few companions, solitude by necessity his lengthened lot, he stands the trial—no slight one, since, next to dying, solitude, rightly borne, is perhaps of fortitude the most rigorous test. But not merely is the backwoodsman content to be alone, but in no few cases is anxious to be so. The sight of smoke ten miles off is provocation to one more remove from man, one step deeper into nature. Is it that he feels that whatever man may be, man is not the universe? that glory, beauty, kindness, are not all engrossed by him? that as the presence of man frights birds away, so, many bird-like thoughts? Be that how it will, the backwoodsman is not without some fineness to his nature. Hairy Orson as he looks, it may be with him as with the Shetland seal—beneath the bristles lurks the fur.

"'Though held in a sort a barbarian, the backwoodsman would seem to America what Alexander was to Asia—captain in the vanguard of conquering civilization. Whatever the nation's growing opulence or power, does it not lackey his heels? Pathfinder, provider of security to those who come after him, for himself he asks nothing but hardship. Worthy to be compared with Moses in the Exodus, or the Emperor Julian in Gaul, who on foot, and bare-browed, at the head of covered or mounted legions, marched so through the elements, day after day. The tide of emigration, let it roll as it will, never overwhelms the backwoodsman into itself; he rides upon advance, as the Polynesian upon the comb of the surf.

"'Thus, though he keep moving on through life, he maintains with respect to nature much the same unaltered relation throughout; with her creatures, too, including panthers and Indians. Hence, it is not unlikely that, accurate as the theory of the Peace Congress may be with respect to those two varieties of beings, among others, yet the backwoodsman might be qualified to throw out some practical suggestions.

"'As the child born to a backwoodsman must in turn lead his father's life—a life which, as related to humanity, is related mainly to Indians—it is thought best not to mince matters, out of delicacy; but to tell the boy pretty plainly what an Indian is, and what he must expect from him.

For however charitable it may be to view Indians as members of the Society of Friends, yet to affirm them such to one ignorant of Indians, whose lonely path lies a long way through their lands, this, in the event, might prove not only injudicious but cruel. At least something of this kind would seem the maxim upon which backwoods' education is based. Accordingly, if in youth the backwoodsman incline to knowledge, as is generally the case, he hears little from his schoolmasters, the old chroniclers of the forest, but histories of Indian lying, Indian theft, Indian double-dealing, Indian fraud and perfidy, Indian want of conscience, Indian blood-thirstiness, Indian diabolism—histories which, though of wild woods, are almost as full of things unangelic as the Newgate Calendar or the Annals of Europe. In these Indian narratives and traditions the lad is thoroughly grounded. "As the twig is bent the tree's inclined." The instinct of antipathy against an Indian grows in the backwoodsman with the sense of good and bad, right and wrong. In one breath he learns that a brother is to be loved, and an Indian to be hated.

"'Such are the facts,' the judge would say, 'upon which, if one seek to moralize, he must do so with an eye to them. It is terrible that one creature should so regard another, should make it conscience to abhor an entire race. It is terrible; but is it surprising? Surprising, that one should hate a race which he believes to be red from a cause akin to that which makes some tribes of garden insects green? A race whose name is upon the frontier a *memento mori*; painted to him in every evil light; now a horse-thief like those in Moyamensing; now an assassin like a New York rowdy; now a treaty-breaker like an Austrian; now a Palmer with poisoned arrows; now a judicial murderer and Jeffries, after a fierce farce of trial condemning his victim to bloody death; or a Jew with hospitable speeches cozening some fainting stranger into ambuscade, there to burk him, and account it a deed grateful to Manitou, his god.

"'Still, all this is less advanced as truths of the Indians than as examples of the backwoodsman's impression of them—in which the charitable may think he does them some injustice. Certain it is, the Indians themselves think so; quite unanimously, too. The Indians, in deed, protest against the backwoodsman's view of them; and some think that one cause of their returning his antipathy so sincerely as they do, is their moral indignation at being so libeled by him, as they really believe and say. But whether, on this or any point, the Indians should be permitted to testify for themselves, to the exclusion of other testimony, is a question that may be left to the Supreme Court. At any rate, it has been observed that when an Indian becomes a genuine proselyte to Christianity (such cases, however, not being very many; though, indeed, entire tribes are sometimes nominally brought to the true light,) he will not in that case conceal his enlightened conviction, that his race's portion by nature is total depravity; and, in that way, as much as admits that the backwoodsman's worst idea of it is not very far from true; while, on the other hand, those red men who are the greatest sticklers for the theory of Indian virtue, and Indian loving-kindness, are sometimes the arrantest horse-thieves and tomahawkers among them. So, at least, avers the backwoodsman. And though, knowing the Indian nature, as he thinks he does, he fancies he is not ignorant that an Indian may in some points deceive himself almost as effectually as in bush-tactics he can another, yet his theory and his practice as above contrasted seem to involve an inconsistency so extreme, that the backwoodsman only accounts for it on the supposition that when a tomahawking red-man advances the notion of the benignity of the red race, it is but part and parcel with that subtle strategy which he finds so useful in war, in hunting, and the general conduct of life.'

"In further explanation of that deep abhorrence with which the backwoodsman regards the savage, the judge used to think it might perhaps a little help, to consider what kind of stimulus to it is furnished in those forest histories and traditions before spoken of. In which behalf, he would tell the story of the little colony of Wrights and Weavers, originally seven cousins from Virginia, who, after successive removals with their families, at last established themselves near the southern frontier of the Bloody Ground, Kentucky: 'They were strong, brave men; but, unlike many of the pioneers in those days, theirs was no love of conflict for conflict's sake. Step by step they had been lured to their lonely resting-place by the ever-beckoning seductions of a fertile and virgin land, with a singular exemption, during the march, from Indian molestation. But clearings made and houses built, the bright shield was soon to turn its other side. After repeated persecutions and eventual hostilities, forced on them by a dwindled tribe in their neighborhood— persecutions resulting in loss of crops and cattle; hostilities in which they lost two of their number, illy to be spared, besides others getting painful wounds—the five remaining cousins made, with some serious concessions, a kind of treaty with Mocmohoc, the chief—being to this induced by the harryings of the enemy, leaving them no peace. But they were further prompted, indeed, first incited, by the suddenly changed ways of Mocmohoc, who, though hitherto deemed a savage almost perfidious as Caesar Borgia, yet now put on a seeming the reverse of this, engaging to bury the hatchet, smoke the pipe, and be friends forever; not friends in the mere sense of renouncing enmity, but in the sense of kindliness, active and familiar.

"'But what the chief now seemed, did not wholly blind them to what the chief had been; so that, though in no small degree influenced by his change of bearing, they still distrusted him enough to covenant with him, among other articles on their side, that though friendly visits should be exchanged between the wigwams and the cabins, yet the five cousins should never, on any account, be expected to enter the chief's lodge together. The intention was, though they reserved it, that if ever, under the guise of amity, the chief should mean them mischief, and effect it, it should be but partially; so that some of the five might survive, not only for their families' sake, but also for retribution's. Nevertheless, Mocmohoc did, upon a time, with such fine art and pleasing carriage win their confidence, that he brought them all together to a feast of bear's meat, and there, by stratagem, ended them. Years after, over their calcined bones and those of all their families, the chief, reproached for his treachery by a proud hunter whom he had made captive, jeered out, "Treachery? pale face! 'Twas they who broke their covenant first, in coming all together; they that broke it first, in trusting Mocmohoc.'"

"At this point the judge would pause, and lifting his hand, and rolling his eyes, exclaim in a solemn enough voice, 'Circling wiles and bloody lusts. The acuteness and genius of the chief but make him the more atrocious.'

"After another pause, he would begin an imaginary kind of dialogue between a backwoodsman and a questioner:

"'But are all Indians like Mocmohoc?—Not all have proved such; but in the least harmful may lie his germ. There is an Indian nature. "Indian blood is in me," is the half-breed's threat.—But are not some Indians kind?—Yes, but kind Indians are mostly lazy, and reputed simple—at all events, are seldom chiefs; chiefs among the red men being taken from the active, and those accounted wise. Hence, with small promotion, kind Indians have but proportionate influence. And kind Indians may be forced to do unkind biddings. So "beware the Indian, kind or unkind," said Daniel Boone, who lost his sons by them.—But, have all you backwoodsmen been some way victimized by Indians?—No.—

Well, and in certain cases may not at least some few of you be favored by them?—Yes, but scarce one among us so self-important, or so selfish-minded, as to hold his personal exemption from Indian outrage such a set-off against the contrary experience of so many others, as that he must needs, in a general way, think well of Indians; or, if he do, an arrow in his flank might suggest a pertinent doubt.

"'In short,' according to the judge, 'if we at all credit the backwoodsman, his feeling against Indians, to be taken aright, must be considered as being not so much on his own account as on others', or jointly on both accounts. True it is, scarce a family he knows but some member of it, or connection, has been by Indians maimed or scalped. What avails, then, that some one Indian, or some two or three, treat a backwoodsman friendly-like? He fears me, he thinks. Take my rifle from me, give him motive, and what will come? Or if not so, how know I what involuntary preparations may be going on in him for things as unbeknown in present time to him as me—a sort of chemical preparation in the soul for malice, as chemical preparation in the body for malady.'

"Not that the backwoodsman ever used those words, you see, but the judge found him expression for his meaning. And this point he would conclude with saying, that, 'what is called a "friendly Indian" is a very rare sort of creature; and well it was so, for no ruthlessness exceeds that of a "friendly Indian" turned enemy. A coward friend, he makes a valiant foe.

"'But, thus far the passion in question has been viewed in a general way as that of a community. When to his due share of this the backwoodsman adds his private passion, we have then the stock out of which is formed, if formed at all, the Indian-hater *par excellence.*'

"The Indian-hater *par excellence* the judge defined to be one 'who, having with his mother's milk drank in small love for red men, in youth or early manhood, ere the sensibilities become osseous, receives at their hand some signal outrage, or, which in effect is much the same, some of his kin have, or some friend. Now, nature all around him by her solitudes wooing or bidding him muse upon this matter, he accordingly does so, till the thought develops such attraction, that much as straggling vapors troop from all sides to a storm-cloud, so straggling thoughts of other outrages troop to the nucleus thought, assimilate with it, and swell it. At last, taking counsel with the elements, he comes to his resolution. An intenser Hannibal, he makes a vow, the hate of which is a vortex from whose suction scarce the remotest chip of the guilty race may reasonably feel secure. Next, he declares himself and settles his temporal affairs. With the solemnity of a Spaniard turned monk, he takes leave of his kin; or rather, these leave-takings have something of the still more impressive finality of death-bed adieus. Last, he commits himself to the forest primeval; there, so long as life shall be his, to act upon a calm, cloistered scheme of strategical, implacable, and lonesome vengeance. Ever on the noiseless trail; cool, collected, patient; less seen than felt; snuffing, smelling—a Leather-stocking Nemesis. In the settlements he will not be seen again; in eyes of old companions tears may start at some chance thing that speaks of him; but they never look for him, nor call; they know he will not come. Suns and seasons fleet; the tiger-lily blows and falls; babes are born and leap in their mothers' arms; but, the Indian-hater is good as gone to his long home, and "Terror" is his epitaph.'

"Here the judge, not unaffected, would pause again, but presently resume: 'How evident that in strict speech there can be no biography of an Indian-hater *par excellence*, any more than one of a sword-fish, or other deep-sea denizen; or, which is still less imaginable, one of a dead man. The career of the Indian-hater *par excellence* has the impenetrability of the fate of a lost steamer. Doubtless, events, terrible ones, have happened, must have happened; but the powers that be in nature have taken order that they shall never become news.

"'But, luckily for the curious, there is a species of diluted Indian-hater, one whose heart proves not so steely as his brain. Soft enticements of domestic life too, often draw him from the ascetic trail; a monk who apostatizes to the world at times. Like a mariner, too, though much abroad, he may have a wife and family in some green harbor which he does not forget. It is with him as with the Papist converts in Senegal; fasting and mortification prove hard to bear.'

"The judge, with his usual judgment, always thought that the intense solitude to which the Indian-hater consigns himself, has, by its overawing influence, no little to do with relaxing his vow. He would relate instances where, after some months' lonely scoutings, the Indian-hater is suddenly seized with a sort of calenture; hurries openly towards the first smoke, though he knows it is an Indian's, announces himself as a lost hunter, gives the savage his rifle, throws himself upon his charity, embraces him with much affection, imploring the privilege of living a while in his sweet companionship. What is too often the sequel of so distempered a procedure may be best known by those who best know

HERMAN MELVILLE

the Indian. Upon the whole, the judge, by two and thirty good and sufficient reasons, would maintain that there was no known vocation whose consistent following calls for such self-containings as that of the Indian-hater *par excellence*. In the highest view, he considered such a soul one peeping out but once an age.

"For the diluted Indian-hater, although the vacations he permits himself impair the keeping of the character, yet, it should not be overlooked that this is the man who, by his very infirmity, enables us to form surmises, however inadequate, of what Indian-hating in its perfection is."

"One moment," gently interrupted the cosmopolitan here, "and let me refill my calumet."

Which being done, the other proceeded:—

XXVII

SOME ACCOUNT OF A MAN OF QUESTIONABLE MORALITY, BUT WHO, NEVERTHELESS, WOULD SEEM ENTITLED TO THE ESTEEM OF THAT EMINENT ENGLISH MORALIST WHO SAID HE LIKED A GOOD HATER

Coming to mention the man to whose story all thus far said was but the introduction, the judge, who, like you, was a great smoker, would insist upon all the company taking cigars, and then lighting a fresh one himself, rise in his place, and, with the solemnest voice, say—'Gentlemen, let us smoke to the memory of Colonel John Moredock;' when, after several whiffs taken standing in deep silence and deeper reverie, he would resume his seat and his discourse, something in these words:

"'Though Colonel John Moredock was not an Indian-hater *par excellence*, he yet cherished a kind of sentiment towards the red man, and in that degree, and so acted out his sentiment as sufficiently to merit the tribute just rendered to his memory.

"John Moredock was the son of a woman married thrice, and thrice widowed by a tomahawk. The three successive husbands of this woman had been pioneers, and with them she had wandered from wilderness to wilderness, always on the frontier. With nine children, she at last found herself at a little clearing, afterwards Vincennes. There she joined a company about to remove to the new country of Illinois. On the eastern side of Illinois there were then no settlements; but on the west side, the shore of the Mississippi, there were, near the mouth of the Kaskaskia, some old hamlets of French. To the vicinity of those hamlets, very innocent and pleasant places, a new Arcadia, Mrs. Moredock's party was destined; for thereabouts, among the vines, they meant to settle. They embarked upon the Wabash in boats, proposing descending that stream into the Ohio, and the Ohio into the Mississippi, and so, northwards, towards the point to be reached. All went well till they made the rock of the Grand Tower on the Mississippi, where they had to land and drag their boats round a point swept by a strong current. Here a party of Indians, lying in wait,

HERMAN MELVILLE

rushed out and murdered nearly all of them. The widow was among the victims with her children, John excepted, who, some fifty miles distant, was following with a second party.

"He was just entering upon manhood, when thus left in nature sole survivor of his race. Other youngsters might have turned mourners; he turned avenger. His nerves were electric wires—sensitive, but steel. He was one who, from self-possession, could be made neither to flush nor pale. It is said that when the tidings were brought him, he was ashore sitting beneath a hemlock eating his dinner of venison—and as the tidings were told him, after the first start he kept on eating, but slowly and deliberately, chewing the wild news with the wild meat, as if both together, turned to chyle, together should sinew him to his intent. From that meal he rose an Indian-hater. He rose; got his arms, prevailed upon some comrades to join him, and without delay started to discover who were the actual transgressors. They proved to belong to a band of twenty renegades from various tribes, outlaws even among Indians, and who had formed themselves into a maurauding crew. No opportunity for action being at the time presented, he dismissed his friends; told them to go on, thanking them, and saying he would ask their aid at some future day. For upwards of a year, alone in the wilds, he watched the crew. Once, what he thought a favorable chance having occurred—it being midwinter, and the savages encamped, apparently to remain so— he anew mustered his friends, and marched against them; but, getting wind of his coming, the enemy fled, and in such panic that everything was left behind but their weapons. During the winter, much the same thing happened upon two subsequent occasions. The next year he sought them at the head of a party pledged to serve him for forty days. At last the hour came. It was on the shore of the Mississippi. From their covert, Moredock and his men dimly descried the gang of Cains in the red dusk of evening, paddling over to a jungle island in mid-stream, there the more securely to lodge; for Moredock's retributive spirit in the wilderness spoke ever to their trepidations now, like the voice calling through the garden. Waiting until dead of night, the whites swam the river, towing after them a raft laden with their arms. On landing, Moredock cut the fastenings of the enemy's canoes, and turned them, with his own raft, adrift; resolved that there should be neither escape for the Indians, nor safety, except in victory, for the whites. Victorious the whites were; but three of the Indians saved themselves by taking to the stream. Moredock's band lost not a man.

"'Three of the murderers survived. He knew their names and persons. In the course of three years each successively fell by his own hand. All were now dead. But this did not suffice. He made no avowal, but to kill Indians had become his passion. As an athlete, he had few equals; as a shot, none; in single combat, not to be beaten. Master of that woodland-cunning enabling the adept to subsist where the tyro would perish, and expert in all those arts by which an enemy is pursued for weeks, perhaps months, without once suspecting it, he kept to the forest. The solitary Indian that met him, died. When a murder was descried, he would either secretly pursue their track for some chance to strike at least one blow; or if, while thus engaged, he himself was discovered, he would elude them by superior skill.

"'Many years he spent thus; and though after a time he was, in a degree, restored to the ordinary life of the region and period, yet it is believed that John Moredock never let pass an opportunity of quenching an Indian. Sins of commission in that kind may have been his, but none of omission.

"'It were to err to suppose,' the judge would say, 'that this gentleman was naturally ferocious, or peculiarly possessed of those qualities, which, unhelped by provocation of events, tend to withdraw man from social life. On the contrary, Moredock was an example of something apparently self-contradicting, certainly curious, but, at the same time, undeniable: namely, that nearly all Indian-haters have at bottom loving hearts; at any rate, hearts, if anything, more generous than the average. Certain it is, that, to the degree in which he mingled in the life of the settlements, Moredock showed himself not without humane feelings. No cold husband or colder father, he; and, though often and long away from his household, bore its needs in mind, and provided for them. He could be very convivial; told a good story (though never of his more private exploits), and sung a capital song. Hospitable, not backward to help a neighbor; by report, benevolent, as retributive, in secret; while, in a general manner, though sometimes grave—as is not unusual with men of his complexion, a sultry and tragical brown—yet with nobody, Indians excepted, otherwise than courteous in a manly fashion; a moccasined gentleman, admired and loved. In fact, no one more popular, as an incident to follow may prove.

"'His bravery, whether in Indian fight or any other, was unquestionable. An officer in the ranging service during the war of 1812, he acquitted himself with more than credit. Of his soldierly character, this anecdote is told: Not long after Hull's dubious surrender at Detroit, Moredock with some of his rangers rode up at night to a log-house, there to rest till morning. The horses being attended to, supper over, and sleeping-places assigned the troop, the host showed the colonel his best bed, not on the ground like the rest, but a bed that stood on legs. But out of delicacy, the guest declined to monopolize it, or, indeed, to occupy it at all; when, to increase the inducement, as the host thought, he was told that a general officer had once slept in that bed. "Who, pray?" asked the colonel. "General Hull." "Then you must not take offense," said the colonel, buttoning up his coat, "but, really, no coward's bed, for me, however comfortable." Accordingly he took up with valor's bed—a cold one on the ground.

"'At one time the colonel was a member of the territorial council of Illinois, and at the formation of the state government, was pressed to become candidate for governor, but begged to be excused. And, though he declined to give his reasons for declining, yet by those who best knew him the cause was not wholly unsurmised. In his official capacity he might be called upon to enter into friendly treaties with Indian tribes, a thing not to be thought of. And even did no such contingecy arise, yet he felt there would be an impropriety in the Governor of Illinois stealing out now and then, during a recess of the legislative bodies, for a few days' shooting at human beings, within the limits of his paternal chief-magistracy. If the governorship offered large honors, from Moredock it demanded larger sacrifices. These were incompatibles. In short, he was not unaware that to be a consistent Indian-hater involves the renunciation of ambition, with its objects—the pomps and glories of the world; and since religion, pronouncing such things vanities, accounts it merit to renounce them, therefore, so far as this goes, Indian-hating, whatever may be thought of it in other respects, may be regarded as not wholly without the efficacy of a devout sentiment.'"

Here the narrator paused. Then, after his long and irksome sitting, started to his feet, and regulating his disordered shirt-frill, and at the same time adjustingly shaking his legs down in his rumpled pantaloons, concluded: "There, I have done; having given you, not my story, mind, or my thoughts, but another's. And now, for your friend Coonskins, I doubt not, that, if the judge were here, he would pronounce him a sort of comprehensive Colonel Moredock, who, too much spreading his passion, shallows it."

XXVIII

Moot Points Touching the Late
Colonel John Moredock

C harity, charity!" exclaimed the cosmopolitan, "never a sound
judgment without charity. When man judges man, charity is less
a bounty from our mercy than just allowance for the insensible lee-way
of human fallibility. God forbid that my eccentric friend should be what
you hint. You do not know him, or but imperfectly. His outside deceived
you; at first it came near deceiving even me. But I seized a chance, when,
owing to indignation against some wrong, he laid himself a little open;
I seized that lucky chance, I say, to inspect his heart, and found it an
inviting oyster in a forbidding shell. His outside is but put on. Ashamed
of his own goodness, he treats mankind as those strange old uncles in
romances do their nephews—snapping at them all the time and yet
loving them as the apple of their eye."

"Well, my words with him were few. Perhaps he is not what I took
him for. Yes, for aught I know, you may be right."

"Glad to hear it. Charity, like poetry, should be cultivated, if
only for its being graceful. And now, since you have renounced your
notion, I should be happy, would you, so to speak, renounce your
story, too. That, story strikes me with even more incredulity than
wonder. To me some parts don't hang together. If the man of hate,
how could John Moredock be also the man of love? Either his lone
campaigns are fabulous as Hercules'; or else, those being true, what
was thrown in about his geniality is but garnish. In short, if ever
there was such a man as Moredock, he, in my way of thinking, was
either misanthrope or nothing; and his misanthropy the more intense
from being focused on one race of men. Though, like suicide, man-
hatred would seem peculiarly a Roman and a Grecian passion—that
is, Pagan; yet, the annals of neither Rome nor Greece can produce
the equal in man-hatred of Colonel Moredock, as the judge and you
have painted him. As for this Indian-hating in general, I can only say
of it what Dr. Johnson said of the alleged Lisbon earthquake: 'Sir, I
don't believe it.'"

"Didn't believe it? Why not? Clashed with any little prejudice of his?"

"Doctor Johnson had no prejudice; but, like a certain other person," with an ingenuous smile, "he had sensibilities, and those were pained."

"Dr. Johnson was a good Christian, wasn't he?"

"He was."

"Suppose he had been something else."

"Then small incredulity as to the alleged earthquake."

"Suppose he had been also a misanthrope?"

"Then small incredulity as to the robberies and murders alleged to have been perpetrated under the pall of smoke and ashes. The infidels of the time were quick to credit those reports and worse. So true is it that, while religion, contrary to the common notion, implies, in certain cases, a spirit of slow reserve as to assent, infidelity, which claims to despise credulity, is sometimes swift to it."

"You rather jumble together misanthropy and infidelity."

"I do not jumble them; they are coordinates. For misanthropy, springing from the same root with disbelief of religion, is twin with that. It springs from the same root, I say; for, set aside materialism, and what is an atheist, but one who does not, or will not, see in the universe a ruling principle of love; and what a misanthrope, but one who does not, or will not, see in man a ruling principle of kindness? Don't you see? In either case the vice consists in a want of confidence."

"What sort of a sensation is misanthropy?"

"Might as well ask me what sort of sensation is hydrophobia. Don't know; never had it. But I have often wondered what it can be like. Can a misanthrope feel warm, I ask myself; take ease? be companionable with himself? Can a misanthrope smoke a cigar and muse? How fares he in solitude? Has the misanthrope such a thing as an appetite? Shall a peach refresh him? The effervescence of champagne, with what eye does he behold it? Is summer good to him? Of long winters how much can he sleep? What are his dreams? How feels he, and what does he, when suddenly awakened, alone, at dead of night, by fusilades of thunder?"

"Like you," said the stranger, "I can't understand the misanthrope. So far as my experience goes, either mankind is worthy one's best love, or else I have been lucky. Never has it been my lot to have been wronged, though but in the smallest degree. Cheating, backbiting, superciliousness, disdain, hard-heartedness, and all that brood, I know but by report. Cold regards tossed over the sinister shoulder of a former friend, ingratitude in a beneficiary, treachery in a confidant—such things may be; but I must take somebody's word for it. Now the bridge that has carried me so well over, shall I not praise it?"

"Ingratitude to the worthy bridge not to do so. Man is a noble fellow, and in an age of satirists, I am not displeased to find one who has confidence in him, and bravely stands up for him."

"Yes, I always speak a good word for man; and what is more, am always ready to do a good deed for him."

"You are a man after my own heart," responded the cosmopolitan, with a candor which lost nothing by its calmness. "Indeed," he added, "our sentiments agree so, that were they written in a book, whose was whose, few but the nicest critics might determine."

"Since we are thus joined in mind," said the stranger, "why not be joined in hand?"

"My hand is always at the service of virtue," frankly extending it to him as to virtue personified.

"And now," said the stranger, cordially retaining his hand, "you know our fashion here at the West. It may be a little low, but it is kind. Briefly, we being newly-made friends must drink together. What say you?"

"Thank you; but indeed, you must excuse me."

"Why?"

"Because, to tell the truth, I have today met so many old friends, all free-hearted, convivial gentlemen, that really, really, though for the present I succeed in mastering it, I am at bottom almost in the condition of a sailor who, stepping ashore after a long voyage, ere night reels with loving welcomes, his head of less capacity than his heart."

At the allusion to old friends, the stranger's countenance a little fell, as a jealous lover's might at hearing from his sweetheart of former ones. But rallying, he said: "No doubt they treated you to something strong; but wine—surely, that gentle creature, wine; come, let us have a little gentle wine at one of these little tables here. Come, come." Then essaying to roll about like a full pipe in the sea, sang in a voice which had had more of good-fellowship, had there been less of a latent squeak to it:

> "Let us drink of the wine of the vine benign,
> That sparkles warm in Zansovine."

The cosmopolitan, with longing eye upon him, stood as sorely tempted and wavering a moment; then, abruptly stepping towards him,

HERMAN MELVILLE

with a look of dissolved surrender, said: "When mermaid songs move figure-heads, then may glory, gold, and women try their blandishments on me. But a good fellow, singing a good song, he woos forth my every spike, so that my whole hull, like a ship's, sailing by a magnetic rock, caves in with acquiescence. Enough: when one has a heart of a certain sort, it is in vain trying to be resolute."

XXIX

The Boon Companions

The wine, port, being called for, and the two seated at the little table, a natural pause of convivial expectancy ensued; the stranger's eye turned towards the bar near by, watching the red-cheeked, white-aproned man there, blithely dusting the bottle, and invitingly arranging the salver and glasses; when, with a sudden impulse turning round his head towards his companion, he said, "Ours is friendship at first sight, ain't it?"

"It is," was the placidly pleased reply: "and the same may be said of friendship at first sight as of love at first sight: it is the only true one, the only noble one. It bespeaks confidence. Who would go sounding his way into love or friendship, like a strange ship by night, into an enemy's harbor?"

"Right. Boldly in before the wind. Agreeable, how we always agree. By-the-way, though but a formality, friends should know each other's names. What is yours, pray?"

"Francis Goodman. But those who love me, call me Frank. And yours?"

"Charles Arnold Noble. But do you call me Charlie."

"I will, Charlie; nothing like preserving in manhood the fraternal familiarities of youth. It proves the heart a rosy boy to the last."

"My sentiments again. Ah!"

It was a smiling waiter, with the smiling bottle, the cork drawn; a common quart bottle, but for the occasion fitted at bottom into a little bark basket, braided with porcupine quills, gayly tinted in the Indian fashion. This being set before the entertainer, he regarded it with affectionate interest, but seemed not to understand, or else to pretend not to, a handsome red label pasted on the bottle, bearing the capital letters, P. W.

"P. W.," said he at last, perplexedly eying the pleasing poser, "now what does P. W. mean?"

"Shouldn't wonder," said the cosmopolitan gravely, "if it stood for port wine. You called for port wine, didn't you?"

"Why so it is, so it is!"

"I find some little mysteries not very hard to clear up," said the other, quietly crossing his legs.

This commonplace seemed to escape the stranger's hearing, for, full of his bottle, he now rubbed his somewhat sallow hands over it, and with a strange kind of cackle, meant to be a chirrup, cried: "Good wine, good wine; is it not the peculiar bond of good feeling?" Then brimming both glasses, pushed one over, saying, with what seemed intended for an air of fine disdain: "Ill betide those gloomy skeptics who maintain that now-a-days pure wine is unpurchasable; that almost every variety on sale is less the vintage of vineyards than laboratories; that most bar-keepers are but a set of male Brinvilliarses, with complaisant arts practicing against the lives of their best friends, their customers."

A shade passed over the cosmopolitan. After a few minutes' down-cast musing, he lifted his eyes and said: "I have long thought, my dear Charlie, that the spirit in which wine is regarded by too many in these days is one of the most painful examples of want of confidence. Look at these glasses. He who could mistrust poison in this wine would mistrust consumption in Hebe's cheek. While, as for suspicions against the dealers in wine and sellers of it, those who cherish such suspicions can have but limited trust in the human heart. Each human heart they must think to be much like each bottle of port, not such port as this, but such port as they hold to. Strange traducers, who see good faith in nothing, however sacred. Not medicines, not the wine in sacraments, has escaped them. The doctor with his phial, and the priest with his chalice, they deem equally the unconscious dispensers of bogus cordials to the dying."

"Dreadful!"

"Dreadful indeed," said the cosmopolitan solemnly. "These distrusters stab at the very soul of confidence. If this wine," impressively holding up his full glass, "if this wine with its bright promise be not true, how shall man be, whose promise can be no brighter? But if wine be false, while men are true, whither shall fly convivial geniality? To think of sincerely-genial souls drinking each other's health at unawares in perfidious and murderous drugs!"

"Horrible!"

"Much too much so to be true, Charlie. Let us forget it. Come, you are my entertainer on this occasion, and yet you don't pledge me. I have been waiting for it."

"Pardon, pardon," half confusedly and half ostentatiously lifting his glass. "I pledge you, Frank, with my whole heart, believe me," taking a draught too decorous to be large, but which, small though it was, was followed by a slight involuntary wryness to the mouth.

"And I return you the pledge, Charlie, heart-warm as it came to me, and honest as this wine I drink it in," reciprocated the cosmopolitan with princely kindliness in his gesture, taking a generous swallow, concluding in a smack, which, though audible, was not so much so as to be unpleasing.

"Talking of alleged spuriousness of wines," said he, tranquilly setting down his glass, and then sloping back his head and with friendly fixedness eying the wine, "perhaps the strangest part of those allegings is, that there is, as claimed, a kind of man who, while convinced that on this continent most wines are shams, yet still drinks away at them; accounting wine so fine a thing, that even the sham article is better than none at all. And if the temperance people urge that, by this course, he will sooner or later be undermined in health, he answers, 'And do you think I don't know that? But health without cheer I hold a bore; and cheer, even of the spurious sort, has its price, which I am willing to pay.'"

"Such a man, Frank, must have a disposition ungovernably bacchanalian."

"Yes, if such a man there be, which I don't credit. It is a fable, but a fable from which I once heard a person of less genius than grotesqueness draw a moral even more extravagant than the fable itself. He said that it illustrated, as in a parable, how that a man of a disposition ungovernably good-natured might still familiarly associate with men, though, at the same time, he believed the greater part of men false-hearted—accounting society so sweet a thing that even the spurious sort was better than none at all. And if the Rochefoucaultites urge that, by this course, he will sooner or later be undermined in security, he answers, 'And do you think I don't know that? But security without society I hold a bore; and society, even of the spurious sort, has its price, which I am willing to pay.'"

"A most singular theory," said the stranger with a slight fidget, eying his companion with some inquisitiveness, "indeed, Frank, a most slanderous thought," he exclaimed in sudden heat and with an involuntary look almost of being personally aggrieved.

"In one sense it merits all you say, and more," rejoined the other with wonted mildness, "but, for a kind of drollery in it, charity might, perhaps, overlook something of the wickedness. Humor is, in fact, so blessed a thing, that even in the least virtuous product of the human mind, if there can be found but nine good jokes, some philosophers are clement enough to affirm that those nine good jokes should redeem all the wicked thoughts, though plenty as the populace of Sodom. At any rate, this same humor has something, there is no telling what, of beneficence in it, it is such a catholicon and charm—nearly all men agreeing in relishing it, though they may agree in little else—and in its way it undeniably does such a deal of familiar good in the world, that no wonder it is almost a proverb, that a man of humor, a man capable of a good loud laugh—seem how he may in other things—can hardly be a heartless scamp."

"Ha, ha, ha!" laughed the other, pointing to the figure of a pale pauper-boy on the deck below, whose pitiableness was touched, as it were, with ludicrousness by a pair of monstrous boots, apparently some mason's discarded ones, cracked with drouth, half eaten by lime, and curled up about the toe like a bassoon. "Look—ha, ha, ha!"

"I see," said the other, with what seemed quiet appreciation, but of a kind expressing an eye to the grotesque, without blindness to what in this case accompanied it, "I see; and the way in which it moves you, Charlie, comes in very apropos to point the proverb I was speaking of. Indeed, had you intended this effect, it could not have been more so. For who that heard that laugh, but would as naturally argue from it a sound heart as sound lungs? True, it is said that a man may smile, and smile, and smile, and be a villain; but it is not said that a man may laugh, and laugh, and laugh, and be one, is it, Charlie?"

"Ha, ha, ha!—no no, no no."

"Why Charlie, your explosions illustrate my remarks almost as aptly as the chemist's imitation volcano did his lectures. But even if experience did not sanction the proverb, that a good laugher cannot be a bad man, I should yet feel bound in confidence to believe it, since it is a saying current among the people, and I doubt not originated among them, and hence *must* be true; for the voice of the people is the voice of truth. Don't you think so?"

"Of course I do. If Truth don't speak through the people, it never speaks at all; so I heard one say."

"A true saying. But we stray. The popular notion of humor, considered as index to the heart, would seem curiously confirmed by Aristotle—I think, in his 'Politics,' (a work, by-the-by, which, however it may be viewed upon the whole, yet, from the tenor of certain sections, should not, without precaution, be placed in the hands of youth)—who remarks that the least lovable men in history seem to have had for humor not only a disrelish, but a hatred; and this, in some cases, along with an extraordinary dry taste for practical punning. I remember it is related of Phalaris, the capricious tyrant of Sicily, that he once caused a poor fellow to be beheaded on a horse-block, for no other cause than having a horse-laugh."

"Funny Phalaris!"

"Cruel Phalaris!"

As after fire-crackers, there was a pause, both looking downward on the table as if mutually struck by the contrast of exclamations, and pondering upon its significance, if any. So, at least, it seemed; but on one side it might have been otherwise: for presently glancing up, the cosmopolitan said: "In the instance of the moral, drolly cynic, drawn from the queer bacchanalian fellow we were speaking of, who had his reasons for still drinking spurious wine, though knowing it to be such— there, I say, we have an example of what is certainly a wicked thought, but conceived in humor. I will now give you one of a wicked thought conceived in wickedness. You shall compare the two, and answer, whether in the one case the sting is not neutralized by the humor, and whether in the other the absence of humor does not leave the sting free play. I once heard a wit, a mere wit, mind, an irreligious Parisian wit, say, with regard to the temperance movement, that none, to their personal benefit, joined it sooner than niggards and knaves; because, as he affirmed, the one by it saved money and the other made money, as in ship-owners cutting off the spirit ration without giving its equivalent, and gamblers and all sorts of subtle tricksters sticking to cold water, the better to keep a cool head for business."

"A wicked thought, indeed!" cried the stranger, feelingly.

"Yes," leaning over the table on his elbow and genially gesturing at him with his forefinger: "yes, and, as I said, you don't remark the sting of it?"

"I do, indeed. Most calumnious thought, Frank!"

"No humor in it?"

"Not a bit!"

"Well now, Charlie," eying him with moist regard, "let us drink. It appears to me you don't drink freely."

"Oh, oh—indeed, indeed—I am not backward there. I protest, a freer drinker than friend Charlie you will find nowhere," with feverish zeal snatching his glass, but only in the sequel to dally with it. "By-the-way,

Frank," said he, perhaps, or perhaps not, to draw attention from himself, "by-the-way, I saw a good thing the other day; capital thing; a panegyric on the press, It pleased me so, I got it by heart at two readings. It is a kind of poetry, but in a form which stands in something the same relation to blank verse which that does to rhyme. A sort of free-and-easy chant with refrains to it. Shall I recite it?"

"Anything in praise of the press I shall be happy to hear," rejoined the cosmopolitan, "the more so," he gravely proceeded, "as of late I have observed in some quarters a disposition to disparage the press."

"Disparage the press?"

"Even so; some gloomy souls affirming that it is proving with that great invention as with brandy or eau-de-vie, which, upon its first discovery, was believed by the doctors to be, as its French name implies, a panacea—a notion which experience, it may be thought, has not fully verified."

"You surprise me, Frank. Are there really those who so decry the press? Tell me more. Their reasons."

"Reasons they have none, but affirmations they have many; among other things affirming that, while under dynastic despotisms, the press is to the people little but an improvisatore, under popular ones it is too apt to be their Jack Cade. In fine, these sour sages regard the press in the light of a Colt's revolver, pledged to no cause but his in whose chance hands it may be; deeming the one invention an improvement upon the pen, much akin to what the other is upon the pistol; involving, along with the multiplication of the barrel, no consecration of the aim. The term 'freedom of the press' they consider on a par with *freedom of Colt's revolver*. Hence, for truth and the right, they hold, to indulge hopes from the one is little more sensible than for Kossuth and Mazzini to indulge hopes from the other. Heart-breaking views enough, you think; but their refutation is in every true reformer's contempt. Is it not so?"

"Without doubt. But go on, go on. I like to hear you," flatteringly brimming up his glass for him.

"For one," continued the cosmopolitan, grandly swelling his chest, "I hold the press to be neither the people's improvisatore, nor Jack Cade; neither their paid fool, nor conceited drudge. I think interest never prevails with it over duty. The press still speaks for truth though impaled, in the teeth of lies though intrenched. Disdaining for it the poor name of cheap diffuser of news, I claim for it the independent apostleship of Advancer of Knowledge:—the iron Paul! Paul, I say;

for not only does the press advance knowledge, but righteousness. In the press, as in the sun, resides, my dear Charlie, a dedicated principle of beneficent force and light. For the Satanic press, by its coappearance with the apostolic, it is no more an aspersion to that, than to the true sun is the coappearance of the mock one. For all the baleful-looking parhelion, god Apollo dispenses the day. In a word, Charlie, what the sovereign of England is titularly, I hold the press to be actually—Defender of the Faith!—defender of the faith in the final triumph of truth over error, metaphysics over superstition, theory over falsehood, machinery over nature, and the good man over the bad. Such are my views, which, if stated at some length, you, Charlie, must pardon, for it is a theme upon which I cannot speak with cold brevity. And now I am impatient for your panegyric, which, I doubt not, will put mine to the blush."

"It is rather in the blush-giving vein," smiled the other; "but such as it is, Frank, you shall have it."

"Tell me when you are about to begin," said the cosmopolitan, "for, when at public dinners the press is toasted, I always drink the toast standing, and shall stand while you pronounce the panegyric."

"Very good, Frank; you may stand up now."

He accordingly did so, when the stranger likewise rose, and uplifting the ruby wine-flask, began.

XXX

Opening With a Poetical Eulogy of the Press and Continuing With Talk Inspired By the Same

Praise be unto the press, not Faust's, but Noah's; let us extol and magnify the press, the true press of Noah, from which breaketh the true morning. Praise be unto the press, not the black press but the red; let us extol and magnify the press, the red press of Noah, from which cometh inspiration. Ye pressmen of the Rhineland and the Rhine, join in with all ye who tread out the glad tidings on isle Madeira or Mitylene.—Who giveth redness of eyes by making men long to tarry at the fine print?—Praise be unto the press, the rosy press of Noah, which giveth rosiness of hearts, by making men long to tarry at the rosy wine.—Who hath babblings and contentions? Who, without cause, inflicteth wounds? Praise be unto the press, the kindly press of Noah, which knitteth friends, which fuseth foes.—Who may be bribed?—Who may be bound?—Praise be unto the press, the free press of Noah, which will not lie for tyrants, but make tyrants speak the truth.—Then praise be unto the press, the frank old press of Noah; then let us extol and magnify the press, the brave old press of Noah; then let us with roses garland and enwreath the press, the grand old press of Noah, from which flow streams of knowledge which give man a bliss no more unreal than his pain.'"

"You deceived me," smiled the cosmopolitan, as both now resumed their seats; "you roguishly took advantage of my simplicity; you archly played upon my enthusiasm. But never mind; the offense, if any, was so charming, I almost wish you would offend again. As for certain poetic left-handers in your panegyric, those I cheerfully concede to the indefinite privileges of the poet. Upon the whole, it was quite in the lyric style—a style I always admire on account of that spirit of Sibyllic confidence and assurance which is, perhaps, its prime ingredient. But come," glancing at his companion's glass, "for a lyrist, you let the bottle stay with you too long."

"The lyre and the vine forever!" cried the other in his rapture, or what seemed such, heedless of the hint, "the vine, the vine! is it not the most graceful and bounteous of all growths? And, by its being such, is not something meant—divinely meant? As I live, a vine, a Catawba vine, shall be planted on my grave!"

"A genial thought; but your glass there."

"Oh, oh," taking a moderate sip, "but you, why don't you drink?"

"You have forgotten, my dear Charlie, what I told you of my previous convivialities today."

"Oh," cried the other, now in manner quite abandoned to the lyric mood, not without contrast to the easy sociability of his companion. "Oh, one can't drink too much of good old wine—the genuine, mellow old port. Pooh, pooh! drink away."

"Then keep me company."

"Of course," with a flourish, taking another sip—"suppose we have cigars. Never mind your pipe there; a pipe is best when alone. I say, waiter, bring some cigars—your best."

They were brought in a pretty little bit of western pottery, representing some kind of Indian utensil, mummy-colored, set down in a mass of tobacco leaves, whose long, green fans, fancifully grouped, formed with peeps of red the sides of the receptacle.

Accompanying it were two accessories, also bits of pottery, but smaller, both globes; one in guise of an apple flushed with red and gold to the life, and, through a cleft at top, you saw it was hollow. This was for the ashes. The other, gray, with wrinkled surface, in the likeness of a wasp's nest, was the match-box. "There," said the stranger, pushing over the cigar-stand, "help yourself, and I will touch you off," taking a match. "Nothing like tobacco," he added, when the fumes of the cigar began to wreathe, glancing from the smoker to the pottery, "I will have a Virginia tobacco-plant set over my grave beside the Catawba vine."

"Improvement upon your first idea, which by itself was good—but you don't smoke."

"Presently, presently—let me fill your glass again. You don't drink."

"Thank you; but no more just now. Fill *your* glass."

"Presently, presently; do you drink on. Never mind me. Now that it strikes me, let me say, that he who, out of superfine gentility or fanatic morality, denies himself tobacco, suffers a more serious abatement in the cheap pleasures of life than the dandy in his iron boot, or the celibate on his iron cot. While for him who would fain revel in tobacco, but cannot, it is a thing at which philanthropists must weep, to see such an one, again and again, madly returning to the cigar, which, for his

HERMAN MELVILLE

incompetent stomach, he cannot enjoy, while still, after each shameful repulse, the sweet dream of the impossible good goads him on to his fierce misery once more—poor eunuch!"

"I agree with you," said the cosmopolitan, still gravely social, "but you don't smoke."

"Presently, presently, do you smoke on. As I was saying about—"

"But *why* don't you smoke—come. You don't think that tobacco, when in league with wine, too much enhances the latter's vinous quality—in short, with certain constitutions tends to impair self-possession, do you?"

"To think that, were treason to good fellowship," was the warm disclaimer. "No, no. But the fact is, there is an unpropitious flavor in my mouth just now. Ate of a diabolical ragout at dinner, so I shan't smoke till I have washed away the lingering memento of it with wine. But smoke away, you, and pray, don't forget to drink. By-the-way, while we sit here so companionably, giving loose to any companionable nothing, your uncompanionable friend, Coonskins, is, by pure contrast, brought to recollection. If he were but here now, he would see how much of real heart-joy he denies himself by not hob-a-nobbing with his kind."

"Why," with loitering emphasis, slowly withdrawing his cigar, "I thought I had undeceived you there. I thought you had come to a better understanding of my eccentric friend."

"Well, I thought so, too; but first impressions will return, you know. In truth, now that I think of it, I am led to conjecture from chance things which dropped from Coonskins, during the little interview I had with him, that he is not a Missourian by birth, but years ago came West here, a young misanthrope from the other side of the Alleghanies, less to make his fortune, than to flee man. Now, since they say trifles sometimes effect great results, I shouldn't wonder, if his history were probed, it would be found that what first indirectly gave his sad bias to Coonskins was his disgust at reading in boyhood the advice of Polonius to Laertes—advice which, in the selfishness it inculcates, is almost on a par with a sort of ballad upon the economies of money-making, to be occasionally seen pasted against the desk of small retail traders in New England."

"I do hope now, my dear fellow," said the cosmopolitan with an air of bland protest, "that, in my presence at least, you will throw out nothing to the prejudice of the sons of the Puritans."

"Hey-day and high times indeed," exclaimed the other, nettled, "sons of the Puritans forsooth! And who be Puritans, that I, an Alabamaian, must do them reverence? A set of sourly conceited old Malvolios, whom Shakespeare laughs his fill at in his comedies."

"Pray, what were you about to suggest with regard to Polonius," observed the cosmopolitan with quiet forbearance, expressive of the patience of a superior mind at the petulance of an inferior one; "how do you characterize his advice to Laertes?"

"As false, fatal, and calumnious," exclaimed the other, with a degree of ardor befitting one resenting a stigma upon the family escutcheon, "and for a father to give his son—monstrous. The case you see is this: The son is going abroad, and for the first. What does the father? Invoke God's blessing upon him? Put the blessed Bible in his trunk? No. Crams him with maxims smacking of my Lord Chesterfield, with maxims of France, with maxims of Italy."

"No, no, be charitable, not that. Why, does he not among other things say:—

> *'The friends thou hast, and their adoption tried,*
> *Grapple them to thy soul with hooks of steel'?*

Is that compatible with maxims of Italy?"

"Yes it is, Frank. Don't you see? Laertes is to take the best of care of his friends—his proved friends, on the same principle that a wine-corker takes the best of care of his proved bottles. When a bottle gets a sharp knock and don't break, he says, 'Ah, I'll keep that bottle.' Why? Because he loves it? No, he has particular use for it."

"Dear, dear!" appealingly turning in distress, "that—that kind of criticism is—is—in fact—it won't do."

"Won't truth do, Frank? You are so charitable with everybody, do but consider the tone of the speech. Now I put it to you, Frank; is there anything in it hortatory to high, heroic, disinterested effort? Anything like 'sell all thou hast and give to the poor?' And, in other points, what desire seems most in the father's mind, that his son should cherish nobleness for himself, or be on his guard against the contrary thing in others? An irreligious warner, Frank—no devout counselor, is Polonius. I hate him. Nor can I bear to hear your veterans of the world affirm, that he who steers through life by the advice of old Polonius will not steer among the breakers."

"No, no—I hope nobody affirms that," rejoined the cosmopolitan, with tranquil abandonment; sideways reposing his arm at full length upon the table. "I hope nobody affirms that; because, if Polonius' advice be taken in your sense, then the recommendation of it by men of experience would appear to involve more or less of an unhandsome sort of reflection upon human nature. And yet," with a perplexed air, "your suggestions have put things in such a strange light to me as in fact a little to disturb my previous notions of Polonius and what he says. To be frank, by your ingenuity you have unsettled me there, to that degree that were it not for our coincidence of opinion in general, I should almost think I was now at length beginning to feel the ill effect of an immature mind, too much consorting with a mature one, except on the ground of first principles in common."

"Really and truly," cried the other with a kind of tickled modesty and pleased concern, "mine is an understanding too weak to throw out grapnels and hug another to it. I have indeed heard of some great scholars in these days, whose boast is less that they have made disciples than victims. But for me, had I the power to do such things, I have not the heart to desire."

"I believe you, my dear Charlie. And yet, I repeat, by your commentaries on Polonius you have, I know not how, unsettled me; so that now I don't exactly see how Shakespeare meant the words he puts in Polonius' mouth."

"Some say that he meant them to open people's eyes; but I don't think so."

"Open their eyes?" echoed the cosmopolitan, slowly expanding his; "what is there in this world for one to open his eyes to? I mean in the sort of invidious sense you cite?"

"Well, others say he meant to corrupt people's morals; and still others, that he had no express intention at all, but in effect opens their eyes and corrupts their morals in one operation. All of which I reject."

"Of course you reject so crude an hypothesis; and yet, to confess, in reading Shakespeare in my closet, struck by some passage, I have laid down the volume, and said: 'This Shakespeare is a queer man.' At times seeming irresponsible, he does not always seem reliable. There appears to be a certain—what shall I call it?—hidden sun, say, about him, at once enlightening and mystifying. Now, I should be afraid to say what I have sometimes thought that hidden sun might be."

"Do you think it was the true light?" with clandestine geniality again filling the other's glass.

"I would prefer to decline answering a categorical question there. Shakespeare has got to be a kind of deity. Prudent minds, having certain latent thoughts concerning him, will reserve them in a condition of lasting probation. Still, as touching avowable speculations, we are permitted a tether. Shakespeare himself is to be adored, not arraigned; but, so we do it with humility, we may a little canvass his characters. There's his Autolycus now, a fellow that always puzzled me. How is one to take Autolycus? A rogue so happy, so lucky, so triumphant, of so almost captivatingly vicious a career that a virtuous man reduced to the poor-house (were such a contingency conceivable), might almost long to change sides with him. And yet, see the words put into his mouth: 'Oh,' cries Autolycus, as he comes galloping, gay as a buck, upon the stage, 'oh,' he laughs, 'oh what a fool is Honesty, and Trust, his sworn brother, a very simple gentleman.' Think of that. Trust, that is, confidence—that is, the thing in this universe the sacredest—is rattlingly pronounced just the simplest. And the scenes in which the rogue figures seem purposely devised for verification of his principles. Mind, Charlie, I do not say it *is* so, far from it; but I *do* say it seems so. Yes, Autolycus would seem a needy varlet acting upon the persuasion that less is to be got by invoking pockets than picking them, more to be made by an expert knave than a bungling beggar; and for this reason, as he thinks, that the soft heads outnumber the soft hearts. The devil's drilled recruit, Autolycus is joyous as if he wore the livery of heaven. When disturbed by the character and career of one thus wicked and thus happy, my sole consolation is in the fact that no such creature ever existed, except in the powerful imagination which evoked him. And yet, a creature, a living creature, he is, though only a poet was his maker. It may be, that in that paper-and-ink investiture of his, Autolycus acts more effectively upon mankind than he would in a flesh-and-blood one. Can his influence be salutary? True, in Autolycus there is humor; but though, according to my principle, humor is in general to be held a saving quality, yet the case of Autolycus is an exception; because it is his humor which, so to speak, oils his mischievousness. The bravadoing mischievousness of Autolycus is slid into the world on humor, as a pirate schooner, with colors flying, is launched into the sea on greased ways."

"I approve of Autolycus as little as you," said the stranger, who, during his companion's commonplaces, had seemed less attentive to them than to maturing with in his own mind the original conceptions destined to eclipse them. "But I cannot believe that Autolycus, mischievous as he must prove upon the stage, can be near so much so as such a character as Polonius."

"I don't know about that," bluntly, and yet not impolitely, returned the cosmopolitan; "to be sure, accepting your view of the old courtier, then if between him and Autolycus you raise the question of unprepossessingness, I grant you the latter comes off best. For a moist rogue may tickle the midriff, while a dry worldling may but wrinkle the spleen."

"But Polonius is not dry," said the other excitedly; "he drules. One sees the fly-blown old fop drule and look wise. His vile wisdom is made the viler by his vile rheuminess. The bowing and cringing, time-serving old sinner—is such an one to give manly precepts to youth? The discreet, decorous, old dotard-of-state; senile prudence; fatuous soullessness! The ribanded old dog is paralytic all down one side, and that the side of nobleness. His soul is gone out. Only nature's automatonism keeps him on his legs. As with some old trees, the bark survives the pith, and will still stand stiffly up, though but to rim round punk, so the body of old Polonius has outlived his soul."

"Come, come," said the cosmopolitan with serious air, almost displeased; "though I yield to none in admiration of earnestness, yet, I think, even earnestness may have limits. To human minds, strong language is always more or less distressing. Besides, Polonius is an old man—as I remember him upon the stage—with snowy locks. Now charity requires that such a figure—think of it how you will—should at least be treated with civility. Moreover, old age is ripeness, and I once heard say, 'Better ripe than raw.'"

"But not better rotten than raw!" bringing down his hand with energy on the table.

"Why, bless me," in mild surprise contemplating his heated comrade, "how you fly out against this unfortunate Polonius—a being that never was, nor will be. And yet, viewed in a Christian light," he added pensively, "I don't know that anger against this man of straw is a whit less wise than anger against a man of flesh, Madness, to be mad with anything."

"That may be, or may not be," returned the other, a little testily, perhaps; "but I stick to what I said, that it is better to be raw than rotten. And what is to be feared on that head, may be known from this: that it is with the best of hearts as with the best of pears—a dangerous experiment to linger too long upon the scene. This did Polonius. Thank fortune, Frank, I am young, every tooth sound in my head, and if good wine can keep me where I am, long shall I remain so."

"True," with a smile. "But wine, to do good, must be drunk. You have talked much and well, Charlie; but drunk little and indifferently—fill up."

"Presently, presently," with a hasty and preoccupied air. "If I remember right, Polonius hints as much as that one should, under no circumstances, commit the indiscretion of aiding in a pecuniary way an unfortunate friend. He drules out some stale stuff about 'loan losing both itself and friend,' don't he? But our bottle; is it glued fast? Keep it moving, my dear Frank. Good wine, and upon my soul I begin to feel it, and through me old Polonius—yes, this wine, I fear, is what excites me so against that detestable old dog without a tooth."

Upon this, the cosmopolitan, cigar in mouth, slowly raised the bottle, and brought it slowly to the light, looking at it steadfastly, as one might at a thermometer in August, to see not how low it was, but how high. Then whiffing out a puff, set it down, and said: "Well, Charlie, if what wine you have drunk came out of this bottle, in that case I should say that if—supposing a case—that if one fellow had an object in getting another fellow fuddled, and this fellow to be fuddled was of your capacity, the operation would be comparatively inexpensive. What do you think, Charlie?"

"Why, I think I don't much admire the supposition," said Charlie, with a look of resentment; "it ain't safe, depend upon it, Frank, to venture upon too jocose suppositions with one's friends."

"Why, bless you, Frank, my supposition wasn't personal, but general. You mustn't be so touchy."

"If I am touchy it is the wine. Sometimes, when I freely drink, it has a touchy effect on me, I have observed."

"Freely drink? you haven't drunk the perfect measure of one glass, yet. While for me, this must be my fourth or fifth, thanks to your importunity; not to speak of all I drank this morning, for old acquaintance' sake. Drink, drink; you must drink."

"Oh, I drink while you are talking," laughed the other; "you have not noticed it, but I have drunk my share. Have a queer way I learned from a sedate old uncle, who used to tip off his glass-unperceived. Do you fill up, and my glass, too. There! Now away with that stump, and have a new cigar. Good fellowship forever!" again in the lyric mood, "Say, Frank, are we not men? I say are we not human? Tell me, were they not human who engendered us, as before heaven I believe they shall be whom we shall engender? Fill up, up, up, my friend. Let the ruby tide aspire, and all ruby aspirations with it! Up, fill up! Be we convivial. And conviviality, what is it? The word, I mean; what expresses it? A living together. But bats live together, and did you ever hear of convivial bats?"

"If I ever did," observed the cosmopolitan, "it has quite slipped my recollection."

"But *why* did you never hear of convivial bats, nor anybody else? Because bats, though they live together, live not together genially. Bats are not genial souls. But men are; and how delightful to think that the word which among men signifies the highest pitch of geniality, implies, as indispensable auxiliary, the cheery benediction of the bottle. Yes, Frank, to live together in the finest sense, we must drink together. And so, what wonder that he who loves not wine, that sober wretch has a lean heart—a heart like a wrung-out old bluing-bag, and loves not his kind? Out upon him, to the rag-house with him, hang him—the ungenial soul!"

"Oh, now, now, can't you be convivial without being censorious? I like easy, unexcited conviviality. For the sober man, really, though for my part I naturally love a cheerful glass, I will not prescribe my nature as the law to other natures. So don't abuse the sober man. Conviviality is one good thing, and sobriety is another good thing. So don't be one-sided."

"Well, if I am one-sided, it is the wine. Indeed, indeed, I have indulged too genially. My excitement upon slight provocation shows it. But yours is a stronger head; drink you. By the way, talking of geniality, it is much on the increase in these days, ain't it?"

"It is, and I hail the fact. Nothing better attests the advance of the humanitarian spirit. In former and less humanitarian ages—the ages of amphitheatres and gladiators—geniality was mostly confined to the fireside and table. But in our age—the age of joint-stock companies and free-and-easies—it is with this precious quality as with precious gold in old Peru, which Pizarro found making up the scullion's sauce-pot as the Inca's crown. Yes, we golden boys, the moderns, have geniality everywhere—a bounty broadcast like noonlight."

"True, true; my sentiments again. Geniality has invaded each department and profession. We have genial senators, genial authors, genial lecturers, genial doctors, genial clergymen, genial surgeons, and the next thing we shall have genial hangmen."

"As to the last-named sort of person," said the cosmopolitan, "I trust that the advancing spirit of geniality will at last enable us to dispense with him. No murderers—no hangmen. And surely, when the whole world shall have been genialized, it will be as out of place to talk of murderers, as in a Christianized world to talk of sinners."

"To pursue the thought," said the other, "every blessing is attended with some evil, and—"

"Stay," said the cosmopolitan, "that may be better let pass for a loose saying, than for hopeful doctrine."

"Well, assuming the saying's truth, it would apply to the future supremacy of the genial spirit, since then it will fare with the hangman as it did with the weaver when the spinning-jenny whizzed into the ascendant. Thrown out of employment, what could Jack Ketch turn his hand to? Butchering?"

"That he could turn his hand to it seems probable; but that, under the circumstances, it would be appropriate, might in some minds admit of a question. For one, I am inclined to think—and I trust it will not be held fastidiousness—that it would hardly be suitable to the dignity of our nature, that an individual, once employed in attending the last hours of human unfortunates, should, that office being extinct, transfer himself to the business of attending the last hours of unfortunate cattle. I would suggest that the individual turn valet—a vocation to which he would, perhaps, appear not wholly inadapted by his familiar dexterity about the person. In particular, for giving a finishing tie to a gentleman's cravat, I know few who would, in all likelihood, be, from previous occupation, better fitted than the professional person in question."

"Are you in earnest?" regarding the serene speaker with unaffected curiosity; "are you really in earnest?"

"I trust I am never otherwise," was the mildly earnest reply; "but talking of the advance of geniality, I am not without hopes that it will eventually exert its influence even upon so difficult a subject as the misanthrope."

"A genial misanthrope! I thought I had stretched the rope pretty hard in talking of genial hangmen. A genial misanthrope is no more conceivable than a surly philanthropist."

"True," lightly depositing in an unbroken little cylinder the ashes of his cigar, "true, the two you name are well opposed."

"Why, you talk as if there *was* such a being as a surly philanthropist."

"I do. My eccentric friend, whom you call Coonskins, is an example. Does he not, as I explained to you, hide under a surly air a philanthropic heart? Now, the genial misanthrope, when, in the process of eras, he shall turn up, will be the converse of this; under an affable air, he will hide a misanthropical heart. In short, the genial misanthrope will be a new kind of monster, but still no small improvement upon the original one, since, instead of making faces and throwing stones at people, like that poor old crazy man, Timon, he will take steps, fiddle in hand, and set the tickled world a'dancing. In a word, as the progress of Christianization mellows those in manner whom it cannot mend in mind, much the same will it prove with the progress of genialization. And so, thanks to geniality, the misanthrope, reclaimed from his boorish address, will take on refinement and softness—to so genial a degree, indeed, that it may possibly fall out that the misanthrope of the coming century will be almost as popular as, I am sincerely sorry to say, some philanthropists of the present time would seem not to be, as witness my eccentric friend named before."

"Well," cried the other, a little weary, perhaps, of a speculation so abstract, "well, however it may be with the century to come, certainly in the century which is, whatever else one may be, he must be genial or he is nothing. So fill up, fill up, and be genial!"

"I am trying my best," said the cosmopolitan, still calmly companionable. "A moment since, we talked of Pizarro, gold, and Peru; no doubt, now, you remember that when the Spaniard first entered Atahalpa's treasure-chamber, and saw such profusion of plate stacked up, right and left, with the wantonness of old barrels in a brewer's yard, the needy fellow felt a twinge of misgiving, of want of confidence, as to the genuineness of an opulence so profuse. He went about rapping the shining vases with his knuckles. But it was all gold, pure gold, good gold, sterling gold, which how cheerfully would have been stamped such at Goldsmiths' Hall. And just so those needy minds, which, through their own insincerity, having no confidence in mankind, doubt lest the liberal geniality of this age be spurious. They are small Pizarros in their way—by the very princeliness of men's geniality stunned into distrust of it."

"Far be such distrust from you and me, my genial friend," cried the other fervently; "fill up, fill up!"

"Well, this all along seems a division of labor," smiled the cosmopolitan. "I do about all the drinking, and you do about all—the genial. But yours is a nature competent to do that to a large population. And now, my friend," with a peculiarly grave air, evidently foreshadowing something not unimportant, and very likely of close personal interest; "wine, you know, opens the heart, and—"

"Opens it!" with exultation, "it thaws it right out. Every heart is ice-bound till wine melt it, and reveal the tender grass and sweet herbage budding below, with every dear secret, hidden before like a dropped jewel in a snow-bank, lying there unsuspected through winter till spring."

"And just in that way, my dear Charlie, is one of my little secrets now to be shown forth."

"Ah!" eagerly moving round his chair, "what is it?"

"Be not so impetuous, my dear Charlie. Let me explain. You see, naturally, I am a man not overgifted with assurance; in general, I am, if anything, diffidently reserved; so, if I shall presently seem otherwise, the reason is, that you, by the geniality you have evinced in all your talk, and especially the noble way in which, while affirming your good opinion of men, you intimated that you never could prove false to any man, but most by your indignation at a particularly illiberal passage in Polonius' advice—in short, in short," with extreme embarrassment, "how shall I express what I mean, unless I add that by your whole character you impel me to throw myself upon your nobleness; in one word, put confidence in you, a generous confidence?"

"I see, I see," with heightened interest, "something of moment you wish to confide. Now, what is it, Frank? Love affair?"

"No, not that."

"What, then, my *dear* Frank? Speak—depend upon me to the last. Out with it."

"Out it shall come, then," said the cosmopolitan. "I am in want, urgent want, of money."

XXXI

A Metamorphosis More Surprising Than any in Ovid

I n want of money!" pushing back his chair as from a suddenly-disclosed man-trap or crater.

"Yes," naïvely assented the cosmopolitan, "and you are going to loan me fifty dollars. I could almost wish I was in need of more, only for your sake. Yes, my dear Charlie, for your sake; that you might the better prove your noble, kindliness, my dear Charlie."

"None of your dear Charlies," cried the other, springing to his feet, and buttoning up his coat, as if hastily to depart upon a long journey.

"Why, why, why?" painfully looking up.

"None of your why, why, whys!" tossing out a foot, "go to the devil, sir! Beggar, impostor!—never so deceived in a man in my life."

XXXII

Showing That the Age of Music and Magicians is Not Yet Over

While speaking or rather hissing those words, the boon companion underwent much such a change as one reads of in fairy-books. Out of old materials sprang a new creature. Cadmus glided into the snake.

The cosmopolitan rose, the traces of previous feeling vanished; looked steadfastly at his transformed friend a moment, then, taking ten half-eagles from his pocket, stooped down, and laid them, one by one, in a circle round him; and, retiring a pace, waved his long tasseled pipe with the air of a necromancer, an air heightened by his costume, accompanying each wave with a solemn murmur of cabalistical words.

Meantime, he within the magic-ring stood suddenly rapt, exhibiting every symptom of a successful charm—a turned cheek, a fixed attitude, a frozen eye; spellbound, not more by the waving wand than by the ten invincible talismans on the floor.

"Reappear, reappear, reappear, oh, my former friend! Replace this hideous apparition with thy blest shape, and be the token of thy return the words, 'My dear Frank.'"

"My dear Frank," now cried the restored friend, cordially stepping out of the ring, with regained self-possession regaining lost identity, "My dear Frank, what a funny man you are; full of fun as an egg of meat. How could you tell me that absurd story of your being in need? But I relish a good joke too well to spoil it by letting on. Of course, I humored the thing; and, on my side, put on all the cruel airs you would have me. Come, this little episode of fictitious estrangement will but enhance the delightful reality. Let us sit down again, and finish our bottle."

"With all my heart," said the cosmopolitan, dropping the necromancer with the same facility with which he had assumed it. "Yes," he added, soberly picking up the gold pieces, and returning them with a chink to his pocket, "yes, I am something of a funny man now and then; while for you, Charlie," eying him in tenderness, "what you say about your humoring the thing is true enough; never did man second a joke better than you did just now. You played your part better than I did mine; you played it, Charlie, to the life."

HERMAN MELVILLE

"You see, I once belonged to an amateur play company; that accounts for it. But come, fill up, and let's talk of something else."

"Well," acquiesced the cosmopolitan, seating himself, and quietly brimming his glass, "what shall we talk about?"

"Oh, anything you please," a sort of nervously accommodating.

"Well, suppose we talk about Charlemont?"

"Charlemont? What's Charlemont? Who's Charlemont?"

"You shall hear, my dear Charlie," answered the cosmopolitan. "I will tell you the story of Charlemont, the gentleman-madman."

WHICH MAY PASS FOR WHATEVER
IT MAY PROVE TO BE WORTH

B ut ere be given the rather grave story of Charlemont, a reply must in civility be made to a certain voice which methinks I hear, that, in view of past chapters, and more particularly the last, where certain antics appear, exclaims: How unreal all this is! Who did ever dress or act like your cosmopolitan? And who, it might be returned, did ever dress or act like harlequin?

Strange, that in a work of amusement, this severe fidelity to real life should be exacted by any one, who, by taking up such a work, sufficiently shows that he is not unwilling to drop real life, and turn, for a time, to something different. Yes, it is, indeed, strange that any one should clamor for the thing he is weary of; that any one, who, for any cause, finds real life dull, should yet demand of him who is to divert his attention from it, that he should be true to that dullness.

There is another class, and with this class we side, who sit down to a work of amusement tolerantly as they sit at a play, and with much the same expectations and feelings. They look that fancy shall evoke scenes different from those of the same old crowd round the custom-house counter, and same old dishes on the boardinghouse table, with characters unlike those of the same old acquaintances they meet in the same old way every day in the same old street. And as, in real life, the proprieties will not allow people to act out themselves with that unreserve permitted to the stage; so, in books of fiction, they look not only for more entertainment, but, at bottom, even for more reality, than real life itself can show. Thus, though they want novelty, they want nature, too; but nature unfettered, exhilarated, in effect transformed. In this way of thinking, the people in a fiction, like the people in a play, must dress as nobody exactly dresses, talk as nobody exactly talks, act as nobody exactly acts. It is with fiction as with religion: it should present another world, and yet one to which we feel the tie.

If, then, something is to be pardoned to well-meant endeavor, surely a little is to be allowed to that writer who, in all his scenes, does but seek to minister to what, as he understands it, is the implied wish of the more indulgent lovers of entertainment, before whom harlequin can never appear in a coat too parti-colored, or cut capers too fantastic.

One word more. Though every one knows how bootless it is to be in all cases vindicating one's self, never mind how convinced one may be that he is never in the wrong; yet, so precious to man is the approbation of his kind, that to rest, though but under an imaginary censure applied to but a work of imagination, is no easy thing. The mention of this weakness will explain why such readers as may think they perceive something harmonious between the boisterous hilarity of the cosmopolitan with the bristling cynic, and his restrained good-nature with the boon-companion, are now referred to that chapter where some similar apparent inconsistency in another character is, on general principles, modestly endeavored to-be apologized for.

XXXIV

In Which the Cosmopolitan Tells the Story of the Gentleman Madman

Charlemont was a young merchant of French descent, living in St. Louis—a man not deficient in mind, and possessed of that sterling and captivating kindliness, seldom in perfection seen but in youthful bachelors, united at times to a remarkable sort of gracefully devil-may-care and witty good-humor. Of course, he was admired by everybody, and loved, as only mankind can love, by not a few. But in his twenty-ninth year a change came over him. Like one whose hair turns gray in a night, so in a day Charlemont turned from affable to morose. His acquaintances were passed without greeting; while, as for his confidential friends, them he pointedly, unscrupulously, and with a kind of fierceness, cut dead.

"One, provoked by such conduct, would fain have resented it with words as disdainful; while another, shocked by the change, and, in concern for a friend, magnanimously overlooking affronts, implored to know what sudden, secret grief had distempered him. But from resentment and from tenderness Charlemont alike turned away.

"Ere long, to the general surprise, the merchant Charlemont was gazetted, and the same day it was reported that he had withdrawn from town, but not before placing his entire property in the hands of responsible assignees for the benefit of creditors.

"Whither he had vanished, none could guess. At length, nothing being heard, it was surmised that he must have made away with himself—a surmise, doubtless, originating in the remembrance of the change some months previous to his bankruptcy—a change of a sort only to be ascribed to a mind suddenly thrown from its balance.

"Years passed. It was spring-time, and lo, one bright morning, Charlemont lounged into the St. Louis coffee-houses—gay, polite, humane, companionable, and dressed in the height of costly elegance. Not only was he alive, but he was himself again. Upon meeting with old acquaintances, he made the first advances, and in such a manner that it was impossible not to meet him half-way. Upon other old friends, whom he did not chance casually to meet, he either personally called, or left his card and compliments for them; and to several, sent presents of game or hampers of wine.

"They say the world is sometimes harshly unforgiving, but it was not so to Charlemont. The world feels a return of love for one who returns to it as he did. Expressive of its renewed interest was a whisper, an inquiring whisper, how now, exactly, so long after his bankruptcy, it fared with Charlemont's purse. Rumor, seldom at a loss for answers, replied that he had spent nine years in Marseilles in France, and there acquiring a second fortune, had returned with it, a man devoted henceforth to genial friendships.

"Added years went by, and the restored wanderer still the same; or rather, by his noble qualities, grew up like golden maize in the encouraging sun of good opinions. But still the latent wonder was, what had caused that change in him at a period when, pretty much as now, he was, to all appearance, in the possession of the same fortune, the same friends, the same popularity. But nobody thought it would be the thing to question him here.

"At last, at a dinner at his house, when all the guests but one had successively departed; this remaining guest, an old acquaintance, being just enough under the influence of wine to set aside the fear of touching upon a delicate point, ventured, in a way which perhaps spoke more favorably for his heart than his tact, to beg of his host to explain the one enigma of his life. Deep melancholy overspread the before cheery face of Charlemont; he sat for some moments tremulously silent; then pushing a full decanter towards the guest, in a choked voice, said: 'No, no! when by art, and care, and time, flowers are made to bloom over a grave, who would seek to dig all up again only to know the mystery?— The wine.' When both glasses were filled, Charlemont took his, and lifting it, added lowly: 'If ever, in days to come, you shall see ruin at hand, and, thinking you understand mankind, shall tremble for your friendships, and tremble for your pride; and, partly through love for the one and fear for the other, shall resolve to be beforehand with the world, and save it from a sin by prospectively taking that sin to yourself, then will you do as one I now dream of once did, and like him will you suffer; but how fortunate and how grateful should you be, if like him, after all that had happened, you could be a little happy again.'

"When the guest went away, it was with the persuasion, that though outwardly restored in mind as in fortune, yet, some taint of Charlemont's old malady survived, and that it was not well for friends to touch one dangerous string."

XXXV

In Which the Cosmopolitan Strikingly Evinces the Artlessness of His Nature

Well, what do you think of the story of Charlemont?" mildly asked he who had told it.

"A very strange one," answered the auditor, who had been such not with perfect ease, "but is it true?"

"Of course not; it is a story which I told with the purpose of every story-teller—to amuse. Hence, if it seem strange to you, that strangeness is the romance; it is what contrasts it with real life; it is the invention, in brief, the fiction as opposed to the fact. For do but ask yourself, my dear Charlie," lovingly leaning over towards him, "I rest it with your own heart now, whether such a forereaching motive as Charlemont hinted he had acted on in his change—whether such a motive, I say, were a sort of one at all justified by the nature of human society? Would you, for one, turn the cold shoulder to a friend—a convivial one, say, whose pennilessness should be suddenly revealed to you?"

"How can you ask me, my dear Frank? You know I would scorn such meanness." But rising somewhat disconcerted—"really, early as it is, I think I must retire; my head," putting up his hand to it, "feels unpleasantly; this confounded elixir of logwood, little as I drank of it, has played the deuce with me."

"Little as you drank of this elixir of logwood? Why, Charlie, you are losing your mind. To talk so of the genuine, mellow old port. Yes, I think that by all means you had better away, and sleep it off. There—don't apologize—don't explain—go, go—I understand you exactly. I will see you tomorrow."

XXXVI

In Which the Cosmopolitan is Accosted By a Mystic, Whereupon Ensues Pretty Much Such Talk as Might Be Expected

As, not without some haste, the boon companion withdrew, a stranger advanced, and touching the cosmopolitan, said: "I think I heard you say you would see that man again. Be warned; don't you do so."

He turned, surveying the speaker; a blue-eyed man, sandy-haired, and Saxon-looking; perhaps five and forty; tall, and, but for a certain angularity, well made; little touch of the drawing-room about him, but a look of plain propriety of a Puritan sort, with a kind of farmer dignity. His age seemed betokened more by his brow, placidly thoughtful, than by his general aspect, which had that look of youthfulness in maturity, peculiar sometimes to habitual health of body, the original gift of nature, or in part the effect or reward of steady temperance of the passions, kept so, perhaps, by constitution as much as morality. A neat, comely, almost ruddy cheek, coolly fresh, like a red clover-blossom at coolish dawn— the color of warmth preserved by the virtue of chill. Toning the whole man, was one-knows-not-what of shrewdness and mythiness, strangely jumbled; in that way, he seemed a kind of cross between a Yankee peddler and a Tartar priest, though it seemed as if, at a pinch, the first would not in all probability play second fiddle to the last.

"Sir," said the cosmopolitan, rising and bowing with slow dignity, "if I cannot with unmixed satisfaction hail a hint pointed at one who has just been clinking the social glass with me, on the other hand, I am not disposed to underrate the motive which, in the present case, could alone have prompted such an intimation. My friend, whose seat is still warm, has retired for the night, leaving more or less in his bottle here. Pray, sit down in his seat, and partake with me; and then, if you choose to hint aught further unfavorable to the man, the genial warmth of whose person in part passes into yours, and whose genial hospitality meanders through you—be it so."

"Quite beautiful conceits," said the stranger, now scholastically and artistically eying the picturesque speaker, as if he were a statue in the

Pitti Palace; "very beautiful:" then with the gravest interest, "yours, sir, if I mistake not, must be a beautiful soul—one full of all love and truth; for where beauty is, there must those be."

"A pleasing belief," rejoined the cosmopolitan, beginning with an even air, "and to confess, long ago it pleased me. Yes, with you and Schiller, I am pleased to believe that beauty is at bottom incompatible with ill, and therefore am so eccentric as to have confidence in the latent benignity of that beautiful creature, the rattle-snake, whose lithe neck and burnished maze of tawny gold, as he sleekly curls aloft in the sun, who on the prairie can behold without wonder?"

As he breathed these words, he seemed so to enter into their spirit—as some earnest descriptive speakers will—as unconsciously to wreathe his form and sidelong crest his head, till he all but seemed the creature described. Meantime, the stranger regarded him with little surprise, apparently, though with much contemplativeness of a mystical sort, and presently said:

"When charmed by the beauty of that viper, did it never occur to you to change personalities with him? to feel what it was to be a snake? to glide unsuspected in grass? to sting, to kill at a touch; your whole beautiful body one iridescent scabbard of death? In short, did the wish never occur to you to feel yourself exempt from knowledge, and conscience, and revel for a while in the carefree, joyous life of a perfectly instinctive, unscrupulous, and irresponsible creature?"

"Such a wish," replied the other, not perceptibly disturbed, "I must confess, never consciously was mine. Such a wish, indeed, could hardly occur to ordinary imaginations, and mine I cannot think much above the average."

"But now that the idea is suggested," said the stranger, with infantile intellectuality, "does it not raise the desire?"

"Hardly. For though I do not think I have any uncharitable prejudice against the rattle-snake, still, I should not like to be one. If I were a rattle-snake now, there would be no such thing as being genial with men—men would be afraid of me, and then I should be a very lonesome and miserable rattle-snake."

"True, men would be afraid of you. And why? Because of your rattle, your hollow rattle—a sound, as I have been told, like the shaking together of small, dry skulls in a tune of the Waltz of Death. And here we have another beautiful truth. When any creature is by its make inimical to other creatures, nature in effect labels that creature, much as an apothecary does a poison. So that whoever is destroyed by a rattle-snake, or other harmful agent, it is his own fault. He should have respected the label. Hence that significant passage in Scripture, 'Who will pity the charmer that is bitten with a serpent?'"

"*I* would pity him," said the cosmopolitan, a little bluntly, perhaps.

"But don't you think," rejoined the other, still maintaining his passionless air, "don't you think, that for a man to pity where nature is pitiless, is a little presuming?"

"Let casuists decide the casuistry, but the compassion the heart decides for itself. But, sir," deepening in seriousness, "as I now for the first realize, you but a moment since introduced the word irresponsible in a way I am not used to. Now, sir, though, out of a tolerant spirit, as I hope, I try my best never to be frightened at any speculation, so long as it is pursued in honesty, yet, for once, I must acknowledge that you do really, in the point cited, cause me uneasiness; because a proper view of the universe, that view which is suited to breed a proper confidence, teaches, if I err not, that since all things are justly presided over, not very many living agents but must be some way accountable."

"Is a rattle-snake accountable?" asked the stranger with such a preternaturally cold, gemmy glance out of his pellucid blue eye, that he seemed more a metaphysical merman than a feeling man; "is a rattle-snake accountable?"

"If I will not affirm that it is," returned the other, with the caution of no inexperienced thinker, "neither will I deny it. But if we suppose it so, I need not say that such accountability is neither to you, nor me, nor the Court of Common Pleas, but to something superior."

He was proceeding, when the stranger would have interrupted him; but as reading his argument in his eye, the cosmopolitan, without waiting for it to be put into words, at once spoke to it: "You object to my supposition, for but such it is, that the rattle-snake's accountability is not by nature manifest; but might not much the same thing be urged against man's? A *reductio ad absurdum*, proving the objection vain. But if now," he continued, "you consider what capacity for mischief there is in a rattle-snake (observe, I do not charge it with being mischievous, I but say it has the capacity), could you well avoid admitting that that would be no symmetrical view of the universe which should maintain that, while to man it is forbidden to kill, without judicial cause, his fellow, yet the rattle-snake has an implied permit of unaccountability to murder any creature it takes capricious umbrage at—man included?—But," with a wearied air, "this is no genial talk; at least it is not so to me. Zeal at unawares embarked me in it. I regret it. Pray, sit down, and take some of this wine."

"Your suggestions are new to me," said the other, with a kind of condescending appreciativeness, as of one who, out of devotion to knowledge, disdains not to appropriate the least crumb of it, even from a pauper's board; "and, as I am a very Athenian in hailing a new thought, I cannot consent to let it drop so abruptly. Now, the rattle-snake—"

"Nothing more about rattle-snakes, I beseech," in distress; "I must positively decline to reenter upon that subject. Sit down, sir, I beg, and take some of this wine."

"To invite me to sit down with you is hospitable," collectedly acquiescing now in the change of topics; "and hospitality being fabled to be of oriental origin, and forming, as it does, the subject of a pleasing Arabian romance, as well as being a very romantic thing in itself—hence I always hear the expressions of hospitality with pleasure. But, as for the wine, my regard for that beverage is so extreme, and I am so fearful of letting it sate me, that I keep my love for it in the lasting condition of an untried abstraction. Briefly, I quaff immense draughts of wine from the page of Hafiz, but wine from a cup I seldom as much as sip."

The cosmopolitan turned a mild glance upon the speaker, who, now occupying the chair opposite him, sat there purely and coldly radiant as a prism. It seemed as if one could almost hear him vitreously chime and ring. That moment a waiter passed, whom, arresting with a sign, the cosmopolitan bid go bring a goblet of ice-water. "Ice it well, waiter," said he; "and now," turning to the stranger, "will you, if you please, give me your reason for the warning words you first addressed to me?"

"I hope they were not such warnings as most warnings are," said the stranger; "warnings which do not forewarn, but in mockery come after the fact. And yet something in you bids me think now, that whatever latent design your impostor friend might have had upon you, it as yet remains unaccomplished. You read his label."

"And what did it say? 'This is a genial soul,' So you see you must either give up your doctrine of labels, or else your prejudice against my friend. But tell me," with renewed earnestness, "what do you take him for? What is he?"

"What are you? What am I? Nobody knows who anybody is. The data which life furnishes, towards forming a true estimate of any being,

HERMAN MELVILLE

are as insufficient to that end as in geometry one side given would be to determine the triangle."

"But is not this doctrine of triangles someway inconsistent with your doctrine of labels?"

"Yes; but what of that? I seldom care to be consistent. In a philosophical view, consistency is a certain level at all times, maintained in all the thoughts of one's mind. But, since nature is nearly all hill and dale, how can one keep naturally advancing in knowledge without submitting to the natural inequalities in the progress? Advance into knowledge is just like advance upon the grand Erie canal, where, from the character of the country, change of level is inevitable; you are locked up and locked down with perpetual inconsistencies, and yet all the time you get on; while the dullest part of the whole route is what the boatmen call the 'long level'—a consistently-flat surface of sixty miles through stagnant swamps."

"In one particular," rejoined the cosmopolitan, "your simile is, perhaps, unfortunate. For, after all these weary lockings-up and lockings-down, upon how much of a higher plain do you finally stand? Enough to make it an object? Having from youth been taught reverence for knowledge, you must pardon me if, on but this one account, I reject your analogy. But really you someway bewitch me with your tempting discourse, so that I keep straying from my point unawares. You tell me you cannot certainly know who or what my friend is; pray, what do you conjecture him to be?"

"I conjecture him to be what, among the ancient Egyptians, was called a ——" using some unknown word.

"A ——! And what is that?"

"A —— is what Proclus, in a little note to his third book on the theology of Plato, defines as —— ——" coming out with a sentence of Greek.

Holding up his glass, and steadily looking through its transparency, the cosmopolitan rejoined: "That, in so defining the thing, Proclus set it to modern understandings in the most crystal light it was susceptible of, I will not rashly deny; still, if you could put the definition in words suited to perceptions like mine, I should take it for a favor.

"A favor!" slightly lifting his cool eyebrows; "a bridal favor I understand, a knot of white ribands, a very beautiful type of the purity of true marriage; but of other favors I am yet to learn; and still, in a vague way, the word, as you employ it, strikes me as unpleasingly significant in general of some poor, unheroic submission to being done good to."

Here the goblet of iced-water was brought, and, in compliance with a sign from the cosmopolitan, was placed before the stranger, who, not before expressing acknowledgments, took a draught, apparently refreshing—its very coldness, as with some is the case, proving not entirely uncongenial.

At last, setting down the goblet, and gently wiping from his lips the beads of water freshly clinging there as to the valve of a coral-shell upon a reef, he turned upon the cosmopolitan, and, in a manner the most cool, self-possessed, and matter-of-fact possible, said: "I hold to the metempsychosis; and whoever I may be now, I feel that I was once the stoic Arrian, and have inklings of having been equally puzzled by a word in the current language of that former time, very probably answering to your word *favor*."

"Would you favor me by explaining?" said the cosmopolitan, blandly.

"Sir," responded the stranger, with a very slight degree of severity, "I like lucidity, of all things, and am afraid I shall hardly be able to converse satisfactorily with you, unless you bear it in mind."

The cosmopolitan ruminatingly eyed him awhile, then said: "The best way, as I have heard, to get out of a labyrinth, is to retrace one's steps. I will accordingly retrace mine, and beg you will accompany me. In short, once again to return to the point: for what reason did you warn me against my friend?"

"Briefly, then, and clearly, because, as before said, I conjecture him to be what, among the ancient Egyptians—"

"Pray, now," earnestly deprecated the cosmopolitan, "pray, now, why disturb the repose of those ancient Egyptians? What to us are their words or their thoughts? Are we pauper Arabs, without a house of our own, that, with the mummies, we must turn squatters among the dust of the Catacombs?"

"Pharaoh's poorest brick-maker lies proudlier in his rags than the Emperor of all the Russias in his hollands," oracularly said the stranger; "for death, though in a worm, is majestic; while life, though in a king, is contemptible. So talk not against mummies. It is a part of my mission to teach mankind a due reverence for mummies."

Fortunately, to arrest these incoherencies, or rather, to vary them, a haggard, inspired-looking man now approached—a crazy beggar, asking alms under the form of peddling a rhapsodical tract, composed by himself, and setting forth his claims to some rhapsodical apostleship. Though ragged and dirty, there was about him no touch of vulgarity; for, by nature, his manner was not unrefined, his frame slender, and appeared the more so from the broad, untanned frontlet of his brow, tangled over with a disheveled mass of raven curls, throwing a still deeper tinge upon a complexion like that of a shriveled berry. Nothing could exceed his look of picturesque Italian ruin and dethronement, heightened by what seemed just one glimmering peep of reason, insufficient to do him any lasting good, but enough, perhaps, to suggest a torment of latent doubts at times, whether his addled dream of glory were true.

Accepting the tract offered him, the cosmopolitan glanced over it, and, seeming to see just what it was, closed it, put it in his pocket, eyed the man a moment, then, leaning over and presenting him with a shilling, said to him, in tones kind and considerate: "I am sorry, my friend, that I happen to be engaged just now; but, having purchased your work, I promise myself much satisfaction in its perusal at my earliest leisure."

In his tattered, single-breasted frock-coat, buttoned meagerly up to his chin, the shutter-brain made him a bow, which, for courtesy, would not have misbecome a viscount, then turned with silent appeal to the stranger. But the stranger sat more like a cold prism than ever, while an expression of keen Yankee cuteness, now replacing his former mystical one, lent added icicles to his aspect. His whole air said: "Nothing from me." The repulsed petitioner threw a look full of resentful pride and cracked disdain upon him, and went his way.

"Come, now," said the cosmopolitan, a little reproachfully, "you ought to have sympathized with that man; tell me, did you feel no fellow-feeling? Look at his tract here, quite in the transcendental vein."

"Excuse me," said the stranger, declining the tract, "I never patronize scoundrels."

"Scoundrels?"

"I detected in him, sir, a damning peep of sense—damning, I say; for sense in a seeming madman is scoundrelism. I take him for a cunning vagabond, who picks up a vagabond living by adroitly playing the madman. Did you not remark how he flinched under my eye?'

"Really?" drawing a long, astonished breath, "I could hardly have divined in you a temper so subtlely distrustful. Flinched? to be sure he did, poor fellow; you received him with so lame a welcome. As for his adroitly playing the madman, invidious critics might object the same to some one or two strolling magi of these days. But that is a matter I know nothing about. But, once more, and for the last time, to return to the point: why sir, did you warn me against my friend? I shall rejoice, if, as I think it will prove, your want of confidence in my friend rests upon a basis equally slender with your distrust of the lunatic. Come, why did you warn me? Put it, I beseech, in few words, and those English."

"I warned you against him because he is suspected for what on these boats is known—so they tell me—as a Mississippi operator."

"An operator, ah? he operates, does he? My friend, then, is something like what the Indians call a Great Medicine, is he? He operates, he purges, he drains off the repletions."

"I perceive, sir," said the stranger, constitutionally obtuse to the pleasant drollery, "that your notion, of what is called a Great Medicine, needs correction. The Great Medicine among the Indians is less a bolus than a man in grave esteem for his politic sagacity."

"And is not my friend politic? Is not my friend sagacious? By your own definition, is not my friend a Great Medicine?"

"No, he is an operator, a Mississippi operator; an equivocal character. That he is such, I little doubt, having had him pointed out to me as such by one desirous of initiating me into any little novelty of this western region, where I never before traveled. And, sir, if I am not mistaken, you also are a stranger here (but, indeed, where in this strange universe is not one a stranger?) and that is a reason why I felt moved to warn you against a companion who could not be otherwise than perilous to one of a free and trustful disposition. But I repeat the hope, that, thus far at least, he has not succeeded with you, and trust that, for the future, he will not."

"Thank you for your concern; but hardly can I equally thank you for so steadily maintaining the hypothesis of my friend's objectionableness. True, I but made his acquaintance for the first today, and know little of his antecedents; but that would seem no just reason why a nature like his should not of itself inspire confidence. And since your own knowledge of the gentleman is not, by your account, so exact as it might be, you will pardon me if I decline to welcome any further suggestions unflattering to him. Indeed, sir," with friendly decision, "let us change the subject."

XXXVII

THE MYSTICAL MASTER INTRODUCES THE PRACTICAL DISCIPLE

B oth, the subject and the interlocutor," replied the stranger rising, and waiting the return towards him of a promenader, that moment turning at the further end of his walk.

"Egbert!" said he, calling.

Egbert, a well-dressed, commercial-looking gentleman of about thirty, responded in a way strikingly deferential, and in a moment stood near, in the attitude less of an equal companion apparently than a confidential follower.

"This," said the stranger, taking Egbert by the hand and leading him to the cosmopolitan, "this is Egbert, a disciple. I wish you to know Egbert. Egbert was the first among mankind to reduce to practice the principles of Mark Winsome—principles previously accounted as less adapted to life than the closet. Egbert," turning to the disciple, who, with seeming modesty, a little shrank under these compliments, "Egbert, this," with a salute towards the cosmopolitan, "is, like all of us, a stranger. I wish you, Egbert, to know this brother stranger; be communicative with him. Particularly if, by anything hitherto dropped, his curiosity has been roused as to the precise nature of my philosophy, I trust you will not leave such curiosity ungratified. You, Egbert, by simply setting forth your practice, can do more to enlighten one as to my theory, than I myself can by mere speech. Indeed, it is by you that I myself best understand myself. For to every philosophy are certain rear parts, very important parts, and these, like the rear of one's head, are best seen by reflection. Now, as in a glass, you, Egbert, in your life, reflect to me the more important part of my system. He, who approves you, approves the philosophy of Mark Winsome."

Though portions of this harangue may, perhaps, in the phraseology seem self-complaisant, yet no trace of self-complacency was perceptible in the speaker's manner, which throughout was plain, unassuming, dignified, and manly; the teacher and prophet seemed to lurk more in the idea, so to speak, than in the mere bearing of him who was the vehicle of it.

"Sir," said the cosmopolitan, who seemed not a little interested in this new aspect of matters, "you speak of a certain philosophy, and a more or less occult one it may be, and hint of its bearing upon practical life; pray, tell me, if the study of this philosophy tends to the same formation of character with the experiences of the world?"

"It does; and that is the test of its truth; for any philosophy that, being in operation contradictory to the ways of the world, tends to produce a character at odds with it, such a philosophy must necessarily be but a cheat and a dream."

"You a little surprise me," answered the cosmopolitan; "for, from an occasional profundity in you, and also from your allusions to a profound work on the theology of Plato, it would seem but natural to surmise that, if you are the originator of any philosophy, it must needs so partake of the abstruse, as to exalt it above the comparatively vile uses of life."

"No uncommon mistake with regard to me," rejoined the other. Then meekly standing like a Raphael: "If still in golden accents old Memnon murmurs his riddle, none the less does the balance-sheet of every man's ledger unriddle the profit or loss of life. Sir," with calm energy, "man came into this world, not to sit down and muse, not to befog himself with vain subtleties, but to gird up his loins and to work. Mystery is in the morning, and mystery in the night, and the beauty of mystery is everywhere; but still the plain truth remains, that mouth and purse must be filled. If, hitherto, you have supposed me a visionary, be undeceived. I am no one-ideaed one, either; no more than the seers before me. Was not Seneca a usurer? Bacon a courtier? and Swedenborg, though with one eye on the invisible, did he not keep the other on the main chance? Along with whatever else it may be given me to be, I am a man of serviceable knowledge, and a man of the world. Know me for such. And as for my disciple here," turning towards him, "if you look to find any soft Utopianisms and last year's sunsets in him, I smile to think how he will set you right. The doctrines I have taught him will, I trust, lead him neither to the mad-house nor the poor-house, as so many other doctrines have served credulous sticklers. Furthermore," glancing upon him paternally, "Egbert is both my disciple and my poet. For poetry is not a thing of ink and rhyme, but of thought and act, and, in the latter way, is by any one to be found anywhere, when in useful action sought. In a word, my disciple here is a thriving young merchant, a practical poet in the West India trade.

There," presenting Egbert's hand to the cosmopolitan, "I join you, and leave you." With which words, and without bowing, the master withdrew.

XXXVIII

THE DISCIPLE UNBENDS, AND CONSENTS TO ACT A SOCIAL PART

I n the master's presence the disciple had stood as one not ignorant of his place; modesty was in his expression, with a sort of reverential depression. But the presence of the superior withdrawn, he seemed lithely to shoot up erect from beneath it, like one of those wire men from a toy snuff-box.

He was, as before said, a young man of about thirty. His countenance of that neuter sort, which, in repose, is neither prepossessing nor disagreeable; so that it seemed quite uncertain how he would turn out. His dress was neat, with just enough of the mode to save it from the reproach of originality; in which general respect, though with a readjustment of details, his costume seemed modeled upon his master's. But, upon the whole, he was, to all appearances, the last person in the world that one would take for the disciple of any transcendental philosophy; though, indeed, something about his sharp nose and shaved chin seemed to hint that if mysticism, as a lesson, ever came in his way, he might, with the characteristic knack of a true New-Englander, turn even so profitless a thing to some profitable account.

"Well" said he, now familiarly seating himself in the vacated chair, "what do you think of Mark? Sublime fellow, ain't he?"

"That each member of the human guild is worthy respect my friend," rejoined the cosmopolitan, "is a fact which no admirer of that guild will question; but that, in view of higher natures, the word sublime, so frequently applied to them, can, without confusion, be also applied to man, is a point which man will decide for himself; though, indeed, if he decide it in the affirmative, it is not for me to object. But I am curious to know more of that philosophy of which, at present, I have but inklings. You, its first disciple among men, it seems, are peculiarly qualified to expound it. Have you any objections to begin now?"

"None at all," squaring himself to the table. "Where shall I begin? At first principles?"

"You remember that it was in a practical way that you were represented as being fitted for the clear exposition. Now, what you call first principles, I have, in some things, found to be more or less vague. Permit me, then, in a plain way, to suppose some common case in real life, and that done, I would like you to tell me how you, the practical disciple of the philosophy I wish to know about, would, in that case, conduct."

"A business-like view. Propose the case."

"Not only the case, but the persons. The case is this: There are two friends, friends from childhood, bosom-friends; one of whom, for the first time, being in need, for the first time seeks a loan from the other, who, so far as fortune goes, is more than competent to grant it. And the persons are to be you and I: you, the friend from whom the loan is sought—I, the friend who seeks it; you, the disciple of the philosophy in question—I, a common man, with no more philosophy than to know that when I am comfortably warm I don't feel cold, and when I have the ague I shake. Mind, now, you must work up your imagination, and, as much as possible, talk and behave just as if the case supposed were a fact. For brevity, you shall call me Frank, and I will call you Charlie. Are you agreed?"

"Perfectly. You begin."

The cosmopolitan paused a moment, then, assuming a serious and care-worn air, suitable to the part to be enacted, addressed his hypothesized friend.

The Hypothetical Friends

C harlie, I am going to put confidence in you."

"You always have, and with reason. What is it Frank?"

"Charlie, I am in want—urgent want of money."

"That's not well."

"But it *will* be well, Charlie, if you loan me a hundred dollars. I would not ask this of you, only my need is sore, and you and I have so long shared hearts and minds together, however unequally on my side, that nothing remains to prove our friendship than, with the same inequality on my side, to share purses. You will do me the favor won't you?"

"Favor? What do you mean by asking me to do you a favor?"

"Why, Charlie, you never used to talk so."

"Because, Frank, you on your side, never used to talk so."

"But won't you loan me the money?"

"No, Frank."

"Why?"

"Because my rule forbids. I give away money, but never loan it; and of course the man who calls himself my friend is above receiving alms. The negotiation of a loan is a business transaction. And I will transact no business with a friend. What a friend is, he is socially and intellectually; and I rate social and intellectual friendship too high to degrade it on either side into a pecuniary make-shift. To be sure there are, and I have, what is called business friends; that is, commercial acquaintances, very convenient persons. But I draw a red-ink line between them and my friends in the true sense—my friends social and intellectual. In brief, a true friend has nothing to do with loans; he should have a soul above loans. Loans are such unfriendly accommodations as are to be had from the soulless corporation of a bank, by giving the regular security and paying the regular discount."

"An *unfriendly* accommodation? Do those words go together handsomely?"

"Like the poor farmer's team, of an old man and a cow—not handsomely, but to the purpose. Look, Frank, a loan of money on interest is a sale of money on credit. To sell a thing on credit may be an accommodation, but where is the friendliness? Few men in their senses, except operators, borrow money on interest, except upon a necessity akin to starvation. Well, now, where is the friendliness of my letting a starving man have, say, the money's worth of a barrel of flour upon the condition that, on a given day, he shall let me have the money's worth of a barrel and a half of flour; especially if I add this further proviso, that if he fail so to do, I shall then, to secure to myself the money's worth of my barrel and his half barrel, put his heart up at public auction, and, as it is cruel to part families, throw in his wife's and children's?"

"I understand," with a pathetic shudder; "but even did it come to that, such a step on the creditor's part, let us, for the honor of human nature, hope, were less the intention than the contingency."

"But, Frank, a contingency not unprovided for in the taking beforehand of due securities."

"Still, Charlie, was not the loan in the first place a friend's act?"

"And the auction in the last place an enemy's act. Don't you see? The enmity lies couched in the friendship, just as the ruin in the relief."

"I must be very stupid today, Charlie, but really, I can't understand this. Excuse me, my dear friend, but it strikes me that in going into the philosophy of the subject, you go somewhat out of your depth."

"So said the incautious wader out to the ocean; but the ocean replied: 'It is just the other way, my wet friend,' and drowned him."

"That, Charlie, is a fable about as unjust to the ocean, as some of Æsop's are to the animals. The ocean is a magnanimous element, and would scorn to assassinate a poor fellow, let alone taunting him in the act. But I don't understand what you say about enmity couched in friendship, and ruin in relief."

"I will illustrate, Frank, The needy man is a train slipped off the rail. He who loans him money on interest is the one who, by way of accommodation, helps get the train back where it belongs; but then, by way of making all square, and a little more, telegraphs to an agent, thirty miles a-head by a precipice, to throw just there, on his account, a beam across the track. Your needy man's principle-and-interest friend is, I say again, a friend with an enmity in reserve. No, no, my dear friend, no interest for me. I scorn interest."

"Well, Charlie, none need you charge. Loan me without interest."

"That would be alms again."

"Alms, if the sum borrowed is returned?"

"Yes: an alms, not of the principle, but the interest."

"Well, I am in sore need, so I will not decline the alms. Seeing that it is you, Charlie, gratefully will I accept the alms of the interest. No humiliation between friends."

"Now, how in the refined view of friendship can you suffer yourself to talk so, my dear Frank. It pains me. For though I am not of the sour mind of Solomon, that, in the hour of need, a stranger is better than a brother; yet, I entirely agree with my sublime master, who, in his Essay on Friendship, says so nobly, that if he want a terrestrial convenience, not to his friend celestial (or friend social and intellectual) would he go; no: for his terrestrial convenience, to his friend terrestrial (or humbler business-friend) he goes. Very lucidly he adds the reason: Because, for the superior nature, which on no account can ever descend to do good, to be annoyed with requests to do it, when the inferior one, which by no instruction can ever rise above that capacity, stands always inclined to it—this is unsuitable."

"Then I will not consider you as my friend celestial, but as the other."

"It racks me to come to that; but, to oblige you, I'll do it. We are business friends; business is business. You want to negotiate a loan. Very good. On what paper? Will you pay three per cent a month? Where is your security?"

"Surely, you will not exact those formalities from your old schoolmate—him with whom you have so often sauntered down the groves of Academe, discoursing of the beauty of virtue, and the grace that is in kindliness—and all for so paltry a sum. Security? Our being fellow-academics, and friends from childhood up, is security."

"Pardon me, my dear Frank, our being fellow-academics is the worst of securities; while, our having been friends from childhood up is just no security at all. You forget we are now business friends."

"And you, on your side, forget, Charlie, that as your business friend I can give you no security; my need being so sore that I cannot get an indorser."

"No indorser, then, no business loan."

"Since then, Charlie, neither as the one nor the other sort of friend you have defined, can I prevail with you; how if, combining the two, I sue as both?"

"Are you a centaur?"

"When all is said then, what good have I of your friendship, regarded in what light you will?"

"The good which is in the philosophy of Mark Winsome, as reduced to practice by a practical disciple."

"And why don't you add, much good may the philosophy of Mark Winsome do me? Ah," turning invokingly, "what is friendship, if it be not the helping hand and the feeling heart, the good Samaritan pouring out at need the purse as the vial!"

"Now, my dear Frank, don't be childish. Through tears never did man see his way in the dark. I should hold you unworthy that sincere friendship I bear you, could I think that friendship in the ideal is too lofty for you to conceive. And let me tell you, my dear Frank, that you would seriously shake the foundations of our love, if ever again you should repeat the present scene. The philosophy, which is mine in the strongest way, teaches plain-dealing. Let me, then, now, as at the most suitable time, candidly disclose certain circumstances you seem in ignorance of. Though our friendship began in boyhood, think not that, on my side at least, it began injudiciously. Boys are little men, it is said. You, I juvenilely picked out for my friend, for your favorable points at the time; not the least of which were your good manners, handsome dress, and your parents' rank and repute of wealth. In short, like any grown man, boy though I was, I went into the market and chose me my mutton, not for its leanness, but its fatness. In other words, there seemed in you, the schoolboy who always had silver in his pocket, a reasonable probability that you would never stand in lean need of fat succor; and if my early impression has not been verified by the event, it is only because of the caprice of fortune producing a fallibility of human expectations, however discreet.'"

"Oh, that I should listen to this cold-blooded disclosure!"

"A little cold blood in your ardent veins, my dear Frank, wouldn't do you any harm, let me tell you. Cold-blooded? You say that, because my disclosure seems to involve a vile prudence on my side. But not so. My reason for choosing you in part for the points I have mentioned, was solely with a view of preserving inviolate the delicacy of the connection. For—do but think of it—what more distressing to delicate friendship, formed early, than your friend's eventually, in manhood, dropping in of a rainy night for his little loan of five dollars or so? Can delicate friendship stand that? And, on the other side, would delicate friendship, so long as it retained its delicacy, do that? Would you not instinctively say of your dripping friend in the entry, 'I have been deceived, fraudulently deceived, in this man; he is no true friend that, in platonic love to demand love-rites?'"

"And rites, doubly rights, they are, cruel Charlie!"

"Take it how you will, heed well how, by too importunately claiming those rights, as you call them, you shake those foundations I hinted of. For though, as it turns out, I, in my early friendship, built me a fair house on a poor site; yet such pains and cost have I lavished on that house, that, after all, it is dear to me. No, I would not lose the sweet boon of your friendship, Frank. But beware."

"And of what? Of being in need? Oh, Charlie! you talk not to a god, a being who in himself holds his own estate, but to a man who, being a man, is the sport of fate's wind and wave, and who mounts towards heaven or sinks towards hell, as the billows roll him in trough or on crest."

"Tut! Frank. Man is no such poor devil as that comes to—no poor drifting sea-weed of the universe. Man has a soul; which, if he will, puts him beyond fortune's finger and the future's spite. Don't whine like fortune's whipped dog, Frank, or by the heart of a true friend, I will cut ye."

"Cut me you have already, cruel Charlie, and to the quick. Call to mind the days we went nutting, the times we walked in the woods, arms wreathed about each other, showing trunks invined like the trees:—oh, Charlie!"

"Pish! we were boys."

"Then lucky the fate of the first-born of Egypt, cold in the grave ere maturity struck them with a sharper frost.—Charlie?"

"Fie! you're a girl."

"Help, help, Charlie, I want help!"

"Help? to say nothing of the friend, there is something wrong about the man who wants help. There is somewhere a defect, a want, in brief, a need, a crying need, somewhere about that man."

"So there is, Charlie.—Help, Help!"

"How foolish a cry, when to implore help, is itself the proof of undesert of it."

"Oh, this, all along, is not you, Charlie, but some ventriloquist who usurps your larynx. It is Mark Winsome that speaks, not Charlie."

"If so, thank heaven, the voice of Mark Winsome is not alien but congenial to my larynx. If the philosophy of that illustrious teacher find little response among mankind at large, it is less that they do not

HERMAN MELVILLE

possess teachable tempers, than because they are so unfortunate as not to have natures predisposed to accord with him.

"Welcome, that compliment to humanity," exclaimed Frank with energy, "the truer because unintended. And long in this respect may humanity remain what you affirm it. And long it will; since humanity, inwardly feeling how subject it is to straits, and hence how precious is help, will, for selfishness' sake, if no other, long postpone ratifying a philosophy that banishes help from the world. But Charlie, Charlie! speak as you used to; tell me you will help me. Were the case reversed, not less freely would I loan you the money than you would ask me to loan it.

"*I* ask? *I* ask a loan? Frank, by this hand, under no circumstances would I accept a loan, though without asking pressed on me. The experience of China Aster might warn me."

"And what was that?"

"Not very unlike the experience of the man that built himself a palace of moon-beams, and when the moon set was surprised that his palace vanished with it. I will tell you about China Aster. I wish I could do so in my own words, but unhappily the original story-teller here has so tyrannized over me, that it is quite impossible for me to repeat his incidents without sliding into his style. I forewarn you of this, that you may not think me so maudlin as, in some parts, the story would seem to make its narrator. It is too bad that any intellect, especially in so small a matter, should have such power to impose itself upon another, against its best exerted will, too. However, it is satisfaction to know that the main moral, to which all tends, I fully approve. But, to begin."

XL

In Which the Story of China Aster is at Second-Hand Told By One Who, While Not Disapproving the Moral, Disclaims the Spirit of the Style

China Aster was a young candle-maker of Marietta, at the mouth of the Muskingum—one whose trade would seem a kind of subordinate branch of that parent craft and mystery of the hosts of heaven, to be the means, effectively or otherwise, of shedding some light through the darkness of a planet benighted. But he made little money by the business. Much ado had poor China Aster and his family to live; he could, if he chose, light up from his stores a whole street, but not so easily could he light up with prosperity the hearts of his household.

"Now, China Aster, it so happened, had a friend, Orchis, a shoemaker; one whose calling it is to defend the understandings of men from naked contact with the substance of things: a very useful vocation, and which, spite of all the wiseacres may prophesy, will hardly go out of fashion so long as rocks are hard and flints will gall. All at once, by a capital prize in a lottery, this useful shoemaker was raised from a bench to a sofa. A small nabob was the shoemaker now, and the understandings of men, let them shift for themselves. Not that Orchis was, by prosperity, elated into heartlessness. Not at all. Because, in his fine apparel, strolling one morning into the candlery, and gayly switching about at the candle-boxes with his gold-headed cane—while poor China Aster, with his greasy paper cap and leather apron, was selling one candle for one penny to a poor orange-woman, who, with the patronizing coolness of a liberal customer, required it to be carefully rolled up and tied in a half sheet of paper—lively Orchis, the woman being gone, discontinued his gay switchings and said: 'This is poor business for you, friend China Aster; your capital is too small. You must drop this vile tallow and hold up pure spermaceti to the world. I tell you what it is, you shall have one thousand dollars to extend with. In fact, you must make money, China Aster. I don't like to see your little boy paddling about without shoes, as he does.'

"'Heaven bless your goodness, friend Orchis,' replied the candle-maker, 'but don't take it illy if I call to mind the word of my uncle, the blacksmith, who, when a loan was offered him, declined it, saying: "To ply my own hammer, light though it be, I think best, rather than piece it out heavier by welding to it a bit off a neighbor's hammer, though that may have some weight to spare; otherwise, were the borrowed bit suddenly wanted again, it might not split off at the welding, but too much to one side or the other."'

"'Nonsense, friend China Aster, don't be so honest; your boy is barefoot. Besides, a rich man lose by a poor man? Or a friend be the worse by a friend? China Aster, I am afraid that, in leaning over into your vats here, this, morning, you have spilled out your wisdom. Hush! I won't hear any more. Where's your desk? Oh, here.' With that, Orchis dashed off a check on his bank, and off-handedly presenting it, said: 'There, friend China Aster, is your one thousand dollars; when you make it ten thousand, as you soon enough will (for experience, the only true knowledge, teaches me that, for every one, good luck is in store), then, China Aster, why, then you can return me the money or not, just as you please. But, in any event, give yourself no concern, for I shall never demand payment.'

"Now, as kind heaven will so have it that to a hungry man bread is a great temptation, and, therefore, he is not too harshly to be blamed, if, when freely offered, he take it, even though it be uncertain whether he shall ever be able to reciprocate; so, to a poor man, proffered money is equally enticing, and the worst that can be said of him, if he accept it, is just what can be said in the other case of the hungry man. In short, the poor candle-maker's scrupulous morality succumbed to his unscrupulous necessity, as is now and then apt to be the case. He took the check, and was about carefully putting it away for the present, when Orchis, switching about again with his gold-headed cane, said: 'By-the-way, China Aster, it don't mean anything, but suppose you make a little memorandum of this; won't do any harm, you know.' So China Aster gave Orchis his note for one thousand dollars on demand. Orchis took it, and looked at it a moment, 'Pooh, I told you, friend China Aster, I wasn't going ever to make any *demand*.' Then tearing up the note, and switching away again at the candle-boxes, said, carelessly; 'Put it at four years.' So China Aster gave Orchis his note for one thousand dollars at four years. 'You see I'll never trouble you about this,' said Orchis, slipping it in his pocket-book, 'give yourself no further thought, friend

China Aster, than how best to invest your money. And don't forget my hint about spermaceti. Go into that, and I'll buy all my light of you,' with which encouraging words, he, with wonted, rattling kindness, took leave.

"China Aster remained standing just where Orchis had left him; when, suddenly, two elderly friends, having nothing better to do, dropped in for a chat. The chat over, China Aster, in greasy cap and apron, ran after Orchis, and said: 'Friend Orchis, heaven will reward you for your good intentions, but here is your check, and now give me my note.'

"'Your honesty is a bore, China Aster,' said Orchis, not without displeasure. 'I won't take the check from you.'

"'Then you must take it from the pavement, Orchis,' said China Aster; and, picking up a stone, he placed the check under it on the walk.

"'China Aster,' said Orchis, inquisitively eying him, after my leaving the candlery just now, what asses dropped in there to advise with you, that now you hurry after me, and act so like a fool? Shouldn't wonder if it was those two old asses that the boys nickname Old Plain Talk and Old Prudence.'

"'Yes, it was those two, Orchis, but don't call them names.'

"'A brace of spavined old croakers. Old Plain Talk had a shrew for a wife, and that's made him shrewish; and Old Prudence, when a boy, broke down in an apple-stall, and that discouraged him for life. No better sport for a knowing spark like me than to hear Old Plain Talk wheeze out his sour old saws, while Old Prudence stands by, leaning on his staff, wagging his frosty old pow, and chiming in at every clause.'

"'How can you speak so, friend Orchis, of those who were my father's friends?'"

"'Save me from my friends, if those old croakers were Old Honesty's friends. I call your father so, for every one used to. Why did they let him go in his old age on the town? Why, China Aster, I've often heard from my mother, the chronicler, that those two old fellows, with Old Conscience—as the boys called the crabbed old quaker, that's dead now—they three used to go to the poor-house when your father was there, and get round his bed, and talk to him for all the world as Eliphaz, Bildad, and Zophar did to poor old pauper Job. Yes, Job's comforters were Old Plain Talk, and Old Prudence, and Old Conscience, to your poor old father. Friends? I should like to know who you call foes? With their everlasting croaking and reproaching they tormented poor Old Honesty, your father, to death.'

"At these words, recalling the sad end of his worthy parent, China Aster could not restrain some tears. Upon which Orchis said: 'Why, China Aster, you are the dolefulest creature. Why don't you, China Aster, take a bright view of life? You will never get on in your business or anything else, if you don't take the bright view of life. It's the ruination of a man to take the dismal one.' Then, gayly poking at him with his gold-headed cane, 'Why don't you, then? Why don't you be bright and hopeful, like me? Why don't you have confidence, China Aster?

"'I'm sure I don't know, friend Orchis,' soberly replied China Aster, 'but may be my not having drawn a lottery-prize, like you, may make some difference.'

"Nonsense! before I knew anything about the prize I was gay as a lark, just as gay as I am now. In fact, it has always been a principle with me to hold to the bright view.'

"Upon this, China Aster looked a little hard at Orchis, because the truth was, that until the lucky prize came to him, Orchis had gone under the nickname of Doleful Dumps, he having been beforetimes of a hypochondriac turn, so much so as to save up and put by a few dollars of his scanty earnings against that rainy day he used to groan so much about.

"'I tell you what it is, now, friend China Aster,' said Orchis, pointing down to the check under the stone, and then slapping his pocket, 'the check shall lie there if you say so, but your note shan't keep it company. In fact, China Aster, I am too sincerely your friend to take advantage of a passing fit of the blues in you. You *shall* reap the benefit of my friendship.' With which, buttoning up his coat in a jiffy, away he ran, leaving the check behind.

"At first, China Aster was going to tear it up, but thinking that this ought not to be done except in the presence of the drawer of the check, he mused a while, and picking it up, trudged back to the candlery, fully resolved to call upon Orchis soon as his day's work was over, and destroy the check before his eyes. But it so happened that when China Aster called, Orchis was out, and, having waited for him a weary time in vain, China Aster went home, still with the check, but still resolved not to keep it another day. Bright and early next morning he would a second time go after Orchis, and would, no doubt, make a sure thing of it, by finding him in his bed; for since the lottery-prize came to him, Orchis, besides becoming more cheery, had also grown a little lazy. But as destiny would have it, that same night China Aster had a dream, in which a being in the guise of a smiling angel, and holding a kind of cornucopia in her hand, hovered over him, pouring down showers of small gold dollars, thick as kernels of corn. 'I am Bright Future, friend China Aster,' said the angel, 'and if you do what friend Orchis would have you do, just see what will come of it.' With which Bright Future, with another swing of her cornucopia, poured such another shower of small gold dollars upon him, that it seemed to bank him up all round, and he waded about in it like a maltster in malt.

"Now, dreams are wonderful things, as everybody knows—so wonderful, indeed, that some people stop not short of ascribing them directly to heaven; and China Aster, who was of a proper turn of mind in everything, thought that in consideration of the dream, it would be but well to wait a little, ere seeking Orchis again. During the day, China Aster's mind dwelling continually upon the dream, he was so full of it, that when Old Plain Talk dropped in to see him, just before dinnertime, as he often did, out of the interest he took in Old Honesty's son, China Aster told all about his vision, adding that he could not think that so radiant an angel could deceive; and, indeed, talked at such a rate that one would have thought he believed the angel some beautiful human philanthropist. Something in this sort Old Plain Talk understood him, and, accordingly, in his plain way, said: 'China Aster, you tell me that an angel appeared to you in a dream. Now, what does that amount to but this, that you dreamed an angel appeared to you? Go right away, China Aster, and return the check, as I advised you before. If friend Prudence were here, he would say just the same thing.' With which words Old Plain Talk went off to find friend Prudence, but not succeeding, was returning to the candlery himself, when, at distance mistaking him for a dun who had long annoyed him, China Aster in a panic barred all his doors, and ran to the back part of the candlery, where no knock could be heard.

"By this sad mistake, being left with no friend to argue the other side of the question, China Aster was so worked upon at last, by musing over his dream, that nothing would do but he must get the check cashed, and lay out the money the very same day in buying a good lot of spermaceti to make into candles, by which operation he counted upon turning a better penny than he ever had before in his life; in fact, this he believed would prove the foundation of that famous fortune which the angel had promised him.

HERMAN MELVILLE

"Now, in using the money, China Aster was resolved punctually to pay the interest every six months till the principal should be returned, howbeit not a word about such a thing had been breathed by Orchis; though, indeed, according to custom, as well as law, in such matters, interest would legitimately accrue on the loan, nothing to the contrary having been put in the bond. Whether Orchis at the time had this in mind or not, there is no sure telling; but, to all appearance, he never so much as cared to think about the matter, one way or other.

"Though the spermaceti venture rather disappointed China Aster's sanguine expectations, yet he made out to pay the first six months' interest, and though his next venture turned out still less prosperously, yet by pinching his family in the matter of fresh meat, and, what pained him still more, his boys' schooling, he contrived to pay the second six months' interest, sincerely grieved that integrity, as well as its opposite, though not in an equal degree, costs something, sometimes.

"Meanwhile, Orchis had gone on a trip to Europe by advice of a physician; it so happening that, since the lottery-prize came to him, it had been discovered to Orchis that his health was not very firm, though he had never complained of anything before but a slight ailing of the spleen, scarce worth talking about at the time. So Orchis, being abroad, could not help China Aster's paying his interest as he did, however much he might have been opposed to it; for China Aster paid it to Orchis's agent, who was of too business-like a turn to decline interest regularly paid in on a loan.

"But overmuch to trouble the agent on that score was not again to be the fate of China Aster; for, not being of that skeptical spirit which refuses to trust customers, his third venture resulted, through bad debts, in almost a total loss—a bad blow for the candle-maker. Neither did Old Plain Talk, and Old Prudence neglect the opportunity to read him an uncheerful enough lesson upon the consequences of his disregarding their advice in the matter of having nothing to do with borrowed money. 'It's all just as I predicted,' said Old Plain Talk, blowing his old nose with his old bandana. 'Yea, indeed is it,' chimed in Old Prudence, rapping his staff on the floor, and then leaning upon it, looking with solemn forebodings upon China Aster. Low-spirited enough felt the poor candle-maker; till all at once who should come with a bright face to him but his bright friend, the angel, in another dream. Again the cornucopia poured out its treasure, and promised still more. Revived by the vision, he resolved not to be down-hearted, but up and at it once more—contrary to the advice of Old Plain Talk, backed as usual by his crony, which was to the effect, that, under present circumstances, the best thing China Aster could do, would be to wind up his business, settle, if he could, all his liabilities, and then go to work as a journeyman, by which he could earn good wages, and give up, from that time henceforth, all thoughts of rising above being a paid subordinate to men more able than himself, for China Aster's career thus far plainly proved him the legitimate son of Old Honesty, who, as every one knew, had never shown much business-talent, so little, in fact, that many said of him that he had no business to be in business. And just this plain saying Plain Talk now plainly applied to China Aster, and Old Prudence never disagreed with him. But the angel in the dream did, and, maugre Plain Talk, put quite other notions into the candle-maker.

"He considered what he should do towards reëstablishing himself. Doubtless, had Orchis been in the country, he would have aided him in this strait. As it was, he applied to others; and as in the world, much as some may hint to the contrary, an honest man in misfortune still can find friends to stay by him and help him, even so it proved with China Aster, who at last succeeded in borrowing from a rich old farmer the sum of six hundred dollars, at the usual interest of money-lenders, upon the security of a secret bond signed by China Aster's wife and himself, to the effect that all such right and title to any property that should be left her by a well-to-do childless uncle, an invalid tanner, such property should, in the event of China Aster's failing to return the borrowed sum on the given day, be the lawful possession of the money-lender. True, it was just as much as China Aster could possibly do to induce his wife, a careful woman, to sign this bond; because she had always regarded her promised share in her uncle's estate as an anchor well to windward of the hard times in which China Aster had always been more or less involved, and from which, in her bosom, she never had seen much chance of his freeing himself. Some notion may be had of China Aster's standing in the heart and head of his wife, by a short sentence commonly used in reply to such persons as happened to sound her on the point. 'China Aster,' she would say, 'is a good husband, but a bad business man!' Indeed, she was a connection on the maternal side of Old Plain Talk's. But had not China Aster taken good care not to let Old Plain Talk and Old Prudence hear of his dealings with the old farmer, ten to one they would, in some way, have interfered with his success in that quarter.

HERMAN MELVILLE

"It has been hinted that the honesty of China Aster was what mainly induced the money-lender to befriend him in his misfortune, and this must be apparent; for, had China Aster been a different man, the money-lender might have dreaded lest, in the event of his failing to meet his note, he might some way prove slippery—more especially as, in the hour of distress, worked upon by remorse for so jeopardizing his wife's money, his heart might prove a traitor to his bond, not to hint that it was more than doubtful how such a secret security and claim, as in the last resort would be the old farmer's, would stand in a court of law. But though one inference from all this may be, that had China Aster been something else than what he was, he would not have been trusted, and, therefore, he would have been effectually shut out from running his own and wife's head into the usurer's noose; yet those who, when everything at last came out, maintained that, in this view and to this extent, the honesty of the candle-maker was no advantage to him, in so saying, such persons said what every good heart must deplore, and no prudent tongue will admit.

"It may be mentioned, that the old farmer made China Aster take part of his loan in three old dried-up cows and one lame horse, not improved by the glanders. These were thrown in at a pretty high figure, the old money-lender having a singular prejudice in regard to the high value of any sort of stock raised on his farm. With a great deal of difficulty, and at more loss, China Aster disposed of his cattle at public auction, no private purchaser being found who could be prevailed upon to invest. And now, raking and scraping in every way, and working early and late, China Aster at last started afresh, nor without again largely and confidently extending himself. However, he did not try his hand at the spermaceti again, but, admonished by experience, returned to tallow. But, having bought a good lot of it, by the time he got it into candles, tallow fell so low, and candles with it, that his candles per pound barely sold for what he had paid for the tallow. Meantime, a year's unpaid interest had accrued on Orchis' loan, but China Aster gave himself not so much concern about that as about the interest now due to the old farmer. But he was glad that the principal there had yet some time to run. However, the skinny old fellow gave him some trouble by coming after him every day or two on a scraggy old white horse, furnished with a musty old saddle, and goaded into his shambling old paces with a withered old raw hide. All the neighbors said that surely Death himself on the pale horse was after poor China Aster now. And something so it proved; for, ere long, China Aster found himself involved in troubles mortal enough.

At this juncture Orchis was heard of. Orchis, it seemed had returned from his travels, and clandestinely married, and, in a kind of queer way, was living in Pennsylvania among his wife's relations, who, among other things, had induced him to join a church, or rather semi-religious school, of Come-Outers; and what was still more, Orchis, without coming to the spot himself, had sent word to his agent to dispose of some of his property in Marietta, and remit him the proceeds. Within a year after, China Aster received a letter from Orchis, commending him for his punctuality in paying the first year's interest, and regretting the necessity that he (Orchis) was now under of using all his dividends; so he relied upon China Aster's paying the next six months' interest, and of course with the back interest. Not more surprised than alarmed, China Aster thought of taking steamboat to go and see Orchis, but he was saved that expense by the unexpected arrival in Marietta of Orchis in person, suddenly called there by that strange kind of capriciousness lately characterizing him. No sooner did China Aster hear of his old friend's arrival than he hurried to call upon him. He found him curiously rusty in dress, sallow in cheek, and decidedly less gay and cordial in manner, which the more surprised China Aster, because, in former days, he had more than once heard Orchis, in his light rattling way, declare that all he (Orchis) wanted to make him a perfectly happy, hilarious, and benignant man, was a voyage to Europe and a wife, with a free development of his inmost nature.

"Upon China Aster's stating his case, his trusted friend was silent for a time; then, in an odd way, said that he would not crowd China Aster, but still his (Orchis') necessities were urgent. Could not China Aster mortgage the candlery? He was honest, and must have moneyed friends; and could he not press his sales of candles? Could not the market be forced a little in that particular? The profits on candles must be very great. Seeing, now, that Orchis had the notion that the candle-making business was a very profitable one, and knowing sorely enough what an error was here, China Aster tried to undeceive him. But he could not drive the truth into Orchis—Orchis being very obtuse here, and, at the same time, strange to say, very melancholy. Finally, Orchis glanced off from so unpleasing a subject into the most unexpected reflections, taken from a religious point of view, upon the unstableness and deceitfulness of the human heart. But having, as he thought, experienced something of that sort of thing, China Aster did not take exception to his friend's observations, but still refrained from so doing, almost as much for the sake of sympathetic sociality as anything else. Presently, Orchis, without much ceremony, rose, and saying he must write a letter to his wife, bade his friend good-bye, but without warmly shaking him by the hand as of old.

"In much concern at the change, China Aster made earnest inquiries in suitable quarters, as to what things, as yet unheard of, had befallen Orchis, to bring about such a revolution; and learned at last that, besides traveling, and getting married, and joining the sect of Come-Outers, Orchis had somehow got a bad dyspepsia, and lost considerable property through a breach of trust on the part of a factor in New York. Telling these things to Old Plain Talk, that man of some knowledge of the world shook his old head, and told China Aster that, though he hoped it might prove otherwise, yet it seemed to him that all he had communicated about Orchis worked together for bad omens as to his future forbearance—especially, he added with a grim sort of smile, in view of his joining the sect of Come-Outers; for, if some men knew what was their inmost natures, instead of coming out with it, they would try their best to keep it in, which, indeed, was the way with the prudent sort. In all which sour notions Old Prudence, as usual, chimed in.

"When interest-day came again, China Aster, by the utmost exertions, could only pay Orchis' agent a small part of what was due, and a part of that was made up by his children's gift money (bright tenpenny pieces and new quarters, kept in their little money-boxes), and pawning his best clothes, with those of his wife and children, so that all were subjected to the hardship of staying away from church. And the old usurer, too, now beginning to be obstreperous, China Aster paid him his interest and some other pressing debts with money got by, at last, mortgaging the candlery.

"When next interest-day came round for Orchis, not a penny could be raised. With much grief of heart, China Aster so informed Orchis' agent. Meantime, the note to the old usurer fell due, and nothing from China Aster was ready to meet it; yet, as heaven sends its rain on the just and unjust alike, by a coincidence not unfavorable to the old farmer, the well-to-do uncle, the tanner, having died, the usurer entered upon possession of such part of his property left by will to the wife of China Aster. When still the next interest-day for Orchis came round, it found China Aster worse off than ever; for, besides his other troubles, he was now weak with sickness. Feebly dragging himself to Orchis' agent, he met him in the street, told him just how it was; upon which the agent, with a grave enough face, said that he had instructions from his employer not to crowd him about the interest at present, but to say to him that about the time the note would mature, Orchis would have heavy liabilities to meet, and therefore the note must at that time be certainly paid, and, of course, the back interest with it; and not only so, but, as Orchis had had to allow the interest for good part of the time, he hoped that, for the back interest, China Aster would, in reciprocation, have no objections to allowing interest on the interest annually. To be sure, this was not the law; but, between friends who accommodate each other, it was the custom.

"Just then, Old Plain Talk with Old Prudence turned the corner, coming plump upon China Aster as the agent left him; and whether it was a sun-stroke, or whether they accidentally ran against him, or whether it was his being so weak, or whether it was everything together, or how it was exactly, there is no telling, but poor China Aster fell to the earth, and, striking his head sharply, was picked up senseless. It was a day in July; such a light and heat as only the midsummer banks of the inland Ohio know. China Aster was taken home on a door; lingered a few days with a wandering mind, and kept wandering on, till at last, at dead of night, when nobody was aware, his spirit wandered away into the other world.

"Old Plain Talk and Old Prudence, neither of whom ever omitted attending any funeral, which, indeed, was their chief exercise—these two were among the sincerest mourners who followed the remains of the son of their ancient friend to the grave.

"It is needless to tell of the executions that followed; how that the candlery was sold by the mortgagee; how Orchis never got a penny for his loan; and how, in the case of the poor widow, chastisement was tempered with mercy; for, though she was left penniless, she was not left childless. Yet, unmindful of the alleviation, a spirit of complaint, at what she impatiently called the bitterness of her lot and the hardness of the world, so preyed upon her, as ere long to hurry her from the obscurity of indigence to the deeper shades of the tomb.

"But though the straits in which China Aster had left his family had, besides apparently dimming the world's regard, likewise seemed to dim its sense of the probity of its deceased head, and though this, as some thought, did not speak well for the world, yet it happened in this case, as in others, that, though the world may for a time seem insensible to that merit which lies under a cloud, yet, sooner or later, it always renders honor where honor is due; for, upon the death of the widow, the freemen of Marietta, as a tribute of respect for China Aster, and an expression of their conviction of his high moral worth, passed a resolution, that, until they attained maturity, his children should be considered the town's guests. No mere verbal compliment, like those of some public bodies; for, on the same day, the orphans were officially installed in that hospitable edifice where their worthy grandfather, the town's guest before them, had breathed his last breath.

"But sometimes honor maybe paid to the memory of an honest man, and still his mound remain without a monument. Not so, however, with the candle-maker. At an early day, Plain Talk had procured a plain stone, and was digesting in his mind what pithy word or two to place upon it, when there was discovered, in China Aster's otherwise empty wallet, an epitaph, written, probably, in one of those disconsolate hours, attended with more or less mental aberration, perhaps, so frequent with him for some months prior to his end. A memorandum on the back expressed the wish that it might be placed over his grave. Though with the sentiment of the epitaph Plain Talk did not disagree, he himself being at times of a hypochondriac turn—at least, so many said—yet the language struck him as too much drawn out; so, after consultation with Old Prudence, he decided upon making use of the epitaph, yet not without verbal retrenchments. And though, when these were made, the thing still appeared wordy to him, nevertheless, thinking that, since a dead man was to be spoken about, it was but just to let him speak for himself, especially when he spoke sincerely, and when, by so doing, the more salutary lesson would be given, he had the retrenched inscription chiseled as follows upon the stone.

'HERE LIE
THE REMAINS OF
CHINA ASTER THE CANDLE-MAKER,
WHOSE CAREER
WAS AN EXAMPLE OF THE TRUTH OF SCRIPTURE, AS FOUND
IN THE
SOBER PHILOSOPHY
OF
SOLOMON THE WISE;
FOR HE WAS RUINED BY ALLOWING HIMSELF TO BE PERSUADED,

Against his Better Sense,
Into the Free Indulgence of Confidence,
And
An Ardently Bright View of Life,
to the Exclusion
of
That Counsel which Comes by Heeding
the
Opposite View.'

"This inscription raised some talk in the town, and was rather severely criticised by the capitalist—one of a very cheerful turn—who had secured his loan to China Aster by the mortgage; and though it also proved obnoxious to the man who, in town-meeting, had first moved for the compliment to China Aster's memory, and, indeed, was deemed by him a sort of slur upon the candle-maker, to that degree that he refused to believe that the candle-maker himself had composed it, charging Old Plain Talk with the authorship, alleging that the internal evidence showed that none but that veteran old croaker could have penned such a jeremiade—yet, for all this, the stone stood. In everything, of course, Old Plain Talk was seconded by Old Prudence; who, one day going to the grave-yard, in great-coat and over-shoes—for, though it was a sunshiny morning, he thought that, owing to heavy dews, dampness might lurk in the ground—long stood before the stone, sharply leaning over on his staff, spectacles on nose, spelling out the epitaph word by word; and, afterwards meeting Old Plain Talk in the street, gave a great rap with his stick, and said: 'Friend, Plain Talk, that epitaph will do very well. Nevertheless, one short sentence is wanting.' Upon which, Plain Talk said it was too late, the chiseled words being so arranged, after the usual manner of such inscriptions, that nothing could be interlined. Then,' said Old Prudence, 'I will put it in the shape of a postscript.' Accordingly, with the approbation of Old Plain Talk, he had the following words chiseled at the left-hand corner of the stone, and pretty low down:

'The root of all was a friendly loan.'"

XLI

Ending With a Rupture of the Hypothesis

W ith what heart," cried Frank, still in character, "have you told me this story? A story I can no way approve; for its moral, if accepted, would drain me of all reliance upon my last stay, and, therefore, of my last courage in life. For, what was that bright view of China Aster but a cheerful trust that, if he but kept up a brave heart, worked hard, and ever hoped for the best, all at last would go well? If your purpose, Charlie, in telling me this story, was to pain me, and keenly, you have succeeded; but, if it was to destroy my last confidence, I praise God you have not."

"Confidence?" cried Charlie, who, on his side, seemed with his whole heart to enter into the spirit of the thing, "what has confidence to do with the matter? That moral of the story, which I am for commending to you, is this: the folly, on both sides, of a friend's helping a friend. For was not that loan of Orchis to China Aster the first step towards their estrangement? And did it not bring about what in effect was the enmity of Orchis? I tell you, Frank, true friendship, like other precious things, is not rashly to be meddled with. And what more meddlesome between friends than a loan? A regular marplot. For how can you help that the helper must turn out a creditor? And creditor and friend, can they ever be one? no, not in the most lenient case; since, out of lenity to forego one's claim, is less to be a friendly creditor than to cease to be a creditor at all. But it will not do to rely upon this lenity, no, not in the best man; for the best man, as the worst, is subject to all mortal contingencies. He may travel, he may marry, he may join the Come-Outers, or some equally untoward school or sect, not to speak of other things that more or less tend to new-cast the character. And were there nothing else, who shall answer for his digestion, upon which so much depends?"

"But Charlie, dear Charlie—"

"Nay, wait.—You have hearkened to my story in vain, if you do not see that, however indulgent and right-minded I may seem to you now, that is no guarantee for the future. And into the power of that uncertain personality which, through the mutability of my humanity, I may hereafter become, should not common sense dissuade you, my dear Frank, from putting yourself? Consider. Would you, in your present need, be willing to accept a loan from a friend, securing him by a mortgage on your homestead, and do so, knowing that you had no reason to feel satisfied that the mortgage might not eventually be transferred into the hands of a foe? Yet the difference between this man and that man is not so great as the difference between what the same man be today and what he may be in days to come. For there is no bent of heart or turn of thought which any man holds by virtue of an unalterable nature or will. Even those feelings and opinions deemed most identical with eternal right and truth, it is not impossible but that, as personal persuasions, they may in reality be but the result of some chance tip of Fate's elbow in throwing her dice. For, not to go into the first seeds of things, and passing by the accident of parentage predisposing to this or that habit of mind, descend below these, and tell me, if you change this man's experiences or that man's books, will wisdom go surety for his unchanged convictions? As particular food begets particular dreams, so particular experiences or books particular feelings or beliefs. I will hear nothing of that fine babble about development and its laws; there is no development in opinion and feeling but the developments of time and tide. You may deem all this talk idle, Frank; but conscience bids me show you how fundamental the reasons for treating you as I do."

"But Charlie, dear Charlie, what new notions are these? I thought that man was no poor drifting weed of the universe, as you phrased it; that, if so minded, he could have a will, a way, a thought, and a heart of his own? But now you have turned everything upside down again, with an inconsistency that amazes and shocks me."

"Inconsistency? Bah!"

"There speaks the ventriloquist again," sighed Frank, in bitterness.

Illy pleased, it may be, by this repetition of an allusion little flattering to his originality, however much so to his docility, the disciple sought to carry it off by exclaiming: "Yes, I turn over day and night, with indefatigable pains, the sublime pages of my master, and unfortunately for you, my dear friend, I find nothing *there* that leads me to think otherwise than I do. But enough: in this matter the experience of China Aster teaches a moral more to the point than anything Mark Winsome can offer, or I either."

"I cannot think so, Charlie; for neither am I China Aster, nor do I stand in his position. The loan to China Aster was to extend his business with; the loan I seek is to relieve my necessities."

"Your dress, my dear Frank, is respectable; your cheek is not gaunt. Why talk of necessities when nakedness and starvation beget the only real necessities?"

"But I need relief, Charlie; and so sorely, that I now conjure you to forget that I was ever your friend, while I apply to you only as a fellow-being, whom, surely, you will not turn away."

"That I will not. Take off your hat, bow over to the ground, and supplicate an alms of me in the way of London streets, and you shall not be a sturdy beggar in vain. But no man drops pennies into the hat of a friend, let me tell you. If you turn beggar, then, for the honor of noble friendship, I turn stranger."

"Enough," cried the other, rising, and with a toss of his shoulders seeming disdainfully to throw off the character he had assumed. "Enough. I have had my fill of the philosophy of Mark Winsome as put into action. And moonshiny as it in theory may be, yet a very practical philosophy it turns out in effect, as he himself engaged I should find. But, miserable for my race should I be, if I thought he spoke truth when he claimed, for proof of the soundness of his system, that the study of it tended to much the same formation of character with the experiences of the world.—Apt disciple! Why wrinkle the brow, and waste the oil both of life and the lamp, only to turn out a head kept cool by the under ice of the heart? What your illustrious magian has taught you, any poor, old, broken-down, heart-shrunken dandy might have lisped. Pray, leave me, and with you take the last dregs of your inhuman philosophy. And here, take this shilling, and at the first wood-landing buy yourself a few chips to warm the frozen natures of you and your philosopher by."

With these words and a grand scorn the cosmopolitan turned on his heel, leaving his companion at a loss to determine where exactly the fictitious character had been dropped, and the real one, if any, resumed. If any, because, with pointed meaning, there occurred to him, as he gazed after the cosmopolitan, these familiar lines:

> *"All the world's a stage,*
> *And all the men and women merely players,*
> *Who have their exits and their entrances,*
> *And one man in his time plays many parts."*

XLII

UPON THE HEEL OF THE LAST SCENE THE COSMOPOLITAN ENTERS THE BARBER'S SHOP, A BENEDICTION ON HIS LIPS

B less you, barber!"

Now, owing to the lateness of the hour, the barber had been all alone until within the ten minutes last passed; when, finding himself rather dullish company to himself, he thought he would have a good time with Souter John and Tam O'Shanter, otherwise called Somnus and Morpheus, two very good fellows, though one was not very bright, and the other an arrant rattlebrain, who, though much listened to by some, no wise man would believe under oath.

In short, with back presented to the glare of his lamps, and so to the door, the honest barber was taking what are called cat-naps, and dreaming in his chair; so that, upon suddenly hearing the benediction above, pronounced in tones not unangelic, starting up, half awake, he stared before him, but saw nothing, for the stranger stood behind. What with cat-naps, dreams, and bewilderments, therefore, the voice seemed a sort of spiritual manifestation to him; so that, for the moment, he stood all agape, eyes fixed, and one arm in the air.

"Why, barber, are you reaching up to catch birds there with salt?"

"Ah!" turning round disenchanted, "it is only a man, then."

"*Only* a man? As if to be but a man were nothing. But don't be too sure what I am. You call me *man*, just as the townsfolk called the angels who, in man's form, came to Lot's house; just as the Jew rustics called the devils who, in man's form, haunted the tombs. You can conclude nothing absolute from the human form, barber."

"But I can conclude something from that sort of talk, with that sort of dress," shrewdly thought the barber, eying him with regained self-possession, and not without some latent touch of apprehension at being alone with him. What was passing in his mind seemed divined by the other, who now, more rationally and gravely, and as if he expected it should be attended to, said: "Whatever else you may conclude upon, it is my desire that you conclude to give me a good shave," at the same time loosening his neck-cloth. "Are you competent to a good shave, barber?"

"No broker more so, sir," answered the barber, whom the business-like proposition instinctively made confine to business-ends his views of the visitor.

"Broker? What has a broker to do with lather? A broker I have always understood to be a worthy dealer in certain papers and metals."

"He, he!" taking him now for some dry sort of joker, whose jokes, he being a customer, it might be as well to appreciate, "he, he! You understand well enough, sir. Take this seat, sir," laying his hand on a great stuffed chair, high-backed and high-armed, crimson-covered, and raised on a sort of dais, and which seemed but to lack a canopy and quarterings, to make it in aspect quite a throne, "take this seat, sir."

"Thank you," sitting down; "and now, pray, explain that about the broker. But look, look—what's this?" suddenly rising, and pointing, with his long pipe, towards a gilt notification swinging among colored fly-papers from the ceiling, like a tavern sign, "*No Trust?*" "No trust means distrust; distrust means no confidence. Barber," turning upon him excitedly, "what fell suspiciousness prompts this scandalous confession? My life!" stamping his foot, "if but to tell a dog that you have no confidence in him be matter for affront to the dog, what an insult to take that way the whole haughty race of man by the beard! By my heart, sir! but at least you are valiant; backing the spleen of Thersites with the pluck of Agamemnon."

"Your sort of talk, sir, is not exactly in my line," said the barber, rather ruefully, being now again hopeless of his customer, and not without return of uneasiness; "not in my line, sir," he emphatically repeated.

"But the taking of mankind by the nose is; a habit, barber, which I sadly fear has insensibly bred in you a disrespect for man. For how, indeed, may respectful conceptions of him coexist with the perpetual habit of taking him by the nose? But, tell me, though I, too, clearly see the import of your notification, I do not, as yet, perceive the object. What is it?"

"Now you speak a little in my line, sir," said the barber, not unrelieved at this return to plain talk; "that notification I find very useful, sparing me much work which would not pay. Yes, I lost a good deal, off and on, before putting that up," gratefully glancing towards it.

"But what is its object? Surely, you don't mean to say, in so many words, that you have no confidence? For instance, now," flinging aside his neck-cloth, throwing back his blouse, and reseating himself on the tonsorial throne, at sight of which proceeding the barber mechanically filled a cup with hot water from a copper vessel over a spirit-lamp, "for instance, now, suppose I say to you, 'Barber, my dear barber, unhappily I have no small change by me tonight, but shave me, and depend upon your money tomorrow'—suppose I should say that now, you would put trust in me, wouldn't you? You would have confidence?"

"Seeing that it is you, sir," with complaisance replied the barber, now mixing the lather, "seeing that it is *you* sir, I won't answer that question. No need to."

"Of course, of course—in that view. But, as a supposition—you would have confidence in me, wouldn't you?"

"Why—yes, yes."

"Then why that sign?"

"Ah, sir, all people ain't like you," was the smooth reply, at the same time, as if smoothly to close the debate, beginning smoothly to apply the lather, which operation, however, was, by a motion, protested against by the subject, but only out of a desire to rejoin, which was done in these words:

"All people ain't like me. Then I must be either better or worse than most people. Worse, you could not mean; no, barber, you could not mean that; hardly that. It remains, then, that you think me better than most people. But that I ain't vain enough to believe; though, from vanity, I confess, I could never yet, by my best wrestlings, entirely free myself; nor, indeed, to be frank, am I at bottom over anxious to—this same vanity, barber, being so harmless, so useful, so comfortable, so pleasingly preposterous a passion."

"Very true, sir; and upon my honor, sir, you talk very well. But the lather is getting a little cold, sir."

"Better cold lather, barber, than a cold heart. Why that cold sign? Ah, I don't wonder you try to shirk the confession. You feel in your soul how ungenerous a hint is there. And yet, barber, now that I look into your eyes—which somehow speak to me of the mother that must have so often looked into them before me—I dare say, though you may not think it, that the spirit of that notification is not one with your nature. For look now, setting, business views aside, regarding the thing in an abstract light; in short, supposing a case, barber; supposing, I say, you see a stranger, his face accidentally averted, but his visible part very respectable-looking; what now, barber—I put it to your conscience, to your charity—what would be your impression of that man, in a moral point of view? Being in a signal sense a stranger, would you, for that, signally set him down for a knave?"

"Certainly not, sir; by no means," cried the barber, humanely resentful.

"You would upon the face of him—"

"Hold, sir," said the barber, "nothing about the face; you remember, sir, that is out of sight."

"I forgot that. Well then, you would, upon the *back* of him, conclude him to be, not improbably, some worthy sort of person; in short, an honest man: wouldn't you?"

"Not unlikely I should, sir."

"Well now—don't be so impatient with your brush, barber—suppose that honest man meet you by night in some dark corner of the boat where his face would still remain unseen, asking you to trust him for a shave—how then?"

"Wouldn't trust him, sir."

"But is not an honest man to be trusted?"

"Why—why—yes, sir."

"There! don't you see, now?"

"See what?" asked the disconcerted barber, rather vexedly.

"Why, you stand self-contradicted, barber; don't you?"

"No," doggedly.

"Barber," gravely, and after a pause of concern, "the enemies of our race have a saying that insincerity is the most universal and inveterate vice of man—the lasting bar to real amelioration, whether of individuals or of the world. Don't you now, barber, by your stubbornness on this occasion, give color to such a calumny?"

"Hity-tity!" cried the barber, losing patience, and with it respect; "stubbornness?" Then clattering round the brush in the cup, "Will you be shaved, or won't you?"

"Barber, I will be shaved, and with pleasure; but, pray, don't raise your voice that way. Why, now, if you go through life gritting your teeth in that fashion, what a comfortless time you will have."

"I take as much comfort in this world as you or any other man," cried the barber, whom the other's sweetness of temper seemed rather to exasperate than soothe.

"To resent the imputation of anything like unhappiness I have often observed to be peculiar to certain orders of men," said the other pensively, and half to himself, "just as to be indifferent to that imputation, from holding happiness but for a secondary good and inferior grace, I have observed to be equally peculiar to other kinds of men. Pray, barber," innocently looking up, "which think you is the superior creature?"

"All this sort of talk," cried the barber, still unmollified, "is, as I told you once before, not in my line. In a few minutes I shall shut up this shop. Will you be shaved?"

"Shave away, barber. What hinders?" turning up his face like a flower.

The shaving began, and proceeded in silence, till at length it became necessary to prepare to relather a little—affording an opportunity for resuming the subject, which, on one side, was not let slip.

"Barber," with a kind of cautious kindliness, feeling his way, "barber, now have a little patience with me; do; trust me, I wish not to offend. I have been thinking over that supposed case of the man with the averted face, and I cannot rid my mind of the impression that, by your opposite replies to my questions at the time, you showed yourself much of a piece with a good many other men—that is, you have confidence, and then again, you have none. Now, what I would ask is, do you think it sensible standing for a sensible man, one foot on confidence and the other on suspicion? Don't you think, barber, that you ought to elect? Don't you think consistency requires that you should either say 'I have confidence in all men,' and take down your notification; or else say, 'I suspect all men,' and keep it up."

This dispassionate, if not deferential, way of putting the case, did not fail to impress the barber, and proportionately conciliate him. Likewise, from its pointedness, it served to make him thoughtful; for, instead of going to the copper vessel for more water, as he had purposed, he halted half-way towards it, and, after a pause, cup in hand, said: "Sir, I hope you would not do me injustice. I don't say, and can't say, and wouldn't say, that I suspect all men; but I *do* say that strangers are not to be trusted, and so," pointing up to the sign, "no trust."

"But look, now, I beg, barber," rejoined the other deprecatingly, not presuming too much upon the barber's changed temper; "look, now; to say that strangers are not to be trusted, does not that imply something like saying that mankind is not to be trusted; for the mass of mankind, are they not necessarily strangers to each individual man? Come, come, my friend," winningly, "you are no Timon to hold the mass of mankind untrustworthy. Take down your notification; it is misanthropical; much the same sign that Timon traced with charcoal on the forehead of a skull stuck over his cave. Take it down, barber; take it down tonight. Trust men. Just try the experiment of trusting men for this one little

HERMAN MELVILLE

trip. Come now, I'm a philanthropist, and will insure you against losing a cent."

The barber shook his head dryly, and answered, "Sir, you must excuse me. I have a family."

XLIII

Very Charming

S o you are a philanthropist, sir," added the barber with an illuminated look; "that accounts, then, for all. Very odd sort of man the philanthropist. You are the second one, sir, I have seen. Very odd sort of man, indeed, the philanthropist. Ah, sir," again meditatively stirring in the shaving-cup, "I sadly fear, lest you philanthropists know better what goodness is, than what men are." Then, eying him as if he were some strange creature behind cage-bars, "So you are a philanthropist, sir."

"I am Philanthropos, and love mankind. And, what is more than you do, barber, I trust them."

Here the barber, casually recalled to his business, would have replenished his shaving-cup, but finding now that on his last visit to the water-vessel he had not replaced it over the lamp, he did so now; and, while waiting for it to heat again, became almost as sociable as if the heating water were meant for whisky-punch; and almost as pleasantly garrulous as the pleasant barbers in romances.

"Sir," said he, taking a throne beside his customer (for in a row there were three thrones on the dais, as for the three kings of Cologne, those patron saints of the barber), "sir, you say you trust men. Well, I suppose I might share some of your trust, were it not for this trade, that I follow, too much letting me in behind the scenes."

"I think I understand," with a saddened look; "and much the same thing I have heard from persons in pursuits different from yours—from the lawyer, from the congressman, from the editor, not to mention others, each, with a strange kind of melancholy vanity, claiming for his vocation the distinction of affording the surest inlets to the conviction that man is no better than he should be. All of which testimony, if reliable, would, by mutual corroboration, justify some disturbance in a good man's mind. But no, no; it is a mistake—all a mistake."

"True, sir, very true," assented the barber.

"Glad to hear that," brightening up.

"Not so fast, sir," said the barber; "I agree with you in thinking that the lawyer, and the congressman, and the editor, are in error, but only in so far as each claims peculiar facilities for the sort of knowledge in

HERMAN MELVILLE

question; because, you see, sir, the truth is, that every trade or pursuit which brings one into contact with the facts, sir, such trade or pursuit is equally an avenue to those facts."

"*How* exactly is that?"

"Why, sir, in my opinion—and for the last twenty years I have, at odd times, turned the matter over some in my mind—he who comes to know man, will not remain in ignorance of man. I think I am not rash in saying that; am I, sir?"

"Barber, you talk like an oracle—obscurely, barber, obscurely."

"Well, sir," with some self-complacency, "the barber has always been held an oracle, but as for the obscurity, that I don't admit."

"But pray, now, by your account, what precisely may be this mysterious knowledge gained in your trade? I grant you, indeed, as before hinted, that your trade, imposing on you the necessity of functionally tweaking the noses of mankind, is, in that respect, unfortunate, very much so; nevertheless, a well-regulated imagination should be proof even to such a provocation to improper conceits. But what I want to learn from you, barber, is, how does the mere handling of the outside of men's heads lead you to distrust the inside of their hearts?

"What, sir, to say nothing more, can one be forever dealing in macassar oil, hair dyes, cosmetics, false moustaches, wigs, and toupees, and still believe that men are wholly what they look to be? What think you, sir, are a thoughtful barber's reflections, when, behind a careful curtain, he shaves the thin, dead stubble off a head, and then dismisses it to the world, radiant in curling auburn? To contrast the shamefaced air behind the curtain, the fearful looking forward to being possibly discovered there by a prying acquaintance, with the cheerful assurance and challenging pride with which the same man steps forth again, a gay deception, into the street, while some honest, shock-headed fellow humbly gives him the wall! Ah, sir, they may talk of the courage of truth, but my trade teaches me that truth sometimes is sheepish. Lies, lies, sir, brave lies are the lions!"

"You twist the moral, barber; you sadly twist it. Look, now; take it this way: A modest man thrust out naked into the street, would he not be abashed? Take him in and clothe him; would not his confidence be restored? And in either case, is any reproach involved? Now, what is true of the whole, holds proportionably true of the part. The bald head is a nakedness which the wig is a coat to. To feel uneasy at the possibility of the exposure of one's nakedness at top, and to feel comforted by the consciousness of having it clothed—these feelings, instead of being dishonorable to a bold man, do, in fact, but attest a proper respect for himself and his fellows. And as for the deception, you may as well call the fine roof of a fine chateau a deception, since, like a fine wig, it also is an artificial cover to the head, and equally, in the common eye, decorates the wearer.—I have confuted you, my dear barber; I have confounded you."

"Pardon," said the barber, "but I do not see that you have. His coat and his roof no man pretends to palm off as a part of himself, but the bald man palms off hair, not his, for his own."

"Not *his*, barber? If he have fairly purchased his hair, the law will protect him in its ownership, even against the claims of the head on which it grew. But it cannot be that you believe what you say, barber; you talk merely for the humor. I could not think so of you as to suppose that you would contentedly deal in the impostures you condemn."

"Ah, sir, I must live."

"And can't you do that without sinning against your conscience, as you believe? Take up some other calling."

"Wouldn't mend the matter much, sir."

"Do you think, then, barber, that, in a certain point, all the trades and callings of men are much on a par? Fatal, indeed," raising his hand, "inexpressibly dreadful, the trade of the barber, if to such conclusions it necessarily leads. Barber," eying him not without emotion, "you appear to me not so much a misbeliever, as a man misled. Now, let me set you on the right track; let me restore you to trust in human nature, and by no other means than the very trade that has brought you to suspect it."

"You mean, sir, you would have me try the experiment of taking down that notification," again pointing to it with his brush; "but, dear me, while I sit chatting here, the water boils over."

With which words, and such a well-pleased, sly, snug, expression, as they say some men have when they think their little stratagem has succeeded, he hurried to the copper vessel, and soon had his cup foaming up with white bubbles, as if it were a mug of new ale.

Meantime, the other would have fain gone on with the discourse; but the cunning barber lathered him with so generous a brush, so piled up the foam on him, that his face looked like the yeasty crest of a billow, and vain to think of talking under it, as for a drowning priest in the sea to exhort his fellow-sinners on a raft. Nothing would do, but he must keep his mouth shut. Doubtless, the interval was not, in a meditative way, unimproved; for, upon the traces of the operation being at last removed, the cosmopolitan rose, and, for added refreshment, washed his face and hands; and having generally readjusted himself, began, at last, addressing the barber in a manner different, singularly so, from his previous one. Hard to say exactly what the manner was, any more than to hint it was a sort of magical; in a benign way, not wholly unlike the manner, fabled or otherwise, of certain creatures in nature, which have the power of persuasive fascination—the power of holding another creature by the button of the eye, as it were, despite the serious disinclination, and, indeed, earnest protest, of the victim. With this manner the conclusion of the matter was not out of keeping; for, in the end, all argument and expostulation proved vain, the barber being irresistibly persuaded to agree to try, for the remainder of the present trip, the experiment of trusting men, as both phrased it. True, to save his credit as a free agent, he was loud in averring that it was only for the novelty of the thing that he so agreed, and he required the other, as before volunteered, to go security to him against any loss that might ensue; but still the fact remained, that he engaged to trust men, a thing he had before said he would not do, at least not unreservedly. Still the more to save his credit, he now insisted upon it, as a last point, that the agreement should be put in black and white, especially the security part. The other made no demur; pen, ink, and paper were provided, and grave as any notary the cosmopolitan sat down, but, ere taking the pen, glanced up at the notification, and said: "First down with that sign, barber—Timon's sign, there; down with it."

This, being in the agreement, was done—though a little reluctantly—with an eye to the future, the sign being carefully put away in a drawer.

"Now, then, for the writing," said the cosmopolitan, squaring himself. "Ah," with a sigh, "I shall make a poor lawyer, I fear. Ain't used, you see, barber, to a business which, ignoring the principle of honor, holds no nail fast till clinched. Strange, barber," taking up the blank paper, "that such flimsy stuff as this should make such strong hawsers; vile hawsers, too. Barber," starting up, "I won't put it in black and white. It were a reflection upon our joint honor. I will take your word, and you shall take mine."

"But your memory may be none of the best, sir. Well for you, on your side, to have it in black and white, just for a memorandum like, you know."

"That, indeed! Yes, and it would help *your* memory, too, wouldn't it, barber? Yours, on your side, being a little weak, too, I dare say. Ah, barber! how ingenious we human beings are; and how kindly we reciprocate each other's little delicacies, don't we? What better proof, now, that we are kind, considerate fellows, with responsive fellow-feelings—eh, barber? But to business. Let me see. What's your name, barber?"

"William Cream, sir."

Pondering a moment, he began to write; and, after some corrections, leaned back, and read aloud the following:

"AGREEMENT
Between
FRANK GOODMAN, Philanthropist, and Citizen of the World, and
WILLIAM CREAM, Barber of the Mississippi steamer, Fidèle.

"The first hereby agrees to make good to the last any loss that may come from his trusting mankind, in the way of his vocation, for the residue of the present trip; *provided* that William Cream keep out of sight, for the given term, his notification of *no trust*, and by no other mode convey any, the least hint or intimation, tending to discourage men from soliciting trust from him, in the way of his vocation, for the time above specified; but, on the contrary, he do, by all proper and reasonable words, gestures, manners, and looks, evince a perfect confidence in all men, especially strangers; otherwise, this agreement to be void.

"Done, in good faith, this 1st day of April 18—, at a quarter to twelve o'clock, P.M., in the shop of said William Cream, on board the said boat, Fidèle."

"There, barber; will that do?"

"That will do," said the barber, "only now put down your name."

Both signatures being affixed, the question was started by the barber, who should have custody of the instrument; which point, however, he settled for himself, by proposing that both should go together to the captain, and give the document into his hands—the barber hinting that this would be a safe proceeding, because the captain was necessarily a party disinterested, and, what was more, could not, from the nature of the present case, make anything by a breach of trust. All of which was listened to with some surprise and concern.

"Why, barber," said the cosmopolitan, "this don't show the right spirit; for me, I have confidence in the captain purely because he is a man; but he shall have nothing to do with our affair; for if you have no confidence in me, barber, I have in you. There, keep the paper yourself," handing it magnanimously.

"Very good," said the barber, "and now nothing remains but for me to receive the cash."

Though the mention of that word, or any of its singularly numerous equivalents, in serious neighborhood to a requisition upon one's purse, is attended with a more or less noteworthy effect upon the human countenance, producing in many an abrupt fall of it—in others, a writhing and screwing up of the features to a point not undistressing to behold, in some, attended with a blank pallor and fatal consternation— yet no trace of any of these symptoms was visible upon the countenance of the cosmopolitan, notwithstanding nothing could be more sudden and unexpected than the barber's demand.

"You speak of cash, barber; pray in what connection?"

"In a nearer one, sir," answered the barber, less blandly, "than I thought the man with the sweet voice stood, who wanted me to trust him once for a shave, on the score of being a sort of thirteenth cousin."

"Indeed, and what did you say to him?"

"I said, 'Thank you, sir, but I don't see the connection,'"

"How could you so unsweetly answer one with a sweet voice?"

"Because, I recalled what the son of Sirach says in the True Book: 'An enemy speaketh sweetly with his lips;' and so I did what the son of Sirach advises in such cases: 'I believed not his many words.'"

"What, barber, do you say that such cynical sort of things are in the True Book, by which, of course, you mean the Bible?"

"Yes, and plenty more to the same effect. Read the Book of Proverbs."

"That's strange, now, barber; for I never happen to have met with those passages you cite. Before I go to bed this night, I'll inspect the Bible I saw on the cabin-table, today. But mind, you mustn't quote the True Book that way to people coming in here; it would be impliedly a violation of the contract. But you don't know how glad I feel that you have for one while signed off all that sort of thing."

"No, sir; not unless you down with the cash."

"Cash again! What do you mean?"

"Why, in this paper here, you engage, sir, to insure me against a certain loss, and—"

"Certain? Is it so *certain* you are going to lose?"

"Why, that way of taking the word may not be amiss, but I didn't mean it so. I meant a *certain* loss; you understand, a *certain* loss; that is to say, a certain loss. Now then, sir, what use your mere writing and saying you will insure me, unless beforehand you place in my hands a money-pledge, sufficient to that end?"

"I see; the material pledge."

"Yes, and I will put it low; say fifty dollars."

"Now what sort of a beginning is this? You, barber, for a given time engage to trust man, to put confidence in men, and, for your first step, make a demand implying no confidence in the very man you engage with. But fifty dollars is nothing, and I would let you have it cheerfully, only I unfortunately happen to have but little change with me just now."

"But you have money in your trunk, though?"

"To be sure. But you see—in fact, barber, you must be consistent. No, I won't let you have the money now; I won't let you violate the inmost spirit of our contract, that way. So good-night, and I will see you again."

"Stay, sir"—humming and hawing—"you have forgotten something."

"Handkerchief?—gloves? No, forgotten nothing. Good-night."

"Stay, sir—the—the shaving."

"Ah, I *did* forget that. But now that it strikes me, I shan't pay you at present. Look at your agreement; you must trust. Tut! against loss you hold the guarantee. Good-night, my dear barber."

With which words he sauntered off, leaving the barber in a maze, staring after.

But it holding true in fascination as in natural philosophy, that nothing can act where it is not, so the barber was not long now in being restored to his self-possession and senses; the first evidence of which perhaps was, that, drawing forth his notification from the drawer, he put it back where it belonged; while, as for the agreement, that he tore up; which he felt the more free to do from the impression that in all human probability he would never again see the person who had drawn it. Whether that impression proved well-founded or not, does

HERMAN MELVILLE

not appear. But in after days, telling the night's adventure to his friends, the worthy barber always spoke of his queer customer as the man-charmer—as certain East Indians are called snake-charmers—and all his friends united in thinking him *quite an original*.

XLIV

In Which the Last Three Words of the
Last Chapter are Made the Text of
Discourse, Which Will Be Sure of
Receiving More or Less Attention From
Those Readers Who Do Not Skip it

Quite an original:" A phrase, we fancy, rather oftener used by the young, or the unlearned, or the untraveled, than by the old, or the well-read, or the man who has made the grand tour. Certainly, the sense of originality exists at its highest in an infant, and probably at its lowest in him who has completed the circle of the sciences.

As for original characters in fiction, a grateful reader will, on meeting with one, keep the anniversary of that day. True, we sometimes hear of an author who, at one creation, produces some two or three score such characters; it may be possible. But they can hardly be original in the sense that Hamlet is, or Don Quixote, or Milton's Satan. That is to say, they are not, in a thorough sense, original at all. They are novel, or singular, or striking, or captivating, or all four at once.

More likely, they are what are called odd characters; but for that, are no more original, than what is called an odd genius, in his way, is. But, if original, whence came they? Or where did the novelist pick them up?

Where does any novelist pick up any character? For the most part, in town, to be sure. Every great town is a kind of man-show, where the novelist goes for his stock, just as the agriculturist goes to the cattle-show for his. But in the one fair, new species of quadrupeds are hardly more rare, than in the other are new species of characters—that is, original ones. Their rarity may still the more appear from this, that, while characters, merely singular, imply but singular forms so to speak, original ones, truly so, imply original instincts.

In short, a due conception of what is to be held for this sort of personage in fiction would make him almost as much of a prodigy there, as in real history is a new law-giver, a revolutionizing philosopher, or the founder of a new religion.

HERMAN MELVILLE

In nearly all the original characters, loosely accounted such in works of invention, there is discernible something prevailingly local, or of the age; which circumstance, of itself, would seem to invalidate the claim, judged by the principles here suggested.

Furthermore, if we consider, what is popularly held to entitle characters in fiction to being deemed original, is but something personal—confined to itself. The character sheds not its characteristic on its surroundings, whereas, the original character, essentially such, is like a revolving Drummond light, raying away from itself all round it—everything is lit by it, everything starts up to it (mark how it is with Hamlet), so that, in certain minds, there follows upon the adequate conception of such a character, an effect, in its way, akin to that which in Genesis attends upon the beginning of things.

For much the same reason that there is but one planet to one orbit, so can there be but one such original character to one work of invention. Two would conflict to chaos. In this view, to say that there are more than one to a book, is good presumption there is none at all. But for new, singular, striking, odd, eccentric, and all sorts of entertaining and instructive characters, a good fiction may be full of them. To produce such characters, an author, beside other things, must have seen much, and seen through much: to produce but one original character, he must have had much luck.

There would seem but one point in common between this sort of phenomenon in fiction and all other sorts: it cannot be born in the author's imagination—it being as true in literature as in zoology, that all life is from the egg.

In the endeavor to show, if possible, the impropriety of the phrase, *Quite an Original*, as applied by the barber's friends, we have, at unawares, been led into a dissertation bordering upon the prosy, perhaps upon the smoky. If so, the best use the smoke can be turned to, will be, by retiring under cover of it, in good trim as may be, to the story.

XLV

The Cosmopolitan Increases in Seriousness

In the middle of the gentleman's cabin burned a solar lamp, swung from the ceiling, and whose shade of ground glass was all round fancifully variegated, in transparency, with the image of a horned altar, from which flames rose, alternate with the figure of a robed man, his head encircled by a halo. The light of this lamp, after dazzlingly striking on marble, snow-white and round—the slab of a centre-table beneath—on all sides went rippling off with ever-diminishing distinctness, till, like circles from a stone dropped in water, the rays died dimly away in the furthest nook of the place.

Here and there, true to their place, but not to their function, swung other lamps, barren planets, which had either gone out from exhaustion, or been extinguished by such occupants of berths as the light annoyed, or who wanted to sleep, not see.

By a perverse man, in a berth not remote, the remaining lamp would have been extinguished as well, had not a steward forbade, saying that the commands of the captain required it to be kept burning till the natural light of day should come to relieve it. This steward, who, like many in his vocation, was apt to be a little free-spoken at times, had been provoked by the man's pertinacity to remind him, not only of the sad consequences which might, upon occasion, ensue from the cabin being left in darkness, but, also, of the circumstance that, in a place full of strangers, to show one's self anxious to produce darkness there, such an anxiety was, to say the least, not becoming. So the lamp—last survivor of many—burned on, inwardly blessed by those in some berths, and inwardly execrated by those in others.

Keeping his lone vigils beneath his lone lamp, which lighted his book on the table, sat a clean, comely, old man, his head snowy as the marble, and a countenance like that which imagination ascribes to good Simeon, when, having at last beheld the Master of Faith, he blessed him and departed in peace. From his hale look of greenness in winter, and his hands ingrained with the tan, less, apparently, of the present summer, than of accumulated ones past, the old man seemed a well-to-do farmer, happily dismissed, after a thrifty life of activity, from the fields to the fireside—one of those who, at three-score-and-ten, are fresh-hearted as at fifteen; to whom seclusion gives a boon more blessed than knowledge, and at last sends them to heaven untainted by the world, because ignorant of it; just as a countryman putting up at a London inn, and never stirring out of it as a sight-seer, will leave London at last without once being lost in its fog, or soiled by its mud.

Redolent from the barber's shop, as any bridegroom tripping to the bridal chamber might come, and by his look of cheeriness seeming to dispense a sort of morning through the night, in came the cosmopolitan; but marking the old man, and how he was occupied, he toned himself down, and trod softly, and took a seat on the other side of the table, and said nothing. Still, there was a kind of waiting expression about him.

"Sir," said the old man, after looking up puzzled at him a moment, "sir," said he, "one would think this was a coffee-house, and it was war-time, and I had a newspaper here with great news, and the only copy to be had, you sit there looking at me so eager."

"And so you *have* good news there, sir—the very best of good news."

"Too good to be true," here came from one of the curtained berths.

"Hark!" said the cosmopolitan. "Some one talks in his sleep."

"Yes," said the old man, "and you—*you* seem to be talking in a dream. Why speak you, sir, of news, and all that, when you must see this is a book I have here—the Bible, not a newspaper?"

"I know that; and when you are through with it—but not a moment sooner—I will thank you for it. It belongs to the boat, I believe—a present from a society."

"Oh, take it, take it!"

"Nay, sir, I did not mean to touch you at all. I simply stated the fact in explanation of my waiting here—nothing more. Read on, sir, or you will distress me."

This courtesy was not without effect. Removing his spectacles, and saying he had about finished his chapter, the old man kindly presented the volume, which was received with thanks equally kind. After reading for some minutes, until his expression merged from attentiveness into seriousness, and from that into a kind of pain, the cosmopolitan slowly laid down the book, and turning to the old man, who thus far had been watching him with benign curiosity, said: "Can you, my aged friend, resolve me a doubt—a disturbing doubt?"

"There are doubts, sir," replied the old man, with a changed countenance, "there are doubts, sir, which, if man have them, it is not man that can solve them."

"True; but look, now, what my doubt is. I am one who thinks well of man. I love man. I have confidence in man. But what was told me not a half-hour since? I was told that I would find it written—'Believe not his many words—an enemy speaketh sweetly with his lips'—and also I was told that I would find a good deal more to the same effect, and all in this book. I could not think it; and, coming here to look for myself, what do I read? Not only just what was quoted, but also, as was engaged, more to the same purpose, such as this: 'With much communication he will tempt thee; he will smile upon thee, and speak thee fair, and say What wantest thou? If thou be for his profit he will use thee; he will make thee bear, and will not be sorry for it. Observe and take good heed. When thou hearest these things, awake in thy sleep.'"

"Who's that describing the confidence-man?" here came from the berth again.

"Awake in his sleep, sure enough, ain't he?" said the cosmopolitan, again looking off in surprise. "Same voice as before, ain't it? Strange sort of dreamy man, that. Which is his berth, pray?"

"Never mind *him*, sir," said the old man anxiously, "but tell me truly, did you, indeed, read from the book just now?"

"I did," with changed air, "and gall and wormwood it is to me, a truster in man; to me, a philanthropist."

"Why," moved, "you don't mean to say, that what you repeated is really down there? Man and boy, I have read the good book this seventy years, and don't remember seeing anything like that. Let me see it," rising earnestly, and going round to him.

"There it is; and there—and there"—turning over the leaves, and pointing to the sentences one by one; "there—all down in the 'Wisdom of Jesus, the Son of Sirach.'"

"Ah!" cried the old man, brightening up, "now I know. Look," turning the leaves forward and back, till all the Old Testament lay flat on one side, and all the New Testament flat on the other, while in his fingers he supported vertically the portion between, "look, sir, all this to the right is certain truth, and all this to the left is certain truth, but all I hold in my hand here is apocrypha."

"Apocrypha?"

"Yes; and there's the word in black and white," pointing to it. "And what says the word? It says as much as 'not warranted;' for what do college men say of anything of that sort? They say it is apocryphal. The word itself, I've heard from the pulpit, implies something of uncertain credit. So if your disturbance be raised from aught in this apocrypha," again taking up the pages, "in that case, think no more of it, for it's apocrypha."

"What's that about the Apocalypse?" here, a third time, came from the berth.

"He's seeing visions now, ain't he?" said the cosmopolitan, once more looking in the direction of the interruption. "But, sir," resuming, "I cannot tell you how thankful I am for your reminding me about the apocrypha here. For the moment, its being such escaped me. Fact is, when all is bound up together, it's sometimes confusing. The uncanonical part should be bound distinct. And, now that I think of it, how well did those learned doctors who rejected for us this whole book of Sirach. I never read anything so calculated to destroy man's confidence in man. This son of Sirach even says—I saw it but just now: 'Take heed of thy friends;' not, observe, thy seeming friends, thy hypocritical friends, thy false friends, but thy *friends*, thy real friends—that is to say, not the truest friend in the world is to be implicitly trusted. Can Rochefoucault equal that? I should not wonder if his view of human nature, like Machiavelli's, was taken from this Son of Sirach. And to call it wisdom—the Wisdom of the Son of Sirach! Wisdom, indeed! What an ugly thing wisdom must be! Give me the folly that dimples the cheek, say I, rather than the wisdom that curdles the blood. But no, no; it ain't wisdom; it's apocrypha, as you say, sir. For how can that be trustworthy that teaches distrust?"

"I tell you what it is," here cried the same voice as before, only more in less of mockery, "if you two don't know enough to sleep, don't be keeping wiser men awake. And if you want to know what wisdom is, go find it under your blankets."

"Wisdom?" cried another voice with a brogue; "arrah and is't wisdom the two geese are gabbling about all this while? To bed with ye, ye divils, and don't be after burning your fingers with the likes of wisdom."

"We must talk lower," said the old man; "I fear we have annoyed these good people."

"I should be sorry if wisdom annoyed any one," said the other; "but we will lower our voices, as you say. To resume: taking the thing as I did, can you be surprised at my uneasiness in reading passages so charged with the spirit of distrust?"

"No, sir, I am not surprised," said the old man; then added: "from what you say, I see you are something of my way of thinking—you think that to distrust the creature, is a kind of distrusting of the Creator. Well, my young friend, what is it? This is rather late for you to be about. What do you want of me?"

These questions were put to a boy in the fragment of an old linen coat, bedraggled and yellow, who, coming in from the deck barefooted on the soft carpet, had been unheard. All pointed and fluttering, the rags of the little fellow's red-flannel shirt, mixed with those of his yellow coat, flamed about him like the painted flames in the robes of a victim in *auto-da-fe*. His face, too, wore such a polish of seasoned grime, that his sloe-eyes sparkled from out it like lustrous sparks in fresh coal. He was a juvenile peddler, or *marchand*, as the polite French might have called him, of travelers' conveniences; and, having no allotted sleeping-place, had, in his wanderings about the boat, spied, through glass doors, the two in the cabin; and, late though it was, thought it might never be too much so for turning a penny.

Among other things, he carried a curious affair—a miniature mahogany door, hinged to its frame, and suitably furnished in all respects but one, which will shortly appear. This little door he now meaningly held before the old man, who, after staring at it a while, said: "Go thy ways with thy toys, child."

"Now, may I never get so old and wise as that comes to," laughed the boy through his grime; and, by so doing, disclosing leopard-like teeth, like those of Murillo's wild beggar-boy's.

"The divils are laughing now, are they?" here came the brogue from the berth. "What do the divils find to laugh about in wisdom, begorrah? To bed with ye, ye divils, and no more of ye."

"You see, child, you have disturbed that person," said the old man; "you mustn't laugh any more."

"Ah, now," said the cosmopolitan, "don't, pray, say that; don't let him think that poor Laughter is persecuted for a fool in this world."

"Well," said the old man to the boy, "you must, at any rate, speak very low."

"Yes, that wouldn't be amiss, perhaps," said the cosmopolitan; "but, my fine fellow, you were about saying something to my aged friend here; what was it?"

"Oh," with a lowered voice, coolly opening and shutting his little door, "only this: when I kept a toy-stand at the fair in Cincinnati last month, I sold more than one old man a child's rattle."

"No doubt of it," said the old man. "I myself often buy such things for my little grandchildren."

"But these old men I talk of were old bachelors."

The old man stared at him a moment; then, whispering to the cosmopolitan: "Strange boy, this; sort of simple, ain't he? Don't know much, hey?"

"Not much," said the boy, "or I wouldn't be so ragged."

"Why, child, what sharp ears you have!" exclaimed the old man.

"If they were duller, I would hear less ill of myself," said the boy.

"You seem pretty wise, my lad," said the cosmopolitan; "why don't you sell your wisdom, and buy a coat?"

"Faith," said the boy, "that's what I did today, and this is the coat that the price of my wisdom bought. But won't you trade? See, now, it is not the door I want to sell; I only carry the door round for a specimen, like. Look now, sir," standing the thing up on the table, "supposing this little door is your state-room door; well," opening it, "you go in for the night; you close your door behind you—thus. Now, is all safe?"

"I suppose so, child," said the old man.

"Of course it is, my fine fellow," said the cosmopolitan.

"All safe. Well. Now, about two o'clock in the morning, say, a soft-handed gentleman comes softly and tries the knob here—thus; in creeps my soft-handed gentleman; and hey, presto! how comes on the soft cash?"

"I see, I see, child," said the old man; "your fine gentleman is a fine thief, and there's no lock to your little door to keep him out;" with which words he peered at it more closely than before.

"Well, now," again showing his white teeth, "well, now, some of you old folks are knowing 'uns, sure enough; but now comes the great invention," producing a small steel contrivance, very simple but ingenious, and which, being clapped on the inside of the little door, secured it as with a bolt. "There now," admiringly holding it off at arm's-length, "there now, let that soft-handed gentleman come now a' softly trying this little knob here, and let him keep a' trying till he finds his head as soft as his hand. Buy the traveler's patent lock, sir, only twenty-five cents."

"Dear me," cried the old man, "this beats printing. Yes, child, I will have one, and use it this very night."

With the phlegm of an old banker pouching the change, the boy now turned to the other: "Sell you one, sir?"

"Excuse me, my fine fellow, but I never use such blacksmiths' things."

"Those who give the blacksmith most work seldom do," said the boy, tipping him a wink expressive of a degree of indefinite knowingness, not uninteresting to consider in one of his years. But the wink was not marked by the old man, nor, to all appearances, by him for whom it was intended.

"Now then," said the boy, again addressing the old man. "With your traveler's lock on your door tonight, you will think yourself all safe, won't you?"

"I think I will, child."

"But how about the window?"

"Dear me, the window, child. I never thought of that. I must see to that."

"Never you mind about the window," said the boy, "nor, to be honor bright, about the traveler's lock either, (though I ain't sorry for selling one), do you just buy one of these little jokers," producing a number of suspender-like objects, which he dangled before the old man; "money-belts, sir; only fifty cents."

"Money-belt? never heard of such a thing."

"A sort of pocket-book," said the boy, "only a safer sort. Very good for travelers."

"Oh, a pocket-book. Queer looking pocket-books though, seems to me. Ain't they rather long and narrow for pocket-books?"

"They go round the waist, sir, inside," said the boy "door open or locked, wide awake on your feet or fast asleep in your chair, impossible to be robbed with a money-belt."

"I see, I see. It *would* be hard to rob one's money-belt. And I was told today the Mississippi is a bad river for pick-pockets. How much are they?"

"Only fifty cents, sir."

"I'll take one. There!"

"Thank-ee. And now there's a present for ye," with which, drawing from his breast a batch of little papers, he threw one before the old man, who, looking at it, read "*Counterfeit Detector*."

"Very good thing," said the boy, "I give it to all my customers who trade seventy-five cents' worth; best present can be made them. Sell you a money-belt, sir?" turning to the cosmopolitan.

"Excuse me, my fine fellow, but I never use that sort of thing; my money I carry loose."

"Loose bait ain't bad," said the boy, "look a lie and find the truth; don't care about a Counterfeit Detector, do ye? or is the wind East, d'ye think?"

"Child," said the old man in some concern, "you mustn't sit up any longer, it affects your mind; there, go away, go to bed."

"If I had some people's brains to lie on. I would," said the boy, "but planks is hard, you know."

"Go, child—go, go!"

"Yes, child,—yes, yes," said the boy, with which roguish parody, by way of congé, he scraped back his hard foot on the woven flowers of the carpet, much as a mischievous steer in May scrapes back his horny hoof in the pasture; and then with a flourish of his hat—which, like the rest of his tatters, was, thanks to hard times, a belonging beyond his years, though not beyond his experience, being a grown man's cast-off beaver—turned, and with the air of a young Caffre, quitted the place.

"That's a strange boy," said the old man, looking after him. "I wonder who's his mother; and whether she knows what late hours he keeps?"

"The probability is," observed the other, "that his mother does not know. But if you remember, sir, you were saying something, when the boy interrupted you with his door."

"So I was.—Let me see," unmindful of his purchases for the moment, "what, now, was it? What was that I was saying? Do *you* remember?"

"Not perfectly, sir; but, if I am not mistaken, it was something like this: you hoped you did not distrust the creature; for that would imply distrust of the Creator."

"Yes, that was something like it," mechanically and unintelligently letting his eye fall now on his purchases.

"Pray, will you put your money in your belt tonight?"

"It's best, ain't it?" with a slight start. "Never too late to be cautious. 'Beware of pick-pockets' is all over the boat."

"Yes, and it must have been the Son of Sirach, or some other morbid cynic, who put them there. But that's not to the purpose. Since you are minded to it, pray, sir, let me help you about the belt. I think that, between us, we can make a secure thing of it."

"Oh no, no, no!" said the old man, not unperturbed, "no, no, I wouldn't trouble you for the world," then, nervously folding up the belt, "and I won't be so impolite as to do it for myself, before you, either. But, now that I think of it," after a pause, carefully taking a little wad from a remote corner of his vest pocket, "here are two bills they gave me at St. Louis, yesterday. No doubt they are all right; but just to pass time, I'll compare them with the Detector here. Blessed boy to make me such a present. Public benefactor, that little boy!"

Laying the Detector square before him on the table, he then, with something of the air of an officer bringing by the collar a brace of culprits to the bar, placed the two bills opposite the Detector, upon which, the examination began, lasting some time, prosecuted with no small research and vigilance, the forefinger of the right hand proving of lawyer-like efficacy in tracing out and pointing the evidence, whichever way it might go.

After watching him a while, the cosmopolitan said in a formal voice, "Well, what say you, Mr. Foreman; guilty, or not guilty?—Not guilty, ain't it?"

"I don't know, I don't know," returned the old man, perplexed, "there's so many marks of all sorts to go by, it makes it a kind of uncertain. Here, now, is this bill," touching one, "it looks to be a three dollar bill on the Vicksburgh Trust and Insurance Banking Company. Well, the Detector says—"

"But why, in this case, care what it says? Trust and Insurance! What more would you have?"

"No; but the Detector says, among fifty other things, that, if a good bill, it must have, thickened here and there into the substance of the paper, little wavy spots of red; and it says they must have a kind of silky feel, being made by the lint of a red silk handkerchief stirred up in the paper-maker's vat—the paper being made to order for the company."

"Well, and is—"

"Stay. But then it adds, that sign is not always to be relied on; for some good bills get so worn, the red marks get rubbed out. And that's the case with my bill here—see how old it is—or else it's a counterfeit, or else—I don't see right—or else—dear, dear me—I don't know what else to think."

"What a peck of trouble that Detector makes for you now; believe me, the bill is good; don't be so distrustful. Proves what I've always thought, that much of the want of confidence, in these days, is owing to these Counterfeit Detectors you see on every desk and counter. Puts people up to suspecting good bills. Throw it away, I beg, if only because of the trouble it breeds you."

"No; it's troublesome, but I think I'll keep it.—Stay, now, here's another sign. It says that, if the bill is good, it must have in one corner, mixed in with the vignette, the figure of a goose, very small, indeed, all but microscopic; and, for added precaution, like the figure of Napoleon outlined by the tree, not observable, even if magnified, unless the attention is directed to it. Now, pore over it as I will, I can't see this goose."

"Can't see the goose? why, I can; and a famous goose it is. There" (reaching over and pointing to a spot in the vignette).

"I don't see it—dear me—I don't see the goose. Is it a real goose?"

"A perfect goose; beautiful goose."

"Dear, dear, I don't see it."

"Then throw that Detector away, I say again; it only makes you purblind; don't you see what a wild-goose chase it has led you? The bill is good. Throw the Detector away."

"No; it ain't so satisfactory as I thought for, but I must examine this other bill."

"As you please, but I can't in conscience assist you any more; pray, then, excuse me."

So, while the old man with much painstakings resumed his work, the cosmopolitan, to allow him every facility, resumed his reading. At length, seeing that he had given up his undertaking as hopeless, and was at leisure again, the cosmopolitan addressed some gravely interesting remarks to him about the book before him, and, presently, becoming more and more grave, said, as he turned the large volume slowly over on the table, and with much difficulty traced the faded remains of the gilt inscription giving the name of the society who had presented it to the boat, "Ah, sir, though every one must be pleased at the thought of the presence in public places of such a book, yet there is something that abates the satisfaction. Look at this volume; on the outside, battered as any old valise in the baggage-room; and inside, white and virgin as the hearts of lilies in bud."

"So it is, so it is," said the old man sadly, his attention for the first directed to the circumstance.

"Nor is this the only time," continued the other, "that I have observed these public Bibles in boats and hotels. All much like this—old without, and new within. True, this aptly typifies that internal freshness, the best mark of truth, however ancient; but then, it speaks not so well as could be wished for the good book's esteem in the minds of the traveling public. I may err, but it seems to me that if more confidence was put in it by the traveling public, it would hardly be so."

With an expression very unlike that with which he had bent over the Detector, the old man sat meditating upon his companions remarks a while; and, at last, with a rapt look, said: "And yet, of all people, the traveling public most need to put trust in that guardianship which is made known in this book."

"True, true," thoughtfully assented the other. "And one would think they would want to, and be glad to," continued the old man kindling; "for, in all our wanderings through this vale, how pleasant, not less than obligatory, to feel that we need start at no wild alarms, provide for no wild perils; trusting in that Power which is alike able and willing to protect us when we cannot ourselves."

His manner produced something answering to it in the cosmopolitan, who, leaning over towards him, said sadly: "Though this is a theme on which travelers seldom talk to each other, yet, to you, sir, I will say, that I share something of your sense of security. I have moved much about the world, and still keep at it; nevertheless, though in this land, and especially in these parts of it, some stories are told about steamboats and railroads fitted to make one a little apprehensive, yet, I may say that, neither by land nor by water, am I ever seriously disquieted, however, at times, transiently uneasy; since, with you, sir, I believe in a Committee of Safety, holding silent sessions over all, in an invisible patrol, most alert when we soundest sleep, and whose beat lies as much through forests as towns, along rivers as streets. In short, I never forget that passage of Scripture which says, 'Jehovah shall be thy confidence.' The traveler who has not this trust, what miserable misgivings must be his; or, what vain, short-sighted care must he take of himself."

"Even so," said the old man, lowly.

"There is a chapter," continued the other, again taking the book, "which, as not amiss, I must read you. But this lamp, solar-lamp as it is, begins to burn dimly."

"So it does, so it does," said the old man with changed air, "dear me, it must be very late. I must to bed, to bed! Let me see," rising and looking wistfully all round, first on the stools and settees, and then on the carpet, "let me see, let me see;—is there anything I have forgot,—forgot? Something I a sort of dimly remember. Something, my son—careful man—told me at starting this morning, this very morning. Something about seeing to—something before I got into my berth. What could it be? Something for safety. Oh, my poor old memory!"

"Let me give a little guess, sir. Life-preserver?"

"So it was. He told me not to omit seeing I had a life-preserver in my state-room; said the boat supplied them, too. But where are they? I don't see any. What are they like?"

HERMAN MELVILLE

something like this, sir, I believe," lifting a brown stool
␣ tin compartment underneath; "yes, this, I think, is a life-
␣r, sir; and a very good one, I should say, though I don't pretend
␣ know much about such things, never using them myself."

"Why, indeed, now! Who would have thought it? *that* a life-preserver? That's the very stool I was sitting on, ain't it?"

"It is. And that shows that one's life is looked out for, when he ain't looking out for it himself. In fact, any of these stools here will float you, sir, should the boat hit a snag, and go down in the dark. But, since you want one in your room, pray take this one," handing it to him. "I think I can recommend this one; the tin part," rapping it with his knuckles, "seems so perfect—sounds so very hollow."

"Sure it's *quite* perfect, though?" Then, anxiously putting on his spectacles, he scrutinized it pretty closely—"well soldered? quite tight?"

"I should say so, sir; though, indeed, as I said, I never use this sort of thing, myself. Still, I think that in case of a wreck, barring sharp-pointed timbers, you could have confidence in that stool for a special providence."

"Then, good-night, good-night; and Providence have both of us in its good keeping."

"Be sure it will," eying the old man with sympathy, as for the moment he stood, money-belt in hand, and life-preserver under arm, "be sure it will, sir, since in Providence, as in man, you and I equally put trust. But, bless me, we are being left in the dark here. Pah! what a smell, too."

"Ah, my way now," cried the old man, peering before him, "where lies my way to my state-room?"

"I have indifferent eyes, and will show you; but, first, for the good of all lungs, let me extinguish this lamp."

The next moment, the waning light expired, and with it the waning flames of the horned altar, and the waning halo round the robed man's brow; while in the darkness which ensued, the cosmopolitan kindly led the old man away. Something further may follow of this Masquerade.

A Note About the Author

Herman Melville (1819–1891) was an American novelist, poet, and short story writer. Following a period of financial trouble, the Melville family moved from New York City to Albany, where Allan, Herman's father, entered the fur business. When Allan died in 1832, the family struggled to make ends meet, and Herman and his brothers were forced to leave school in order to work. A small inheritance enabled Herman to enroll in school from 1835 to 1837, during which time he studied Latin and Shakespeare. The Panic of 1837 initiated another period of financial struggle for the Melvilles, who were forced to leave Albany. After publishing several essays in 1838, Melville went to sea on a merchant ship in 1839 before enlisting on a whaling voyage in 1840. In July 1842, Melville and a friend jumped ship at the Marquesas Islands, an experience the author would fictionalize in his first novel, *Typee* (1845). He returned home in 1844 to embark on a career as a writer, finding success as a novelist with the semi-autobiographical novels *Typee* and *Omoo* (1847), befriending and earning the admiration of Nathaniel Hawthorne and Oliver Wendell Holmes, and publishing his masterpiece *Moby-Dick* in 1851. Despite his early success as a novelist and writer of such short stories as "Bartleby, the Scrivener" and "Benito Cereno," Melville struggled from the 1850s onward, turning to public lecturing and eventually settling into a career as a customs inspector in New York City. Towards the end of his life, Melville's reputation as a writer had faded immensely, and most of his work remained out of print until critical reappraisal in the early twentieth century recognized him as one of America's finest writers.

A Note from the Publisher

Spanning many genres, from non-fiction essays to literature classics to children's books and lyric poetry, Mint Edition books showcase the master works of our time in a modern new package. The text is freshly typeset, is clean and easy to read, and features a new note about the author in each volume. Many books also include exclusive new introductory material. Every book boasts a striking new cover, which makes it as appropriate for collecting as it is for gift giving. Mint Edition books are only printed when a reader orders them, so natural resources are not wasted. We're proud that our books are never manufactured in excess and exist only in the exact quantity they need to be read and enjoyed. To learn more and view our library, go to minteditionbooks.com

MINT EDITIONS

Enjoy more of your favorite classics with Bookfinity,
a new search and discovery experience for readers.
With Bookfinity, you can discover more vintage
literature for your collection, find your Reader Type,
track books you've read or want to read,
and add reviews to your favorite books.
Visit www.bookfinity.com, and click on
Take the Quiz to get started.

Don't forget to follow us
@bookfinityofficial and @mint_editions

bookfinity & MINT EDITIONS

Enjoy more of your favorite classics with Bookfinity,
a new search and discovery experience for readers.
With Bookfinity, you can discover more vintage
literature for your collection, find your Reader Type,
track books you've read or want to read,
and add reviews to your favorite books.
Visit www.bookfinity.com, and click on
Take the Quiz to get started.

Don't forget to follow us
@bookfinityofficial and @mint_editions

Printed in the USA
CPSIA information can be obtained
at www.ICGtesting.com
LVHW010243290723
753661LV00005B/505